A WIDOWMAKER JONES WESTERN

SO-BDL-264

GUNPOWDER EXPRESS

BRETT COGBURN

WHEELER PUBLISHING
A part of Gale, a Cengage Company

GALE
A Cengage Company

Copyright © 2020 by Brett Cogburn.
Wheeler Publishing, a part of Gale, a Cengage Company.

Following the death of William W. Johnstone, the Johnstone family is working with a carefully selected writer to organize and complete Mr. Johnstone's outlines and many unfinished manuscripts to create additional novels in all of his series like The Last Gunfighter, Mountain Man, and Eagles, among others. This novel was inspired by Mr. Johnstone's superb storytelling.

Wheeler Publishing Large Print Western.
The text of this Large Print edition is unabridged.
Other aspects of the book may vary from the original edition.
Set in 16 pt. Plantin.

**LIBRARY OF CONGRESS CIP DATA ON FILE.
CATALOGUING IN PUBLICATION FOR THIS BOOK
IS AVAILABLE FROM THE LIBRARY OF CONGRESS**

ISBN-13: 978-1-4328-7788-0 (softcover alk. paper)

Published in 2020 by arrangement with Pinnacle Books, an imprint of Kensington Publishing Corp.

Printed in Mexico
Print Number: 01   Print Year: 2020

GUNPOWDER EXPRESS

CHAPTER ONE

The punch was the kind of blow that comes out of nowhere, and the kind you're never really set and ready to take. It was the kind that'll knock you flat like a Texas tornado; the kind that can make tough people slobber and crawl, and the weak ones won't ever get back up.

The big man, as ugly and scarred as he was tall, took that punch square and true on his jaw. He felt the sharp bite of knuckles crash into the marrow of his bones and the hard thud of the ground rising up to meet him. The dust rose up and floated around him as wispy and ephemeral as the dull roar of the crowd cheering and screaming for his demise. Truly, he couldn't have told you where he was in that instant, or even so much as his name. But the pain was real, and it was something to lay hand to.

Slowly, his senses returned until he was aware of other things outside the throbbing of his skull. He tasted the dirt in his mouth mixing with the blood, and the grit of sand scraping under his eyelids. He rolled onto his back and stared up at the face of the referee floating in the furnace sky above him and waving his hands to signal the end of the round.

The big man got one hand under him and then the other, followed by his knees, and pushed his belly up from the ground. The ropes that marked off the fight ring came into focus, at first a blur, and then one, two of those ropes with the screaming crowd behind them cheering and slopping beer down the fronts of their sweat-stained shirts. None of those things came to the big man in clear, individual thoughts, but rather as a wave of impressions, a blur of sights and sounds. He was sure of none of those impressions, and only one thing, one instinct, screamed for attention above it all. He had to get up or they would ring the bell. The bell meant you were done; the bell meant you lost. You had to beat the bell. You had to toe the mark.

The crowd went silent, if only for a brief instant, when he got a leg up under him and wobbled to his feet. But their shock quickly turned to anger over the audacity of the man to take what most couldn't, to fight back against the narrative of his demise. They heckled him while he nodded drunkenly at the referee and raised his fists to show that he was ready to fight again. Somebody flung an empty beer bottle at him, but it went wide of his head and sailed into the crowd on the opposite side of the ring from whence it had come. He didn't even notice the flying bottle and kept shuffling his feet to keep his balance, lest he fall again. All the while, he was listening for the sound of the bell. He was half-afraid it might have sounded without his hearing it.

But the bell had not rung, and he was still in the fight. In a determined, weaving march, he made his way back to his corner, turned, and propped his shoulder blades against the corner post and draped an arm over the top rope to either side of him. His whole body sagged, and only his hollow eyes seemed alive when he stared across the ring at the man who had knocked him down.

And then there came a slight quirk at one corner of his mouth and the parting of his lips to reveal a slit of bloody, clenched teeth. Slow to form, this expression, like the breaking apart of an old scab or wound. Maybe it was only a muscle spasm on the face of a man as punch-drunk as they came, or simply a grimace of pain. Regardless, to the crowd, it looked like a defiant snarl.

The big man pawed at his forehead with one hand and slung the sweat from it to the sand at his feet. He blinked once, twice, at the fighter across the ring from him, as if he was still having a hard time focusing his vision. He blinked a third time, and then that quirk formed at the corner of his mouth again, every bit as wolfish as it had been the first time it cracked his face.

The devilish name and the reputation of the man passed through the crowd like a slow whisper riding the tobacco smoke hovering over them, blown from one to another like an accusation until more than one of them voiced his name as if it explained what they were seeing. Most of them had bet good, hard-earned money against him, yet, there he stood with that snarling expression and glaring back at them and the whole damned world in general. He should have stayed down; he should have been out cold no matter how damned mean he was supposed to be.

Should have. It dawned on some in the crowd then that the damned fool wasn't snarling at all, and that realization made them all the madder. He was trying to grin like the whole thing was funny. Who grinned at a time like that? Poor bastard was out on his feet. That had to be it. One more round and he would go down for good and get what he deserved.

They wouldn't have understood his expression even if they had been sober, or even if they had known him better. He was an unusual man in any place or time, and they wouldn't have understood even if he had the words to explain it to them, which he didn't.

But the crowd had guessed one thing right. The odd contortion at the corner of his mouth was truly a grin, or at least the closest his battered face could come to such an expresion at the moment. And to his way of thinking, he had plenty of reason to grin. Yes, he was punch-drunk and hurt and hanging on by a thread, but there was still the chance to walk across that ring and draw back and knock the living hell out of the bastard who had downed him. That mattered a lot to him. However, what mattered most, and the real reason he grinned, was simply because he was back on his feet and not a one of them had gotten to ring that bell and take him out of the fight. Not yet.

And then he heard someone in the crowd speak his name, and then another — that old name that was none of his choosing but that he wore like another of his scars.

"Widowmaker . . . Widowmaker . . . Widowmaker," the whisper went.

CHAPTER TWO

There were some who said Vulture City got its name because the prospector that founded it spotted some buzzards hovering over the site, a simple enough and slightly romantic tale. While it was true that even such humble and homely creatures gliding high overhead on a thermal wind would have added some romance and color to an otherwise drab place, it was also true that the story of its naming was undoubtedly nothing more than a folktale. Or, in other words, a load of horse pucky to those cynical sorts with enough common sense to realize certain facts.

For starters, such a place held little interest for even a single buzzard. Yes, there was often death — a thing one would think would attract such avian scavengers — but even the promise of a ready meal wasn't enough to tempt the city's namesake birds. Vuture City was simply too damned hot and miserable for anyone, even buzzards, to live there given any other choice.

Secondly, it was really no city at all, except in name, but rather a ramshackle sprawl of construction scattered on a brushy, gravel flat amidst the litter of rocks, cacti, and cast-off junk at the foot of an eroded, red ridge rising up out of the desert. Some might say it was unremarkable, and others less kind could have reasonably claimed it was ugly. Thirsty men usually pointed out that Vulture City had three saloons, a thing worthy of overlooking the place's other faults.

Three saloons or not, there was no denying Vulture City's builders apparently gave little thought or effort toward aesthetic appeal and pleasant architecture. Every bit of man-made habitation seemed to exist only for practical purpose, mainly that it would grant the occupants some modicum of shade when the worst of the afternoon heat bore down on the camp. The buildings were a mismatch of framed lumber, sheet iron, stacked stone, or poorly plastered adobe bricks. None were built exactly the same and were similar only in the uniform coating of dust they shared.

If substance counted for anything, the commissary was the only building that held promise at first glance. Although it was built of dull brown and burnt red native stone stacked in a most common way and coated in more than its share of common dust, it was at least tall — two stories tall — and all that imposing height and those tons of rock were meant one day to hold the offices, assay room, and the treasure vault for the Central Arizona Mining Company. That ownership and any mention of treasure should have made it at least an iconic tower of optimism and civilization in such a frontier hamlet, no matter how plain and ordinary its rectangle design, but sadly, it was still under construction and only three-quarters complete. Its walls had been slower to take shape than they would have been in an ordinary place. Three months of work so far, to be exact, because the piles of sun-baked stone and mining rubble gathered around it and meant to add to its structure would unfortunately blister your hands any time except at night or in the earliest hours of the morning. As it was, for a newcomer, it was hard to tell if the commissary was a new building under construction or an ancient rock tomb whose walls were slowly crumbling down over the centuries.

Beyond the commissary and slightly uphill stood an eighty-stamp mill, usually pounding away incessantly with a mind-numbing racket at the gold ore its crews fed it, but ominously silent for the afternoon. And beyond that, slightly more upslope and rising above everything, stood the massive hoist and headframe of the Vulture Mine. The hard-rock shaft burrowing deep into the earth beneath it and the vein of high-grade ore it promised were the only reasons that such a place came to be at all in that expanse of desolate nothingness. And the shiny tin water pipeline snaking out of camp to the east toward the Hassayampa River ten miles away was the only means by which Vulture City survived long enough for anyone to dig their hearts away for gold or to take a break from the grueling monotony long enough to get drunk and watch a Saturday-afternoon boxing match.

And such a boxing match was currently under way.

The promise of getting to see two men pummel each other wasn't to be missed, considering how much Vulture City's citizens admired a good fight. And no usual fight, this one, but a genuine, imported professional pugilist had come to the mining camp, a thing as rare as it promised to be bloody. Bloody was good.

The peeled cedar posts that had been used to build the crude boxing ring glared under the desert sun like old ivory tusks, and the two large strands of grass rope strung through holes bored in those wooden supports sagged under the oppressive afternoon heat as much as they did because of the press of the crowd of cheering miners they held back. A single, massive ironwood tree stood on one side of the ring, and the furnace breeze periodically gusting through its grotesquely twisted and gnarled limbs cast dappled shadows across both the spectators and the two shirtless and sweating combatants doing their best to punch each other into bloody oblivion inside the ropes. The sounds of those two fighters' bare fists smacking flesh and their grunts of exertion filled in the brief moments when the crowd of spectators paused to catch their breath, mop their brows, or to purchase another mug of lukewarm beer.

Some five hundred hardy souls called Vulture City their home, most of them working for the Central Arizona Mining Company, and the rest consisted of those trying to make a living off those miners, honestly or otherwise. Add another score or so of itinerant types passing through on their way to hell or some other similar place more promising and pleasant than Vulture City, and you had a sizable population, especially considering that neither God nor nature probably ever intended a single human soul to reside there for so much as a minute. And it seemed as if every one of that population had turned out to watch the fight.

All but two.

A man and a woman stood at the completed end of the commissary building in the narrow shade it cast. From their vantage point they had a good view of the fight, and although only thirty yards away, their position behind the crowd let them go unnoticed.

The man was middle-aged and indistinct of look from almost any other adult male of the camp, from the thatch of grizzled, gray hair sprouting out from under the slouching brim of his hat, to the sweat-stained white shirt pinned to his torso with a pair of suspenders, and to the faded canvas pants and lace-up work boots scuffed so badly that they looked as if an entire pack of coyotes had gnawed on them. He puffed thoughtfully on a curve-stemmed pipe, eyes squinted slightly in thoughtful repose.

The woman beside him, on the other hand, would have caused most of the camp to do a double take at the sight of her had they looked away from the fight long enough to notice she had come outside, and not only because she resided in a place in short supply of females. In truth, there were things about her so unusual that she would have drawn stares no matter where she stood, in backwater Vulture City or anywhere else.

It was hard to tell whether she was young or old, for next to nothing of her was revealed, but the way she dressed was unique, to say the least, and lent her an air of mystery that she might or might not deserve. She wore a long-sleeved, red cotton dress, despite the afternoon heat, and where the ends of those sleeves should have revealed the flesh of her hands a pair of tight, kid leather gloves covered them. Where a bit of ankle perhaps might have shown at the bottom of her dress when the furnace breeze lifted it, there were only the high tops of her riding boots with a dainty pair of silver-overlaid California spurs strapped to them. A broad, flat-brimmed felt hat of Spanish style sat atop her head, and a black lace veil was secured around the crown of it. That veil entirely covered her face and shoulders to the extent that her features were hidden to the world.

The shade cast by the commissary was slowly retreating toward the foot of its stone wall, and for a brief instant the sun caught a few scattered strands of pale blond hair beneath the edge of her veil. She moved quickly back into the shadows, as if that brief touch of the sun might melt her, and as if she were as out of place beneath the burning sky as was hair the color of snow in the desert.

The man with the smoking pipe noticed her retreat into the shade, but remained where he was, now half cast in sunlight. He gave a brief, scornful glance at the sky as if it were an old enemy that he could do nothing about.

"It's a hot one today, sure enough," he said more to himself than to her, like a man long used to spending time alone with his thoughts will do.

She did not reply, instead, continuing to watch the fight playing out down the hill from them.

Inside the roped-off boxing ring, the two fighters shuffled their feet and circled each other, their movements lifting dust from the raked sand. One of them was a redheaded man, half a foot taller than anyone in camp. He wore a pair of black tights with a green sash tied around his waist and a pair of high-topped, lace-up boxing shoes on his feet.

The man with the pipe muttered, "The damned fools put up a collection and ordered that boxing getup for him. Had it sent here all the way from San Francisco."

"Hmm," was all the woman gave in reply.

"Guess we couldn't have our local champ looking like any old country bumpkin, could we?" the man with the pipe continued.

Instead of answering him, the woman shifted her gaze to the other fighter squared off against the redhead.

He was a big man himself, although not so professionally attired for a bout of pugilism. He was stripped to the waist like his counterpart, but instead of tights he wore only ragged work pants, and his feet were encased in, of all things, a pair of Indian moccasins. Well over six feet at a guess, still tall, but a couple of inches shorter than the redheaded giant he faced.

She studied him closer to see what it was that had given her the initial impression that he was larger than he was. He was an abnormally big-jointed and big-boned man, true, and all angles and jutting jaw. Maybe that was it. And the muscles and tendon cords stretched over that outsized frame were visible even from a distance, as if every bit of spare fluid and finish had been sucked out of him. His waistband was bunched in

21

wads and cinched tight over his gaunt belly with a piece of rope that served as a belt, as if the pants were two sizes too big for him or as if he hadn't eaten regularly in a long, long time.

Truly, he should have seemed almost a sad, comical figure standing in that ring in his ratty, oversized pants and Indian moccasins, and with the shaggy mop of his black hair hanging lank and sweat damp over his brow as if he hadn't had a haircut in months. And to add to that impression was the still, almost bored expression on his face, as if it didn't matter that the mining crowd was cheering for the redhead to cave his head in. Just a raggedy man too far from where he had come from and too far from his last good luck. But still, there was something about him. Maybe it was the scars.

To say that the big man's face was scarred was putting it nicely. Maybe he had been handsome once, and maybe he still was if you liked them rugged, but it was hard for her to look away from the scars. In between the broad swath of his forehead and the jut of his blunt chin, the bridge of his nose was knotted and bent, obviously having been broken more than once. And his eyebrows were so scarred that one of them was all but hairless, and similar scars marked his cheek-bones and the rest of his face. All like a roadmap of pain, and story symbols of a life of battles painted on him for all to see.

While she was contemplating such things, the redhead swung a wide, awkward fist that clipped the scar-faced man on the jaw. Even with no more than she knew about boxing, she could see that the redhead had little skill for such things. But skill or not, he was powerful. And that slow, ponderous fist he threw had enough power in it to knock his opponent down, even though it had only grazed him. The scar-faced man lay in the dust while the referee called for the end of the round and made sure the redhead went back to his corner.

"I thought he was supposed to be a professional," she said to the man with the pipe. "*Professional,* you said."

"I didn't use that word," the man answered. "I said he was tough, or at least that's the rumor."

"Well, his reputation isn't doing him much good."

The man beside her nodded, but didn't seem especially bothered by what they had seen. "They say he brought Cortina's head back to Texas in a sack."

Her voice was quiet like she was short of

23

the air required to speak in a normal tone, breathless and slightly husky, as if the afternoon heat had sucked the oxygen from her lungs. "A tramp boxer who cuts off heads in his spare time? Not exactly inspiring, and a poor recommendation for employment if I ever heard one, if that's really even him."

"Oh, it's him, all right. I'm certain of that. Same one that tamed that mob in Shakespeare a few years back, and the one that got back that Redding boy from the Apaches last fall. Read it in the newspaper and I heard it from an army officer I ran across in Tucson," the man said. "And there's another rumor going round that he spent the winter in Mexico hunting after another kid he lost down there while he was after the Redding boy."

"You know how people like to talk."

"Maybe."

"How did he end up here?"

The man took another thoughtful puff on his pipe and shrugged before he answered. "Rode in about two weeks ago wearing rags and riding a horse about as starved as he was. Said he'd been in Mexico and lost his traveling stake. Wanted a job."

"Is that why you believe that story about him going back to Mexico after the other kid? Because he said he had been in Mexico?"

"No, I didn't even know who he really was until somebody who had seen him box up in Silver City recognized him and came and told me. But that story fits with what I saw. He came from the south, and unless I miss my guess, he'd ridden a far piece on nothing but guts and bad water." The gray-haired man pulled his pipe from his mouth and used it to gesture at the scar-faced man in the ring. "Notice what kind of Injun moccasins he's wearing?"

"They're Apache, I presume."

He put the pipe back in his mouth and nodded while he drew on it. "You always were a smart girl."

"What else?"

He shrugged. "Shows up to work every day. Doesn't complain. Doesn't say much at all, for that matter. Best man with a double-jack I've got unless it's Ten Mule there. That redheaded devil can swing a sledgehammer, I promise you, but that man yonder isn't far behind him."

"That's not much to go on."

"Any man that will pester an Apache has got plenty of guts, and he got Cortina. Cortina was good with a gun. Real good."

"Still . . ." She put a gloved pointer finger

25

to where her mouth would have been if not for the veil, as if rethinking what she had been about to say and shushing herself.

"Who else could I hire?" he asked. "There aren't many around here that might handle the job and fewer that wouldn't laugh at us if we asked them. There was a man over at the store yesterday claiming he saw Irish Jack and two of his gang on the road between here and White Tank."

The mention of that name caused the woman to turn her head and look at him, and she took a deeper breath before she spoke again. "You said we need at least four men."

He nodded. "Six or eight would be better."

"I don't think you're going to find six or eight, and neither do you. So, let's say four guns." She gave an inclination of her veiled face toward the boxing ring and the scar-faced man only then getting up off the ground. "Say that's one. Who else have you got in mind?"

"The Dutchman will come."

"Waltz? You trust him more than I do."

"He's tough, knows the trail, and if he says he'll go, he'll go."

"Who else?"

"The Stutter brothers."

26

She nodded again, as if she, too, had thought of them but didn't like it. "I'd trust them farther than I would the Dutchman, but they aren't exactly the brightest stars in the sky."

"Maybe not, but they've both got good rifles and they've offered to let us use the company coach."

"I still don't like it," she said.

"You forget that this isn't your run. It's mine." The man squinted at her through his pipe smoke.

Her reply came no louder than any of those that came before, but her voice was stronger. "I've got as much riding on it as you do. Don't you forget that."

They stood in silence once more, watching the fight. By then, the scar-faced man in the moccasins had gotten himself back up and to his corner.

"Got to give that to him. Not many can take a lick from Ten Mule and get back up." The man beside her jabbed a thumb in the direction of the boxers, and the corner of the man's mouth curled in an ironic smirk around the stem of his pipe.

"Widowmaker," she said. "That's what they call him, isn't it? The Widowmaker?"

"That's what they call him."

She turned as if to go, not toward the box-

27

ing ring below them, but the opposite way. She had taken several steps before she called over her shoulder, "It will take more than a name to get that gold to the railroad."

"Are you saying we ought to try and hire him?"

"If Ten Mule doesn't kill him first," she said without looking back.

CHAPTER THREE

Ten Mule Mike, that's what they called the overgrown devil glaring back at Newt Jones, and if ever a name fit a man it was that one. The red-haired Irish puke had a head made of pure gristle and bone, and every punch he landed on you felt like a team of mules had run over you and kicked you twice in passing for good measure. Hard as nails, that one.

Newt Jones leaned his back against the corner post and swiped a wet sponge at the sweat and the blood running down into his right eye where an old scar had been laid wide open above his eyebrow. He stared across the ring to where Ten Mule stood in the opposite corner of the prize ring. Ten Mule was sweating heavily, too, and there was a red knot over one cheekbone where Newt had clipped him one. But he didn't seem especially bothered by it. Newt spat a stream of bloody spittle onto the sand between his feet and tongued the jaw tooth that Ten Mule had loosened for him. He'd be lucky not to lose that tooth.

Heavy. Not just his arms and the fists hanging at the end of them, but Newt's whole body and something on the inside of him suddenly felt outsized and sagging, weighing him down like a wet blanket. And it wasn't only the battering he had taken in the first round or the punch Ten Mule had landed out of nowhere. Newt was plain and simple weary, and had been for a long time. Tired of it all. And that bonehead across the ring was staring at him like this was something new, as if knocking him down was really special.

Maybe there was something to be said for a man who will keep getting back up no matter how many times he's knocked down, at least that's what some claimed. But Newt didn't know what it was that was worth saying. "Don't know the meaning of *quit.*" That's what Mother Jones used to repeat almost proudly, as if that were a thing a man could hang his hat on and something that would get her boy somewhere. True, maybe, or maybe that kind of fellow just doesn't have enough sense to quit. Either way, getting back up never got easier, like the whole world was packing fists and swinging at him every time he raised his head. And it never seemed to get him anywhere other than back in the same tracks he'd been standing in before. Fighting for nothing but the sake of fighting, where even winning didn't feel much different from losing.

And here he was again, getting his face pummeled for nothing more than the entertainment of people he didn't know and for a lousy one-hundred-dollar purse.

"Time!" one of the umpires cried as he held up his stopwatch.

"Fighters, to your mark," the referee in the center of the ring shouted.

There was a confident grin on Ten Mule's swollen mouth as he rolled his neck and loosened his hairy shoulders. He came forward at a lean with his chin tucked and his elbows out like some redheaded bull coming to gore everything in its path.

Newt moved toward the line scratched in the dirt at the center of the ring so slowly that he was almost shuffling, and so lost in his own thoughts that the referee had to ask him twice if he was ready and good to go for another round. Newt only nodded. Maybe that blank expression on his face was a daze from the hard lick he had taken to the head, or maybe he was simply daydreaming. And maybe either one of those

31

two reasons was why the cheap shot Ten Mule took at him to begin the second round worked so well.

The referee hadn't finished his hand motion to start the new round before Ten Mule poked a stiff jab at Newt's face, practically throwing the punch over the top of the referee. The crack of the fist striking Newt's chin was loud, and it snapped his head back like his neck was made of India rubber. The crowd of miners pushed against the top rope and cheered louder than ever when Ten Mule followed that jab up with a straight, hard right that knocked Newt down to one knee.

The referee called for the end of the round and stepped between the two fighters, but not before Ten Mule took another cheap shot and grazed a left hook across the top of Newt's forehead. Newt went from kneeling to lying flat on his back for a second time and was still staring up at the blue sky when the referee finished wrestling Ten Mule back to his corner.

"Get up, you puke!" one of the miners leaning over the top rope yelled at Newt. "Get up, you lily-livered poser."

Knocked down for a second time in as many rounds, Newt shoved himself up on one elbow and glared in the direction the voice had come from, but let it go at that. It was all he could do to get the rest of the way to his feet and stagger to his corner, much less bother with a smart-aleck drunk. And on top of that, it wasn't like that one was the only loudmouth in the crowd rooting against him. Ten Mule was a local favorite, and most of Vulture City was jeering and throwing catcalls Newt's way. And never was there born a mining camp crowd with some whiskey under their belts that could exactly be called anything close to *reserved* or *polite* when they got their blood up.

He took the same sponge he had used earlier, threw it aside, and lifted the whole bucket of water and poured it over his head. Then he turned and leaned his back against the corner post again, waiting for the cobwebs to clear from his head and gripping the top rope to either side of him until his legs felt steadier.

Whereas Newt was alone in his corner, Ten Mule had a pair of men to help him. One of them, a little Mexican fellow, was trying to wipe Ten Mule's face with a wet sponge, but the big redheaded fighter pushed it away with an impatient scowl.

The other man in Ten Mule's corner, wearing a derby hat and stripped down to

33

his vest and rolled-up, gartered sleeves, was trying to give his fighter some kind of instructions. But Ten Mule wasn't having any of that, either. He brushed him off, same as he had the Mexican, and turned his head and accepted the cigar somebody in the crowd behind him shoved in his mouth. He took two good puffs on the smoke stick before he handed it back. A mug of beer was next passed over the top rope to him, and he turned it up and downed it in one long pull while the Mexican massaged his shoulders. Ten Mule handed the mug back while he wiped the foam from his mouth with the back of his hand, still watching Newt. A gloating smirk slowly spread across Ten Mule's mouth, and he put one fist in the other, cracking his knuckles so loud that the sound of those popping joints carried across the ring.

Newt returned Ten Mule's stare without changing expression. *Smug bastard. Smoking cigars and drinking beer in the corner to show how easy it is for him. Caught me like a fool with the cheap trick at the mark and thinks I'm easy pickings.*

Newt felt the old devil rising up inside of him — the devil that liked this kind of thing; the devil that didn't have enough sense to quit; the devil that was slowly coming awake and wanted nothing more than to walk over there and gouge out both of Ten Mule's eyes and drag him around by his skull.

"Fighters, to your mark!" the referee called out.

Newt started to complain to the referee about the quick punch and Ten Mule sneaking in another lick after he was down, but held it in. The fact that the referee hadn't so much as given Ten Mule a warning meant that he wanted to see the Irishman win as badly as most of the crowd did. Anything said about it would be nothing but wasted breath. And besides, the old devil was blowing smoke inside Newt, and it was hard to talk any time the devil started smoking like that.

Ten Mule came forward quickly with that same confident, smug look on his face. Newt moved slowly to meet him, milking every bit of time he could to clear his head and to get his legs under him. The referee began to count off the eight seconds Newt, as the downed man, was allowed to reach the mark under the London Prize Ring Rules.

"Get out there, you puke!" the same one in the crowd that had heckled him before leaned far over the top rope and all but screamed in his ear. "Some kind of fighter you are! Haw, haw! The Widowmaker, my ass!"

Newt reached the mark just as the referee reached a count of seven. The referee nodded at him to get his fists up, and Newt did so sluggishly, as if it took all the energy he had to do that much. Ten Mule saw that, and that nasty grin of his got bigger.

The referee glanced at each fighter to see that they were ready, and then with a chop of his hand between them and a quick step back, he motioned for the round to begin. Ten Mule was big and he was tough, but his size didn't extend to his intellect. He saw the sag in Newt's shoulders and the slow way Newt had readied his fists and elected to try the same cheap trick that had worked the round before. And that was exactly what Newt wanted him to do. At the same instant the referee's hand was dropping, Ten Mule poked his left fist out aimed at Newt's chin, only this time it didn't connect.

From the crowd's point of view — and Ten Mule was probably no less shocked — Newt moved with surprising quickness for a man who had only an instant before appeared out on his feet. He bobbed his head to the right and let Ten Mule's jab slide past him and then leaned back and bobbed the other way to slip the looping overhand right that Ten Mule followed with. The punch meant to end Newt merely flew over his right shoulder, and in doing so, Ten Mule found himself off-balance and his whole right side exposed. Newt split the redhead's ear with a left hook and then followed that blow with a right uppercut under the edge of Ten Mule's breastbone. Ten Mule went up on his tiptoes and doubled over, and the air gushed out of him in a groan. His legs wobbled and he would have fallen on his face then and there, but Newt bull-rushed into him and pinned him against the ropes.

Oh no, you don't. You stay up and take it. He laid his forehead against Ten Mule's chest, holding him upright, and hammered blow after blow to the man's guts, liking the feel of his hard fists sinking into giving flesh. Ten Mule's mouth was sagging open by the time Newt stepped back and swung another uppercut from the hip that caught Ten Mule under the chin. The punch was slightly off the mark, only just clipping off the point of Ten Mule's chin, but Newt felt the man's teeth clack together with an awful snap. Ten Mule's whole body twisted and tottered before he fell slowly like a cut tree held up by the wind for an instant before crashing down.

The referee jumped in front of Newt and waved his arms for the end of the round. The crowd went quiet as Newt dropped his fists and headed back to his corner. Every one of them was trying to get a handle on how a man who had appeared beaten had so quickly downed their local tough. Newt's walk was as slow and methodical as his approach to the mark had been, and he hadn't quite made it all the way when the crowd finally got over their shock and began shouting for Ten Mule to get up.

The same heckler as before leaned out over the top rope again. "Lucky punch, you ugly bastard."

The drunk was close enough that Newt could feel the spittle flecking the side of his face and smell the man's sour breath; close enough that he could see the twisted, crooked teeth in the front of that leering mouth. Without stopping, Newt swung a short, quick right aimed at those teeth. The blow was so compact that most of the audience didn't realize what he had done, and all that most of them saw was the drunken heckler collapse and wind up folded in two and hanging unconscious from the top rope The unconscious heckler looked like nothing so much as a wet, limp piece of laundry hung out to dry, as if he had simply passed out from the liquor he was imbibing. Only a few of those standing closest to him had seen what actually happened, and they shook their fists at Newt and made other gestures more obscene to show their displeasure at the treatment of their friend. In their heated passion they forgot about their abused comrade for the moment, and while they were threatening Newt, the drunk's body slipped headfirst into the ring and hit with a sodden thump.

Newt was standing with his back to the corner post again and making a show of ignoring the mob by the time the referee came over and looked down at the drunk lying in his ring. He looked a question at Newt, but Newt merely shrugged. The referee was about to ask something, but by then the camp marshal was dispersing the unruliest of the crowd. A few licks of his pistol barrel smacked against the heads of the most stubborn soon had things under control. The referee gave Newt one last frown while a couple of men grabbed the downed heckler by the heels and dragged him under the bottom rope and out of the ring.

Newt shifted his attention to Ten Mule. Ten Mule's cornermen had him sitting on a stool, and while one mopped his face with a wet sponge, the other held smelling salts under his nose. Ten Mule slowly managed to lift his chin off his chest slightly, but even from across the ring Newt could see that the Irish brute's eyes weren't focusing properly.

How's that fit your pistol? Newt summoned the effort and the energy to throw the same kind of grin at Ten Mule that the Irishman had been giving him earlier. *Hurts, don't it? Where's your damned cigar now?*

"Time!" one of the umpires outside the ring called.

"Fighters, to your marks," the referee said from the center of the ring.

Newt started forward quicker than before, and that devil in him filled him to the point that he was actually beginning to enjoy himself. So, Ten Mule had landed a few on him. No big deal. He never had been able to really get going in a fight until he had taken a couple of punches.

The man in the gartered sleeves was squatting in front of Ten Mule's stool, mostly blocking Newt's view of the redhead. The referee began counting off the time Ten Mule had to reach the mark. He reached three before the man in the gartered sleeves rose and slipped through the ropes. Ten Mule stood and came forward. Slowly and somewhat unsteady on his feet, but he came, regardless. But this time, instead of that smug smirk on his face there was nothing but grim determination. And something else.

Ten Mule didn't try to quick-punch Newt for the start of the fourth round. Perhaps he had learned his lesson and was more cautious, or perhaps he simply was buying time to regain his strength. He worked a slow half circle around Newt and made a few weak feints at Newt's head with his left hand.

Newt sensed how badly Ten Mule was hurt and knew it was time to finish things. One hundred dollars wasn't much of a purse, but that was more money than he had held in his hands for a long time. He closed the distance between them in two quick slides of his feet, throwing a combination straight and hard for Ten Mule's head and then following that with another combo to Ten Mule's body. "Hit 'em where they live, son, if you want to take the fight out of 'em." That's what Mother Jones always said.

Ten Mule tried to slip out the side as Newt moved to pin him in the corner, and Newt shifted that way to head him off and landed a hard right to Ten Mule's rib cage. Newt pressed forward behind a flurry of punches, and Ten Mule offered almost no counterpunching, only flailing out weakly with his left hand and backpedaling toward his corner. A quick thought flashed through Newt's mind, and he wondered if the big redhead had broken his right hand. That was the problem with bare-knuckle matches, and Ten Mule wouldn't be the first to crack a knuckle on Newt's skull.

Newt threw a left jab of his own, more confident now, and intending to go under it and to shoulder Ten Mule against the corner post, where he could finish him, close and personal.

Maybe it was some sixth sense, but whatever it was that warned Newt, it came too late. He was halfway there and ducked low and slightly off-balance when it dawned on him that Ten Mule's right hand wasn't broken at all. Given more time, he might have figured out exactly why the Irishman had been holding back that hand, but as it was, that fist came out of nowhere and landed below Newt's left eye with a force that was like a sledgehammer had struck him and as if his face cracked open and all the stars and swirling sky in the whole wide world spilled from his skull.

And then there was nothing but pain and then merciful blackness.

CHAPTER FOUR

Pale angels hovering over him. That was the first thing Newt thought when he came awake. He tried to squeeze his eyes shut to clear his blurred vision, but found that only one of his eyelids was working properly. He thought he caught a one-eyed glimpse of a sharp-chinned face and head of pale hair framed from behind with a glowing halo, but that image was fleeting.

He squinted at the bright, heavenly light hitting him full in the face while he wondered why such a light would make his head hurt so badly and while he listened to the sound of the angel's footsteps leaving him. It took him some time to realize that he was not dead, no matter how badly he hurt, and that he was actually flat on his back on a narrow cot in a tiny room with rock walls and a low ceiling. And the bright light was actually the sun shining through the single glass window at the foot of the cot.

43

He lifted an arm out from under the sweaty sheet that covered him and laid that forearm across his face to block the sun. He heard the footsteps again and felt someone standing beside him. "Cover that window."

"What?" a woman's voice answered.

He realized that his speech was slurred and that his mouth wouldn't seem to work right, but he tried again, anyway. "The window."

The footsteps moved at the foot of the cot, and shortly the room went darker. He lifted his forearm away from his face and saw the figure standing before the window. She had lowered the blanket that served as a curtain, but it was undersized and let a little sunlight around its edges — enough to give her some substance and enough to reveal that she was a woman.

He watched her shadow as she came back beside him and took a seat in a chair. She held out a glass of water, and it shamed him the way he snatched it from her. It was as if he had never been so thirsty. Most of the water slopped over his chin because his mouth still didn't want to work right, but what he swallowed was as good as anything he had ever tasted.

"More," he thought he said, holding out the empty glass, but what he actually managed was more like "mmmo."

She filled it again from a tin pitcher on a small table at the head of the bed, and he drank a second glass in the same fashion as before. The water was cool where it soaked through the sheet and touched his bare chest. She started to pour him another, but he fended it off with a lifted hand and a shake of his head that caused him more pain.

Although he couldn't make her out well, he could tell that she had long hair. The feeble sunlight spilling around the blanket in the window caught bits of that hair, and it was indeed as white as the vision of the angel he had earlier. He inhaled and caught the scent of lavender or some kind of flowers. He remembered another woman who also sometimes smelled of lavender. A woman with dark hair instead of angel hair, but that was so long ago he couldn't quite make out her face from memory, any more than he could this stranger who currently sat beside him.

He pulled his gaze away from her shadow and studied what he could of his surroundings more carefully. He wasn't sure if he was in a room, or if the space surrounding him was the entirety of the structure that housed him. He shifted slightly to his side so that he could see the floor. It was dirt. In fact, the whole room smelled of dirt. A dark, musty room with stringers of cobwebs hanging from the pole rafters like ghost rags lit by the tiny pinholes of sunlight showing in the sheet-iron roof where the wind had loosened it around the nails that pinned it down. It was as if he lay in a cave. A coffin.

"Where am I?" he managed after he swallowed a couple of times and focused intensely on making his mouth work. Even so few words caused his jaw to ache all the way to where it joined his ear.

"You need to rest." Her voice was quiet and soft as the sunlight on her pale hair. "We'll talk again once you're on your feet."

He closed and opened his good eye again, trying to focus on her, and not at all sure that it was the dark room that was making her so indefinite and blurry. Maybe he was going blind. He put gentle fingers to his bad eye and felt the puffiness there.

"Mmmeer," he slurred, and then tried again. "Mirror."

"Perhaps later, Mr. Jones."

She knew his name.

"Why can't I talk right?" At least he thought he did a fairly good job of getting those words out — a small victory.

"Your jaw may be broken," she said.

"There's a bandage under your chin, and the doctor said it's probably best you don't talk too much."

A broken jaw — he recalled seeing a boxer in Kansas who had taken a bad lick and had to have his jaw wired shut for a month or so. The only thing the poor fellow could eat was soup slurped through a straw between his clenched teeth.

He ran his tongue inside his mouth to check his teeth. The jaw tooth that Ten Mule had knocked loose was still there. At least there was that. Another small victory, and he needed all the victories he could get.

Ten Mule, the bastard, had hit him with a loaded fist. That was the only explanation for it. A piece of pipe or a tiny bag of shot hidden in his fist, or anything that had some weight to add to the power of his punch. An old, nasty trick that appeared more often in rigged glove matches, but that's what it had to have been. The mangled eye and his bum jaw were testimony that there had been something in Ten Mule's hand.

He made as if to get up, but the quick movement set his head to spinning.

"I wouldn't do that if I were you," she said.

He groaned, as much to disagree with her as it was because of the headache. His head had been rattled more than once and it had

47

yet to keep him down for long. The cot was uncomfortable, and already he could feel sore spots on his back from lying on it. Time to be up. He would find Ten Mule and settle things.

But his second attempt to get up was no better than the first, and he decided to lie back for a moment. No sense in rushing things. A minute or two and he would try it again.

He hadn't tried again by the time the woman stood.

"Horse," he said through clenched teeth. He speech wasn't any plainer that way, but it hurt less to talk. "My horse."

"I don't know anything about your horse," she said.

"Liv . . . livery."

"I'm sure your mount is still there and being well taken care of, but I'll have someone check to make sure."

Another stream of sunlight splashed across him as she opened the door. He knew it was the door because he could hear the bottom of it grating on the doorframe or the ground where it sagged against the hinges.

"How long have I been here?" he asked before she could leave him.

His only answer was the sound of that grating door again, and then the room was once more cast in darkness. He wished he had thanked her for doctoring him. Most of all, he wished he hadn't asked her to cover the window. It was lonely in the dark, and lonely was an old acquaintance that he had never been able to get shuck of and that he had never been able to learn to truly like.

The pale-haired woman didn't return for two days. At least Newt thought it was two days. It was hard for him to tell.

In her place came a young Mexican girl who occasionally brought him more water and a bowl of soup. He had never liked any kind of soup. Never felt like real food, but he didn't complain. His sore jaw and his loose tooth wouldn't have taken real food anyway.

By the second day he was sitting up on his cot for longer periods and had even managed standing up long enough to jerk the blanket off the window. That gave enough light for him to see her. She sat shyly with her eyes on the floor while he ate. He tried to ask her questions in both English and in Spanish, but got no answers. Either his Spanish was that bad or she couldn't understand his slurred attempts at it. When he finished his meal she took his chamber pot out the door and returned with it empty. That chore done, she checked that he had enough water in his tin pitcher, then took his dishes and left.

And he lay back on his cot again, unsure whether the pounding in his head was nothing but the stamp mill crushing rock or if his skull was cracked beyond healing.

By the fourth day when the pale-haired woman came back he was up and about. It was too hot inside the rock shack, and he had opened the door and was sitting in the chair just outside and watching the camp. Watching it out of one eye, that is.

She stopped several feet away from him, giving him a careful looking over. Or at least he thought she was. She was wearing some kind of veil over her face and it was hard to tell where she was looking.

"Do I look that bad?" he asked.

"Yes."

He let that soak in. There was something to be said for her honesty, but that wasn't exactly the answer he had been hoping for.

"Does your head still hurt?" she asked.

"Some."

"Do you enjoy fighting, Mr. Jones?" The questions came rapid-fire out of her, giving him the impression she was an impatient sort.

He didn't answer her, not sure what she

50

was getting at or what the answer would be if he was to give her one.

She gave him a polite amount of time, the ball of one foot patting the ground like clock strokes, but added to her questioning when he wasn't forthcoming. "I'm told you fight often for prize money."

"You ask a lot of questions."

"I need a lot of answers," she said as flatly as she had before.

It was odd talking to someone you didn't know when you couldn't see her face. He had once tried confessing his sins to a Mexican priest, and her line of questioning and that veil on her face gave him the same feeling, as if giving the wrong answer, or even the right one, might have penalties or consequences he would just as soon not know about or care to suffer. And her accent threw him off. It was from someplace he'd never been and couldn't place, and so subtle that he wasn't sure it was even there.

The bandage wrapped over his head and under his jaw and the pain every time he moved his mouth didn't especially make him more inclined for conversation. Not that he ever found much to say, especially to a woman, even when his face wasn't wrecked.

Her hands were encased in skintight, black

51

leather gloves, but he could see that her fingers were long and slender. He also thought it was odd that she wore a ring over her gloves — a ring on one pointer finger with a red gemstone that looked big enough to choke a horse.

"Are you a man for hire, Mr. Jones? That's what I want to know."

"I don't know if I like the way you make that sound, but I'd guess you'd have to say that it depends."

"Depends on what?"

"On what you want to hire me for."

"You come see me when you're feeling better." She pointed to the clapboard building, not fifty yards away and directly in line with the door of the shack he had been sleeping in. "You can see that far, can't you?"

That question let him know how bad his other eye must look. "I can see it."

"You come see me when you feel up to it."

"All right."

"Here." She handed him a small square mirror and a bar of soap, both bundled in a towel.

"Thanks."

"Think nothing of it. You need to shave, and a bath would do you even more good."

She turned and walked away as soon as she said that, and he watched her go, noting the sway of her hips and somewhat surprised that she wore spurs. He watched her until she disappeared into the back door of the saloon she had pointed out. He was beginning to realize who she was, but that made her no less of a mystery to him.

53

CHAPTER FIVE

It was the fifth day before his balance came back and his head felt up to walking. He dragged the table outside and propped the mirror she had given him on it and against the wall. The Mexican girl had brought him his saddlebags, and from them he took his shaving kit and placed it on the table before him. He looked into the mirror almost reluctantly. He was a man who had seen his face maimed more than once, but it was never a pleasant experience, that first look. And this time was no different. It wasn't that he didn't recognize himself; it was simply that he didn't like what he saw.

He knew he wasn't handsome, but Ten Mule hadn't helped him any. It was no wonder that he still couldn't see much out of his left eye, for it was nothing but a purple knot. But the swelling in that eyelid had at least gone down enough so that he could open it to a narrow slit, and enough to reveal an ugly slice of bloodshot eye behind it. And the cheekbone below it wasn't much better. His whole face was puffy and swollen, and made more pronounced because of the bandage scrunching it all together like mud. Someone, presumably the doctor, had put three stitches where the old scar above his other eyebrow had been laid open. He studied those stitches and decided the doctor would make a poor seamstress and that the scar was going to be even worse this time around.

He unwrapped the bandage and set it aside. That helped some. He turned his head to one side and put fingers tenderly to the hinge of his jawbone. He studied the knots and gristle of that cauliflower ear above his hand while he gingerly worked his mouth open and closed to test the state of his healing. The maimed, misshapen ear was courtesy of a stout arm and three feet of pine board swung by a claim jumper in the days of his youth, and there was no taking that moment back or fixing it. But he thought that his jaw felt better as long as he didn't get carried away with it. Then he ran a hand through the stubble of black whiskers that had grown out during his convalescence. At least he could do something about the whiskers. The rest of his face, well, it was what it was, bad ear and all.

After he shaved, he wet a rag with water from the pitcher and took a whore's bath, scrubbing his hands and face, armpits, and other places most in need of attention. It didn't leave him truly clean, but at least he felt fresher and maybe smelled enough better that the dogs wouldn't follow him through the camp. He couldn't find his toothbrush, but he did find a pint bottle of whiskey in his bags. He took a slug from it, gingerly swished it around in his mouth, gargled some, and then spat it out. It was far from good whiskey, and he wasn't sure that his mouth didn't taste worse than it had before.

He looked down at his saddlebags lying open at his feet. Two battered leather bags small enough to hang behind a saddle without getting in your way, and yet, they held almost everything he owned. What had it been, fifteen years since he first went westward? More? *A lot of years and a long damned way, either way.* A *far piece* was what they called that back in the hills of Tennessee, and nothing to show for it but what was in those bags.

He took out a shirt and slipped it over his head. It was once red but had faded to more of a dim pink with white salt streaks and grime stains in the fabric that no soap could take out, and both elbows were crudely patched with canvas scraps that he had cut out of an old coffee sack and sewn on himself. Tucking in the shirt made him notice how his pants sagged down on his hips. The waistband was already bunched up in folds, but he cinched the piece of rope he used for a belt tightener and reknotted it. He told himself then and there that he was going to have to start eating more regularly or get a smaller pair of pants.

Next, he took out his gun belt from the bag and slung it around his hips and buckled it. Unlike his clothes, the leather and the pistol it held were well cared for and both dark with oil. He flexed his right hand. His knuckles were split and swollen, but nothing seemed broken. Satisfied, he slid the Smith & Wesson .44 with the blue turquoise crosses in its walnut grips from the double-loop holster, broke the pistol open and checked the loads, and then closed it again and slid it back in place and hooked the keeper thong back over the hammer.

Last came his hat. He frowned when he first pulled it from the bags. The black felt of it was somewhat crumpled and creased

57

and the brim of it bent out of shape. He set store by that hat and would never have stuffed it inside his saddlebags, but he was glad someone had at least gathered it for him after the fight. Better a little mistreatment than to have lost it.

He spun the hat brim around in his hands, briefly studying the band around the bottom of the crown. It was decorated with turquoise, like the crosses in his pistol butt. He put the hat on and looked again at himself in the mirror. Crumpled or not, it was still a damned fine hat.

He was going to put on his boots, but when he tried to bend over and tug one of them on it threatened to bring back his headache, so he went inside and sat on the cot and slipped his moccasins back on. The buckskin footwear were Apache style and were supposed to lace up on his calves, but he didn't bother to tie them and simply left them sagging down around his ankles when he went back outside.

He wove through a patch of greasewood and around a lone saguaro cactus growing out of a pile of red rocks that lay between his most recent residence and the back of the Blind Drift Social House, stopping when he neared the back door to that establishment. He had never been inside it, for it was said the drinks cost twice as much as they did at the other two watering holes in camp. A twelve-hour shift in the mine netted him a whopping two dollars a day, and considering he hadn't been working there long enough to draw any wages, yet, he was as broke then as he was when he first came to Vulture City. And an empty purse and nothing but lint in your pocket wouldn't pay for a drink or the other "recreation" the Blind Drift supposedly offered.

There was other business he needed to attend to, but it would be discourteous if he didn't talk with the woman first. He had no clue what she wanted to talk to him about, but he at least owed her his thanks and a squaring of his doctor bill.

The saloon was built up on rock piers, and the back side of it was waist-high due to the sloping ground. Three wooden steps led up to the door. He climbed them and paused with his hand on the doorknob. No sounds came from the inside of the building, and he thought again about tending to other rat killing and coming back later. It was late morning, but still too early for the sorts that operated such places to be awake and stirring around.

But the doorknob wasn't locked and turned freely under his hand. He pushed inside and found himself in a small kitchen. The Mexican girl who had tended him in the shack stood at a cast-iron stove cooking breakfast. He started to ask her a question, but she gave a quick nod of her head toward the door on the far side of the kitchen and then looked down at the skillet of huevos rancheros she was cooking. The smell of the eggs and beans and fresh salsa reminded him how hungry he was. *Anything that isn't soup.*

A narrow hallway led from the kitchen into the saloon proper. A long walnut bar ran the length of the right side of the room, and he took a stand at the end of it while he took everything in, from the swept wooden floor with its scatterings of rugs, to the polished brass rail at the foot of the bar. The building consisted of two stories, but the second floor didn't extend out over the bar area, leaving a high, spacious ceiling all the way to the roof. Such high walls left a lot of room for decoration.

No typical deer horns, out-of-date advertising calendars, or fly-specked window glass here. Floral wallpaper had been pasted on those walls, and a number of paintings in imitation gilded gold frames were hung about. They depicted everything from bugle-blowing rich Englishmen in red jackets chasing a fox and jumping their horses over hedges, to well-endowed women reclining nude on Roman couches while they ate grapes. Newt wondered what kind of woman could eat grapes naked while someone painted her likeness.

His gaze shifted, and he saw the biggest painting of all above the bar's back mirror. It was of some kind of goddess rising up out of a giant clamshell with her arms spread wide like she wanted to hug you. As near as he could tell, she must have been taking a bath in the clamshell, for she, like the women in the other paintings, was as naked as the day she was born, and a mist of water encased her feet and the broad swell of her hips, as if rising from a fountain. For the life of him, he couldn't imagine who came up with such stuff. Many a man devoted some thought to naked women of all sorts, but whoever ran across one taking a bath in a clamshell?

Someone cleared their throat to get his attention. His eyes flitted across the plush velvet curtains hanging above the tall windows looking out over the front porch and facing the street, and to the long staircase with its wrought-iron banister leading up to a balcony on the second floor. Nobody stood on the balcony looking down at him, but there were two people sitting at a table with their backs to the foot of the staircase.

Newt recognized the man. He was Tom Skitch, foreman and manager of the Vulture Mine, and he was smoking his crooked pipe as usual while he stared at Newt. The woman beside him had white hair, and she wasn't wearing her veil.

CHAPTER SIX

"Have a seat," Tom Skitch said.

Newt picked his way slowly through the arrangement of upholstered chairs and couches, and for the second time he considered how the room looked more like a parlor than it did a saloon or anything else. He pulled a chair from under the table and took a seat opposite the mine foreman and the woman.

The two of them passed a look between each other as if to decide who would do the talking, and Newt had a feeling that he had interrupted some kind of meeting. But that gave him time to study the woman more. No hat and no veil on this morning, and no gloves — only that long-sleeved dress. One look at her sitting there, and it was obvious that her choice in outdoor apparel wasn't the only thing unusual about her.

Not quite white hair, but so fine and the yellow of it so pale that it looked white at a

63

glance. And her skin was the same. Ivory skin, he had heard it called, but this was lighter than that — so pale that he could see a faint tracing of blue veins in the back of one of her hands lying there on the table. He would have guessed her an albino at first glance, but her eyes were blue instead of pink — light blue, like ice with the light hitting it just right. The frosty eyelashes above them flickered once when she saw him looking her over, and her bloodred lips tightened together. He didn't know what to make of her, for never had he seen a woman such as she. *A frost queen in the middle of the desert.*

Newt pulled his gaze from the woman and noticed that the pipe in Skitch's mouth wasn't lit. However, the man kept it between the jaw teeth on one side of his mouth, anyway, and talked with his teeth clenched because of that.

"You look like the dickens," Skitch said.

"I ought to be fit to work in another couple of days if I still have a job," Newt replied.

Skitch took a box of matches from his vest pocket and started to strike one of them on the tabletop, but noticed the irritated look the white-haired woman aimed at him. He gave her back an apologetic grin and a shrug before he struck the match on his belt buckle, instead. He lit the pipe while he looked across the table at Newt through the puffs of tobacco smoke that lifted every time he drew on the pipestem. He shook his head somberly while he pinched out the match flame, and Newt took that to mean he might not have a job at the mine anymore. But he couldn't blame the man. Skitch hadn't asked him to step into the prize ring and get his jaw busted.

"No," Skitch said when he got the pipe going good enough to take it out of his mouth and hold it to one side.

"You know I'm a good worker."

"That you are, but I don't want you working in the mine anymore."

"Well, can't say as I blame you for firing me, considering I've missed five days of work," Newt said.

Skitch shook his head. "You're misunderstanding me."

Again, Skitch and the woman shared a look between them, and Newt had the uneasy feeling that they had only then come to some kind of an agreement. And that agreement had something to do with him.

"We've got another job in mind for you. One that will pay better than busting your back down in that hole swinging a double-jack or pushing a muck stick."

"You said *we.*" Newt held Skitch's stare for an instant longer, then looked pointedly at the woman. "I've talked to you twice now, ma'am, but I don't know you and I've never caught your name."

"Jenny," she said. "Jenny Blake."

Newt had already assumed who she was. Many a lunch break or a night's discussion in the boardinghouse had revolved around the woman sitting across from him and her establishment, the Blind Drift. But her last name was new to him, for everyone he had heard speak of her simply called her Jenny Silks. An eccentric woman, according to what was said of her, and everything he had seen so far made that no less true. Not at all what he would have expected for the camp's notorious cathouse madam.

Something of his thoughts must have been revealed on his face, for one of her frosted eyebrows raised slightly.

"I take it you've heard of me, although I can't say I recall you ever coming into my establishment," she said. "And I have a very good memory, Mr. Jones."

"I guess everyone in camp knows of you," Newt answered, and then felt embarrassed for the way that sounded.

Her lips parted slightly in what might have been a thin smile, either because she was enjoying his embarrassment or because she didn't mind him saying it. "What do they know of me, Mr. Jones?"

He wasn't sure why she kept calling him Mr. Jones. Plain Newt would have served just fine. The way she said it sounded like some kind of accusation, rather than a polite way of addressing someone you had only recently met. And something about that white skin of hers made him feel dirty, like a man with muddy feet staring at the white marble floor in some palace and knowing he needed to walk across it but wishing there was a way around it.

He had almost thought of how to answer her, but she cut in before he could put his thoughts to words.

"I suppose they say I'm a whore," she said.

That was one of the things Newt had heard, but again, she didn't give him time to answer her.

"But what I don't suppose they tell is how I was one of the first to come to this camp," she continued. "I was here when Henry Wickenburg was still charging fifteen dollars a ton to anyone that wanted to dig ore out of his claim."

Tom Skitch nodded at that while he looked for a place to throw away his matchstick. "I heard you operated out of a tent when old Henry was still running things."

She gave Skitch a look like she had a certain way she wanted to tell whatever she was going to tell and didn't like him interrupting her. Or maybe she was only watching to see that he didn't throw the matchstick on her clean floor and set one of her fancy rugs on fire. Newt couldn't decide which it was. Even without the veil, she was hard to read.

"Henry felt sorry for me and rented me that tent for two dollars a week," she said. "There were only me and Tulip then, but Tulip caught pneumonia the second year and died."

Again, Skitch nodded. "Never knew her, but they said she was really something. One of a kind."

Jenny Silks scoffed, or at least what passed for a scoff from her but was only a little hiss of air out her nose and no more. "She was a heartless bitch, but she taught me the business. Yes, she did. I'll give her that."

Newt shifted uncomfortably, and even Skitch, no doubt used to Jenny's ways, fidgeted and looked at the ceiling like it suddenly interested him.

Jenny noticed the way they were acting and blew an incredulous gust of air out her nose again. "Men, I swear. You think nothing of tramping into my house and plunking down your coin to have your way with my girls, and then you blush and look all judgmental at the sound of one little curse word."

"It ain't that, Jenny," Skitch said, stealing a glance at her to better gauge her temper and then studying the ceiling some more.

"Oh yes, it is, but I don't know why I mention it or let it bother me," she said. "It's been the same since forever, I guess. Always will be. Tulip used to say that the trick of it was to get your money and not to worry about the injustice of it."

Newt tried again to place her foreign accent and the slight, lilting lift of her speech, but was as lost to the origin of it as he had been the first time he heard her voice. And he noticed for the first time that one side of her face was paler than the rest. One cheek, to be exact. You had to look close to notice it, but it was there, nonetheless. The skin was less smooth and webbed with fine cracks. It dawned on him then she had pasted some kind of flour-white cosmetic over that cheek, and the more he looked the more he thought he could see faint dimples and indentations beneath that white makeup, as if she had suffered the pox sometime in the past and sought to cover up the scars it had left her with.

He shifted his seat on his chair while he was thinking, and in doing so he caused one chair leg to screech on the hardwood floor. That sound pulled her attention back to him, and that wasn't something he wanted. Jenny Silks seemed full of words, and he always found that words were hard to handle. A man could top a bad horse, dig a hole, hunt his meat, chop his firewood, build a house, or do most anything without talking. But Jenny Silks seemed overflowing with talk. And once she had a man cornered there wasn't any way to fend off those words, nor was there anything to guide him on how he could answer that wouldn't lead to more talk.

"Mr. Jones," she said, perhaps noticing that his attention was drifting off and wanting to corral him, "I speak of this, not because I don't realize this is a man's world and there is nothing I can do about it, but because I long ago told myself that I would find a way out of Vulture City short of putting a pistol to my head."

Newt's chair leg screeched again. If she would only quit talking long enough he would ask her how much he owed her for the doctor bill and be on his way. Chatty soiled doves with ghost skin talking about shooting themselves made him restless.

She must have noticed his unease, for she held up a pale palm, as if to hold him in place or to fend off whatever she thought him about to say.

"Long before I built this social house and before Skitch's company took over the mine, I loaned Henry Wickenburg two thousand dollars at ten percent annual interest," she said.

Newt took another glance around the room. He had never heard such a place referred to as a "social house."

"Two thousand at ten percent simple interest annually — did you hear that, Mr. Jones? That was nineteen years ago. Do you know what that two thousand dollars plus interest represents?" she asked.

Newt didn't try to perform the math.

"That's over thirteen thousand dollars," she said. "You would agree that's a lot of money, wouldn't you, Mr. Jones?"

Newt nodded, but he was trying to guess how old she was rather than counting money. He came to no conclusions as to her age, other than she had to be older than she looked. Other than the blemish she was covering up on that one cheek, her skin showed not a wrinkle, yet, according to her own story, she had been in Vulture City for nineteen years and working as a soiled dove for that long, too. She must have been nothing but a kid when she started. Hard life for a kid, and he knew without her saying it that nobody with her complexion chose a desert to make a living. Not with other options. But he himself had ended up in a lot of places like Vulture City over the years. Places he wouldn't have picked for pleasure, although with each one of them he could think of a whole string of bad choices that led him there. He wondered what bad choices Jenny Silks had made.

"At the time I made the loan to Henry it seemed a sound investment," she continued. "After all, he owned the best gold strike in the Arizona Territory, or anywhere, for that matter. He was considering his own stamp mill and trying to pay for it. A stamp mill, and then he'd be rich and I'd get my money back with interest."

Again, Newt could only nod.

"But he was never able to put his mine in the black. Trouble, you know, mainly that his miners robbed him blind. High-graded him every time they got the chance. Poor Henry was never made of the stuff required to become a gold baron. He was more the kind that finds mines than the type that can develop them," she said. "But what matters is that the Vulture Mine has sold twice since I loaned Henry that money. The first new owners cheated Henry of most of the purchase price, and as you can imagine, I didn't get my money back. Nor have I since."

"Hard luck," Newt said, and wished he hadn't said anything at all from the way she looked at him when he said that.

"Yes, hard luck, as you put it. Isn't that the excuse for everything out here?" she asked after she drew a breath. The long, thin fingers of the hand she rested on the table drummed at the wood before she spoke again. "The debt Henry owes me, my lien on the mine, if you will, has continued to be carried on the books since the mine first sold, from one owner to the other. And that's a debt I would like to collect."

Newt thought he knew where the conversation was going, no matter that it had been a one-sided conversation thus far. He cleared his throat and tried to quit staring at her face. It was an unusual face — unusually pale and delicate of bone, and unusually pretty. A man had to be careful around pretty women. Most of them were used to getting their way and had an uncanny knack for getting even the most stubborn men to do their bidding. No matter, he didn't intend to do whatever she was working her way toward asking him. It wouldn't be the first time someone had asked him to perform some strong-arm work — make a few threats, break a bone or two so that debts were paid or slights punished.

"I think you've got the wrong man," he said.

"Perhaps." Her voice was as cool as the expression on her face, and those blue eyes gave him a feeling like icicles touching him. Usually, pretty women didn't make him feel cold.

"You'll have to find somebody else to get your quart of blood out of this Henry fellow," he said.

Skitch cleared his throat, obviously trying to get Jenny Silks's attention, but she never once pulled her gaze away from Newt. She stared so intently that Newt could count her pulse through the tiny throb of a vein in her pale temple.

"I understood that your gun is for hire," she said. "They do call you the Widowmaker, don't they?"

"Bunch of drunk fools started that one night, and I can't seem to get shut of the name."

"Nonetheless, you are a man with a reputation."

"Maybe I'm picky about what I hire out for."

"So proud you are." Jenny leaned over the table closer to Newt, peering intently at him with that strange, brittle gaze.

Newt glanced at Skitch. What was a mine foreman doing partnered with a prostitute with a tongue too sharp for her own good? There was an angle there, but Newt hadn't quite put his finger on it, yet. Whatever it was, he had about enough of it.

"If you'll tell me what I owe you for my keep and the doctor bill I'll settle up with you and be gone," Newt said to her.

There was something new in Jenny Silks's icicle eyes now, but Newt couldn't fathom what it was. If she wasn't purposely being flippant, it was as if she found something funny about him. And it was worse because he didn't know what that was. He had never had that effect on anyone else. To the contrary, most people took one look at him and gave him extra space. He wasn't normally a man who caused laughter, nor was he a man who caused people to be overly familiar with him.

"And what could you afford to pay me if I were to present your bill, Mr. Jones?" she asked. "I'm guessing you don't have more than a dollar or two to your name, if that."

Newt's temper started to rise. He had been broke so often that it rarely bothered him to consider his meager finances, but being broke and having a cathouse madam laughing at you because of it were entirely two different things, even if she was laughing only with her eyes.

He looked at Skitch. "I guess I've got almost two weeks' wages coming to me."

"You do," Skitch answered.

"Twelve days at two dollars a day comes to twenty-four dollars, minus the two dollars you loaned me to buy myself a pair of gloves and a lamp hat at your store," Newt said. "Twenty-two dollars ought to square us and we'll part ways."

"Please sit back down, Mr. Jones," Jenny Silks said. "It seems we've gotten off on the wrong foot."

Her voice was so soft that Newt found himself sitting back down without realizing that he had done it. He wondered if that soft, silky voice was how she got her nickname, or if it was because of other things that went with her profession and plush houses of ill repute. Either way, she had asked him to sit and there he was sitting again. Troublesome, was what it was, obeying when you didn't intend to obey. Pretty women were dangerous that way. He felt more restless than ever.

"I don't want you to kill Henry, or hurt him in any way, or whatever it is that you're thinking," she said. "Henry is one of my dearest friends."

"So what is it you want?" Newt asked. "And no more games. I don't guess you saw to my tending out of the goodness of your heart."

"Straight to the point, huh? All business. I like that," she said. "I do want to hire your gun, Mr. Jones, that I don't deny."

Skitch cut in before she could go further. "What she means is that we're hiring express guards for a mine shipment and thought you might be interested. Simple as that."

"And what do you have to do with this shipment?" Newt looked at Jenny Silks when he asked it.

"That loan I made Henry has passed along to the current owners of the mine," she said. "Despite hiring the best counsel I can afford, I've been unable to get a red cent of what is owed to me. Until most recently, that is."

"What changed?" Newt asked.

"Imagine my surprise when I received a letter not long ago informing me that the Central Arizona Mining Company would settle with me for the sum of five thousand dollars."

"Must have been good news, that," Newt said.

"But there was a catch to their offer," she answered.

"Always is."

"I'm to take my payment in bullion here in Vulture City and sign a receipt for such. There is a very dull, but insistent lawyer from New York waiting down the street at the hotel for me to do that very thing, a representative of the mining company."

"And something about that's got you edgy?"

"No . . . maybe. Five thousand dollars in gold in Vulture City doesn't spend well if I can't get it out of here. And I do intend to leave, Mr. Jones. I've sold the Blind Drift, and I'm going to take the proceeds of that sale and my settlement from the mining company and leave for good."

"And you want to hire me to guard you to the railroad?"

"I do."

"And where is it that you come in?" Newt asked Skitch. "She's done most of the talking so far, but you said it was a mine shipment you want me to guard."

"Jenny is going to ride with my gold shipment."

"And I suppose that if I hire on I'm working for you, too?"

"That's right. A hundred dollars to ride shotgun on my shipment."

"I'll add another hundred dollars to your pay once we get to the railroad. Call it a bonus for paying special attention to my welfare," Jenny said. "Part of the gold will belong to Tom and the mining company and part to me. Naturally, I care most about my part."

Newt stood and stepped away from the chair. "No thanks."

"Two hundred dollars is a lot of money," Skitch said.

"Speaking of money," Newt replied. "Can you pay me here, or do I have to go get my wages from your clerk?"

"I never said you were fired," Skitch said.

"I'll save you the trouble of firing me. I'm thinking she has it right, and it might be best to get out of Vulture City. Climate doesn't sit well with me now that I've taken its measure."

Skitch counted out twenty-two dollars in coins and paper money on the table, and Newt raked it in.

"How much do I owe you?" Newt asked Jenny. "For the doctoring."

She waved him off. "Forget it. You aren't

the first bad investment I've made in this camp. Not by a long shot."

He laid five dollars on the table. "That ought to cover your expenses. Thanks for putting me up."

"Some thanks. I help you when you're down and out, and you refuse to help me in turn," she said. "Get out of here."

He should have gone right then without another word, knowing that she had helped him only because she thought she could get something out of him. But still, she had helped him.

"Ma'am, you aren't telling me everything. Neither one of you are."

"I said leave."

"Mr. Skitch, it's been good working for you," Newt said.

He bent the brim of his hat to both of them and crossed the room to the front door. But he stopped there and looked back at them. "Either of you know where I might find Ten Mule? I'd like to have a talk with him."

"Ten Mule's gone," Skitch said.

"How's that?"

"He left yesterday," Skitch said. "He was afraid you'd come hunting him once you were on your feet again."

"He hit me with a loaded fist."

Skitch nodded as if Newt's revelation of Ten Mule's cheating didn't surprise him. "Probably why he left. Afraid you figured that out. Ten Mule is as strong as an ox, but he's no hand with a pistol."

"I aim to dent his head a little to get my evens, but I won't pull on him."

"I suppose he didn't figure it that way. Folks probably got to telling him stories about you, I guess, and he thought it best to light a shuck."

"Which way did he go?"

"I don't know."

"You don't know, or you won't say?"

"Like Jenny said, you've got a reputation as a man who's not one to let a slight or an insult go unattended. As dumb as Ten Mule is, he's worked for me for a long spell, and I wouldn't care to see him killed."

Newt opened the door and looked out at the street that ran in front of the porch. "I've got a hard name, Mr. Skitch, but I've also got ears. And those ears have heard things since I come to your mining town."

Skitch frowned and looked down at the table in front of him, as if he had already written Newt off and was moving on to other thoughts.

"And what have they told you?" Jenny asked.

Newt stepped out on the porch and motioned at the street and where it turned into the trail that led out of Vulture City. "I heard about your gold road and what some folks are calling it."

"Coward," she all but hissed.

"Say what you will, but two hundred dollars ain't enough. No, ma'am, not if it's anything like I heard."

"What's your price, then?"

"No price. And even if I hadn't heard those stories about that road out there, I'd still say no. I'd say it, no matter what you two were asking me to do or what you were paying," he said.

"Why is that?" she asked.

"Because you're desperate, and desperate people tend to do stupid things. No kind of money is worth dying over. You might do well to remember that."

"Leave," she said for the third time. "You aren't the man they told me you were."

"No, ma'am, I'm not that desperate." And then he shut the door behind him.

CHAPTER SEVEN

Newt waited for a big freight wagon to pass
before he stepped out into the rutted road
that served as a street through the middle
of the settlement. The wagon passed before
his eyes, the rattle of the trace chains on the
six-mule team slowly faded, and when the
dust the wagon stirred up slowly dissipated
Newt was still standing there in the middle
of the road — the same road, the same
wagon-rutted, rock-littered trail that the
more colorful types in Vulture City called
the Gunpowder Express.

He looked to the east to where the wagon
ruts crossed a desert flat on their way
toward the old stagecoach route on the Hassayampa that led down across the Salt and
Gila rivers to the Southern Pacific Railroad,
and then he looked to the north side of
Vulture City where the road climbed over a
ridge on its way to Wickenburg and Prescott
and the AT&SF railroad beyond. The repu-

tation of the route leading either way was equally dismal. Locals claimed that the Gunpowder Express had been the end of at least twenty men and a handful of women over the years, and those were only the bodies that someone had stumbled upon so as to add to the official count of the dead. First it had been the Apaches picking off backcountry travelers, and more recently it was bandits. The citizens of Vulture City were still talking about the last gold shipment to leave there some three months before Newt arrived — the driver blasted from the box at short range with a shotgun in ambush, two express guards gunned down, two more wounded, one mortally, and the strongbox taken.

Newt shook his head, bothered by his thoughts. Crazy, white-haired woman thinking getting her money over that trail was going to be some kind of cakewalk. And Skitch wasn't much better. The mine foreman was in some kind of trouble himself, whether he said it or not, and that stage road was likely the reason for it. And the amount that they were offering to pay him gave it away that it wasn't a normal express run they were expecting. In his experience, he could always tell how bad a job would be by how much somebody offered him to take it. Two hundred dollars for a couple of days' work represented a lot of trouble, by his formula of judging such things.

But the woman had helped him, no matter what her reasons or intentions, and Skitch had been good enough to give him a job when he badly needed one. There was that, and not things to be taken lightly.

He squinted both ways along the road again, then strode toward the livery at the edge of town. He had a horse, and the best thing he could do was to get on it and ride. A man couldn't win sticking his nose into other people's trouble, and he had the scars to prove it.

The liveryman was forking hay out of the back of a wagon into the mangers hung on the side of the corral when Newt walked up. He was a thin man in a pair of sagging overalls and with an equally saggy straw sombrero on his head. He was so intent on his grunting and straining with the pitchfork in his hands that he didn't notice Newt's arrival at first.

There were a double handful of horses in the corral, but Newt quickly spotted the Circle Dot horse. The stocky, short-coupled brown gelding stood alone on the far side of the corral, pinning its foxlike ears and snaking its neck in a threatening manner at the other horses and stingily guarding the hay manger it had claimed as its own. Despite that dominant, antisocial behavior, the gelding was the kind of horse that it would have been easy to look past. Not a glossy palomino or buckskin or loud-colored paint, but simply a brown horse, so dark brown it was almost black in places, with a light brown nose, and not a white mark anywhere on its body. A knowledgeable horseman might have noticed the gelding's strong back and hip, good bones, sturdy, dark hooves, and the broad, intelligent forehead. The scar of an old brand ruffled the hair on the gelding's left hip. It was a circle with a single dot in the center, an unusual brand on a plain and ordinary brown horse.

Newt put his arms through the fence rails and whistled at the gelding to get its attention. It didn't come to him, but it did lift its head long enough to give him a sleepy, bored look while it ground a mouthful of hay between its bulldog jaws. Newt whistled again, but that time the Circle Dot horse didn't bother to look at him.

"You expecting that horse to come to you?" the liveryman asked.

The liveryman was leaning on his pitch-fork in the back of the hay wagon, with one leg cocked and one hand braced on his hip, like a horse resting three-legged. Newt wondered if the man had tended horses so long that he had taken on some of their habits.

"I said, are you expecting that horse to come when you whistle?" the liveryman repeated.

"No, he generally has a mind of his own."

"He's a damned buzz saw, is what he is. Kicked half the hide and hair off my customers' horses since you left him here," the liveryman said. "I'll be damned glad to get that unsocial bag of soupbones out of my corral. You are taking him, aren't ya?"

"I am." Newt went under the metal-roofed, sideless shelter that passed as a livery barn and found his saddle and other tack hanging on a string from the rafters. He took the saddle down and lugged it back to the corral. He was about to open the gate and go bridle the Circle Dot horse when the liveryman stopped him.

"Seventeen dollars," the liveryman said.

"What?"

"That's what you owe me." The liveryman worked his chew of tobacco around in his cheek and splashed a stream of thick brown tobacco juice on the ground beside the wagon for emphasis. "Thirteen days at a

dollar a day, plus three dollars for the shoe-
ing, and another dollar for patching that
stirrup leather on your saddle you wanted
fixed."

"A dollar a day? Don't you think that's a
might steep? I get a room for myself and
three meals a day down at the boardinghouse for four bits."

"Maybe you should have figured that out
before you left your animal in my care," the
liveryman said.

"You never said."

"You never asked."

"I've known highwaymen that were kinder
with a dollar." Newt's head was starting to
hurt again, and he was in no mood to argue
further with a crooked hay forker.

The liveryman waved a hand at the desert
around them. "You see anything around
here fit to feed a horse? I got to go all the
way to the river to cut hay and then haul it
back here. Man's time has got to be worth
something, or there ain't no reason what to
go in business."

Seventeen dollars, that was every bit of
the pay Newt had only just received from
Tom Skitch, and the fruit of many days
busting his back two hundred feet down in
a pitch-black mineshaft. And he still had a
bill to pay for his room at the boarding-

house. He looked up at the liveryman on the wagon, squinting against the bright glare of the sun. He supposed that the liveryman didn't really charge that much and ran his racket only on newcomers and an occasional tenderfoot to see if they would fall for it.

"How about you quit joshing me and give me a fair bill?" Newt said.

"A man working for two dollars a day down in Skitch's glory hole ought to consider that he might not be able to afford the keep of a horse, or at least turn him out in the brush like everyone else and not go wasting money he ain't got," the liveryman answered.

"I'll give you ten dollars, and that's still twice as much as what I've paid anywhere else." Newt laid the money on the edge of the wagon bed and unlatched the corral gate.

The liveryman jumped down off the wagon with his pitchfork pointing out in front of him as if he intended to stab Newt. "You don't open that gate unless you hand over seven more dollars."

"You put that pitchfork down or me and you are going to have trouble." Newt kept his hand on the gate, but dropped his saddle. His right hand clenched into a fist.

"This man bothering you, Skinny?" another voice said from behind Newt.

Newt swiveled so that he could see the newest participant in the conversation. A short, broad man wearing a hair-on, brindle-colored cowhide vest stood under the barn roof, leaning against one of the support posts. He was somewhere on the front side of middle-aged and stood fairly straight, but he had been living too easy and his belly was pushing his vest buttons tight and his cheeks were turning to jowls. Dewdrops of sweat glistened on his flushed cheeks above the close-trimmed, thick mustache that shadowed his upper lip. He had his right hand on the butt of the Colt pistol holstered on his hip, and what was more troubling than that hand on his pistol was the badge pinned on his cowhide vest.

"Ain't no trouble at all, Marshal. This man opens that gate so much as a smidgen more and I'm going to bury this pitchfork in his gizzard, easy as that," the liveryman said.

"You there, are you trying to cut Skinny out of his fees?" the marshal asked.

The fact that the marshal already had his hand on his pistol and his timely arrival let Newt know that the whole thing was a setup. He wondered how big of a cut the marshal got when they ran their scam.

"You tell him to put that pitchfork down," Newt said. "I'm about out of patience."

"You got a bossy way for a man I just caught trying to steal a horse," the marshal said. "And now here you are, threatening one of our local businessmen."

Newt shifted his feet to where he could better see both men. He had the liveryman holding the needle-pointed tines of the pitchfork at his left shoulder and the marshal twenty feet to his right with his hand on the butt of that shooter.

"I gave him ten dollars," Newt said.

"He owes me seventeen," the liveryman quickly added.

"How about you hand over the rest of the money you owe, and maybe I can talk Skinny into putting that pitchfork down? Or if you haven't got it, you come back when you do. I'm sure Skinny will keep your tab running." The marshal said that last part with a smirk.

The old devil was starting to smoke inside Newt again; he could feel it as plain as day. Maybe it showed on his face or in the way he stood, for the marshal noticed.

"I heard about what a hard man you're supposed to be," the marshal said. "Might be you don't respect the law."

Newt said nothing.

"This town doesn't tolerate troublemakers. I don't tolerate troublemakers." The marshal pushed against his pistol butt, and the holster leather that held it creaked. "Everyone knows how Ten Mule run off because he was scared of what you'd do, and only because he whipped you in a fair fight. Now I find you here making trouble for Skinny."

Newt wanted nothing more right then than to knock that smug look off his face, but the fidgety way the marshal kept hold of his pistol made it plain that it wouldn't be so simple a thing as a head-butting between them if the issue was pushed.

Newt realized that his own hand was hanging alongside his .44 and that he had somehow taken the keeper thong off the hammer without knowing he did it. That was the thing about trouble, and with packing a gun on your hip like it was some appendage you were born with. What started off with next to nothing, maybe no more than harsh words, could turn real bloody in a blink of an eye — what people back in the mountains where Newt came from used to call *hell in a handbasket,* yes, sir. And the shame of it was that it was too damned easy to let things go that far.

Newt took a deep breath and tried to keep

the devil in him down. There was trouble, and then there was trouble. And tangling with a city marshal was of the second kind of trouble. You didn't win those kinds of fights. Things could get complicated in a bad way with the law against you, and he was as tired of complications as he was of trouble.

Newt had to repeat to himself several times to do the smart thing for once before he finally reached down and picked up his saddle. He went past the marshal into the barn and set the saddle on top of one of the horse stall partitions.

"There now, that's better," the marshal said. "We'll make a respectable citizen out of you, yet."

Newt was out of the barn and on the street before those words soaked in, and he stopped there with his back to the marshal. He took another deep breath, and his exhale was ragged. *Do the smart thing. Do the smart thing.*

"You tell him not to come back unless he's got my money." The liveryman's voice went up an octave.

"Easy, Skinny," the marshal said. "He can pay his bill or not. If he don't, then we'll put his horse and gear up for public auction. That horse doesn't look like much, but that's a good saddle that ought to fetch a fair price."

Newt turned slowly to face them. He didn't bother with the liveryman, and focused his stare on the marshal.

"You get on now, before I take a notion to lock you up," the marshal said.

Newt continued to stare at the marshal, saying nothing.

"You're about to get your ass locked up," the marshal said. "That's what you're about to do."

"Arrest him, Marshal," the liveryman said. "I bet there's papers on him somewhere. He's got that look about him."

From the strained expression on the marshal's face, he seemed about to pull his pistol, or else he was having a bad gut pain. It was hard to tell.

"Damned if you two aren't a pair." Newt turned on his heel and started up the street.

"Where are you going?" the marshal called after Newt.

"I don't think I'm in the mood to be arrested today," Newt said while he kept on walking.

Newt's anger hadn't cooled much by the time he reached the boardinghouse, where he took lunch in the dining room. He sat where he could see out the front window, half expecting the marshal to show up to finish what they had started between them.

After a healthy bowl of chicken and dumplings and a cup of coffee he was of half a mind to walk back down there and take his horse, crooked marshal be damned. But he had already seen the little rock hut that the town used for a jail. Place like that would be hot and miserable, and everybody in Vulture City liked to tell how many men had been hung off the twisted limbs of that big ironwood tree not far from it. No, nobody but a fool bucked the system, and that's just what he would be doing if he twisted that marshal's ear any more than he already had. The thing to do was to be smart for once and think his way through his troubles, the way normal folks did things.

And the longer he thought, the worse his head hurt, and chewing the doughy, half-raw dumplings had set his jaw to aching. He would have liked nothing more than to go to his room and lie on his bed, but instead, he paid the landlady for thirteen days of board, gathered his Winchester rifle and a roll of blankets from the closet in his room, and headed back down the street. Almost two weeks in Vulture City, and he was as flat broke as he had been when he arrived. Flat broke, and with a crooked marshal about to auction off his horse and saddle.

There was a time for thinking and a time for doing. Weighing his options, he came up with only one course of action. It wouldn't turn out well, he was sure of it, but there was no sense dwelling on things he couldn't do a damned thing about. He quickened his pace and aimed himself in the direction of the Blind Drift.

Tom Skitch was gone, but Jenny Silks was still sitting at her table nursing a cup of coffee when he pushed into her parlor for a second time. The bartender behind the bar wiping glasses gave him a cautious look while two half-dressed prostitutes smiled sleepily down at him from the balcony above, but Jenny only held her coffee mug to her lips and watched him through the steam with a bland but faintly pleased expression on her face. As if she already knew what he had come to say, and as if she had been expecting it.

"How many other express guards have you got?" he asked, standing before her.

She set down the coffee mug. "You'd make four."

"You think that's enough?" He watched closely to see if that hot coffee steam would melt her poker face away and let him know what she was really thinking.

"I thought you said you weren't desperate enough to hire on with us," she said, as icy as ever.

"I was wrong."

"Oh?"

"Yes, ma'am, I guess you could say I'm a thoroughly desperate man. Maybe I only got that way recently, or maybe I always have been."

CHAPTER EIGHT

The stars were clear overhead, and the stagecoach was only a midnight shadow in the single pool of lamplight in front of the commissary's door. Three men also stood in that lamplight, all of them holding rifles cradled in the crooks of their elbows and paying close attention to Newt when he stepped past them and went inside.

Tom Skitch was waiting in the vault room. He stood over a square hole in the floor with a lantern in one hand and a short, double-barreled Parker 12-gauge in the other. He lowered the shotgun when he saw it was Newt, but the nervous look on his face and the twitch about him didn't leave.

Newt looked down into the vault, a small concrete cellar about six feet deep with a wooden ladder leading down into it. The steel lid covering the hatchway had been removed, and he could make out the iron express box lying on the floor of the vault.

"Is that it?" Newt asked.

Someone else rustled in a dark corner across the room before Skitch could answer him. Jenny Silks stepped into the lamplight. She wore her veil and the Spanish hat, but for the moment, the veil was lifted in the front and resting on her hat brim so that her face showed. Newt also noticed that she was wearing her spurs again, and that a broad, tooled leather belt was cinched around the narrow waist of her dress. A nickel-plated Merwin Hulbert pistol was holstered on her left hip at a cross draw, and a sheath knife rode on her other hip. Both knife and pistol had pink mother-of-pearl grips.

Jenny was studying him out of those weird blue eyes of hers, and her gaze was as intense and unreadable as usual. Newt ran his finger inside the neck of his shirt. He had outfitted himself the evening before from the proceeds of an advance that Skitch had made him on his guard wages, but his new pin-striped white shirt and brown denim pants were suddenly itchy, and his new high-topped boots pinched his feet.

"Help me get it out," Skitch said, gesturing down in the hole at his feet.

Newt went down the ladder, wrestled with the steel box, and handed it up to where

Skitch could take it from him. The box thumped loudly on the floor when Skitch sat it down.

"Heavy," Newt said as he climbed out of the vault. "You know, pulling out of here in the dark isn't going to fool anybody. You can't keep this much gold a secret."

"You let me worry about that."

"Worry is what you ought to be doing."

"We'll make it."

"Maybe, but you aren't telling me everything, are you?"

Skitch looked more uncomfortable than ever, not only like a manager worrying over a shipment, but like a man with other stakes on the line. Not only his job, but everything.

"Be honest with him, Tom. He'll find out anyway," Jenny said.

Skitch shook his head.

"He's having some difficulties of late," she said when Skitch wouldn't. "Mainly, the mine is about to go broke."

"Don't you spread that around," Skitch said to Newt, and then he glanced at the door to see if the other guards were close enough to listen. "You know a rumor like that can stir things up."

"Quit acting like it's a secret," she said. "Everybody already knows the company is having trouble. You haven't made a shipment in three months."

"What's the trouble?" Newt asked. "The rumor that I heard is that the crews in the Number Three stope have hit a pay streak. Found the vein again. High-grade stuff. Jewelry rock."

"We have," Skitch said, but like it didn't solve anything.

"Tell him, Tom," Jenny repeated.

"Thieves," Skitch replied. "High-graders and road agents. I don't know which is worse."

High-grading was an old story to Newt, who had spent much of his time in mining camps since coming west. More than one dishonest miner had stashed a bit of gold on his person or in his lunch pail while working a high-grade vein. Some companies had gone so far as to make their workers strip naked after a work shift under the examination of paid guards who searched their clothes and other gear for signs of stealing.

And as for Skitch's mention of road agents, Newt had heard a few stories about that, too — the Gunpowder Express, the last attempted shipment, other robberies all over the territory, and all of that.

"How bad is it?" Newt asked.

"Bad enough that if I don't get this shipment to the railroad I won't be able to make payroll next week."

Newt thought about the miners and other company employees and contractors in the camp and how they would take not being paid. It would likely get very ugly. From the look on Skitch's face, he seemed to be considering the same thing.

"And what's been stopping you from shipping your gold up to now?" Newt asked.

"Irish Jack O'Harrigan, that's the what of it," Skitch said. "That Mick road agent and his gang hit my last shipment. Got away with every ounce of it."

"Sounds like a swell fellow, this Irish Jack."

"Territorial governor has a price on his head, but it hasn't done a lick of good so far."

"Why don't you hire Wells Fargo? For a cut of the pie they'll supply their own express guards and insure your shipment."

"I tried, but they've temporarily ceased operations until they can get the roads safe again. They've taken too many losses over the last several years, and they'll only take my shipment at the railroad."

"Let me guess, Irish Jack."

"Jack isn't the only owlhoot in this territory that likes to rob stagecoaches. This territory seems to sprout a road agent behind every rock," Skitch said. "But, yeah. Irish Jack is the worst of them."

"You need more express guards."

Skitch only nodded as if he had the same thought, but couldn't do a thing about it.

"Nobody else will hire on, will they?" Newt added. "Nobody that's fool enough to risk their necks, you mean, or that you think you can trust."

"Only the four of you, plus me and Jenny and a passenger," Skitch replied. "That'll have to do."

"What passenger?"

"Why, that would be me." A short, rotund fellow in a dapper suit limped into the room and tipped his bowler hat enough to reveal a brief glimpse of his bald scalp. "Cyrus McPhee, at your service."

Newt gave the newcomer a careful once-over and then jerked a thumb at him while at the same time giving Skitch and Jenny Silks a *who the hell is he?* look.

"This is the lawyer I told you about," Jenny said, and then gave a shrug of her shoulders as if that explained the whole situation and the odd man before them.

"Yes, indeed," the lawyer said. He was long of torso and short of leg. The balloon-legged, pin-striped pants he wore and the tail of his coat made what legs he had seem

103

almost nonexistent, as if a pair of knees and those two oversized shoes came directly out of his hip bones. That, and his feet were so big for a man of his stature and turned out so far at the toe that they added to the legless perception.

"I'm sure you've heard of Simon and Crusher," McPhee added.

"I never," was all that Newt could muster for an answer.

The stubby lawyer wrinkled his broad, pug nose and shoved his eyeglasses up the bridge of his nose and tilted his head back to get a better look at Newt. "Simon and Crusher? Attorneys-at-law?"

Newt shook his head again.

"One of the preeminent law firms in the country? Vested owners and investors in various shipping ventures? Railroads? The brand-new cannery in Maine that all the newspapers were writing about a month ago?"

"I don't get many newspapers."

"New York, New York?"

"Heard of the place a time or two. You've come a long way, then."

That statement seemed to please McPhee, and he patted the leather satchel suspended from a strap over his left shoulder and sighed, as if that sound explained it all. "I admit that I first thought this trip was some sort of punishment, but I've come to see it as an opportunity. The whole endeavor has been challenging, to say the least, but in a few more days I will have seen the whole thing to fruition, surely something that my superiors will notice."

"They sent you all the way out here to get her to sign papers?" Newt jerked his head at Jenny.

Again, McPhee patted his satchel. "Oh yes, my firm holds a two-thirds majority interest in the Central Arizona Mining Company, and Mr. Simon himself would not settle for anything short of the necessary documents being hand-delivered to Miss Blake and that I personally audit the mine's operation and report back to them with my findings."

"You don't say?" Newt said weakly, because he didn't know what else to say, no more than he knew what to make of the little lawyer.

"Oh yes, I look most forward to telegraphing Mr. Simon once we get to the railroad and letting him know that Miss Blake's situation has been brought to closure and to relay to him the findings of my audit. Mr. Crusher can be most patient, but that is not one of Mr. Simon's virtues, I can assure you. He is most demanding when it comes to timely reporting and closure on matters he deems important."

Newt had the strange feeling that he had met or encountered the odd lawyer before, but that didn't seem possible. He tried to remember someone else he knew who might remind him of McPhee, but came up with nothing on that line, either.

McPhee didn't appear to be armed, nor did Newt appraise the lawyer as the kind of man trained in any sort of combat, firearms or otherwise. There was an air of timidity about the man, or perhaps that impression was only a result of his blinking, bewildered expression. Newt wondered if McPhee had a clue what he could be getting himself into by taking a seat aboard the stagecoach waiting for them outside.

"Catching a ride, huh?"

McPhee nodded so quickly that he unsettled his bowler hat so much that it tipped down to his eyebrows, and he had to shove it back on his head and readjust his eyeglasses. "They tell me that it is a relatively quick jaunt to the Southern Pacific tracks. I'll catch a train there for Galveston and then on to New York by steamer."

Everything Newt had heard about the way south to the Southern Pacific tracks said it was a two-day trip, but McPhee was in for a rude shock if he thought two days' travel over a rutted, rocky trail was going to be a pleasant sightseeing excursion.

Skitch cleared his throat, obviously impatient with the conversation. "Well, best you get aboard then, McPhee."

"Ah yes, I'm sure you want to get the shipment loaded and be away, and although my trip to your fine territory has been . . . huhhum . . . let's say, interesting, I'm not above telling you that I'm most ready to return to more civilized places." McPhee turned quickly and hobbled to the door, clutching his leather satchel tightly to his hip and with his other hand on top of the crown of his hat as if expecting to hit a stiff breeze once he was outside. His limping gait hinted of some past injury or disease that had affected one or both of his legs.

"Odd fellow," Newt said when McPhee was gone.

"Yeah, he's a little quirky," Skitch said.

"It's been my experience that most folks are a little quirky," Newt replied. "Fact is, I prefer the ones that don't hide it. Less surprises that way."

"No surprises to that one." Skitch's irritated gaze was aimed at the retreating lawyer's back. "If I had a nickel for every time I've met his kind I'd be a rich man. Just another slimy lawyer and bean counter set on keeping better men from their work."

Newt looked up at the pinpricks of stars overhead in the night sky, visible through a hole in the commissary's unfinished roof. "You should have talked him into taking the next stage."

Skitch frowned. "Tried to, but he claims his instructions are to ride with the shipment until it's handed over to Wells Fargo at the Maricopa Station."

"Well, a ride in that stagecoach will likely be like no kind of lawyering he's ever done."

"He's a pain in the neck is what he is," Skitch said. "Here I am trying to get this shipment ready, and I've got him under my feet. He's got nine kinds of questions and did everything but insist I take him down in the mine and show him the new shaft I'm digging and the new vein we've struck in Number Three, as if he knows one thing about mining or what it takes to get ore out of the ground."

"What about the three men out there?" Newt pointed outside toward where the stagecoach was parked and the other express guards waited.

"Good enough men," Skitch answered. "I trust them."

"You don't trust anyone with this much gold."

"Even you?" Jenny asked with a heavy dose of sarcasm.

"Even me."

"Help me with this box," Skitch said, ignoring the byplay between the two of them.

Newt took one handle at the end of the express box, and Skitch the other. Jenny followed in their wake.

"There's Jacob Waltz," Skitch said between grunts as he strained at his end of the heavy box. "Most around here call him the Dutchman."

"German, I take it?"

"Yep," Skitch said. "He's worked for me for a long time, and for the previous managers before me. Cranky sort, but he knows mining and he's good with a rifle. I've seen him shoot the head off more than one jackrabbit with that Ballard gun of his."

"If we have trouble, it won't be with jackrabbits," Newt said. "What about the other two?"

"The Stutter brothers. Ned and Fred."

Newt looked a question at him.

"Not the brightest sorts, but they're young and strong. Mississippi boys. Know the trail like the back of their hands."

The instant they got the express box out of the door, two men standing by the stagecoach stepped forward and took hold of it. Newt guessed that they were the Stutter brothers. The other man, presumably the Dutchman, stayed in the shadows at the rear of the coach.

Newt watched while the brothers stowed the express box. It was too dark to get a good look at them, but they seemed strong. He also noticed that they put the box inside the passenger compartment and not on the luggage rack behind or under the driver's seat up front as was traditional.

Skitch must have been reading his mind. "I want that box where I can see it."

"How do you want to play this?" Newt asked.

"We go north to Wickenburg. It's a longer way, but anybody that might be laying for us will probably guess we'd take the new road straight east to Seymour instead of coming at it from the north later," Skitch answered.

"You've given this some thought, haven't you?"

"Forty thousand dollars' worth of thoughts."

The amount in the strongbox that Skitch mentioned didn't go unnoticed by Newt, and he ran those numbers in his head, weighing how much trouble each ounce of gold and the corresponding dollar value upped their risk. He was shocked that Skitch had been so trusting as to mention the number, for there was risk in such loose talk. Half the holdup men in the territory would be champing at the bit and slobbering at the mouth if word leaked out that Skitch was hauling that much gold in one shipment.

"So, it's the Southern Pacific we're headed for?" Newt asked.

"That's the right of it. Thought about trying for the AT&SF, but there's a lot of rough country between here and Prescott and beyond. More places we could be ambushed," Skitch said. "No, the way I see it, once we hit Wickenburg we double back and head south down the Hassayampa. Maybe make someone think that we're headed north to Prescott when we really aren't. Travel fast until we hit the tracks at Maricopa Station. Be there before anybody has long enough to think on stopping us."

"Maricopa Wells? Heard of that."

"Not the old wells on the Butterfield Road. They moved the town south and east when the Southern Pacific came through. Two days to get us there, at most, less maybe."

"What else?"

"I figured me and Jenny would ride in the coach with McPhee, and the Stutter brothers will drive and ride shotgun. You and the Dutchman will come along beside us on horseback. Flankers and scouts, you know."

"Sounds like a plan." Newt started toward the hitching rail in front of the commissary.

"I see you got your horse back." Skitch gestured at the shadow of a horse standing at the hitching rail. "Hope you didn't cause any trouble."

"Nah," Newt said without looking back at him. "Wasn't any trouble at all."

"Good. That Skinny is as crooked as he is disagreeable, and damned hard to deal with sometimes."

"Like I said, no trouble."

"Well, I wouldn't have paid what you said he was asking for any kind of a horse. You should have let him have it and I'd have loaned you another one."

"He's my horse."

"Still, I wouldn't have let Skinny crook me like that."

"The more I think on it, the more I think I got my money's worth."

"Glad to hear you and Skinny worked it out."

112

"That reminds me of something," Newt said. "How come Skinny's marshal buddy isn't coming along with us? Can't say I'd welcome his company, but it seems odd."

"Ernie Sims? He isn't Skinny's buddy. He's his brother-in-law," Skitch scoffed. "Skinny's married to Ernie's sister, or was, until some Coyotero Apaches run off with her some years back."

"What happened to her?"

"Skinny never got her back. Whether she's dead or still living with those heathens is anybody's guess."

"That's tough."

"I don't know about that. After her time with Skinny even living with the Apache might have been more to her liking."

Newt couldn't help but chuckle, but felt a little ashamed for it. Skinny was a sorry sort, but Newt knew firsthand the ordeal an Apache captive faced, certain memories still fresh in his mind, and he wouldn't wish that on anyone.

"You never said why the marshal isn't coming along," Newt said. "Fact is, we've spent a whole day waiting around here for you to tell us you're ready to pull out, and I haven't seen hide nor hair of him."

"Ernie says he was hired as town marshal and his jurisdiction doesn't extend past that.

No telling where he's gone off to, but I imagine he'll have one reason or another for not being here when we leave," Skitch said. "He's got lots of excuses. Always does, but mainly Ernie likes bedding whores and cheating at cards and shaking down newcomers more than he likes real lawman work."

"My guess is that your mining company pays his wages," Newt said. "You ought to have some leverage with him."

"You'd think," Skitch replied. "Chalk him up to another one of the problems I haven't gotten around to yet. Ernie's made it plain that any man intending to replace him as marshal is going to have to rip that badge off his chest."

"Is that so?"

"That's his brag, and so far I haven't found anyone willing to try him," Skitch said. "And don't let Ernie fool you. I know he doesn't look the part, but looks can be deceiving. He got the job because he's a mean little bastard in high-heeled boots. Killed a man up at Prescott a while back, and that isn't the first notch on his pistol if you listen to the talk."

Jenny Silks was already getting inside the stagecoach. One of the Stutter brothers was holding the door open for her. Newt heard the rattle of her spurs and wondered why she was wearing them when she wasn't going to be riding a horse.

Newt went to the hitching rail and found the brown gelding lying on its side with his neck stretched at an awkward angle where the reins were still wrapped around the hitching rail.

"I wouldn't put up with that if he was mine," Skitch said, eyeing the Circle Dot horse.

"He's partial to his rest when he can get it," Newt replied.

"Lazy and stubborn if you ask me."

"I'm stubborn myself."

"I don't doubt that one bit, but I still wouldn't tolerate such an animal. That's a way to ruin a perfectly good saddle, letting him wallow around on it like that."

"He's all right, he's just a peculiar animal, that's all."

Skitch frowned, then followed Jenny into the coach. The Stutter brothers took up their rifles and climbed up on the box while the Dutchman mounted his horse. Newt toed the Circle Dot horse in the hip and waited for him to get up.

"You better be glad Skitch doesn't own you," Newt said to the horse when it finally rose, grunting and shaking the dust from its body.

The horse yawned, showing its teeth, and lifted its tail and expelled a large and noisy amount of gas.

Newt talked while he tightened the cinch. "Yawn if you want to, but he'd feed you to the dogs if he knew half of your quirks. Best you try acting like a normal horse."

The Circle Dot horse farted again, then shook its head, coating Newt in a fine layer of fresh dust.

Newt checked his Winchester in the saddle boot to make sure it hadn't been damaged and that it was shoved in tight, then took up his split reins and stepped into the saddle. The Dutchman's shadow rode past him going to the lead of the stagecoach.

"Take us out of here easy and quiet like," Skitch leaned out of a window and said to the driver.

The six-horse team hitched to the coach must not have heard his instructions. The instant the driver released the brake and gave them some slack in the ribbons, all six horses scrambled and snapped against their harness, and the stage left Vulture City at high-lope, rattling and bouncing with the driver sawing on the reins and cursing the half-wild horses. That noise caused several dogs to start barking and to run out into the street, and the barking caused several windows to suddenly glow with lamplight.

Newt was passing by one of those house windows when he saw a face peering back at him. Newt was traveling fast in order to keep up with the runaway team, but he saw enough, even at such speed. It was Skinny's face in the window. The liveryman's narrow, pinched features were plain where they pressed against the dirty glass and backlit by the lamp behind him. And also plain in that instant were the puffy bruises on his face and his swollen, busted lips. Newt grinned for a second time.

"Good doing business with you," he said loudly to Skinny's window and waved at him with a hand bearing some freshly scraped and split knuckles as he spurred ahead to catch up with the stage.

The dogs scattered before Newt's horse, and then they barked some more. And when he looked back one last time there were more lights being lit. So much for secrecy. By dawn, the entire population of Vulture City was going to know that the ore shipment had left town headed toward Wickenburg. But at least the express made good time. They were over the ridge and two miles on their way before the driver got the

117

horses to check and slowed to a walk.

Newt rode alongside the stagecoach, and Skitch pushed back a canvas window curtain and looked out at him.

"Fresh horses you've got there," Newt said wryly.

"We need fast horses," Skitch replied, irritation in his voice.

"Yeah, but couldn't you find some broke, fast horses? That team there doesn't have but two speeds, dead stop or go."

"I imagine they'll settle down now that they've got the fresh off of them."

Newt rode along, silent for a spell, and Skitch remained equally silent leaning out the window and looking at the dark road ahead.

At that very moment a gagging, retching sound came from inside the stagecoach, as if someone was vomiting. Whoever was making that sound was very, very sick.

The window curtain on the other side of the coach door was shoved back and Jenny's face appeared. She leaned out the open window as far as she could. "I fear Mr. McPhee has taken road sick."

"Oh?" Newt said just as McPhee started gagging again, coupled with more than a few weak moans. "Do we need to stop?"

"I'm fine," came McPhee's voice. "Really,

don't mind me."

Skitch looked into the coach, then quickly back outside, as if he was fighting off a gag or two himself.

Newt was glad he wasn't riding with McPhee. The lawyer wasn't the first passenger to become nauseous after a ride in a stagecoach. The rocking and swaying of the carriage and its leather strap suspension over the rough trail gave many a case of motion sickness equivalent to being seasick. Newt wondered if the lawyer had already reconsidered his notion of a quick jaunt on the stage.

After another mile, Newt twisted in the saddle to where he could look back the way they had come. "I don't know what this says about us."

"What's that?" Skitch asked.

"That we're the only fools in Vulture City that think we can get a box of gold over a hundred miles of desert without getting ourselves killed."

"Try to be more optimistic, Mr. Jones," Jenny's soft voice whispered from inside the shadowed coach.

At that very moment McPhee started vomiting again. The sounds were most unpleasant, and both Skitch and Jenny Silks leaned farther out the windows.

"Well, we're off to a good start," Newt said while he reined the Circle Dot horse a little farther away from the coach. "Aren't we, Mr. McPhee?"

"Pardon me, pardon me. This is most unpleasant and embarrassing," McPhee's voice sounded, more than a touch breathless and weakened during a pause in his violent and noisy attempts to void his stomach. "No mess here."

Newt looked to McPhee's fellow passengers and could only imagine what the inside of the coach was like.

Skitch threw a quick glance behind him at McPhee, but turned away just as quickly. "He's puking in his hat."

"Tidy fellow, that Mr. McPhee," Newt said. "Real considerate and mannerly."

CHAPTER NINE

"You in or you out?" the bucktoothed gambler across the table said.

Irish Jack O'Harrigan didn't look up at him, and instead continued to study the pasteboards on the edge of the table before him. He wrinkled his broad nose and sniffled, and squinted against the dim light of the room.

"You're on a rare streak of luck tonight, Seamus," he said when he finally lifted his chin and the brim of his derby hat enough to look across the table at the bucktoothed gambler. Only the two of them were left in the hand, and a considerable pile of coins and paper money lay on the table between them.

"Every man gets on a run now and again," the bucktoothed one called Seamus said, and licked the sweat off his upper lip after he said it.

It was a hot room, made worse due to the

fact that it was the hottest part of the afternoon, and Seamus was sweating profusely. Sweating so much that his own hat had slipped uncomfortably down to the tops of his ears. He had big ears that stuck out almost perpendicularly from the sides of his head, something that he was uncomfortable with and normally tried to keep covered with his hair, but those ears, for once, were coming in handy to keep his sweaty hat held up. It would have been bothersome to have to resituate his hat given the quality of the poker hand he had before him and given Irish Jack's worsening mood.

Irish Jack, on the other hand, didn't seem bothered by the heat, nor was there a bead of sweat visible on his freckled face or the stubble of red whiskers lining his jaws. He finished the last of the whiskey in his glass with his hand not examining his hole cards, and then took hold of his fancy gold watch chain with a finger bone decorating the end of it and serving as a fob. It was a real human finger bone, polished and shiny white, and Seamus thought it an unusual and morbid decoration. Jack pulled his pocket watch from his silk vest and glanced at the timepiece, as if it would somehow make the decision for him whether to fold, call, or raise.

Seamus observed Irish Jack closely, his attention not so much on the watch, but instead on Jack's hand that held it. A pair of short-barrel Remington revolvers rode in shoulder holsters under each of Jack's armpits, and that hand that held the watch was dangerously close to the butts of either of those pistols. Seamus had gambled in the territory long enough to hear that Jack was a notoriously sore loser, as well as a volatile man. Seamus, having never progressed beyond a questionable and intermittent third-grade education in a country schoolhouse back in Missouri, wasn't exactly sure what *volatile* meant, but he knew enough to keep an eye on Jack's gun hand.

"Your play," Seamus said more quietly than he had before.

"I don't recall that there's any time limit on how long a man can take thinking over his cards," Jack said.

Seamus was some relieved when Irish Jack put the watch away and lowered his gun hand. But then again, that hand had disappeared under the table's edge, and that was a whole new set of worries. Seamus had one of his own hands under the table, trying to work the cuff of his coat sleeve up so that he could expose the little derringer he carried strapped to his forearm, and he had no reason to believe that Jack wasn't doing something equally devious under his own side of the table.

"I think I've made up me mind," Jack pronounced in a tone Seamus didn't like.

"You callin' or raisin'?" Seamus asked. He almost had his sleeve pushed up to where the derringer would be handy, rubbing his forearm against his thigh, but not so wiggly that Jack would catch on to what he was doing.

"I'm raising you," Jack said, and pushed the last of his table stakes into the pot.

"What you got there? Thirty dollars?" Seamus asked.

"Thereabouts. I'm all in, I am."

Seamus looked down at the pair of aces he had showing among his four up cards and then took a peek at the other ace he had as his hole card. He was considerably shocked that Jack had raised him. He knew that Jack held only a pair of queens, for he had purposely dealt them to Jack that way. Odds were that Jack had paired up another of his cards. Still, a man being foolish enough to raise on two pair, queen high, with a pair of aces showing on the board across from him was enough cause to have taken away some of Seamus's guilt at cheating — if Seamus had been one to feel any guilt about such doings, which he wasn't. Being a professional gambler meant you had to win regularly enough to make a living, and playing fair was no way to win regularly.

Seamus tried not to grin when he counted out thirty dollars and slid the money into the pot to match Jack's bet. "I call."

"Go ahead and put the rest of it in," Jack said quietly.

Seamus was slow to catch on. "What? I matched your thirty. Pot's right."

"Put all your money in." The tone of Jack's voice caused the other two gamblers on either side of him and Seamus to scoot back their chairs, hoping for more distance from the table and to get out of Jack's sight.

"Pot's right, I tell you," Seamus said. "Count it if you wish."

"All of it."

Seamus started to complain, but Jack shook his head slowly. That was enough to give Seamus pause. He wondered how he could get his other hand under the table without making Jack's mood deteriorate any further, especially when Jack got to see that his two pair was the losing hand.

"What you got in the hole?" Jack asked. "Another ace? You been scratching the corners of the aces ever since you sat down here, and I suspect you aren't above hiding

125

one or two of them if the mood strikes you."

"I don't like what you're hintin' at." Seamus thought he did a reasonable job of appearing both shocked and offended. He was often proud of his dramatic skills, something that was useful in the gambling business. Even his second-grade teacher, a smelly but pleasant woman, had bragged on his performance as a shepherd in the school-house Christmas play. Of course, that was in his younger days, but he liked to think that with time and practice he had become a much better actor. And had that teacher the chance to cast him again for her play he would, no doubt, garner a speaking role, perhaps the narrator, no less.

Jack seemed not to have heard him, or was at least no connoisseur of the thespian arts. He continued in a dull drone, the hint of the Irish brogue in his speech. "You're slick, Seamus, I'll give you that. But you ought not win so much when it's your turn to deal. Suspicious is what it is."

Seamus intended to scoot back from the table and grab for his derringer all in one quick motion, but Jack had taken a cross-armed hold on both of his pistol butts before Seamus could so much as move.

"You're a damned cheat," Jack said. "A shyster if I ever saw one."

"I never . . . ."

By then, the other two players had left their chairs and were well clear of the table and standing with the rest of the onlookers over by the bar. Several of them had more schooling than Seamus and knew what *volatile* meant. They also knew that word fit Irish Jack quite accurately, and accordingly, the odds of gunplay and dangerous stray bullets were increased.

Seamus knew there was a way out of his predicament, if he could only think of the right words. In his experience, a man who could say the right thing could get out of almost anything, even when caught cheating. He had spent years trying to learn some bigger words, for they seemed more effective, even if only to make lesser men pause while they tried to figure out what those words meant. And a pause could buy you time to run or to pull a weapon.

Most of the gents and rich folks that he had observed had plenty of big words and made good use of them. But big words and the right big words had always been a strain for Seamus. He picked the most intriguing ones out of newspapers and off the labels of store-bought goods, the more letters to a word the better. His spelling of such words was iffy, but he rarely had cause to write and no one to write to should he have wanted to send a letter. The worst problem about using one of the new words he found was that he wasn't always sure where it fit properly or how it should be pronounced. What if he should happen to be in some random conversation with a stranger, and that stranger should happen to know the very word Seamus was pronouncing wrong? That could be highly embarrassing, to say the least, and would surely ruin any effect he had intended. But at the moment he doubted there was much risk of Irish Jack outwording him. Jack seemed to care little for word choice, placing more emphasis on the pistols he was grasping.

"You seem to have concerns about the propriety and the fairness of my play," Seamus said. *Propriety* wasn't an especially long word, but it was the only recent acquirement that came to mind. Seamus had no doubt that he could think of a bigger and better word if Irish Jack would quit pressuring him so.

"Propriety?" Jack asked, somewhat perplexed, or perhaps annoyed.

Seamus was pleased that he knew a word that Jack didn't. Maybe he could work him off his guard, for Jack obviously didn't spend enough time reading.

"I would not have a stranger claiming that he got less than an equitable shake from my dealing." *Equitable* was another big word, and Seamus was proud to have thought of it in such a bind. "What say you take your money out of that pot and let's call it quits. No hard feelings, huh? That would be the sporting thing, eh?"

Irish Jack shook his head while he sat there cross-armed and studying Seamus. "No, you got two ways out of this. You leave all your money on the table and skitter your hind legs out of here, or you pull that hideout gun you've been playing with under the table and see if you can kill me."

Seamus licked his upper lip again. His coat, a requirement for a man who needed to hide small pistols on his arm or possibly stash a card here and there, was unreasonably hot, and his hat had slipped a little farther down his head. He sweated some more and wondered if Jack would let him get his other hand under the table before he started drawing those Remington pistols under his armpits.

"How do I know you won't murder me when I stand up?" Seamus asked.

"Like you said, you've been on a good run. You'll have to see if it lasts," Jack said. One of his shaggy eyebrows and the eyelid that went with it were twitching by then.

Seamus glanced at the money piled in the pot, and then at what he had before him on his side of the table that Jack insisted on also having. It was a goodly amount to surrender and far more than Jack had lost since sitting in on the game, but nothing Seamus couldn't stand to lose. After all, he had a healthy stake remaining in his vest pocket and enough to get in another game elsewhere with less *acrimonious* and *vindictive* opponents. His brain seemed to be finally working properly to have plucked out two such complicated and difficult words out of the thin air, but there wasn't much solace in that, considering the decision at hand.

He brought his hand from under the table slowly and braced himself against the tabletop, preparing to rise. Irish Jack's eye was still twitching, and Seamus couldn't tell if that was a normal thing or if it wasn't. He stood even more slowly, so slowly that his legs barely managed the feat after sitting so long. There was no word that Seamus knew of for such an awkwardly embarrassing and terrifying condition.

Irish Jack didn't shoot him, but Seamus knew that it was still a long ways to the front door. Fifteen feet and six inches, to be exact. He had measured it only the day before in case he should be able to sucker someone less informed into making a bet with him on who could guess closest to the distance.

"I'm going to leave now," Seamus said.

Jack only nodded.

"You won't shoot me in the back, will you? I admit that would be bothersome on my part."

To answer him, Jack drew both his Remingtons and thumped them on the tabletop before him. The draw had been surprisingly fast, and Seamus was glad that he hadn't chosen to go for his own derringer or the knife or other pistol at his belt. Knives and pistols worked fine on some, but not on those with the hand speed and coordination such as Irish Jack. Seamus promised himself to remember that. Perhaps he ought to hire someone with faster hands to watch his back in the future. A hired man not busy with the game could keep his gun out at all times and thus not have to worry about drawing fast.

Jack let go of his pistols and laid his hands in his lap, leaning back slightly and making a peaceful show of distancing himself from his weapons. "There, how's that?"

Seamus took one last longing look at the money he was leaving on the table, then turned and took his first step toward the door that led outside. He kept his neck craned over his shoulder and a careful watch on Jack, but Jack left his guns on the table and acted as if he had no intent of reaching for them. The look on his face was almost pleasant other than that twitching eye, and Seamus hoped that he had decided to let bygones be bygones.

Three more gingerly steps and Seamus was halfway across the room, but the brief distance to the door somehow seemed expanded. And his back felt as if it were wider than normal, despite his being an uncommonly thin man. He took another step.

The front door had been left open, and a splash of sunlight spilled into the room. And that beam of sunlight looked better than anything that Seamus had ever seen. Before long he quit watching Jack over his shoulder and focused on getting to that light. He even began to think he was going to make it.

CHAPTER TEN

The roar of the gun echoed in the confines of the room and caused dust to fall from the low ceiling. The shot took Seamus squarely between the shoulders and flung him flat on his face two steps short of the door. One outstretched hand was all that lay in the sunlight.

Those watching from the bar or pinned back against some wall took their hands off their ears once the concussion was over and looked from the dead man to Irish Jack. Jack's pistols were still resting where they had been, untouched, but he held a smoking sawed-off shotgun across the tabletop that he had obviously been hiding in his lap all along. He rose and holstered his pistols, broke the shotgun open, and ejected the spent brass cartridge and inserted a fresh one while he walked across the room to Seamus's body. He snapped the gun closed and bent over and began to search the dead

133

gambler's sleeves and the rest of the inside of his coat, taking special care to avoid the blood.

Another redhead, similar in his freckles and fat nose to Irish Jack but almost twice as big, came through the front door and joined him beside the body. He was a mountain of a man and had to stoop to keep his head from banging the low rafters. Ten Mule was his name, the very same redhead who had left Vulture City so recently. His face still bore the swelling and bruises from his prizefight.

Ten Mule stood there stooped over like that, frowning at the mess the charge of buckshot had made of the gambler's back. "I thought you told him you weren't going to shoot him in the back."

Irish Jack gave Ten Mule a quick glare. "How come you have to stand bent over that way? It annoys me to no end."

"It's the only way I can keep from whacking my head."

"Well, you don't have to stoop around me. It makes you look like you're stupid. Stand straight and whack your head, or leave me be," Jack said. "And don't you hang around doors eavesdropping on me when I'm about to shoot someone. You could get hit by accident like that."

Ten Mule seemed not to hear him. "I said, how come you shot him in the back after you said you wouldn't?"

"Changed my mind," Jack said as he straightened from his search of the body. "Can you believe that his hat stayed on?"

"Well, he's wearing it pulled way down and he's got those big ears," Ten Mule offered.

Irish Jack stuffed a roll of greenbacks in his vest pocket and then held up a playing card for Ten Mule to see. It was the ace of hearts.

"What's with the card?" Ten Mule asked.

"I was going to let him walk, but I got to thinking on this ace," Jack said. "I hadn't seen it for a good while."

Jack hung his sawed-off scattergun in the crook of one elbow and went back to the table and gathered his winnings before he took a quick survey of the other occupants of the room.

"I guessed he had this ace stashed, and here it is," he added as he held up the card he had found on Seamus's body, as if that said it all.

Nobody in the room had any comment to make about the card, or Jack's shooting of Seamus, for that matter. Either Seamus hadn't been well liked, or else nobody wanted any trouble with Irish Jack.

Jack went toward the door, but stopped again over the gambler's body. "I should've given the cheating bastard both barrels."

"I'd say one did the trick," Ten Mule replied.

"True, but I bet his hat wouldn't have stayed on his head that way if I gave him both barrels, screwed down on those big ears or not."

Ten Mule wondered why it mattered that the dead card cheat's hat had stayed on after being murdered. Jack liked to be thorough in all things, and maybe a hat staying on one of his victim's head made him doubt the quality of his shotgun cartridges.

Jack went out the door with Ten Mule following him. Ten Mule was still stooping, but he did hit his head twice on the rafters, no matter how he bent over. The last time he knocked his hat off and had to come back and get it. He gave those watching him an embarrassed look due to having lost his hat in front of them when the dead man on the floor had done a much better job of keeping his own headwear in place, weak buckshot charge or not.

Irish Jack was studying Ten Mule's lathered horse tied in front of the cantina when Ten Mule appeared outside. "You're too heavy for that horse. You ought to find a bigger horse or take to walking instead of riding."

Truly, the horse did look tired and miserable, and it was a small horse. Anyone looking at Ten Mule and then the horse would have found it hard to believe he had ridden the poor animal very far without it dropping.

"How long have you been here?" Jack asked.

"Long enough to hear you shoot that gambler," Ten Mule answered. "He was so talky I thought he might wear you down and make you forget you intended to kill him."

"Yes, he was a talker, for sure," Jack said, behaving a little less surly. "I thought you were in Vulture City."

"I was till I had to leave."

"Who gave you the beating?" Jack asked, taking note of Ten Mule's battered face.

"The Widowmaker."

"Who?"

"Widowmaker Jones. He's in Vulture City. Me and him had us a boxing match. You heard of him, haven't you?"

"How'd he whip you?"

"He didn't whip me. I hit him a good one and knocked him out. That's why I had to leave."

"You tore his meat house down, but you're the one that had to leave?"

"I had a little bag of shot hid in my fist. He's bound to come gunning for me."

"Well, maybe you did right. You're handy to have around to put your boots to a man, but you never have been much good with firearms," Irish Jack said. "Though I don't like the thought of everyone knowing you ran from him. There's not many that know you're my nephew, but it would be a blight on the family name if they did."

"I brought you some news. That's part of why I come."

"What news besides the Widowmaker's hunting you?"

"Tom Skitch is planning on trying a shipment. Could be they'll try leaving soon. Skitch's been asking around camp for express guards, and I heard that the Stutter brothers and the Dutchman have taken him up on his offer."

"The Stutter brothers?"

"That's right. And the Dutchman."

"The Stutter brothers don't worry me, but the Dutchman I could do without."

"That old man? I wouldn't have figured you even knew him."

"He's the kind you've got to watch."

Ten Mule didn't particularly like the

Dutchman. The old man was entirely too cranky and didn't like to talk while at work. But at least the Dutchman was something Jack seemed willing to talk about. "I like to have smashed the Dutchman's hand once when he was holding a drill for me. He was wobbling it all around and couldn't hold it steady. He's shaky like that, and I don't suppose a man that old and shaky would be much of a gun guard."

Irish Jack gave Ten Mule a wicked look and shook his head. "If you weren't my nephew . . ."

Jack didn't finish what he was going to say, but he was still frowning when he shoved his stubby little shotgun in a pommel holster beside his saddle horn. The stock of it had been cut off at the pistol grip and the double barrels sawn off so short that it hardly got in his way when he mounted.

Jack reined his horse around, but held it in place while he watched Ten Mule preparing his own horse. "You'll be lucky if that pony makes it much farther."

"Think I should steal another one?" Ten Mule looked at the line of horses in front of the cantina.

"None of them are any bigger or stouter-looking than the one you have and just as

139

likely to cripple under you," Irish Jack said. "Besides, you can sooner get away with taking a man's money than you can his horse. It's been my experience that's a sure way to eventually get your neck stretched, taking horses that don't belong to you."

"What if this one I'm riding doesn't make it?" Ten Mule asked. "I paid Skinny thirty dollars for him, but you're right, he doesn't look so good."

"Then I'll leave you afoot. You're too big to ride double with me." Irish Jack was already riding away, leaving the little cantina on the outskirts of Phoenix in his dust.

Some farmer's pigs had gotten loose, and they stood in the middle of the road coated in mud from a nearby irrigation ditch and grunting and squealing over something they had found. Ten Mule saw that it was a snake they had caught when one of the shoats broke free of the cluster shaking the limp form of the reptile in its mouth and causing more squealing and grunting as the other hogs tried to steal the recently caught morsel.

Jack spurred his horse through the hogs, obviously trying to trample as many as he could, but they dodged his efforts and stood in the road watching him after he passed. Ten Mule thought they looked at Jack's retreating back skeptically, if pigs could look skeptical.

"Damned hogs," Jack said when Ten Mule booted his tired horse in the belly and caught up with Jack.

"I like hogs just fine if they kill snakes," Ten Mule mused.

"You what?" Jack asked.

"I said I don't mind hogs, especially if they'll cut down on the rattlers," Ten Mule said. "I ever tell you about the time I squatted down over a rattlesnake? There I was with my bare arse hanging out and about to do my business when I look down between my legs and see this great old big snake. Well, I'll tell you I . . . ."

Jack glared at him. "Where there's pigs there's diggers."

Diggers were what Jack called farmers, and any man hearing him say that understood by the way he said it how much he disliked diggers. Jack had spent his youth on a farm back in County Cork in the old country and subsequently hated anything to do with agricultural endeavors, especially farmers. He claimed that years of starving and slaving on that Irish farm had been what led him to flee to America in the first place and to look for easier ways to make a living after serving in the war.

The once-tiny settlement of Phoenix had grown into a town proper and showed signs of growing bigger yet, all due to the diggers that Jack was currently getting all worked up over simply due to a few hogs getting in his way. But Jack was like that, and liable to go from a perfectly pleasant mood to anger when something got in the way of what he wanted to do or at the appearance of something he particularly disliked.

Several small farms were in sight, worsening Jack's mood. The green of crops marked the course of the irrigation ditch, one of many of the old Indian canals that the pioneers of Phoenix had cleaned out or modified and extended to tap the water supply provided by the Salt River. Ten Mule couldn't even imagine how many shovelfuls of dirt had been removed to water the land, but knew Jack was right in that sense, for the farmers truly were diggers.

"I imagine if they dug straight down instead of sideways they'd be to China by now." Ten Mule thought it was a fairly witty observation, but Jack only glared at him again.

"Damned fool diggers," was Jack's answer.

Ten Mule thought Jack was wrong to dislike farmers so. Farmers were rarely well armed and easy to rob on the rare occasion they had anything you wanted to steal. But he didn't voice those thoughts with Jack still glaring at him and obviously on the prod. Ten Mule regretted having mentioned that he wasn't bothered by pigs, regardless of whether they killed snakes or not. One of these days Jack might get bitten by a rattlesnake and thus come to understand pigs weren't all bad, but until then it was best to keep quiet about the matter.

Jack was turned in the saddle and staring at the pigs in the road as if he was thinking of turning back and trying to trample them again. But after a time the pigs were out of sight and they had left the farm country behind. The farther away he got, the more Jack seemed to calm.

"Where are we going?" Ten Mule asked, taking the chance to move the conversation on to a less dangerous topic.

"We got us a bit of road work to do, if what you've told me is true," Jack answered.

Ten Mule nodded at that. Jack never used the words *robbery* or *stealing,* or anything like that. He always referred to the way he made his living as *road work.*

"How much money you think we'll get? Plenty, right?"

"Make that horse keep up," Irish Jack said. "The only thing that makes traveling with you bearable is that you're big enough to cast a good patch of shade."

Ten Mule wrinkled his face in thought while he weighed whether or not he should ask any more questions. Shooting the cheating gambler and then running afoul of a herd of disrespectful pigs had Jack feeling bloody, and asking too many questions when Jack was like that was risky. Ten Mule had seen him gut-shoot men for less, or cut them with the long, slender dagger that he carried in his boot top. But Jack was prone to riding long stretches without saying much at all, and questioning him was sometimes the only way to get a conversation out of him. And talking helped to pass the miles, especially when Ten Mule had to keep kicking his tired horse in the belly to keep it moving.

Ten Mule urged his horse back up alongside Jack's and decided to risk it. "You didn't say how much money you figure we can get."

Irish Jack pulled out the playing card again that he had taken from Seamus's body, studied it for a moment, then flicked it away. "All of it. That's what we're going to get. Every damned last ounce of it."

Irish Jack spurred his horse to a trot as the pasteboard he had flung away fluttered in the wind behind him until it finally lodged itself in a bush. It was still there when they rode out of sight, headed for an appointment with a stagecoach.

CHAPTER ELEVEN

The stagecoach changed horses at Wicken-burg, thirteen miles to the north of Vulture City. A wizened old man puffing on the glowing stub of a cigar was waiting for them at the station in the middle of the sleepy settlement. The Stutter brothers and the old man harnessed the fresh team in the dark, while lawyer McPhee weakly hugged the rear wheel and watched Jenny slosh out the floor of the coach with a bucket of water.

The new horses were, if anything, more rambunctious than the first team, and Newt guessed that the stage company was buying half-gentled mustangs instead of trained draft stock to save a dollar. One of the Stutter brothers took a glancing kick to his thigh, and the old man had to dodge twice to avoid being pawed or bitten.

"You better keep an eye on dem horses, Herr Skitch," the old man said between draws on his cigar and while he scratched at

146

his whiskers. "Only zee second time zey've been in harness, and zey're apt to throw a runaway, you bet."

Tom Skitch's face was lit briefly as he drew on his pipestem. "Seen anybody strange hanging about?"

"Strange? Hav of zee peoples in zis territory are strange," said the old man.

"I mean anybody suspicious."

"You mean Irish Jack or some of his men? I zee none of them, nope."

"Maybe we fooled them."

"Maybe, but you still got to go right through Seymour, same as if you had taken zee road east, you bet. Maybe you go out of your ways for nuzzing."

"I intend to keep anybody guessing that has ambitions," Skitch said. "Leastwise, I won't let 'em get good and set before they try to waylay us."

"Sounds good in zeory, but I'm glad I'm not riding wiz you to see how it works out."

"I've got a few tricks left in my bag," Skitch said, but he didn't sound as confident as he probably intended. "You're welcome to come along. We could use another gun."

"No, I done been shot over zat mine once already, and I don't favor taking another bullet, you bet. Last one about took my head off, and I don't zink straight since."

The old man lifted his hat a little and probed in the hair on one side of his head, as if that proved something, even though it was too dark to see what kind of wound or old scar he was pointing out.

"Be seeing you, Henry. Thanks for helping us out and keeping this on the quiet."

The old man gestured with his cigar at the Dutchman sitting his horse a ways off from them and at the rear of the stage. His voice lowered to a little above a whisper. "Tom, you're a fool to trust zat one. He used to work for me and he was zee worst high-grader I ever saw, yep. I would have had him hung if I could have caught him at it. I would have, you bet."

"The Dutchman's always been on the up-and-up with me," Skitch said.

"You watch him, I tell you. Herr Waltz, he's a cagey one. Always on the lookout for himself."

"So long, Henry."

"Hold on." The old man grabbed Skitch by the upper arm. "You asked before if zhere had been any strangers here."

Skitch pulled away gently from the old man's clutches, but leaned close to him. "Go ahead."

The old man's cigar ash glowed brightly when he inhaled, and his next words were mixed with the faint, ghost tendrils of tobacco smoke. "Two men were here yesterday evening. Two men in long coats and riding black horses that looked so alike they would have made a matched buggy team."

"And you've never seen them before?"

The glowing ash of the cigar waved back and forth. "No, and zey didn't even come to introduce zemselves, nor to have a drink at my store. Just sat zeir horses up on a hill for a couple of hours, watching, and I zink I saw ze reflection shining off binoculars or a spyglass before it got dark."

"You got any idea what they were about?"

"No good, I zink."

"Thanks." Skitch headed for the stagecoach's door.

"Funny-talking fellow," Newt said to Skitch when the old man had walked back inside his station.

"Henry's a good one," Skitch said.

"That little Prussian is Henry?" Newt asked. "The one she talked about?"

"That's him, Henry Wickenburg, but Austrian, I think. He founded the Vulture Mine and loaned that reb, Jack Swilling, the money to start digging his water canals down at Phoenix and put it on the map. Henry's a real pioneer in these parts."

Newt thought about the relatively unimpressive old man and studied the shadows of the village around them. There were only the stage station, what looked like a saloon, a few other abandoned commercial buildings in various states of disrepair, and a cluster of humble houses. Nothing about the place named after Henry Wickenburg could be truly called a town, but maybe it had seen better days, same as the man it was named after. "He doesn't look exactly prosperous."

"He made the biggest gold strike in the history of the territory. Nobody can take that away from him," Skitch said. "He's just hit a rough stretch of late."

Newt nodded. "What is it they say? Gold is easier to find than it is to keep?"

"Don't remind me."

"What do you make of what he said about those men on black horses?"

"Could be anybody."

"Could be someone waiting for your gold shipment."

"We'll cross that bridge when we come to it," Skitch said as he climbed into the stagecoach.

Jenny Silks and McPhee were already inside the coach, and Newt couldn't help but admire the little lawyer's pluck. He doubted that if his own self was that sick he would have been willing to crawl back inside the stage.

One of the Stutter brothers was holding the bridle of one of the lead horses to keep the team from taking off, and he waited until Skitch had climbed inside and closed the door, and until the Dutchman and Newt were mounted before he let go and ran to join his brother up on the box. He barely made it and had to leap for the driver's box on the fly, as once more the coach lurched forward at high speed. The new team of horses was faster and wilder than the first set, but the Stutter brother on the ribbons sawed on their bridle bits and cursed them enough to keep them to a relatively safe trot.

The trail followed the course of the Hassayampa River for a short ways before it entered a tight canyon. The narrow confines forced them to travel practically in the riverbed at times. Newt kept nervous watch on the bluffs above them. There was plenty of cover on both sides of the river to hide ambushers in the daylight, much less at night, and he was relieved when the canyon began to open up and the trail climbed up on the side of a hill to hug the east bank of the river.

There was soon light glowing on the horizon, and Newt was able to make out that the trail ran along the edge of some rugged, barren foothills scored with gullies and littered with jumbled rock. The stage-coach caused a considerable amount of dust, and because he brought up the rear he rode as wide of it as he could and kept a rag tied around his face to filter out the worst of it. The Circle Dot horse, while peculiar, was ever eager to travel, and the brown gelding kept pace at a trot, his little foxlike ears perked forward and his head bobbing with every stride.

The road became too narrow and the dust too thick, and Newt moved forward to ride alongside the stage. The coach was no stripped-down mud wagon such as many backwater lines used to carry passengers over rough trails or during the muddy season, but a genuine Concord-style coach with solid wooden sides painted bright green and gold and with a luggage boot on the back of it with a leather drape covering it. A painted shield on the door read GILMER & SALISBURY.

Skitch leaned out the window and saw Newt looking at the sign on the door.

"The stage company's giving you a special run?" Newt asked.

"The Stutter brothers work for the line, but they were more than willing to roll out their stage for the bonus I'm paying them," Skitch replied.

"Whether their bosses at Gilmer and Salisbury know about it or not?"

"I don't know. Maybe," Skitch growled.

Newt leaned down in the saddle to where he could see through the window into the interior of the coach. "How's our lawyer making it?"

"He hasn't thrown up in his hat since we left Wickenburg."

"And the woman?"

"It isn't like I can't hear you," Jenny's voice replied. "But, for your information, *the woman* is making it fine."

Newt straightened in the saddle and nudged his horse even with the driver's box to get a better look at the road ahead and to avoid having to talk with Jenny Silks. The Stutter brothers nodded at him.

"How . . . ddd . . . do?" the one driving said.

He was the brother Skitch referred to as Ned, a sandy-haired kid, maybe in his twenties, with a scraggly dusting of fine whiskers on his cheeks. Young or not, he kept his rifle propped up against his shoulder like he was used to one, and handled the six-horse ribbons like a veteran driver. The other brother, Fred, riding shotgun beside him, looked exactly the same, so similar that they could have been twins, if, indeed, they weren't.

"You men making it all right?" Newt asked.

"Mmm . . . making it fuh . . . fff . . . fine," Ned said.

"Easy muh . . . money," Fred added.

It was readily apparent how they got their nickname, for both of them stuttered fiercely, even over the simplest words.

"Where you from?" Newt asked.

"The . . . guh . . . guh." Ned stalled out trying to spit out whatever he wanted to say and nudged Fred in the ribs. "Ya . . . you tell 'im."

Fred bowed his chest out and threw back his head like a rooster about to crow. "We'uz from the . . . guh . . . grear . . . sssss . . . state of . . . Muh . . . Muh . . . Mississippi."

Both brothers looked at Newt carefully as if to gauge how much that pronouncement impressed him. Newt nodded somberly so as not to let them down.

"Keep your eyes peeled," Newt said. "It's been too easy so far."

Fred Stutter, or at least Newt thought it was Fred — he was having a hard time keeping their names straight — yes, Fred reached down into the box at his feet and came up with a 10-gauge coach gun and brandished it in one hand and his Winchester carbine in the other. Holding those two guns like that, and with the bandolier of brass shotgun shells slung across his chest and the headwind folding back the broad brim of his hat, he looked like nothing so much as some silly photographer's idea of a wild, western scout, or maybe a Mexican bandito.

"Old Irish . . . Juhyack . . . sh . . . shows his topknot up the rrr . . . road, I'll bust his guh . . . guh . . . gourd . . . plll . . . plumb center," Fred swore.

Ned nodded in agreement. "Tell 'im, brother. Suh . . . suh . . . savage chillen we is and . . . crrrrr . . . kruh . . . crack shots, too."

It was Fred's turn to nod. "From the guh . . . guh . . . grrr . . ."

"The great state of Missssissippi," Newt finished for him.

"You got it mmm . . . mister," Ned said.

Waltz, the one called the Dutchman, was riding about forty yards ahead. Newt had been looking for a chance to talk with him and take his measure. Daylight had revealed the Dutchman to be a scowling sort, scowling at the road ahead or scowling at whoever or whatever happened to pass through his vision. And Newt thought about what

155

Henry Wickenburg had said about the Dutchman, that he was a thief and a man who couldn't be trusted.

"How much farther to the next station?" Newt asked the Dutchman as he rode alongside of him.

The Dutchman gave him a hard look and acted as if he wasn't going to answer before he finally spoke. "Four miles, maybe, to Seymour."

Seymour Station, not far from Vulture City, and where they would have arrived if they had gone due east instead of going north to hit the stage road at Wickenburg. As it was, they had gone a long circle out of their way, but one that might have thrown off the timing of anyone lying in wait for them. It was also a route that might make any spies watching their departure from Vulture City believe that the stagecoach intended to go north to Prescott.

Newt took another look at the Dutchman. The man looked every bit as old as Henry Wickenburg, at least in the eyes and in the white of his bushy beard that reached to his chest, but where Wickenburg had been bent and withered, this man sat his saddle straight. Old maybe, but a powerful man no doubt, broad of shoulder and a couple of inches under six feet. The hands that gripped his bridle reins and held his big-bore No. 4 Ballard rifle were gnarled and scarred and burned brown from years under the desert sun. Those hands reminded Newt of nothing so much as the roots of a juniper bush he had once seen clinging to a bare rock ledge where no kind of plant should have been able to survive.

"What are the odds of us catching trouble before we hit the station at Seymour?" Newt asked. He got the impression from the way the scowling old man's eyes searched the trail ahead and the surrounding terrain that the Dutchman knew the country well. More important, he might know some of the most likely places for an ambush.

The Dutchman's face above his beard was shaded by the dip of his hat brim, and he took long in responding, as if Newt's question had interrupted whatever he was thinking about while looking at the desert and as if that interruption annoyed him to no end.

"Lots of places for trouble," the Dutch-man said. "It's a long way to the railroad."

The Dutchman's accent still held a slight hint of German, but no more than that. He spoke like most of the other workingmen of the West, and his voice was hard-edged and cracked like brittle twigs breaking some-where down inside him, as if his throat was perpetually dry.

"I've heard talk of Phoenix. Much of a place?" Newt asked.

"Regular town now, and some that live there are calling it a city," the Dutchman replied with more of a scowl, as if the word *town* was as distasteful to his mouth as taking a swig of alkali water. "Wasn't a bad place once, before Swilling and his farmers went to digging their ditches and over-crowded it. Now it's gone to church houses, red brick, and uppity ways. Give 'em a few more years and they'll get the railroad built up from Maricopa Station like they've been howling about."

"Times change." Newt wasn't much good at small talk, but he tried anyway. The Dutchman seemed to be a man who knew the country and might orient him as to what lay ahead and around them.

The Dutchman had nothing to say to that and leaned over the side of his horse and spat, although he didn't have any tobacco in his mouth. How a man with a voice like that found the moisture to spit, Newt couldn't say.

"What about Seymour?" Newt asked.

"Talky sort, ain't ya?" the Dutchman growled.

That brought a chuckle from Newt. Nobody had ever accused him of being talkative. Quite the contrary, in fact.

The Dutchman wrinkled his eyebrows and frowned at Newt's levity, but managed an answer. "Nothing there but a stage station and the water pump for Vulture City."

Newt looked back at the stagecoach and the trail behind it and then at the road ahead. "It's gone too easy so far."

"I suspect that'll change," the Dutchman replied, doing his own studying of the road ahead.

They rode a ways in silence before the Dutchman looked at Newt carefully from head to toe and then back again. "How come you hired on for this?"

"A man's got to work if he wants to eat," Newt answered.

The Dutchman gave a soft grunt as if he didn't believe it. "You'll smell powder smoke before this is over, mark my words. Irish Jack's got a taste for gold, and once a man has it he won't quit. Makes a man crazy, it does. Lay the tiniest chunk of it in a man's hand and watch how his eyes light up. A fever is what it is. Hits some worse than others, but nobody's immune."

Newt noticed how the Dutchman's voice changed when he spoke of gold, but he was too busy thinking his own thoughts to make

159

much of it. Gold fever, he'd seen it himself in camp after camp and boomtown after boomtown. Some fool made a lucky strike, and then the word went out that there were new rich diggings to be had for all comers. Soon, men would start showing up from everywhere to give it a try. Most of them would get nothing for their labor, but a few might strike it rich. And stories of those lucky few were part of what kept the hard-luck scrabblers moving on to the next strike to try it all again.

"Who's this Irish Jack I keep hearing about?" Newt asked.

"You ask him when you meet him, but if I was you I would spend my time ducking or fighting and not asking too many questions," the Dutchman said. "Jack's not much for talking when he's on the shoot."

"You asked me how come I hired on for this," Newt asked. "What about you?"

"Damned fool, I guess. Thought maybe I'd take my guard wages and do me some prospecting up in the mountains after this. A man can't get ahead sweating himself dry digging someone else's ore."

Newt looked at the purple-shadowed mountains far to the west that he had noticed earlier. "Got you a claim, do ya?"

The Dutchman gave him a suspicious

look. "What makes you think that? Maybe I do, maybe I don't."

The Dutchman's reaction wasn't a surprise to Newt. He never had been good at casual conversation the way most folks were. Always said the wrong thing.

"Those Mississippi boys on the box look steady enough," Newt said, trying to change the subject. "Skitch might have it right. Four good guns would make me think twice before I tackled this stage. Could be we'll make it through clean as a whistle."

"Them?" The Dutchman looked back at the Stutter brothers and gave another of his dismissive grunts.

"You don't trust them?"

The Dutchman jerked his head back at the stage. "That's a lot of gold."

Newt started to tell him that he had already learned that lesson well and long ago, but he didn't. And that lack of trust on his own part was one of the reasons he talked to the grumpy old man at all.

It paid to be cautious. The Dutchman might be on the up-and-up, no matter what Henry Wickenburg had said, or he might not. Choirboys didn't usually volunteer for the ugly jobs, and what you got was men with a little bark on them, rough men with rough ways. And Newt couldn't think of a single man he had ever known who hired out his gun, a man with scalps on his belt, who was what he would call a truly good man. Some were touchy, some were shifty, and every one of them had a streak of mean. And that went for men with badges, as well. He'd spent almost half his life working with such men that he didn't really know or couldn't trust, and wondering who would play it straight when the fat was in the fire and who wouldn't.

"Is that Seymour I see up ahead?" Newt asked after another stretch of silent riding.

"No. A fellow came here a few years back intent on trying his hand at farming. Damned fool built his barn and planted his orchard too close to the river and it washed him out. Nothing but the old house still standing," the Dutchman said begrudgingly. His mood seemed to have worsened since Newt had a mentioned a mining claim.

"Think we ought to ride up ahead and scout things out?"

The Dutchman squinted at him. "No, I'm getting paid for guarding. Not for scouting. But be my guest. Irish Jack usually isn't particular about who he shoots, and I'd rather it be you than me."

The stage rolled slowly behind them, and up ahead Newt could see the roof of a building sticking up above a belt of desert brush. The coach road seemed to pass between that building and the river and through that tangle of brush, forming a narrow choke point that he didn't like at all. The riverbank to his right dropped off sharply for ten feet or so, and once the stage was committed to that choke point there would be nothing to do but charge ahead if anyone was using the abandoned house for cover to lay an ambush.

"You know, what I hate worse than actually getting shot is feeling like I'm about to get shot," Newt said.

The Dutchman only grunted at that.

Newt's rifle was an Express Model 1876 Winchester chambered in .45-75, with folding-leaf rear sights and a half-round, half-octagonal barrel that had been cut down to carbine length by some gunsmith in the past. He shucked the Winchester from his rifle boot, cracked the action open enough to see that there was a round in the chamber, and then grounded the butt stock on his thigh with the rifle pointing skyward in his right hand. His left hand was light on the bridle reins, letting the Circle Dot horse pick its own pace.

The belt of low-growing brush was some fifty or sixty yards deep and the tangle of limbs and thorns pressed in close on either side of the trail until he and the Dutchman could see little except for the daylight directly ahead of them where the thicket finally ended and the trail once more entered open desert.

Without being cued and of its own volition, the Circle Dot horse stopped with its head raised and its ears perked at the far edge of the brush belt. Newt let the horse stand, because he had long ago learned to trust the gelding's instincts, no matter how odd some of the animal's actions were.

The Dutchman stopped his own horse, and he and Newt scanned the desert before them. The country beyond the brush belt opened up considerably to a gravel flat dotted thinly with dry clumps of buckskin-colored grass and scattered cactus, and a little less than two hundred yards away stood a single, dirt-roofed jacal with walls built of slim ironwood poles jammed in the ground and with mud plastered between them to chink the cracks. A few crooked fence posts stuck up like rib bones to mark where a corral had once been, the fence rails and the rest having been scavenged and carted off to build other things or burned for firewood. No other structures were visible. Newt had seen many such places, ghost towns, ruins, and the wind-scoured remains of well-intended ambitions that didn't survive. Pick the wrong location, the wrong moment, and a place didn't last.

Newt remained where he was for a long time, studying the jacal carefully. Behind him he could hear the occasional stamp of a horse's hoof or the rattle of a trace chain as the stagecoach closed the distance behind him.

"Trouble?" Skitch called to him from the stage.

Trouble? No trouble at all, because trouble is what you're paying me for. Newt scolded himself for the way his thoughts were running. If a man took a job, then he ought to do it without complaining. But for the thousandth time Newt wondered why he hadn't had the good sense to learn a safer trade. He could think of all kinds of professions where there was scant chance of getting your guts blown out through your backbone on any given day, and he wondered what failing there was in him that kept him living such a life. Why couldn't he have been a doctor or a schoolteacher, a craftsman or a storekeeper, a farmer or a peddler, or anything normal and less likely to see you laid in a shallow grave sooner rather than later?

165

He grimaced and pushed such thoughts away. What was it that Mother Jones used to say? "You made your bed, now lie in it." "No crying over spilt milk." And all such old sayings like that. Damned if the woman didn't sound smarter and smarter over the years, and damned how he missed her. How long since she was gone now? The years had a way of fading one into the other. His mother had been uncommonly thoughtful and had proven to be somewhat of a sage in his opinion, but he doubted even she could have predicted her prodigal Tennessee son would have ended up in a sweaty thicket in the Arizona Territory wondering where the first bullet was going to come from and when. And all for a few dollars of wages, no more than a man could lose in a night's worth of overpriced liquor and bad gambling. It was a pitiful price to put on a man's life.

The stage road passed barely fifty yards in front of that jacal on its way southward, and for that matter, the jacal held a commanding field of fire, and there was no way to approach it from any direction without putting yourself at risk from the marksmanship of anyone who might have decided to use it as an ambush point. A fool express guard riding in the lead of his shipment would be especially under the gun if that was the case, and for all he knew a gun could be aimed at him that very moment.

He took another deep breath and nudged the Circle Dot horse ahead. He counted his horse's steps, one by one. *So far, so good.* A man had to look at the bright side.

On a rocky ridge a mile to the west across the Hassayampa River, two men wearing long, pale linen dusters sat their black horses, watching the stagecoach. Newt might have seen the brief flash of sunlight on their spyglass if he hadn't been too busy worrying about how he was going to keep himself alive and get the Vulture Mine's shipment a little farther down the Gunpowder Express.

CHAPTER TWELVE

Inside the stagecoach, Tom Skitch closed his eyes and leaned back against his seat, either because he was tired or simply to take a moment's reprieve against the stress. It was barely past sunup, but already the inside of the coach was growing hot. Lawyer McPhee fanned his face with his hat. Some color had returned to his face.

"A good hat comes in handy out here," Skitch said without opening his eyes, and with a hint of chuckle in his voice.

The fact that he was fanning his face with the same hat he had puked in earlier must have been very embarrassing for the lawyer, because he ignored Skitch's remark as if he hadn't heard it.

Unlike Skitch, Jenny Silks couldn't have closed her eyes and slept if she wanted to. She avoided tangling legs with McPhee and scooted across the rear bench and leaned against the side wall where she could look out the window. The sunlight was hitting that side of the coach the hardest, and she dropped her veil over her pale face and leaned her head slightly out of the window to better see the trail ahead. To her disappointment, there was nothing really to see, other than a narrow lane of wagon ruts passing through the scrub. But at least there was some fresher air to be had. Despite her rinsing of the coach, it still bore the sickly sweet smell of McPhee's vomit.

"Where did the Dutchman and the Widowmaker go?" she said up to Fred Stutter where he rode shotgun on the box.

"Ggg . . . got a tight sss . . . spot ahead. Mmm . . . might be somethin', mmm . . . might not." Like his brother, Fred sounded as if he was straining and half strangling to make the words come out right, and as a result he was slightly breathless at the end of each outburst.

Jenny squinted over the top of the brush that encroached tightly on the sides of the trail, and she thought about the Widowmaker. Maybe only another hard case — she had seen plenty of them come and go — but what a strange one he was. Dark and with violence oozing out every sweaty pore of him, if she didn't miss her guess, but something else, too, that didn't fit with the rest of him. Those tired, stubborn eyes of his staring out of that scarred face, so calmly and almost wise; as if he had seen it all before, and as if nothing that could happen to him were anything but an old game, no matter that he couldn't have been much older than her, if any.

And she had reason to know that look and the feelings that caused it. A human being could take only so much before you became numb to the game, calloused to misfortune, and until there was no such thing as surprise. She'd taken enough licks herself, but she promised herself then and there, as she had so many times before, that she was getting out a winner this time. She had paid her dues, waiting for this very moment. Some said you had to crawl before you walked, and damned if she hadn't done more than her share of crawling, and suffered enough indignities for two lifetimes. She had groveled and stooped and sold herself to whoever had the coin.

Her glance fell on the express box in the floor of the coach for an instant. Everything depended on that box, all she had worked for, and enough to go somewhere else, go back as if it had all never happened. Start anew. Make things right.

Her lips were dry and she debated on asking Skitch to hand her one of the canteens they had packed, but nobody else was drinking, and not even the lawyer seemed bothered by the heat. If they could take it, she could.

She looked out the window at the dry, desolate countryside they passed through. Desert, she was sick of it. Water was precious in the desert and not to be wasted, she had heard them say when she had first come west. If that was true, then they ought to make her the damned queen of the desert, for she hadn't wasted so much as a tear in a long, long time.

Criers and whiners were losers, that was the way of things, desert or no desert, only it was easier to see for some out on the sand — the way things really were. The stunted and grotesquely twisted plants strained against the dry soil begging for moisture only to see the mouse eat their seeds. The snake ate the mouse, the hawk and the coyote ate the snake, and the sun tortured them all . . . and so on, a vicious cycle of taking and making the weaker suffer until it was your turn to suffer at the hands of someone bigger, tougher, or more cunning and ruthless. Some found shade and a moment's respite from time to time, a full belly or somebody to curl up with in the dark, but nobody won in the end, not really. Not unless they changed the rules of the game or found a way out of the food chain.

She glanced at the gold again, and then she noticed that Tom Skitch had opened his eyes and had caught her looking at the express box.

"Thinking about your money in there?" he asked.

She nodded. "Yes, there's a lot of money in there. A lot at stake."

Tom Skitch was worried until he was almost sick. She could see it plainly written all over him. He had always been basically square with her and a good enough man in a world where there were far, far worse. But the recent weeks and days had changed him, eaten away at him, until he was a little more hollow-eyed than usual and a lot less talkative.

He said he wanted to see her get the money the mine owed her and had let that money ride in his strongbox. But no matter how long she had known him, Tom still worked for the mining company and had his own troubles and plans that had nothing to do with her.

Then there were the Stutter brothers and the Dutchman, men she was familiar with but didn't really know . . . and the Widowmaker, the newest joker in the deck. She wondered what kind of man he really was. A part of her wanted to believe that everything she had worked for was riding on a hundred miles of desert road and a little luck, but the other part of her knew it always came down to the people — who took what side and when, and who you could trust and who you couldn't.

There were those back in Vulture City who said she was a slut and a harlot and a cold, money-hungry albino bitch who didn't belong in the desert unless she was flat on her back in a whorehouse. But they didn't know her. She smiled a hidden smile behind her black veil. No, they didn't know her. A harlot and a bitch, she couldn't deny either, for she had been both; too fair and soft for a sun like the one overhead right then, true also. She burned red and blistered when the skin of others only tanned and turned brown. She covered her pale, soft flesh and hid it from the sun behind lace and cloth, feminine and weak in a place that exploited weakness above all.

But the desert had taught her things, despite how she hated it; Vulture City had taught her things; even Tulip, curse her cruel soul, had taught her things in the early days. All of them had seared it into her that she didn't belong, but they had also taught her that nobody looked after you but yourself, and that soft and pale and female didn't mean you were weak, for it wasn't the strongest that always won. It wasn't the smartest, either. It was the one who had a plan and the will.

She drew herself back into the coldness that balled tightly inside her, kept everything else wrapped inside that icy ball until not even the hot sun glaring down on the stagecoach could make her sweat. One corner of her red lips ticked downward when she caught a glimpse of the Widowmaker ahead in the trail.

Use every weapon at hand to keep what was yours and what belonged to you, what was owed to you. And let them all think she was a weak woman in a land of strong men. Let them think that all they wanted, for she knew more than anything that she was strong now. She never would have made it this far if she were anything else.

CHAPTER THIRTEEN

No sooner had Newt and the Dutchman ridden forward than a man on a gray horse barreled out from the other side of the jacal in the distance. The rider put the spurs to his horse and hit the stage road at a gallop. Before they could react, that rider was lost to sight in a cloud of dust that slowly disappeared to the south. Newt got only a quick glimpse of that rider, but there was something familiar about him.

Whoever it was, he had obviously been using the house for shelter, at the very least, or using it for cover to spot the coming of the stage, at the worst. Newt's guess was the latter, and he also guessed that rider was helling it down the stage road to tell others of their coming.

Newt grimaced and readjusted his hold on his Winchester, not liking the implications. He kept the Circle Dot horse to a slow walk that would have made an under-

175

taker's hearse in a funeral procession look fast, and so slow that the trickle of sweat running down the crease of his spine underneath his shirt seemed to take an eternity to reach his belt. The abandoned jacal had only one window facing the stage road, and he kept an eye on it and the open front doorway.

The Dutchman pulled up in the middle of the trail and waited for the stage to catch up with them while Newt rode over to the jacal. The Circle Dot horse stopped of its own accord when its nose brushed the adobe plaster, and the eave of the roof was so low that Newt could see the open holes in the dilapidated roof. He slid from the saddle and dropped a rein on the ground. The plank door was hanging open, swung outward with one strap-leather hinge dry-rotted and torn in two and letting it sag against the ground. He moved to the front window, standing to one side and peering at an angle through a cracked glass pane and a cloud of cobwebs. He ducked below the window and moved to the door, then went around it into the doorway with his rifle leading the way.

The inside of the jacal consisted of a single room, and there was nothing more threatening in its shadows than a table and some overturned chairs on the dirt floor over by the beehive adobe fireplace at one end. Somebody had busted up a couple of the chairs and burned them for firewood, and the ashes in the fireplace were cold and damp to Newt's touch, as if the man on the gray horse had doused his fire with water sometime before daylight.

Newt flicked the wet ashes from his fingers, scraped the residue off on the fireplace, and took note of the horse droppings and hoof-torn floor at the opposite end of the room. Whoever that rider was, he had kept his horse tied inside the jacal. He had a good idea who that somebody was, but couldn't figure out how he played into things.

The sound of the stagecoach pulling up outside drew his attention, and he went out to meet it. The stage was stopped and Ned Stutter was talking soothingly to his half-wild team to keep them in place. He didn't stutter at all when he talked to horses.

Tom Skitch was standing with his door open on the far side of the stage and looking at Newt over the top. He glanced down the stage road to the south at the fading cloud of dust that marked the retreat of the man on the gray horse. "Who was that?"

Newt studied the dust for a moment

before he replied. "Didn't get a real good look at him, but my guess is that it was that town marshal of yours. Does he ride a gray horse?"

Skitch didn't give an answer about the color of the horse, but Newt guessed that Skitch would have said so if Marshal Ernie Sims didn't usually ride a gray horse.

"What would Ernie be doing here?" Skitch asked.

"From the looks of it, he laid up here overnight." Newt jerked a thumb over his shoulder to the jacal behind him. "Kept his horse inside and put out his fire before daylight. My guess is that he was waiting for us."

"Waiting for us?"

"Quit acting like you don't hear him," Jenny said from inside the stage.

Newt went to retrieve his horse.

"I meant, waiting for what?" Skitch threw after him.

Newt checked his cinch and then swung up on the Circle Dot horse. He rode over and stopped in front of the stagecoach team. "Right now I would guess that your marshal has gone to tell somebody else that we're coming."

"You think someone's waiting for us at Seymour?" Jenny asked, and her tone was as matter-of-fact as Newt's had been.

"Could be there," Newt answered. "Could be anywhere. Lot of country in front of us, and wherever they pick, it looks like your town marshal has him a side job helping rob stagecoaches."

All of them were either looking at or thinking about what lay down the trail, and it was plain to Newt that they were doing the same as he had been earlier — all of them considering that there were a hundred more miles of trail between them and the Southern Pacific train tracks and imagining how many places somebody could be waiting to ambush them. And if their faces were any measure, they weren't enjoying it any more than he had.

"Ain't bbb . . . but a fff . . . few more miles to Sss . . ." Ned Stutter started to say, but got hung up on the words and couldn't finish.

"Sss . . . Seymour," his brother Fred finished for him with a gasp that sounded somewhat like a hiccup, and pushed the floppy brim of his hat up against the crown.

"How much bottom is left in your horses?" Newt asked Fred Stutter on the ribbons. "If they're waiting for us at Seymour we'll have to run for it without a change of teams."

Fred shrugged and shook his head as if to suggest Newt's guess was as good as his own.

"How much farther past Seymour to the next station?" Newt asked.

"Twenty miles or better on to Agua Fria," the Dutchman answered instead of one of the Stutter brothers.

Jenny Silks threw the Dutchman a displeased look. Maybe she simply didn't like the Dutchman's manners then, or maybe it was simply that she didn't like the Dutchman anytime. Newt couldn't tell which.

Newt wrapped his reins around his saddle horn, lifted his hat slightly, and rubbed gently at his temple beside his knotted cheekbone. His headache was coming back and steadily getting worse as the morning wore on.

"Might be best to save those ponies while we can." Newt pointed at the six-up stage team when he said that. "Might be we'll need all they've got before long."

"Don't matter what Irish Jack pulls, or anybody else, for that matter," Skitch said, and then grimaced as if he hadn't intended to say that. And when they all looked his way he added, "Anybody that wants to steal this shipment is going to play hell with a cavalry escort riding along with us as far as

Phoenix."

"What makes you think the army will help us?" Jenny asked with a cautious, measuring tone, as if she was rethinking something.

For a brief moment, the worried, drawn look that had been on Skitch's face changed to something close to a crafty hint of a grin. "Because I talked to them, that's why."

"What else are you keeping to yourself?" Newt asked as he settled his hat back on his head.

The same almost smug look stayed on Skitch's face, but it was less strong and a tad more defensive. "The captain over at Fort McDowell owes me a favor and a cavalry patrol is meeting us on the road. That was the plan. I've already lost one shipment, and I don't intend to lose another. Thought a little insurance would be the thing."

Newt twisted in his saddle and made a show of looking at the countryside around them. "Begging your pardon, but I don't hear any bugles."

Skitch's mouth tightened. "They'll meet us soon."

Newt gathered his bridle reins. Like the rest of the party, he was more than a little surprised by Skitch's revelation, but it was good news, nonetheless. Apparently, Skitch

181

was craftier than Newt had first supposed.

Skitch made as if to duck back inside the stagecoach, but Jenny's voice stopped him. "When and where are the soldiers supposed to meet us, Tom?"

Skitch hesitated, halfway in and halfway out, and there was reluctance in his voice. "They're running late, that's all. I'm sure we'll meet them down the road a ways."

"You didn't say where you had arranged to meet them," Jenny said.

Skitch seemed to be getting mad, and that was all that was needed to let the rest of them know that the army was supposed to meet them earlier in their journey, and the fact that the cavalry patrol hadn't showed up yet meant something had gone wrong.

"Muh . . . maybe there's your army puh . . . puh . . . patrol now," Fred said from his vantage point up on the box.

"I told you," Skitch said with an equal blend of smugness and relief.

All eyes shifted to a tiny dust cloud, dark as smoke on the face of the rising sun, and boiling across the desert to the east. They watched that dust cloud steadily grow as it came closer.

"Told you," Skitch said, straightening from his former pose and hanging on to the roof and watching the dust cloud.

"Not much dust for an army patrol." The Dutchman jabbed in the direction of the dust cloud with the barrel of his Ballard rifle for emphasis. "How many troopers you figure?"

Ned Stutter squirmed on his seat, re-adjusted the ribbons between his fingers, and squinted at the dust cloud. "Ain't bbb . . . but one rrr . . . rider."

"Wh . . . what?" Skitch did a little stammering himself when he heard what his driver said.

"He's right." The Dutchman gestured at the dust cloud with his rifle again. "One soldier. I can see his blue jacket."

Newt squinted into the sun, but could make out nothing blue. The Dutchman's eyes must have been sharp as a buzzard's. Newt glanced at the old miner beside him and decided that the Dutchman's eyes did, indeed, remind him of a buzzard's, beady and keen and shiny beneath the hooding of his bushy eyebrows.

"Yep, one rider," the Dutchman said. "He must have cut off the trail and come cross-country to save time."

Newt only half considered what the Dutchman said, his mind too busy determining what it was that bothered him about the old miner. He didn't have long enough to come to a conclusion, for the form of a cavalry trooper became plain at the front of the dust cloud.

It wasn't long before the soldier loped a lathered horse up to them and pulled it down to a hard stop. The cavalry private's uniform jacket was marked with white salt streaks, and Newt wondered about a man who didn't have the good sense to shed his jacket on a hot morning. Most soldiers out West were more practical when it came to their dress, shedding formal uniform requirements in the field and anywhere they could, and leaving the traditional brass buttons and sabers and such for the parade grounds and visiting dignitaries.

"Which one of you is Tom Skitch?" the trooper asked.

"That'd be me." Skitch stepped down from the stagecoach.

"Captain Noyes sends his regards," the trooper said.

"That's well and fine, but where's the rest of your patrol?" Skitch said louder than was necessary.

"Cholera," the trooper blurted out.

"What?"

"We aren't sure, but the post surgeon thinks it might be cholera."

184

"So when will my escort be here?" Skitch asked.

The trooper cleared his throat. "I don't think you get my meaning. Your escort ain't running late. It ain't coming at all."

CHAPTER FOURTEEN

Seymour Station lay four miles to the south. The stage road ran virtually on the edge of the riverbank there, and the station itself lay on the east side of the road. It consisted of a wide, single-story adobe house with a small set of corrals and a shed to hold horses for Gilmer & Salisbury's stagecoach runs. Several other buildings that had once housed other businesses in more prosperous times before the Vulture Mine's stamp mills had been moved away to the mine were now abandoned. A scattering of hovels and a couple of rock houses were scattered among the low desert brush behind the station.

Straight across from the front of the station the high banks of the river channel had been cut down to make a crossing for the trail that led west to Vulture City, and a steam engine water pump sat under a shed on the far bank.

Marshal Ernie Sims whipped his lathered horse into Seymour at a run. He was in such a hurry that he waited until he was almost on top of the long front porch that lined the front wall of the adobe stage station before he made any attempt to stop. The gray gelding he rode was tired and a poor stopper, and when it finally responded to the bit it bounced hard three times on its front end before coming to a jarring halt.

Ernie wasn't a very good rider, and his preference for beer and a good chair in a comfortable town over a more strenuous outdoor lifestyle had recently showed itself in the form of his growing waistline. The horse's jarring stop caused his saddle horn to jab him twice in that overhanging belly, punching the air out of him and almost sending him flying over the animal's neck. And as it was, both man and beast were gasping for air when Ernie made a stiff-legged dismount. To make matters worse, Irish Jack and Ten Mule were waiting for Ernie on the porch and saw the whole embarrassing event.

"You're either going to have to get rid of that belly or saw off your saddle horn," Irish Jack observed as he leaned back against the adobe wall behind him.

Ten Mule laughed at that. In Ernie's

opinion, the giant Irishman, besides being extraordinarily dumb, had a braying laugh that sounded like nothing so much as a jackass. Ernie was too out of wind to give Ten Mule the cussing he deserved, even if Irish Jack would stay out of any trouble made for his nephew.

"What are you laughing at?" Ernie finally managed to wheeze at Ten Mule. "You ain't so trim yourself."

Ernie thought his observation was fairly witty considering he had the air knocked out of him, but Ten Mule only laughed again and patted his stomach with both of his big paws. Although much younger than Ernie, he didn't seem at all bothered by having his girth pointed out. Ernie assumed that was because a big belly didn't look as bad on a man of Ten Mule's size, while it certainly looked more pronounced on his own more average frame.

"What the hell are you doing here?" Irish Jack asked. "I never knew you to be up this early unless you hadn't gone to bed yet."

Ernie was still bent over at the waist with his hands on his thighs, trying to catch his breath, but he dearly wanted to tell Jack what he thought of him. He weighed the odds of making an issue of what Jack had said, but didn't like the possible ramifications of such action. Irish Jack was always touchy and unpredictable, but he was apt to get especially antsy before a robbery. Talking to Jack at such times was like playing with a rattlesnake with your bare hands and your eyes closed. Still, having to walk softly around Jack didn't sit well with Ernie any more than taking his insults. A little professional respect shouldn't be too much to ask from Jack.

Ernie had killed three men in pistol fights. Although contrary to the stories he cultivated around those killings, he had considerable advantage in two of those fights. Primarily, that his opponents didn't know a fight was about to happen, and secondly, that he already had his pistol out and was shooting at them at close range before they figured out he meant them harm.

But one of his killings had been a true gunfight. He and an old horse thief named Calico Bob had stalked each other up and down the streets of Prescott taking potshots at each other. Calico Bob was old enough by then that his vision was as feeble as his aim, but he still retained a reputation earned in his younger years as a badman. Accordingly, all anybody remembered afterward, especially those who weren't there, was that Ernie had bested Calico Bob, a bold feat, indeed. Served the old thief right for calling him *Fats* behind his back. A man with two notches filed on his pistol butt and touchy about his waistline couldn't let such talk pass, even if it came from an arthritic outlaw somewhere just short of the century mark.

Surprisingly, Ernie found that people were nicer to him after he killed Calico Bob. They complained less and didn't become overly offended when he got too drunk and urinated on the saloon floor, or insulted their women with rough talk or kicked their dogs. He liked it how many men physically stronger and more handsome than him often gave him wide berth, and how the first thing they often did when it came to harsh words was to glance at the pistol he wore. That's what came with a reputation, and Ernie thoroughly enjoyed being a known man in the territory. In fact, he had always been quite sure that he would become a man of stature someday, even when still a teenager and it was looking pretty certain that he would never reach much past five and a half feet tall.

But what Ernie liked best of all was the badge that his gunfight with Calico Bob had earned him. Admittedly, nobody was more shocked than he was when the mining company that ran Vulture City offered him the job, but he was quick to take advantage of the situation. Without the badge there was only so much he could do in a financial sense, no matter how many old horse thieves and drunks he shot, and that piece of shiny tin pinned on his chest, combined with his pistol and his reputation, made even more people likely to bow down to him. He regretted not thinking of the badge-and-pistol combination sooner in life. Being the marshal of Vulture City let him run all kinds of rackets, from pocketing the majority of the fines he levied on those who broke city ordinances (ordinances he sometimes made up on the spot), to the protection money he made every gambler pay him, to his shares in the occasional fleecing he and his cousin Skinny gave tenderfeet and newcomers down at the livery barn.

His job didn't make him rich, but it did keep him in more than enough money to buy into a nightly poker game or pay for a woman when the mood struck him. And there were other perks of being the marshal, and that's how he had come to work with Irish Jack. But the downside of working with Jack was being continually reminded that Jack wasn't impressed with his badge or gun, nor did knowing who it was that had killed Calico Bob give him any pause. Arrogant and condescending is what Jack was, and not one to be considerate of others' reputations.

Ernie knew positively that he was fast with his hands and a good shot — better than anyone. He proved that to himself twice a week shooting empty cans and bottles at the trash pile outside of town, but for some reason, when it came to Jack he didn't feel that way. He couldn't say how he knew that Jack could best him, because he had never once seen Jack in a fight. But there were lots of stories about Jack, from how the bloody-minded Irishman had once stuck that knife he carried in his boot top into a camp cook's throat for breaking the yolk on one of his fried eggs, to that damned medal he wore pinned on his vest that he won in the war killing secesh rebels. A dozen men supposedly killed with gun or knife or his bare fists, that's what everyone said about Irish Jack, and that was a hard thing not to think about when considering a fight with him. Early on in his forays with Jack, Ernie had tried to think of other things when Jack was looking at him; tried to give Jack the icy glare that he had practiced so much on other people. But none of that worked with Jack.

And that was most of the reason why he

tried not to be around Jack any more than he had to, because it had dawned on him not long after he first met the man that, like it or not, he was scared of Jack. After a time, Ernie had somewhat made peace with the notion, for it wasn't so bad to be scared of only one man in the whole wide world. Most people were probably scared of dozens. He could have found mediocre solace in that notion if Jack wasn't always rubbing it in that he was the top dog.

"I said, what the hell are you doing here?" Jack asked for a second time.

"The stage is coming," Ernie blurted out.

"I know the damned stage is coming. Ten Mule told me about the shipment two days ago, and I've had a man watching the mine office ever since," Jack said. "What I want to know is how come you didn't send me word instead of me having to wait to hear it from him? Short notice like that, and Skitch could have slipped right past me before I even knew what he was about."

"I'm telling you now." Ernie managed to catch his wind and straighten himself. Irish Jack wasn't any taller than him, but looked considerably taller looking down at him from the porch. Standing up straight diminished some of the difference in their respective elevations and made Ernie feel better.

"I would have told you sooner, but I had to go up to Skull Valley to identify a stolen mule."

"You were most likely passed out drunk. Or has that Mexican goat tender gone off with his herd again and left that ugly wife of his alone and ready for you to come calling?"

Ten Mule laughed at that, too. "She's ugly, sure enough, but I reckon she'd do just fine for Ernie."

"I waited all night up at that old farm for the stage, and sure enough, it come along this morning. I knew you and the boys would likely be waiting here and I come to tell you to get ready," Ernie said.

"What makes you think I need any help?" Jack was playing with that finger bone watch fob of his while he talked. "I pay you too damned much as it is for letting me know when there's a shipment about to go over the trail."

"How many guns have you got? Skitch has got two guards on horseback, and the Stutter brothers on the box. There's another couple riding on the inside, if I don't miss my guess." Ernie tried to peer through the open door to the station to see who Jack had with him, but Ten Mule was standing in the way. There was also no sign of the family that tended that station, and Ernie wondered what Jack had done with them.

"Tell me something I don't know," Jack said, barely looking up from his finger bone plaything long enough to glance at Ernie, as if he had already written him off. "And while you're at it, tell me why I ought to let you in for a cut. First thing I learned about road work is that gold splits better when you don't have so many to share it."

"I bet I know one thing you'd like to hear."

"Speak up. You're tiring me."

"Skitch hired Newt Jones, the Widow-maker."

"Is that so? Lot of talk about this Widow-maker." Irish Jack gave Ten Mule an irritated glance.

No matter how Irish Jack tried to play off the news about the Widowmaker, it was plain from the look on the outlaw's face that he was interested, and Ernie thought he saw a moment of advantage. "You don't have to pay me a full share, since I'm coming in on the deal late. The only thing I ask is that I get to be the one that puts the Widowmaker down."

"My guess is that most of the stuff about him is mostly talk," Jack said.

"You give the word, and I'll knock him out of his saddle first."

"You'll do what I tell you to do," Jack said, stepping down off the porch. "What's got you all fired up to notch the Widowmaker?"

"He beat up Skinny, and then he run off before I could find him."

Jack took a step closer to Ernie. "Let me guess. You and Skinny tried to pull one of your games on the Widowmaker?"

"You don't know . . ."

"If you're so all-fired set to kill him, how come you didn't pop a shot off at him up the road when you had the chance?"

"The rest of them would have pinned me down, plus it would have ruined your ambush," Ernie said. "You let me in on this, and I'll show you how I handle him."

"No, the Widowmaker's mine." Jack kept staring at him until Ernie looked away. "They say he's got a fancy pistol with pretty blue crosses on the grips. That true?"

"He does." Ernie told himself he ought to grab hold of Jack's right arm and draw his own gun before Jack could wrestle free, but the thought was short-lived. Jack wore two pistols for a reason, and he was said to be equally dangerous with either hand. Not many men had earned a reputation for using a single pistol, much less two. Ernie had been telling himself for a long time that he ought to practice with his left hand so that he could wear two pistols, but had never gotten around to it. "I saw that pistol myself. He and I like to have went toe-to-toe, but he went yellow when I called his bluff."

"You backed him down, huh?" Jack's stare was intense and unblinking.

"I was ready for him, and he wasn't having any part of it," Ernie said. "If I had known how he was going to treat Skinny the way he did I would have gone ahead and handled it then."

Irish Jack turned suddenly and started back up the porch steps. He must have shared some private look with Ten Mule that Ernie couldn't see, for Ten Mule laughed.

Ernie took the laughing without complaint and started up the porch behind Jack. Let Ten Mule laugh all he wanted to. There would come a day, but the thing to do now was to keep a low profile and make sure he got in on the action. Jack might say he wanted the Widowmaker for himself, but who was to say what might happen when things started popping? Jack wasn't likely to hold it against the man who got a shot at any of the express guards as long as the holdup went as planned.

Ernie almost ran into Jack's back when

the Irish outlaw suddenly stopped at the top of the steps. He turned and looked down at Ernie with a scowl.

"Where do you think you're going?" Jack asked.

"That stage will be here anytime. Thought I would get inside with you and find me a likely spot to shoot from."

"No, you get down in the riverbed with the rest of the boys," Jack said. "Me and Ten Mule will take watch here."

"But . . ."

"You hurry now. Get that horse out of sight, and don't you fire a shot unless I do. You hear me? I want that coach to roll in here nice and easy like business as usual."

Ernie took one last look into the open door of the stage station, but saw no one inside. In fact, nobody but Jack and Ten Mule were visible anywhere he looked. "What did you do with the station tender?"

"He and his woman ran off through the brush when they saw us coming," Jack said.

"How do you know he won't double around and warn the stage you're waiting for them?"

Jack grinned, his teeth as white as that finger bone he was playing with. "No, I suspect he'll be content to lay up in the brush until we're gone."

Ernie wondered if Jack had killed the station keeper. What was his name? Conger or something or the other. Not a bad fellow. Always impressed with a badge, and making a point to serve Ernie a free meal and some respectful talk any time Ernie came through on business.

Ernie went to his horse and started leading it across the road, trying all the while to keep an optimistic view on things. Irish Jack wasn't getting any younger, and at the very least there would come a time when he didn't see or shoot any better than Calico Bob had back in Prescott.

"And one more thing," Jack called out to him when he was only halfway to the riverbank and barely across the road.

Ernie stopped and looked back.

"You remember, the Widowmaker is mine," Jack said. "I doubt he's much, but I can't say I would mind that fancy pistol of his for a souvenir."

Chapter Fifteen

There were a lot of grim faces in and around the stagecoach when the cavalry trooper delivered the news about the cholera outbreak.

"How bad is it?" Newt asked.

"Bad," the trooper answered. "Half of the post has come down sick."

"I'm sure it's as bad as you say, but that doesn't explain where my escort is," Skitch said. "Your captain promised me."

"Nobody for him to spare."

"Bbb . . . best them . . . sss . . . soldiers stay where . . . they . . . they's at," Ned Stutter said.

"Tuh . . . tell 'em, brr . . . brother," Fred Stutter chimed in. "We ain't . . . we ain't chuh . . . chancin' . . . cuh . . . catchin' the blue . . . wuh . . . whistler shits. Nuh . . . no, sir."

"Watch your language," Newt said. "There's a lady present."

Jenny Silks gave a sarcastic giggle.

"Shuh . . . she ain't no . . . luh . . . lady," Fred Stutter said. "She's a huh . . . huh . . . whore."

"Hush, bbb . . . brother," Ned said, seeing how the Widowmaker was looking at them.

Jenny Silks didn't snicker this time. It was true laughter, throaty and full of sarcasm. "Oh, you men. You damned silly fools. A whore is what I am, as if any of you had any room to talk."

Newt shifted uncomfortably in his saddle when the focus of her gaze shifted to him.

"As for this cholera outbreak," Jenny continued. "I've had it myself and don't care to see if I can survive it one more time."

The brothers nodded agreement, but not too passionately, for the Widowmaker was acting sort of unfriendly-like.

"You're a hard woman to look out for," Newt said.

"I'm paying you to look out for my money and not my virtue," Jenny said. "I lost all that years ago."

"You wouldn't have hired me if you thought you could take care of yourself," Newt replied.

Jenny started to snap something else at him, but stopped short. Newt shifted his attention back to the Stutter brothers.

"You boys talk like that in front of women back in Mississippi?" he asked.

Ned stuttered and attempted a reply, but Newt didn't let him finish.

"I don't like rude talk in front of women or children," Newt said, and then he gave every one of them an individual look to pound his point home, landing last on Jenny. "A man ought to be polite where he can."

Fred Stutter shifted his grip on his shotgun.

"Fff . . . Fred," Ned warned.

Fred ignored his brother's warning. "Yuh . . . you fight one of us, you . . . you fight the both of us."

Ned Stutter nodded grimly beside his brother, uneasy, but his jaw clamped stubbornly, nonetheless.

The Circle Dot horse stamped beneath Newt with a creak of saddle leather, and a blowfly buzzed by his head. The soldier was looking like he wanted to be somewhere else. Only the Stutter brothers seemed unfazed, and they stared at him like a pair of sulking, stubborn donkeys, both of them willing to take it as far as he wanted.

Newt's tone lost some of its edge. "You know, you two don't stutter near so much when you're mad."

The brothers' posture loosened a little, but the tension between them and Newt was still a thing so thick on the air that it was like mud.

Skitch gave a relieved, nervous chuckle of his own, but it came off as the fake thing it was.

"There will be no fighting, you understand me?" he said when the awkward silence remained after he tried his laugh. "Widowmaker, you . . ."

"Don't call me that."

Skitch swallowed the knot in his throat, evident by the slow bob of his Adam's apple in his skinny throat. "Jones, you let it lie. I'll have no trouble amongst my men."

Newt weighed the Stutter brothers more carefully than he had before, already getting more of a feel for them.

"Are you boys going to be this nervy when we go down that road and run into whoever's waiting for us?" Newt asked with one corner of his mouth lifting in what he meant as a grin.

The Stutter brothers must have taken that as the peace offering he meant it to be, for both of them nodded and Fred Stutter set his shotgun butt-down on the dashboard.

"Duh . . . don't you be . . . luh . . . lookin' behind you when . . . truh . . . trouble comes," Fred said. "Cuh . . . 'cause we'll be . . . rrr . . . right on your . . . huh . . . heels."

"Yeah," Ned added. "Rrr . . . run this . . . cuh . . . coach right up yore . . . I muh . . . mean yore . . . Wuh what's the word, brrrr . . . brother? A polite one, I . . . mmm . . . mean."

"I think you mean his posterior," Jenny said with a hint of laughter in her voice and her veiled face swiveling from the Stutter brothers to Newt, then back again.

Ned blushed. "Nnn . . . now, Mmm . . . Miss Jenny, don't you . . . buh . . . be using . . . ddd . . . dirty words like that. Yuh . . . you're gonna make the . . . Wuh . . . wuh . . . Widowmaker wuh . . . want to ssshh . . . shoot us again."

Newt smiled for a second time. Although a real smile this time, he kept it on the inside. He couldn't help but like the brothers, no matter how trying it was to talk to them, and no matter how stubborn they were. And he had no doubt that fighting one of them meant you tackled them both.

That was family; that was kin. It had been that way back in the east Tennessee mountains of his youth. He recalled a neighbor boy getting in a fight with another kid. The neighbor boy won the fight, but the kid he whipped had three brothers. Every day a different one of those brothers showed up to fight him. He whipped the first two of the brothers, but gave it up after that and let the third one give him a beating and get their evens. He knew that if he didn't let one of them win they would come again and again, one at a time, or maybe all four of them at once. Or maybe their cousins and other kin would come.

It had been a long time since Newt had known how that felt himself — that no matter whether you were wrong or right, and no matter what was against you, your family had your back, that somebody stood with you through thick and thin. Family. He turned the Circle Dot horse to where the gelding faced down the stage road to the south.

Jenny's voice sounded behind him, careful, but with an edge to it. "Listen to you preach. You, with a name like bloody sin following you wherever you go."

"Out here, a man comes at you, you got a decision to make. You either take a beating or you fight. A man pulls on you, you put him down or you die. After a while, if you survive long enough, sometimes you get a reputation, a name. And maybe not a name of your choosing."

"Mr. Jones, I've been out here a long time myself," she threw back at him, but her voice remained calm. "I only find it humorous that a brawler like you would lecture anyone on manners."

"Sometimes we can't help what trouble that comes our way," Newt replied, hating that she was making him angry and at the same time making everything he said seem foolish. But he plunged ahead, trying to shape his thoughts for something he had never tried to explain to anyone. "Even a poor man can afford to carry himself like a . . ."

"Like a gentleman?" Jenny scoffed.

"Like a man."

"You . . ."

"I know I'm ugly, and maybe I've done a few things I wish I could take back, but when I lay down at night I know I mostly stuck to my rules."

"Rules?"

Newt nodded. "Yes, rules. The things a man sets store by and those he doesn't. The things he'll fight for and those he won't."

"And what if I said I think you're a hypocrite?"

"Ma'am, arguing with you won't change your mind, but as long as I'm guarding you, you'll be treated like a lady, whether you act like one or not."

Jenny Silks inhaled so sharply that they all heard her, but said nothing in reply. At a loss for words, perhaps, but her veiled face remained tilted down at Newt, and although he couldn't see her eyes, he could practically feel them glaring at him.

"I've delivered my message," the soldier said when the break in the conversation gave him the chance, and plainly uncomfortable being caught in the middle of an argument that didn't belong to him. "Best I be going now."

They watched him until he was once more only a dust cloud in the distance. Instead of taking the road south, the trooper went across country as he had before.

"Too bad he didn't come through Seymour Station," the Dutchman said. "We could have asked him if anybody out of the normal was hanging around there."

"We could turn back and go north to Prescott," Newt said.

"No, we go ahead, just like we planned," Skitch said. "If somebody wants to take a shot at this shipment, they could be waiting for us anywhere. And we won't get this done if we keep second-guessing ourselves."

Every one of them knew the truth in what he said. The best thing they had going for

them was speed, and yet, there they sat going nowhere. Skitch got back inside the
stage and the Stutter brothers started the
team down the trail.

Newt rode even with the brothers on the
box and called up to Ned, "Keep them
moving relaxed and easy."

"It's not far to the station from here," the
Dutchman said from the other side of the
stage team. "There's a little hill between
here and there, and if anyone's waiting for
us there they'll be able to see us as soon as
we top out."

"Yeah," Skitch muttered from inside the
coach, and his tone told that he had been
thinking the same thing and not liking it at
all. "There won't be time to turn around if
we're under their guns."

"Best we go careful, then," Newt replied.
"The Dutchman and me will ride ahead.
Check things out."

The Dutchman scowled across the team
at him but nodded his agreement. The two
of them rode forward with the coach coming along some twenty yards behind them.

For the next few miles the stagecoach kept
to an easy trot, eating up the distance. Newt
looked south across the desert. The country
was slowly opening up more as they left the
broken foothills, and he was glad of it, for

there was less cover for any kind of ambush.

The Dutchman pointed ahead. "That's the hill I was talking about. Seymour's just the other side of it."

The hill that the Dutchman pointed out was really a low ridge that ran across the trail a quarter of a mile ahead of them. Newt motioned for the stage to stop when they reached the foot of it, and he and the Dutchman continued on to the top. Both men stopped their horses as soon as they could see to the other side and before they were truly skylined and easily visible to anybody from the station who might look their way.

They stayed like that for a while, studying what lay before them for any hint of trouble ahead. Other than the long adobe house that served as the stage stop, there was nothing much to the place other than a few scattered shacks scattered about the desert scrub behind the station, and the big barn and horse corrals on the opposite side of the trail along the riverbank. The pump house for Vulture City's water pipeline was just across the river. Not so much as a single soul could be seen stirring, and other than the trickle of smoke coming out of one of the chimneys at the station house, the entire place might have been abandoned.

"Peaceful down there," the Dutchman said.

"Yeah, maybe too peaceful," Newt replied.

The two of them watched the station for a while longer and then turned their horses around and rode back up the trail. Newt reined up on Jenny's side of the stagecoach with the Dutchman behind him. Jenny had her window curtain tied back and looked out at him but didn't speak.

Skitch appeared in the window across from her seat. "What's it look like?"

"Ordinary, but if I was a holdup man that's the way I'd want it to look," Newt answered.

"Only horses we could see were those in the company corrals," the Dutchman added. "No saddle horses tied about, but they could be hid."

Skitch looked from one man to the other. "Well, what do you think? Do we try it?"

"It's that or we turn back," Newt replied. "This won't be the last place we could get hit, and we'll never make it anywhere sitting when we should be moving."

"Let's be going, then." Skitch reached out the window and slapped the side of the coach, and Ned Stutter chucked to his team and put them to a trot.

Newt kept pace with the stage, and said

to the brothers, but loud enough for those inside the coach to hear it, too, "If they're there, they'll probably want us in close before they start anything."

The Stutter brothers nodded at that.

"So, we go slow and give ourselves time to look things over," Newt said. "But if I say the word, or if you see anything that doesn't look right, I want you to lay the whip to those ponies. You hear?"

Again, both brothers nodded their understanding, and Fred Stutter nodded so intensely that it caused his hat brim to flop comically. The brothers were gritty young men, but they were nervous, too. Newt could see it in the tense way they sat up on the box and the grim set of their jaws. But, he was nervous himself. Only a fool wouldn't be.

"Me and the Dutchman will lead the way, but the first hint of trouble and you get going. If it comes to a fight it can get hard to think straight, but you remember one thing if you don't remember anything else," Newt added. "Those crazy horses you're driving have been trying to run off all morning, and if the time comes to run, you let 'em."

A broad, wild grin spread across Ned Stutter's mouth, and he screwed his own hat tighter down on his head. He shifted the ribbons all to one hand and with his other hand took hold of the buggy whip mounted on the side of the box.

"Not yet, Ned. Not yet," Newt said. "You keep that buggy whip handy, but let's see how it plays out, first."

Beside him, he saw that Jenny had her head partially out of the window so that she could see the trail ahead. The black veil was pressed tight to the profile of her face, a lovely shape without detail, and making her look like some kind of carving of a goddess on the prow of a ship. He kicked the Circle Dot horse forward until he caught up with the Dutchman twenty yards in front of the stagecoach.

It was only a short way to the top of the low ridge, but it seemed to take forever. Newt glanced to his side and noted that the Dutchman had his Ballard rifle out of its scabbard and laid it across his saddle swells.

"Here we go," Newt said as they topped the ridge and rode into plain sight of anybody at the station who might be waiting for them.

One of the horses at the station corrals spotted them and nickered, and two of the coach horses nickered back. Newt's vision cut over the layout in front of him, searching for threats. His hand went inadvertently to the butt of his pistol and he left it resting there.

Both men spoke quietly to each other when they spoke again.

"So far, so good," the Dutchman said when the stage had rolled down the hill.

"You notice anything funny about that water pump?" Newt asked.

"You mean that it isn't running?" the Dutchman answered in an even quieter voice.

Both men made a show of not looking directly at the pump house across the river, but watched it out of the corner of their eyes.

"Not only that, but that fellow tending to it," Newt said.

Normally, the pump tender pumped water down the pipeline to Vulture City twice a day, morning and evening, to fill the tanks, and was on call for the rest of the day should water need to be pumped to the stamp mills. That pump tender was visible sitting in a chair under the pump shed just like he ought to be, and somebody had gone to the trouble to make sure it looked that way. The only problem was that the pump wasn't running like it ought to be, and one more thing.

"Is that a rifle he's got propped up against

213

that engine?" the Dutchman rasped.

"I've never seen an engine that you had to threaten with a rifle to get it to work," Newt replied.

The Dutchman leaned over and spit and nodded when he straightened back up in the saddle. "Yeah."

They were within fifty yards of the station when a mutt of a dog came running out of the barn and crossed the trail in front of them. It scampered with its tail tucked between its back legs and looked back once at the barn as if it had been scolded, and as if there was someone in the barn that might not want it in there.

"See that?" the Dutchman asked.

"Yeah. I'd say if we're going to do something, now would be the time," Newt said.

"I reckon," was all that the Dutchman gave for an answer.

The Dutchman hooked his thumb over the hammer of his Ballard and tried to cock it quietly, but the click of it sounded loud to Newt's ears. Newt twisted in the saddle to look back at the stagecoach, but a rifle cracked from somewhere along the riverbank ahead of them before he shouted a warning to Ned Stutter.

The gunshot must have been intended for Newt, for the bullet hummed so close past

214

his head that he swore he could feel the hot lash of it. He yanked his pistol from his holster and put the spurs to the Circle Dot horse beneath him. The brown gelding bolted ahead like a racehorse.

Behind Newt, Ned Stutter reared back with the lash of his buggy whip. He cracked it once, twice, over the team's backs and the startled horses immediately jerked against their harnesses and bolted ahead in a run. First Ned, and then Fred, let out a high-pitched yell. The brothers didn't stutter at all when they screamed like that, and their shrill cries sounded like nothing so much as Indian war whoops.

More gunshots sounded, a lot of them, and the stagecoach bounced and teetered along the trail in a mad attempt to dash past the stage station and out of the ambush.

CHAPTER SIXTEEN

"Damned fool!" Jack swore from where he was hunkered down behind an open window in the thick adobe walls of the stage station.

It had been his intention to let the stagecoach roll quietly into the station, thinking about nothing but a change of horses and a stretch of the leg. Let them roll right up to the front door all unsuspecting, that had been the plan, but one of his men on the riverbank lost his patience or his nerve and fired a shot before the trap could be sprung as he had planned it.

"Pour it to them!" Jack shouted to his men as the stagecoach barreled toward the station.

It wasn't as if the gang needed encouragement, because every one of them was already firing. He shouldered his Marlin rifle, resting on the windowsill, and tried to draw a bead on one of the two guards racing ahead of the stagecoach. But both men were riding fast, rising and falling over the rutted trail, and both of them were leaned low over their horse's necks, making poor targets. He recognized the Dutchman. The cantankerous old German's long white beard whipped over one of his shoulders like a flag. Try as he might, Jack couldn't get a good sight picture on the Dutchman or the big man riding beside him.

Jack squeezed the trigger and the explosion of the .45-70 cartridge and 405 grains of flat-nosed lead hammered the rifle's butt stock against his shoulder. He absorbed the recoil and worked the lever to jack another round into the chamber, all in one motion, and in that instant he thought he saw the Dutchman's horse falter and stumble slightly. But the horse, if hit, found its stride again, and both of the lead riders charged on with the stagecoach right behind them.

Ten Mule had taken a position at a window at the far end of the room, and his gun roared and roared again. The two shots were so close together that they almost sounded like one, and the report of his '73 carbine's .44-40 cartridges going off was in stark contrast to the dull, deep boom of Jack's big-bore Marlin. Jack peeked at Ten Mule out of the corner of his eye and saw his nephew working the lever on his Winchester so fast that there was no way he was taking the time required to aim.

Jack cursed Ten Mule's ineptitude with firearms and then snapped another shot at the big man riding in the lead of the coach. He knew as soon as he touched the shot off that he had missed again. And he knew in the same instant that the man he had shot at, the big man on the brown horse, had to be the Widowmaker.

And Jack and Ten Mule weren't the only ones missing their shots. There was a veritable hail of gunfire from the other side of the road, and yet, both lead riders, the Widowmaker and the Dutchman, were still unscathed. The first thing the gang should have done was to knock down the horses pulling the stagecoach and stop it in its tracks, but the six-up team didn't seem to have a scratch on them, and they were running like jackrabbits with their tails on fire.

Jack's crew of road agents were an experienced lot, usually as steady as they were mean, and able to shoot fairly straight when it came to that. But for some reason they were off their game.

It had been like that in the war. Jack had learned that a man who performed admirably in a tight spot one day might be so shaken that he refused to fight the next.

Some men folded if you gave them too much warning about trouble to come and too much time to dwell on it. Others were the opposite, and became shaken if a fight came on them too quickly and didn't give them ample time to brace themselves. If he had learned one thing during the war and in the years afterward, it was that few men were natural, even-keel fighters.

And then there was plain, simple luck. That was always a factor. It could go against you or for you, as shifty as the wind. Sometimes the most damned fool stunt worked when there was no way it should, and sometimes it just wasn't your day.

For instance, the man riding shotgun on the stagecoach, one of the Stutter brothers, bouncing on the seat so wildly that he looked to fall off at any second, let go with one barrel of the shotgun he was aiming at someone along the river. The shotgun boomed, and then the other barrel went off. A man bouncing like that shouldn't have been able to hit anyone, scattergun or not, but somebody down in the river channel screamed bloody murder with the second roar of that shotgun.

By then, the stagecoach was passing in front of the station. Guns cracked, both from the ambushers Jack had put in place and from inside the stagecoach. Bullets kicked up dust in the road, and more than a few of them knocked chunks out of the adobe station house, sounding like nothing so much as buckets of rocks being thrown against the walls. Most of those bullets weren't coming from the guns of the express guards, but rather from Jack's own men. The bloodlust and excitement had taken hold of the outlaw gang, and they had forgotten the dangers of a cross fire as they shot at the coach passing between them and the station house. One of those gunshots shattered the window that Ten Mule was shooting out of, showering him with glass, and another bullet whipped through the same window and rang off the cast-iron cookstove at the back of the room. Ten Mule quit firing at the stagecoach and dropped onto his side below his windowsill and curled into a ball.

Jack cursed again, shouting a long string of profanities this time. How many times had he told those fools to be careful where they put their shots?

Jack didn't have time to dwell on his nephew's cowardice, for he was a big believer in the adage that if you wanted something done right you did it yourself. He rose slightly from his crouch and leaned out the window to take another snap shot broadside into the passing stagecoach. It was point-blank range, barely ten yards between the end of his rifle barrel and a target as big as a . . . well, as big as a wagon, but he never got the chance to pull the trigger. Up he popped with his rifle ready, and there was Jenny Silks framed in one window of the coach, wearing that ridiculous black veil of hers. He barely had time to catch the flash of sunlight on the nickel-plated pistol she was poking out the window right before she tried to kill him with it.

He had expected a lot of things that morning, but not an eccentrically dressed whore pointing a pistol at him. Her shot struck the window frame, pelting him with plaster and splinters.

Jack fell to the floor with his rifle hugged to his chest and looked across the floor at Ten Mule curled up on his side beneath his own window.

"Keep low and they can't hit you," Ten Mule said.

Jack wanted to scream at his idiot nephew and remind him that they had to stop the stage before they could rob it, but in that same moment a trickle of adobe dust rained down on his head and a bit of it got in his ear. His temper was already to a boiling point, and the indignity of finding himself cowering behind a wall while the express shipment passed by, not to mention his ticklish ear, was the proverbial straw that broke the camel's back. He lunged to his knees and struggled to get his rifle up and ready to kill someone, all the while cursing pistol-packing whores, runaway horses, and outlaws who didn't have the good sense not to shoot at one another.

But the stagecoach was already gone, passed by and leaving nothing behind but a cloud of dust as it ran south.

CHAPTER SEVENTEEN

The Dutchman's horse fell over dead less than half a mile past Seymour Station. It was running one moment and the next it simply folded up and took a lifeless nose-dive, sending the Dutchman flying over its outstretched neck. Newt reined out of the way of the stagecoach and doubled back to the downed man and horse. He barely had time to notice the bullet wound in the dead horse's flank and the slow, lavalike pulse of blood bubbling out of that hole before the Dutchman scrambled up off the ground. Miraculously, the bitter old miner didn't seem too maimed from his fall, and even more impressive was that he had managed to hang on to his Ballard rifle.

Newt freed a boot from a stirrup and offered an assisting hand. The Circle Dot horse was anxious and bothered to be held in place while the coach horses were running off and leaving him, and, hooves chopping the sand, he danced in place beneath Newt. The Dutchman looked up from under the brim of his hat with his usual scowl and maybe a bit of surprise that Newt had come back for him, but it was a brief thing, and he took Newt's outstretched hand with grim determination and a grip like a wolf trap. He never bothered to use the empty stirrup, but instead, swung up behind Newt with the agility of a circus trick rider and a man half his apparent age.

Newt let the Circle Dot horse run again, and the Dutchman slapped the gelding's hip with the barrel of his rifle. The rifle spanking him and two pairs of human legs drumming his belly had the brown horse running wide open in a few powerful strides.

Their sprint was short-lived, for they had barely rounded a curve ahead of them before they came on the stagecoach stopped in the middle of the trail. Even as Newt pulled the Circle Dot horse to a stop again, Fred Stutter leapt from the box and raced to the head of the six-up team while Ned stayed and kept hold of the ribbons. One of the leaders was down and thrashing in the harness, causing a tangle of kicking horses. The Dutchman slid off from behind Newt just as Fred reached the downed horse.

The fallen leader, struck by a bullet in the

ambush the same as the Dutchman's horse had been, was too wild with pain to allow Fred to properly unhook it from the traces. Newt saw the young shotgun guard wade into the tangle of kicking hooves, followed by the brief flash of a knife blade. The wounded horse gave a groan and its hind legs convulsed, and then it went still with a gaping, bloody gash below its jawbone where Fred had cut its throat. There was no time to pity the lost coach horse, and the Dutchman immediately began to help Fred unhook the horse and roll it out of its harness.

Newt glanced at the stagecoach and saw Jenny watching out her window. Her black veil had somehow been torn loose during the wild race through Seymour Station and her face was paler than ever. But he also noticed her pistol barrel resting on the windowsill. Scared or stricken, she had still possessed the grit and gumption to participate in the fight they had just escaped.

Only then did he notice the numerous bullet marks in the side of the coach. Everywhere he looked, the carriage body's green paint was marred with little white rings of splintered wood. And she had been inside through the whole thing.

Most holdup men caught their prey on a

long, steep climb or at another point where the conveyance would be traveling slow or stopped. And many an express box had been taken over the years without anyone getting hurt. But the gang that had hit them in Seymour was a bloody bunch, no doubt. That had been a killing ground if Newt had ever seen one, and he was almost sure that regardless of whether or not they had stopped to change horses at the station, as a normal run on the stage line would have, they would have been killed without a chance to give in and hand over the express box. Whoever was leading that gang, Irish Jack or some other of his sort, would stop at nothing to get his hands on that much gold, or perhaps it was worse than that. It was a cold, hard thing to think on, but dead men told no tales. Gun down the entire express party and there would be no witnesses and nobody to tie you to the crime.

Rarely was there an easy way to face down trouble. When men were willing to risk it all to take what they wanted, you had to be willing to take the same risks to defend what was yours. He had knowingly chosen to take those risks when he hired on to guard the shipment, same as Jenny had when she insisted on coming along despite warnings from both Newt and Tom Skitch, as well as others. She was obviously a smart, independent-minded woman used to taking care of herself, proven by the kind of money she had riding in the express box, but still it bothered Newt to have a woman along. Had she really known what she was getting herself into when she climbed in that stagecoach back in Vulture City?

He put the Circle Dot horse in the middle of the trail behind the coach, facing back the way they had come while Ned Stutter and the Dutchman worked to get them going again. The stagecoach was barely out of sight and gunshot of the station, and he knew without seeing it that the outlaws who had ambushed them were at the moment mounting horses to come after them and finish what was started.

He had no idea how many men would be coming, for the ambush had happened too fast, the roar of guns all blending together and the brief flashes of the outlaws firing from cover seemed to have happened in a blurred instant. He guessed six or seven guns, but it could have been twice as many. No matter, the express party was outnumbered, and things didn't look pretty if the stagecoach's horses couldn't be patched back into some semblance of a team — a team that could run. Flat, sparsely vegetated desert surrounded them for miles on the east side of the river where the coach road ran, and there was nothing in sight that even faintly resembled a suitable place to fort up and make a stand.

He broke open his pistol and was surprised when four empty cartridge cases ejected. He could remember firing only once, maybe twice, but it was always like that in a scrap, when the odds were against you and it was root-hog-or-die. There was no time to think, only to react. Thinking meant you were hesitant and slow, and the slow were always the first to fall. The quick and the dead, wasn't that what he'd heard from scripture? But he doubted that Mother Jones meant the word *quick* the same as he had come to understand it when she used to crack open that old black Bible and read from it, time to time. She set store by her faith and in the words of that heavy black book, the way some counted on the .44 on their hip. Him, perhaps he ought to be ashamed, but he tended to the latter, more often than not. Yes, sir, it paid to be quick, and he'd take quick over dead anytime.

He thumbed fresh cartridges from the loops on his gun belt and fed them one by one into the Smith's cylinder chambers, watching the trail to the north where it disappeared around the bend. At any moment he expected to see horsemen come running into sight, and although the stagecoach had been stalled for only a few short minutes, the waiting seemed like an eternity.

He holstered the Smith pistol and slid his Winchester from his saddle boot. The best that he could hope for when Irish Jack's gang appeared — if it was them back there — was to keep the disagreement at a distance as long as he could to buy time to get the stagecoach rolling again.

He threw a quick glance over his shoulder and saw Fred Stutter climbing back up to the box. The remaining leader had been unhooked from the team, and the Dutchman was sitting astride it, bareback over the harness it still wore. He had hacked the long driving reins short with a knife to make them manageable for riding.

Newt moved back to the stagecoach on Jenny's side and looked down into her window. What he saw was Cyrus McPhee lying across the seat with his head in Jenny's lap. McPhee had lost his hat, and in place of it was a bloody, blue bandage torn from Jenny's dress.

"How bad is he hit?" Newt asked. The lawyer's eyes were closed, but he was breathing.

Jenny frowned, as if unsure how to answer. And there was something else in her look. "The bullet skirted around his head, but it left a nasty gash and there's bits of bone in it."

"Will he make it?" Newt immediately felt foolish for asking such, for none of them were doctors, and she was doing all she could.

She shrugged.

"I'm not dead, yet, Mr. Jones," came McPhee's voice, speaking through clenched teeth against the pain.

The coach creaked and lurched ahead, Ned Stutter keeping the team to a walk, and now driving four horses instead of six. The young driver looked unharmed, and he nodded at Newt, as if to confirm that he was good to go. Fred on the seat beside him seemed also to have gotten through the barrage of gunfire without mishap, other than he had lost that big ugly hat of his.

"You lost your hat," Newt thought aloud.

Fred nodded vigorously. "Sss . . . son of a bbb . . . bitches shot it off mmm . . . me." He looked down at Jenny's window as soon as he said that. "Ppp . . . pardon . . . me, Mmm . . . Miss Jenny."

"No offense taken," Jenny replied.

Fred put the team to a trot, letting them

breathe and cool down a little, and when he did Newt noticed that not only had they lost two horses in the fight, but that the off-wheeler was limping badly. A closer look proved that it, too, had taken a bullet. A raw gouge of flesh had been knocked out of the muscle at the bottom of the horse's hindquarters and above the curve of its hock. And the other stage horses were lathered and blown and in no shape for another run.

Newt took another look at their back trail.

"See them yet?" Skitch asked from inside the coach.

"Not yet."

Skitch scooted across the coach's front seat until he was at the window next to Newt. "How many of them were there?"

"Seven, eight, who knows? They didn't give me time to count."

Skitch absorbed that information grimly, nodding while he thought it through.

"How far did you say it is to the next station?" Newt asked.

"Twenty-five miles or more."

"We won't make it," Newt said. "If we could take an easy pace, maybe, but not with them pushing after us."

"We'll make it," Skitch said, but didn't sound like he believed his own words.

A gunshot sounded behind them, and then another. Both reports sounded like they had come from Seymour Station, although why the outlaws would still be shooting back there was a mystery.

"They ought to be coming by now." The Dutchman, too, was looking back in the direction of Seymour.

"They'll come." Jenny said what they all knew.

"What's at Phoenix?" Newt asked. "If we could make it that far."

"What do you mean?" Skitch asked.

"I mean how big of a place is it?"

"Big enough, I guess."

"Have they got any law there?"

"City marshal, and there's a county deputy stationed there," Skitch said."

"How much farther until we make it there, if we could make it?" Newt asked.

"Trail runs to the station at Agua Fria and then another long run into Phoenix," Skitch answered.

"They guh . . . got them a . . . bbb . . . big red . . . brr . . . brick . . . bank we could . . . ppp . . . put this . . . muh . . . money in," Fred Stutter said. "Old Irish Jack, he'd . . . ppp . . . play hell . . . guh . . . gittin' that gold outta there."

"That was my plan," Skitch said. "Move

the shipment to that bank and lock it up for the night, then make the last rush to the Southern Pacific tomorrow morning."

"Well, your plan's done for," the Dutchman said. "You got about fifty or so more miles of desert between you and that red-brick bank, and these horses won't make it."

No more gunshots had sounded from back at Seymour, and the fact that the outlaws who had ambushed them hadn't showed yet was bothering Newt. It didn't figure.

When he returned his attention to what lay ahead, he saw a fork in the trail with one course continuing along the river southward and the other branching off to the east.

"What's that?" Newt asked.

"Stage road goes east till it hits the Agua Fria River and then ducks down to Phoenix."

"Where does the other road go?"

"Freight road. Skirts the mountains by White Tank and comes by Phoenix on the south end."

"Which way's closer to the railroad?"

The Dutchman gave him a curious look. "The freight road's shorter by a good bit, but there's not a stop between here and

Maricopa Station."

"What are you thinking?" Jenny asked from her window in the coach.

Newt took a glance at their back trail and then at the wounded and lightened stage team. "We won't make it to the next station if they push us. Horses can't take it. And they'll run us down, no matter if we have fresh horses or not."

"Nobody's after us, yet," Skitch said. "Maybe they've had enough."

"Are you willing to gamble your gold on that? Your life?" Newt asked.

"Have you ever heard of holdup men trying a second time when they botch the deal?" Skitch asked. "No, none of us have. It doesn't work that way. They're probably hightailing it right now before the law comes after them."

"Whoever that was back there is as bloody a bunch as I've ever run across. They'll be coming after us, you can bet the farm on it," Newt said as calmly as he could, willing patience into his voice.

Skitch only mumbled something that none of them could understand, and it was obvious he knew that Newt had spoken the truth.

"My guess is that they'll expect us to stick to the stage road," Newt said.

"You're saying we ought to duck off and follow the freight road?" Jenny asked.

"We can't slip off from them," the Dutchman observed. "Not a chance with this stagecoach and the amount of sign we're leaving behind. A child can follow wagon tracks."

"I don't know the country, but maybe we could fool them," Newt said. "If they have to hunt for us, that buys us time. And every bit of time it buys us puts us closer to the Southern Pacific."

"It won't work," Skitch said.

"Tom, you aren't thinking straight," Jenny said. Unlike Skitch, she was strangely calm. "We can't outrun them, fresh horses or not, and I've got my money in that box, same as you."

Skitch rubbed his face and glanced at his palm and the dust and grime there with a frown. "If we stick to the stage road, maybe we run across some help. Maybe we're already through the worst of it."

"I wouldn't count on good luck," Newt said. "I'd say it's been an unlucky morning and likely to get worse."

"If we took the freight road we could fort up at White Tank if it came to that," the Dutchman said. "If we could make it that far."

Skitch was silent for a bit, but finally gave a grim, reluctant nod. "Let's try it, then."

"All right, keep them moving, and I'll catch up to you." Newt stopped the Circle Dot horse and swung down to the ground.

"What are you doing?" Skitch had to lean out the window to keep sight of him.

"I'm going to try and buy us some time," Newt said.

Ned Stutter kept the team at a steady trot and headed down the freight road, and there was no time for further discussion. Newt glanced one last time at the stage then took down the lariat rope from where it was tied to his saddle horn. He went to the edge of the trail and hacked the limbs off a spindly creosote with his sheath knife and then did the same to another nearby bush. He bundled the brush together and cinched it together in the loop of his rope and then climbed back into the saddle. He put the Circle Dot horse to a long, easy lope, headed east on the stage road with the bundle dragging behind him from his saddle horn.

He looked often behind him, both at the dust he was raising with his improvised drag, and for signs of anyone on his back trail. He had heard of Apaches using such drags to create the illusion of a larger party as a decoy to lead off pursuit from the main band, but the dust cloud he raised was more meager than he had hoped. It was probably a fool trick, but it was all he could think of. He urged the Circle Dot horse to a little more speed.

CHAPTER EIGHTEEN

Irish Jack came out of the station house cursing and shouting as his men brought up their saddle horses from where they had been hidden in the barn. He was made even madder by the fact that his own horse refused to stand still for him to mount. The horse was tall and made it difficult to reach a stirrup in normal times, but now the fractious animal, still frightened from the recent gunfire and excitement, danced a circle around him and jerked away every time he lifted his boot. Several others of his gang were having the same problem.

At the moment he finally got his horse to stand still, a rifle boomed and the man next to him gave out a cry and dodged out of the way as his own horse fell dead. The men already mounted spun about in confusion and tried to spot where the bullet had come from.

"What the hell?" Jack shouted as he

dragged his horse by one rein toward the cover of the station.

The rest of the gang were trying to do the same, but those already mounted were caught in the wide open with little to do but sit there and get shot at. Another gunshot cracked across the desert, and a second bullet kicked up dust and then ricocheted and thumped into the side of the station, knocking a big chuck of plaster from the wall.

Jack thought he had the direction that the shots were coming from down, but not the source. Whoever was doing the shooting at them was atop the hills across the river. By then, several of his gang were firing off their weapons blindly without a clue of where to shoot or who to shoot at.

"You damned fools, they're across the river!" Jack shouted again.

Whatever marksmen were across the river ceased firing, and that gave the gang time to ride behind the station or one of the other buildings, or to duck back inside the barn.

Jack led his horse up onto the station porch and close enough to the door that he could hunker inside and still hang on to the bridle rein and keep the animal with him. With his rifle ready he peered at the hill across the river and tried to spot whoever was shooting at him.

"You hit?" Ten Mule called from the barn.

"How about instead of asking about me, you find that son of a bitch across the river and shoot him!" Jack answered.

Despite Jack's instructions, neither Ten Mule nor any of the others were willing to step out from cover to do any reconnaissance, much less make a target of themselves. Jack found a dark spot on the hillside some three hundred yards away and fired a shot at it. He fired more out of frustration than any hope that what he had seen was actually their attackers, but it made him feel better.

"Damn it, lay it to that hill!" he shouted again.

Either his gang was over its initial surprise or they had finally gotten their courage up, for immediately bullets began knocking up puffs of dirt on that far hillside. None of their shots were particularly aimed at anything but the side of that hill, but Jack hoped that the quantity of their fire, if not the accuracy, might convince whoever was out there to give it up.

After a long spell of firing, the gunfire began to slow and eventually came to a stop. Jack, along with the rest of his gang, reloaded and waited to see what would happen next. No more shots were fired from the hill, but none of the gang were convinced enough that it was over to come out from cover and risk getting shot.

The wait gave Jack the time to curse more. He was a man prone to profanity, especially when in the middle of a fight. The escape of the stagecoach infuriated him, and the fact that he was now delayed in pursuing the gold shipment had him in such a rage that he could barely breathe. He spotted Ten Mule peering sheepishly from the barn. Although he knew that Ten Mule hadn't been the one to fire the premature shot that ruined his ambush of the stagecoach, the sight of his nephew staring out of the barn door with that slack look of his was infuriating, considering his mood.

"You see anything?" Jack called out to his men.

Nobody answered him, and Jack took that as a *no.* The thing he hated worse than a plan gone wrong because of ineptitude was having to wait for anything. But he also knew that patience was an undervalued aspect of fighting, no matter how hard it was to come by. The first fool to move in such a situation was often the first fool to die.

Who the hell is out there?

What seemed like an eternity, but in reality was only a matter of a quarter of an hour or so, went by while Jack waited and watched and cursed everything he could think of. It was hot inside the station and growing hotter, even in the shade. A fly buzzed around his face and he swatted at it until he could stand it no more. The mine shipment was getting farther away by the minute.

He half hoped that one of his men would be the first to move and test things, but no such luck. It was another case of having to do things yourself if you wanted them done right.

He came out on the porch slowly and stood there in the shadows under the roof for a while, still searching that hill across the river. Slowly, his men began to come out of hiding.

"Reckon we got 'em?" Ten Mule asked.

Jack threw a vicious glance his way, but didn't reply. He was busy trying to figure out who it was that had shot at them. There was no way that one of the express guards had the time to double back and take a stand across the river.

He took a deep breath and willed himself not to think about the target he could be making of himself and came down off the porch and mounted his horse. "I think they've given it up."

"I don't know," Ten Mule said.

"Get on your horse."

Ten Mule did as he was told, as did the rest of the gang.

"You sure about this?" one of the outlaws that had his horse killed asked. "I don't like the thought of maybe somebody up there waiting for the right moment to take another potshot at us."

Jack glared at him. The man was always a whiner and a complainer.

"I aim to have that gold," Jack said for all of them to hear him. "You're either staying or you're coming with me. Now, let's ride."

"But I ain't got a horse," the same outlaw said.

"Your tough luck," Jack said.

"You can't leave me."

Jack had made as if to go, but he spun his horse back to face the man and cocked his Marlin rifle and shot him in the chest. The heavy bullet knocked a grunt out of the outlaw and he staggered back two steps and then slowly folded and fell to the ground. Jack worked the lever on his rifle and shot a second time into the fallen man's body. He rode his horse almost on top of the man and circled around him until he was sure that he was dead.

"I can't stand a complainer," Jack said when he looked up and caught the rest of the gang staring at him.

Nobody had anything to say in response.

"Now, let's go get us some gold." Jack spurred his horse and started off in a run, followed by the rest of the gang.

Two men rose from the stand they had taken across the river. They shared a glance with each other, but said nothing while they watched Irish Jack's gang riding out of Seymour. They were both tall, thin men, but the rest of their features were hidden beneath the drooping brims of the matching black hats they wore. One of them picked up a Remington Hepburn rifle, folded down the tang peep sight, and cradled the heavy rifle in the crook of one elbow. The other man bent over and picked up the folded linen duster that his partner had used as a shooting rest.

When the outlaw gang was out of sight, the two watchers went down the back side of the hill to where they had left their horses hobbled. They tightened their cinches and mounted, still without a word to each other. When they rode away they went southward toward the White Tank Mountains, but they did not follow the freight road that ran that way, the same road that the stagecoach was then taking. Instead, they stayed on the west bank of the river, paralleling it and keeping the terrain between them and the road wherever they could.

CHAPTER NINETEEN

Newt traveled roughly three miles eastward, stopping a few times to check his back trail for any signs of pursuit. Yet, there was no sign of the gang that had attacked the stage. Again, he scolded himself for trying such a silly ruse. Apaches might make the dust thing work, but they would have several warriors dragging dust makers, enough to raise a big enough cloud to possibly fool pursuers.

But he was raising some dust. There was that.

The stage road climbed up a low saddle between two knobs that flanked it to the north and south, and he stopped there atop that rise. He dismounted and parked the Circle Dot horse off to one side in a small cactus thicket. The country was wide open with nothing but low-growing desert scrub and the occasional finger of a saguaro cactus or a Joshua tree rising up above it. He could see for a long ways back the way he had come, and so he waited.

He had all but given up hope that his ruse might have worked when he saw the riders coming in the distance. They were too far off to make them out with any detail, but there were several of them and they were coming fast.

Six, no, seven of them, he saw when they were nearer. The man riding in the lead was on a big sorrel horse that must have been every bit of sixteen hands tall. The horse's red coat stood out plainly, even at such a distance.

Newt moved the Circle Dot horse until it was standing broadside and perpendicular to the stage road, and he rested his Winchester across his saddle. He waited until he guessed the riders were within five hundred yards or so, and until he could get a better look at them. Twice, sunlight reflected off steel, and Newt was sure that a couple of them, at least, were riding with rifles in their hands. Their pace and that flash of steel made him almost sure that they were the gang who had hit the stage back at Seymour.

He waited another span of breaths and let them come closer until he was sure who they were. The range was too far for Newt's skill with a rifle, and he couldn't get them all, even if he were such a long-range marksman. However, that wasn't his intention. Either they had assumed the stage would stick to the regular road, or his dust trick had worked. No matter, his goal was simply to delay them, and to buy time to get the stage a head start. He slid the graduated elevator on the Winchester's rear sight until it was set on the mark for four hundred yards. He squeezed off a round and the big-bore rifle bucked and bellowed, and his round scattered gravel thirty yards ahead of them.

The party of riders pulled their running horses to hard stops while he jacked a fresh round in the Winchester. Somehow, they must have spotted him or they were simply firing blind in his general direction, for bullets were soon whistling past him. None came close.

His second shot hit the road in front of them and a little closer than the first. The debris scattered from that shot must have hit one of the horse's legs, for it shied violently and almost threw its rider from the saddle. The frightened horse also served to disrupt the other horses until the outlaws were a milling mess.

Newt moved the rear sight elevator to five

hundred yards and took a sight picture on the man on the big sorrel horse. He let out a breath, saw the front sight steady, and squeezed the trigger. He knew he had missed even before the recoiling rifle muzzle dropped back on target.

Someone in the gang got his horse settled enough to fight back, and the bullet he fired came uncomfortably close to Newt. Whether they had spotted him or whether it was a lucky shot, it was time to move out of there.

Newt fired, again and again, working the lever on the Winchester as fast as he could while still taking some kind of loose aim. He shot until the Winchester was empty. He saw one horse kick out like he might have burned it, and one of the outlaws grabbed at one arm and fell from his saddle.

Newt didn't wait around longer to check the effects of his fire. He shoved the Winchester down in his saddle boot and gathered the Circle Dot horse's bridle reins. The gelding hadn't so much as moved a muscle during the entire episode. In fact, it didn't seem at all disturbed at the commotion. It bent its neck and craned its head around to look at him and yawned, as if to ask what all the commotion was about.

"What are you looking at?" Newt asked the horse. "You think you can do better, you do the shooting next time."

He jammed a boot in the stirrup and then kicked the Circle Dot horse into a running start as soon as he hit the saddle seat. He raced over the rise, then left the road at the foot of it and headed across the desert to the south. The slope blocked his retreat from view of the outlaws as long as they were on the far side, and he let the Circle Dot horse really run, wanting to get all the distance he could while he had the chance. Man and horse wove in and out of the scattered brush and cacti, leaping over what low obstacles and rough terrain they couldn't go around.

He kept to that wild pace for almost half a mile, then slowed the gelding to a walk. There was no sign of pursuit.

"That ought to slow them down," he said to himself as much as to the horse, and there was a hint of a wolfish grin on his face.

An hour later and many miles farther along, he circled his way to the west until he struck the freight road and fell in behind the wheel tracks the stagecoach had left. He followed those tracks for another good while. The Hassayampa River to his right was now nothing but a dry streambed with sparse green vegetation marking its banks, and looked like nothing more than a huge wash like so many others that scarred the desert. The clear, shallow water that had marked its course earlier had gone under the sand. The Circle Dot horse was caked in dust and dried sweat, and although the horse showed no signs of faltering, Newt wished he could find some water to quench his thirst.

He left the road and dropped over the riverbank to follow its course in hopes of finding a place where the water might resurface again. Such places were rare, but not unknown in that country, and Newt had seen it in other deserts. A man might dig a hole in the sandy riverbed and find water, but that was a chancy thing. You could die of thirst easily while you dug holes.

He dismounted and poured the last of the water in his canteen for the horse, one cupped handful at a time, then he moved on. The Dutchman had mentioned something about a water hole ahead, and he gambled that either he could catch up to the stage and get water from the bags it carried or that he could find that water hole — simply another gamble in a life full of such.

Intending to rejoin the road, he found a break in the riverbank that allowed an easy climb out of the channel, and he had just topped out on level ground when he looked to the west and saw the two riders sitting horses off in the distance. They were so far away he could barely make them out, but there they were. And they were watching him. Making no move his way, but they were definitely watching.

He put the Circle Dot horse to the road while he kept an eye on the newcomers. Once, he thought he caught the glint of sunlight on glass. What was it Henry Wickenburg had said about two men with binoculars?

Newt took a deep breath and moved his head around to work some of the stiffness out of his neck. He reached down and gave the Circle Dot horse a pat on the neck.

"I never did have a lick of luck," he said, and then looked at the men spying on him one last time. "Well, let 'em come."

CHAPTER TWENTY

He found the stagecoach an hour later where the road ran along the foot of a high set of mountains that had been growing steadily in the distance since they left Wickenburg. Ned Stutter had slowed the team to a walk to save them, or simply because the horses were too worn out to manage a faster pace.

The Dutchman held up when he saw Newt coming, and fell in beside him. "You look all tuckered out."

Newt merely looked at him and gave a deep grunt that said it all. The Dutchman stayed beside him until they caught up to the stage. Ned Stutter stopped the team when he saw Newt.

Skitch swung a door open and put one foot out on the step. "We heard a lot of shooting a while ago."

Newt nodded and dismounted and took a bucket from the luggage boot and poured it full from one of the leather-and-canvas water bags hanging there. He let the Circle Dot horse drink and took a handful himself and sipped from it slowly. The water was lukewarm, but good.

"Did you get any of them?" Skitch asked.

Newt waited for the water to moisten his parched throat before he answered. "Might have winged one."

"That so?"

Again, Newt nodded. "If I did or I didn't, I imagine I put a little caution into them."

"Was it Irish Jack?" Jenny asked from inside the coach.

"Can't say. There was one man on a big red horse that stood out, and that's all I can tell you."

"That's him," the Dutchman said. "Everybody in these parts knows that horse. Jack sets as much store by that animal as he does that finger bone watch fob he wears."

"Could be."

"I've heard some hard things about you, Jones," Skitch said. "But you're a man with the bark on, I'll say that. We get to the railhead and I'm going to double your pay."

Newt filled his canteen and hung the water bag back on the stage. He checked the tightness of his saddle girth and then climbed back on the Circle Dot horse.

"That's fine and dandy, but we've got to make it there first."

Skitch got back inside the stage and Newt headed up to the driver's box to talk with the Stutter brothers. As he passed one of the windows he saw Jenny Silks staring at him. Her veil was up and she was giving him an odd look. It wasn't a look of admiration at all, but rather a cold, calculating expression that he couldn't put a handle on.

"How are you making it?" Newt asked Ned Stutter.

"Sss . . . slow as . . . lll . . . lasses in wintertime," Ned stuttered.

The four horses remaining in harness did look bad. The wheeler with the bullet wound was holding that leg up to relieve the pain, and all the horses in the hitch were coated in dried sweat and salt marks.

"Can we make it?" Newt already thought he knew the answer.

"Mmm . . . maybe," Ned said.

"Hhh . . . how . . . fff . . . far behind us yuh . . . you think they are?" Fred asked. His forehead and his face were already red with sunburn since he had lost his big hat.

"Couldn't say, but it's best we get moving."

Both brothers nodded. Ned had to peck

255

the team several times with his buggy whip to coax them into a walk.

Newt had forgotten to mention the two men glassing him back on the Hassayampa, but for some reason he didn't after he thought of it.

The Dutchman fell in alongside him again. Newt glanced at him and thought how uncomfortable it must be for a man his age to have ridden so far bareback. But the old German didn't seem any worse for the wear. He still had a good hold on that heavy Ballard rifle and sat with his back straight as a rail. That riding posture, what some called a parade-ground seat, made Newt guess that the Dutchman had served in the cavalry at some time in his past.

"You all of a sudden aren't so talky," the Dutchman said after a time.

"Like you said, maybe I'm all tuckered out."

The Dutchman gave him an appraising look. "Like hell."

Two hours later the team was trying to balk every time they came to a rise in the road. Newt was considering suggesting that they somehow hitch his and the Dutchman's horses to the stage to help with the pull when they came to a set of wagon wheel ruts ducking off toward the mountain looming over them.

Newt asked the question by simply nodding at those wagon ruts.

"White Tank is up there in a canyon," the Dutchman said. "Rough trail up toward the end, but there's good water there. Lots of travelers camp there time to time."

Newt looked up at the mountain and at the high rock bluffs that marked the canyon the Dutchman spoke of. And then he looked again at the worn-out team.

"What kind of place would it be to take a stand and rest the horses?" he asked.

The Dutchman shrugged. "Good place. The tank's set back at the head of that canyon. Nobody's going to come at you horseback except for up that trail."

Skitch overheard the discussion. "Trouble with a place with one way in is that there's only one way out."

"What do you think about holing up for a while?" Newt asked.

"I don't like it, but it's our only option."

Ned turned his team into the trail. They followed it up a flat in the mouth of a wide draw that narrowed the closer they got to the mountain ahead of them. The trail wound through a thick stand of low-topped paloverde trees with their odd yellow-green trunks and thick clumps of cactus. The farther up the draw they went the rockier the terrain became, and the worse the going went. Ned drove slowly, cringing with each jarring jolt of the stagecoach and fearful of busting a wheel or damaging the undercarriage.

Beyond the stand of paloverde trees they entered the canyon proper, and thicket gave way to more open ground. High, white granite bluffs rose straight up to either side of them, and in places the canyon floor was littered with large rocks and boulders the size of a wagon that had broken off from those bluffs. And at the very head of the dead-end canyon they found the water hole they were looking for. There were actually two tanks, both stone basins nestled inside a field of boulders and carved out from runoff waters from above over the centuries.

Several old fire rings from previous occupants of the hideaway marked a small circular area that was the only flat ground to be found in the rugged canyon. They parked the stagecoach as close to the boulder field as they could, positioning it broadside to the way they had come in case they should need it as breastwork if Irish Jack's gang were to come upon them. Jenny spread a blanket underneath the stagecoach and helped lawyer McPhee onto the improvised pallet and began examining his head wound. There was a narrow footpath winding through the boulder field, and Newt, the Dutchman, and Ned Stutter led the horses along it to water them at the lowest tank while Skitch and Fred remained behind to set up camp. Once the horses' thirst was quenched, they rigged a picket line close to the tank and left the animals tied there.

The Stutter brothers had a sack of victuals stashed away up in the driver's box, and Fred was hacking open a tin can of corned beef when they returned from tending to the horses. Ned dug further in the sack and produced several biscuits he had gathered before leaving Vulture City. The meat was rancid tasting and the biscuits were stale, but the men took places in the rocks and wolfed down a late lunch without complaint while they watched the trail into the canyon. Jenny Silks refused to eat and lay down on the blanket beside McPhee to take a nap.

"I never did care for canned meat," the Dutchman said.

"I've ate worse," Newt said.

"Like what?"

"There was a time when I saw pack rat served for supper," Newt said. "Apaches favor it, but I don't recommend it unless you've got a powerful hunger."

259

The Dutchman grunted and there was a twinkle to his eyes. "Rat, huh? I was snowed in with a party out to California once. Rations got short and we ate one of the dogs."

"Dog ain't bad if you've got a bit of red pepper to doctor it up," Newt replied, not to be outdone.

The Dutchman cocked an eyebrow. "Well, we didn't have any red pepper."

"Met a man down on the Rio Grande a while back. A judge, he was," Newt said. "Claimed he once ate a man in a blizzard."

The Dutchman was watching the trail again. "How'd he like it?"

"He didn't say."

"I don't imagine he had any red pepper."

"No, I imagine not."

The Dutchman pulled a pipe from his tobacco pouch, packed the bowl with tobacco, and lit it with a parlor match. He took a couple of contented puffs before he spoke again around the pipestem clenched in his teeth. "They say Alfred Packer ate five men up in Colorado."

"Heard that when I was working as a mine guard in Silver City," Newt said. "Never did know whether to believe it. You think he did?"

"He could have. A man gets hungry

enough for a thing he's liable to do anything."

Newt glanced at the Dutchman out of the corner of his eye. The heat of the afternoon was sapping the energy from most of them, but the old German seemed unbothered by the sun beating straight down into the canyon and was strangely talkative, given his surly nature. What had brought about his desire to talk was a mystery, but then again, Newt had known other men who liked to talk when trouble was at hand. Newt understood how that could take your mind off things, but he was a man who had grown used to being around strangers and keeping his thoughts to himself.

Mother Jones used to say that restless people were the ones who can't make peace with the thoughts jumbling around in their own heads. Newt had thought about that saying of hers many times over the years. The years and the miles of solitude had given him questions he could not answer, and he never sat still in one place for very long. He had swung a hammer with an Irish tracklaying crew to build the Katy railroad through the Indian Territory to Texas when he first came west, and since then he had worked at a bit of everything, from digging graves one winter to working as a blacksmith for a time. And then came the years of working the mines all over the New Mexico and Arizona territories, at first as a miner and then as a company guard. And he had fought with his fists for prize money where he could, knocking heads when he could get a match, sometimes for the hell of it, but mostly to earn a little extra coin to keep the wolf from the door. Footloose, he had been for most of his adult life, what some called a knockabout man.

According to her, his father had been like that before he married and finally settled down, always ready to see new country and always looking for something he couldn't find. Newt had never known that side of his father, for he hadn't been much more than a long-legged boy when the man fell dead behind his plow cutting rocky furrows to plant a patch of mountain corn.

Newt didn't consider himself a wise man, but the years since that boyhood version of himself had packed a sack over his shoulder and left for the West made him often reflect on such things. And one thing he was certain of was that a man rarely picked the place or moment of his demise. His old daddy probably never thought he would fall in a furrow with a busted heart, no more than his own self would have guessed he would find himself hunkered down in pile of rocks in the Arizona Territory with his life on the line.

"You ever think on how we end up where we are?" Newt let the way his thoughts were running come out aloud without really meaning to.

"What do you mean?" the Dutchman asked.

"I mean here and now."

The Dutchman seemed irritated by the question.

"I heard a man speak in Shakespeare years ago," Newt continued. "He was some kind of a scholar or scientist. For a half-dollar he would run his fingers over your head and tell things about you simply from feeling your skull."

"Feeling your skull?"

"Yeah, but he also gave a little speech in the theater house after he got finished feeling heads. Said fate was nothing but the result of decisions and consequences. *Cause and effect* is what I believe he called it," Newt was talking to himself as much as he was talking to the Dutchman. "It was kind of like you put together all the things you've done and it comes to a particular result, like if you could do the math it would tell you where you end up."

The Dutchman glanced at Newt. "You ought to find some shade. I think the heat's getting to you."

"You ever guess you would end up here? Right now?"

"Never gave it much thought," the Dutchman said. "Just the way it is."

Newt shifted his body position to ease the pain in his joints. Down the canyon a roadrunner showed in the trail. The bird had a lizard in its beak.

"Yeah, the way it is," he said.

"Huh?" The Dutchman was watching the roadrunner like Newt was.

"I said I guess you're right. Seems like ever since I strapped on a gun I've been waiting for a fight or a funeral," Newt said. "I guess this canyon is as good a place as any."

"If it comes to a fight, I'd as soon give the other fellow the funeral," the Dutchman said. "I've lived a fair share of years, and nobody's managed to put me under yet."

The roadrunner disappeared behind a clump of cholla cactus, and Newt rose and moved over a few yards to sit down against the lee side of a different rock. Maybe the Dutchman was right and he needed some shade.

CHAPTER TWENTY-ONE

Irish Jack was riding in the lead through the paloverde thicket when he stopped his horse. The men behind him did likewise and waited in silence. The only sound was the occasional sound of a horse's hoof stomping at a fly and the creak of saddle leather.

"Smell that?" Jack asked in a quiet voice while he studied the rock bluffs that rose up ahead of them and marked the entrance to the canyon that held White Tank.

"I don't smell anything," one of the outlaws answered behind him.

Jack inhaled deeply. "Tobacco smoke, that's what it is."

"You figure they're still up there?" Ten Mule asked in too loud of a voice for any kind of stealth.

"Of course they're there." Jack frowned at his nephew. "There's not but one way in and out of there with a wagon."

Ten Mule nodded and tried to act like he

265

had known that all along. Jack was a bit surprised that his nephew had spoken at all, for he hadn't made a sound other than to let out an occasional moan of pain, not since he had been shot by whoever had waylaid them back on the stage road. Jack glanced at him again and at the weary slump of Ten Mule's back and the crude bandage tied below one shoulder. The bullet that had struck him had left a nasty wound. Jack hadn't said it, but Ten Mule would be lucky not to lose that arm.

Jack turned his attention back to the canyon ahead. He could see nothing of it other than the top of the bluffs, due to the paloverdes and the scattered, thick clumps of cactus and desert scrub blocking his view. He had been to the water hole only once in the past, and the inability to see ahead and to remember the exact topography of the old campsite in the canyon irritated him to no end.

"We've got 'em now," Jack said. "Time to put an end to this."

"We damned sure owe 'em one," Ernie Sims said.

Jack gave the marshal a cold look. He was half convinced that Ernie was the one who had gotten antsy and fired the shot that had spoiled his setup at Seymour Station and caused the stage to get away. And Ernie was always as irritating as he was nervous. Jack wanted to berate the man for this latest observation on the current state of their road work, even though it was true. They should have taken the gold and made their getaway long ago.

The lot of them had been so hot on the chase that like a bunch of greenhorns they had been fooled by a fake dust cloud. He prided himself on a calm, calculated approach to his business, yet they had charged right past the White Tank freight road without checking it. Finding the bundle of brush in the road used to lure them away had almost made him madder than anything that had gone wrong so far. And then they had lost valuable time trying to track whoever had made that drag across the desert instead of cutting back to the freight road and locating the stage that way. While he realized he should have done things differently in that regard, he also made a mental note to find a better tracker for his gang. Neither he nor his current men were capable when it came to following sign.

And then there was the fact that he had been fired upon, not once, but twice. One posse or another on his tail after a job was part and parcel of the business, but it was always after the fact and not during the course of his road work. Normally, he either laid an ambush and held the coach driver and shotgun guard at gunpoint while he took what he wanted or, according to his most recent technique, he recruited enough firepower to put the numbers in his favor and simply gunned down everyone on the stage. While he was proud of the efficiency of that latest tactic, as it left no bothersome witnesses, neither style usually resulted in much resistance from the opposing side.

But it was not that he had been shot at that bothered him, but rather not knowing who had shot at him. The last attack was self-explanatory. It had to have been one of the gold guards who had remained behind to lead them off course and scatter a few shots at them to delay their pursuit. That was made plain by that marksman's flight across the desert in the direction of the freight road that the stage had taken.

However, those shots from the hill back at Seymour were an entirely different matter, and there were only a few explanations that made sense. All of them were troublesome, but some worse than others.

The territorial government was offering a reward for his capture or demise, and he had considered whether or not it might be bounty hunters taking potshots at him. He could tell by the rifle report that there had been only one gun shooting at them from that hill and a mere two shots fired at them. That might imply a lone gunman or a small party, but he doubted that meant bounty hunters. A bounty hunter, or maybe two of them, weren't likely to take their shots unless they caught their bounty alone.

Another option was that peace officers might be using the mine shipment as a means to run him down. Again, he doubted that theory for much the same reasons, and because it made sense that if the stagecoach was meant as bait, a posse of lawmen would have closed the trap on him instead of sniping at him from afar and not pushing the fight.

Perhaps he had underestimated Tom Skitch, and the mine foreman was craftier than he supposed. A cunning man might have held back a party of guards to follow behind. He had never encountered or heard of such, although an express box full of gold was enough to make its owner go to extremes.

The last possibility was the one that bothered him most, and it had to do with the little Wells Fargo shipment he and his men had hit outside Tucson the previous winter. The company not only had messengers riding shotgun on the shipments it handled, but it also had detectives working with local law enforcement and the U.S. marshal to investigate robbery cases in the territory. It could have been one or more of those Wells Fargo detectives who shot from the hill at Seymour.

Wells Fargo tended to hire tough, competent men, and they were a whole other breed of animal compared to the local peace officers who bumbled around to make a show of doing their job and then ran back to town the first chance they got. The last thing he needed was those detectives on his trail, not with the gold so close and ripe for the taking. His sources had assured him that Wells Fargo had temporarily suspended operations over the road from Prescott to Phoenix, due in large part to his taking of the last shipment from the Vulture Mine and the recent rash of stagecoach hits elsewhere. Knowing that the company didn't have an interest in the haul and that there wasn't to be one of their express messengers on board had made the job seem all the easier. But that suspension might be the very reason they had detectives out hunting the territory to get them back in business.

Ten Mule's voice brought Jack back into

the moment.

"Jack, my arm's hurting bad." Ten Mule still hadn't gotten the hint to keep his volume down. "I need a doctor."

"Do you see any doctors here?" Jack hissed under his breath.

"You don't care, because you're not the one that's shot."

Jack whirled on him and pointed up the canyon. "Do you know what's up there? That's gold. Likely a good bit of it. I'm not leaving here until I get it. You toughen up and you'll get some, too. Make you forget about that arm."

Jack turned away. He could feel a black rage coming on. He had been shot twice himself in the war, and he'd be damned if it ever stopped him from doing what he needed to do. No, not Ten Mule or any damned Wells Fargo detectives were going to stop him from getting that gold.

His anger was such that it took a great deal of effort to keep his voice down to a whisper when he turned back to his men. "We leave our horses here."

The outlaws immediately began to dismount.

Jack climbed down from his big sorrel and shucked his rifle out of his saddle scabbard. "We don't let that stagecoach out of this canyon."

"What about the woman?" one of them asked.

"No witnesses," Jack said. "If you can't stand that, say so right now."

None of them complained. While he often grumbled about the failings of his gang, they were as rough a bunch of renegades and cutthroats as he could gather, and what they lacked sometimes in skill they made up for with an aptitude for violence and a total lack of morality.

"I saw her once in that whorehouse of hers at Vulture City," one of the men said while he found a place to tie his horse. "Too uppity for my tastes, but a good-looking slut. Woman like that could use a little humbling."

"You put a bullet in her head, just like the rest of them, and then we get gone," Jack said. "I aim to be on my way to California come nightfall."

He hadn't thought about California until then, but it sounded like a fine idea now that he had said it, especially if Wells Fargo had put their hounds on his trail. A mild winter and a little time on a sunny beach with a bottle of tequila in his hand and one of those California senoritas to rub his back was just what he needed.

Jack checked that his rifle was ready and started on foot through the thicket toward White Tank with his men spread out and picking their way quietly behind him. The smell of tobacco smoke grew steadily stronger.

CHAPTER TWENTY-TWO

Newt thought he caught a bright flash of light from somewhere behind and above him. He turned to where he could watch the bluffs at the head of the canyon, but whatever it was did not happen again. Perhaps his tired eyes were playing tricks on him under the bright glare of the sun, and his head was hurting again and maybe it was affecting his vision.

He placed his attention back on the trail where it ran through the thicket, and it was later when he heard someone behind him and glanced over his shoulder to see Jenny Silks approaching him. She was coming from the path through the boulders as if she had paid a visit to the water hole. He had assumed she was still sleeping under the stagecoach, and it bothered him that he hadn't heard her get up and leave.

She folded her dress up under her with one hand and sat on the ground next to him where she could peer out between the waist-high rocks and see the trail leading up to the water hole. She said nothing, nor did she look at him. At least he thought she didn't look at him, but it was hard to tell with her face hidden behind that black lace.

"Have a good nap?" Newt said, because the silence between them was awkward, and it felt impolite not to speak.

"It's too hot to sleep," she answered. "Thought I would go wash my face."

He noticed then that she was carrying a hand mirror and must have been using it when she freshened herself at the tank. He would have sworn that the reflection he had seen came from much higher up the canyon, but then again he had noticed the flash only out of the corner of one eye and was no doubt mistaken.

He considered going to the tank. A splash of cool water on his face and neck would feel good, at that. He looked up at the sky above them. It was miserably hot — so hot that he had to keep his rifle in the scant shade of the rock he leaned against or the steel of it would blister his hand. His shirt and hatband were wet with sweat and he was rank enough that he could smell his own stink and the musty odor of the dried crust of horse sweat on his pant legs.

"Think they'll find us?" she asked.

He started to tell her that they were the farthest thing from hidden, but held back such harsh words and simply said, "Yes, ma'am."

"Will it be bad?"

"I counted seven of them."

"We should be able to hold them off, then?"

"I see you've got sand, but have you ever been in a fight?" Newt pointed at the stagecoach where McPhee lay. "And that lawyer doesn't know one end of a gun from the other, and he's in no shape to fight even if he did."

"I'd think we could stay in these rocks and keep them away," she said. "I thought that's why you chose this place."

"Never been here before in my life, but I've fought out of worse places, that's for certain," he said.

"You sound like we're already beaten."

"No, not by a long shot, but it is what it is."

"You get me out of here and I'll double your wages. If you can kill Irish Jack in the process, I'll double that." Her voice had taken on an edge of, not fear or nervousness, but anger.

The passion when she mentioned Irish

Jack surprised him. But then again, she struck him as a woman who didn't like to be thwarted. "A man like him will get his in the end, whether it be the law or another one like him that does him in."

"You don't know that."

"Why him? There are six others likely out there in the brush just as bad as he is."

"He's trying to take what's mine. That's all. Maybe my share of what's in that express box isn't much to some, but it is to me," she said. "Didn't you ever wish you had enough money to start all over? Make things like they should have been in the first place?"

"Never was much for wishing, but I do know that money can't buy back your past. Can't buy half the things that people seem to think it can. Not the things that matter."

She snorted at that. "Money might not buy the things that matter to you, but it will buy me out of this territory. And if there's a chance that it will buy a bullet in Irish Jack's heart, I'd count that as money well spent."

Newt looked across the desert and nodded. "It's the waiting that's hard. Always hate waiting for a fight."

She turned her veil his way and looked at him head-on. "I guess if half of what they say about you is true, then this must be old hat to you."

"I've been in a scrap or two," he said.

"You remember, I'll double your wages. But whatever comes, don't you forget, you work for me."

"I'll take the pay we agreed upon at the start of this, no more. If my word wasn't good when this started, are you going to trust that you can buy me now?" he asked.

"I never met a man I'd trust."

"Well, trust a man you can buy even less." As soon as he said that several small birds flew up from the thicket like something had flushed them. "Best you go back to the horses with McPhee, and keep your head down while you're at it. I think the fight's about on us."

She stood as if to move away from him, and she had only half risen when a bullet struck the top of the rock she had been sitting behind and ricocheted off with a high-pitched whine. The boom of the gun that fired it was still roaring in Newt's head when he grabbed Jenny by the arm and yanked her back down behind the rocks. By then, more bullets were spanging off the rocks, and it sounded like the whole world was shooting at them.

CHAPTER TWENTY-THREE

Irish Jack's gang was scattered out in the brush in a long line sixty yards out from the stagecoach. Jack had fired the first shot, and the rest of the gang took that as the signal to open up on their own. They were firing fast and pouring everything they had into those rocks.

Ernie Sims wound up a little behind the rest of the line because he had encountered an especially thick stand of cholla as they snuck through the brush. He was a man with tender skin and had always had a special aversion to anything with thorns, and the cholla had the worst thorns he knew of. Nasty things, those thorns; so bad that it often seemed like all you had to do was get close to one of those cactus plants and the needle-sharp tines jumped at you. Get a cluster of those needles buried in your skin and it hurt terribly and would likely leave you with a festered wound that could take a month to heal, and there was no one in Jack's gang that he trusted to be gentle picking thorns out of him should he become stuck. Accordingly, Ernie picked his way carefully through that cholla, regardless of whether it made him fall behind or not.

And he had other reasons besides thorns to go slower than the rest of them. He thought it prudent that he keep behind Jack, especially given the way Jack had been looking at him occasionally since they had let the stage get away from them. Jack hadn't said it, but it was obvious that he had definite notions about who had fired the first shot at Seymour and spoiled the ambush. Jack thinking a thing like that could be unhealthy for whoever he was thinking it about. Every time Jack looked at him that way he was reminded of how Jack had gunned down one of his own men back there at Seymour simply because he had let his horse get shot. Ernie didn't intend to get shot due to one of Jack's bloody whims. No, he would stay in back of the rest of them where he could keep an eye on Jack.

Ernie moved ahead with his pistol held ready before him. And after a step or two, he saw Jack through the brush slightly to his left and ahead of him. The Irishman was so intent on shooting at the stagecoach party that he was unaware of Ernie's approach.

Ernie stopped and studied Jack for a moment. Given that he couldn't shake the feeling that Jack might try to kill him at some point, or at the very least try to cut him out of his share of the gold, he considered putting a bullet in Jack's back right then. It would be an easy thing to kill him while all of the shooting was going on, and none of the rest of them would know that Ernie was the one who did it.

Ernie cocked his pistol. He almost had it raised when something made Jack glance back over his shoulder, catching him in the act.

Ernie debated on going ahead and shooting Jack, but doing it while the gang leader was looking at him was a different matter and one not to be taken lightly or performed without proper time to think it through. Erne continued to bring his pistol up, but made a show of aiming it at the rock pile beyond the edge of the brush. He fired off a shot, not aiming at anything in particular, but hoping to throw off any suspicions on Jack's part. When he looked at Jack again he found the Irishman still watching him with a cunning look. For a moment, Ernie thought Jack had seen right through his act and knew his real intentions.

A bullet whipped through the brush right over Ernie's head, and he was too busy diving to the ground to give the matter further thought. His hat was knocked off his head by a limb and fell down over his eyes, and when he felt something poke him hard in the ribs he was immediately afraid that he had fallen on a cholla. He righted his hat while he scrambled on his belly to a different point in the thicket. One of the stage party must have spotted him to have taken a shot at him that came so close, and he wanted to be sure that he was hidden properly. The first thing he did when he felt he was behind adequate cover was to examine his side for signs of any cactus stickers. There were none to be found, and it must have been only a sharp rock or the stub of a limb that had stuck him in the ribs. No more bullets came through the brush in his immediate vicinity, and he had avoided encountering any cholla in his fall. Those two things should have been more than enough to leave him feeling relieved and a bit on the lucky side, but at that moment Jack laughed at him.

Ernie glared in Jack's direction, but Jack laughed again. Jack obviously thought it funny that Ernie had been so quick to duck for cover. In fact, two bullets cut through the brush near Jack while Ernie was glaring at him, but Jack didn't even stop laughing, nor did he flop on his belly. Instead, Jack continued to kneel against the green trunk of a paloverde tree as if there were no risk of him being hit by return fire. Ernie was quick to note that Jack kneeling like that was a much more dignified pose than lying on your belly.

"Where's your fight, Marshal?" Jack taunted. He placed special emphasis on the word *marshal.*

Ernie wanted to kill Jack more than ever. He knew himself to have plenty of fight, however he saw no reason that a man couldn't kill the members of the stage party while he kept his head down. There was no sense in taking foolish risks. Jack led the gang and was undoubtedly making a show of ignoring the risk to lift the spirits of his men. Ernie was sure that Jack would be down on his own belly if he didn't have the gang to think of. Still, it hurt to have Jack belittling him that way and questioning his mettle, but Jack was fond of belittling people.

There was no way to shoot Jack in the back while he was looking at Ernie, so the marshal found an open spot of daylight through the brush and fired another shot at the jumble of rocks. Although he couldn't spot any of the stage party, his aim was sufficient enough for his bullet to ricochet with an angry whine off one of the rocks around the water hole.

When he looked back at Jack he found that the Irishman was no longer watching him and was once again intent on killing other folks besides Ernie. Ernie favored things to stay that way. Let Jack's wrath rest on someone else while he waited for another time when Jack's back presented itself and Jack wasn't so alert — maybe when Jack was half-asleep sitting by a campfire and gone night-blind staring at the flames, or when Jack was drunk. On second thought, he ought to go with the former tactic. Jack drank whiskey often, but instead of making him unsteady, the booze never seemed to affect his motor skills. Also, Jack tended to get meaner the more he drank. Ernie decided catching Jack at a fire was by far the best course.

Calico Bob, and then Irish Jack — notching his pistol with those two names ought to get him plenty of respect, so much respect that nobody in the territory would ever dare laugh at him again.

Ernie was so lost in his thoughts that he

realized he had gone a good while without firing another shot. He crawled farther forward until he could see better and peered closely at the jumble of rocks and the stagecoach parked among them. It was a frustrating kind of fighting. It was generally hard enough to hit a man with a pistol at such distance, much less when you couldn't see him for all the rocks in the way. Twice he thought he saw someone moving behind those rocks, but they were gone before he could take aim.

Then he saw the black hat appear between two of those big rocks. And on that black hat was a hatband dotted with blue turquoise. He remembered that hat. It belonged to the Widowmaker.

Ernie took careful aim with his pistol. Truly, his luck had finally turned for the better. He had missed his shot at the Widowmaker at Seymour, but he wasn't going to miss this one.

Calico Bob, Irish Jack, and oh yes, the Widowmaker — quite the impressive list. He would be the talk of the territory.

CHAPTER TWENTY-FOUR

It was hard to keep his head down and try to spot their attackers at the same time, but Newt dared a glance between two rocks and thought he saw a puff of black powder smoke flutter up out of a bush sixty yards dead in front of him. He cocked his Winchester and tucked the buttstock against his shoulder, all in one smooth motion, and aimed a shot into that puff of smoke. He didn't get to see if his shot went true, for as soon as he pulled the trigger another round of bullets started smacking against the rocks around him. He hit the ground again, hugging close to the big boulder that fronted him.

Jenny was already down on her side with her knees drawn up to her chest in order to make as small a target as possible. He landed with his face inches from hers. Her hat had fallen off, and along with it, the veil. Those blue eyes of hers seemed twice as big as they ought to be, and her nostrils flared and pumped with the fear and excitement. There were dirt and bits of dried grass stuck to one side of her face where she had pressed it to the ground. When she rubbed at it with one hand he saw that she had wiped away not only the grime, but also other things. He had suspected when he first met her that she wore some kind of white cosmetic on one cheek, meant to match her pale skin and to conceal some blemish. And now that blemish was revealed.

The faint indentations in her skin that had been barely visible beneath her makeup were now fully revealed as a scar that covered the hollow of her cheek. He had seen pox scars before, and although similar, hers were different. Shallow, pitted indentations and what looked like hardened blisters dotted her skin, as if something red-hot had splattered her or as if she had taken a charge of shotgun pellets there. It wasn't an ugly scar or a big scar, and he was a judge of such things. And no bigger than it was, even an ugly scar would have done little to mar her good looks, for she was truly a stunning woman. But whatever had caused that had hurt her, and hurt her badly.

She must have been very self-conscious about the scar, because she immediately put her hand up to cover that side of her face when she realized he was looking at her. She gave him an expression that was undoubtedly some kind of unspoken message, but it was one that he could not fathom. She rolled onto her back and tugged her Merwin Hulbert pistol free of its holster, and whatever she might have been about to say was forgotten.

"Keep your head down," he said to her as he rose to his knees and chanced another look at the thicket.

"You think?" she threw back at him.

Somebody on their own side of things was firing often, and Newt moved closer to the stagecoach and saw Fred Stutter lying on his belly firing his Winchester through a small hole in the stack of rocks that served as his breastwork. Fred shot his carbine dry and rolled onto one side and started feeding fresh cartridges from his bandolier into the loading gate. His face was beet-red, from his sunburned forehead caused by his lost hat, to his swollen right cheekbone irritated by the kick of his rifle. Fred saw Newt looking at him and gave a reckless grin.

"They . . . wuh . . . wanta . . . fff . . . fight. Www . . . well, by ggg . . . golly they're ggg . . . gittin' it," he stuttered.

One of the outlaws must have heard him and fired at nothing more than the sound of his voice, for a bullet struck Fred's rock pile. He stuttered something incomprehensible and rolled back on his belly and poked his rifle barrel through his firing hole.

Newt moved slowly down the line of rocks, staying low and keeping cover between himself and the thicket. He found Ned Stutter not far past his brother. Ned was apparently the more cautious fighter of the pair, for he had wallowed himself a hole in the ground behind a low rock, and the only time he showed any part of himself to the enemy was to raise up his arms and point his shotgun in the general direction of the thicket. He would let off a round from that 10-gauge coach gun and then lower it and wait awhile before doing it again. He wasn't likely to hit anything like that, but he wasn't going to get shot, either. The outlaws in the thicket, from the number of shots they were firing into the rocks, seemed to have an unlimited supply of ammunition and hadn't let up at all.

The Dutchman, like Fred Stutter, had stacked himself a knee-high parapet of head-sized stones between two boulders, and he had laid a ragged old coat across that stack of rocks. His Ballard rifle rested on the coat, and he was squinting down its long barrel at the thicket. He didn't fire while Newt was watching him, but it was plain to see that he was looking for one of the outlaws in the thicket to show themselves.

Skitch was just beyond the Dutchman, and Newt made it to him at the same moment there was a break in the shooting from the thicket. Either the outlaws were moving position or they were reloading and thinking up a new strategy. The silence itself seemed overly loud after so much gunfire.

"How's it going?" Newt asked in a hushed tone.

"Can't see them to shoot at them," Skitch said.

"They'll move closer before long and you'll get your chance."

"That's what I'm afraid of," Skitch said. "Think we can hold them off?"

"We'll have to."

Skitch rubbed his right hand up and down the straight grip of his Winchester buttstock in a nervous gesture. He lifted his chin a little.

"Breeze has picked up a bit," he said.

Newt hadn't noticed it before, but there was a breeze now, straight out of the south. It had been still as death not long before.

"I think it might rain before evening," Skitch added.

Newt stared across the desert. It appeared as much of a scalded furnace as it ever did. He had never cared much for deserts.

"What makes you think that?" Newt asked.

"See that dark cloud to the south? That's carrying a gully washer if it keeps coming our way."

The mouth of the canyon mostly blocked Newt's view to the south, but he could see a bit of the flat country there with the dark wall of the Sa de la Estrella mountains in the background. A big thundercloud was there along those mountains just as Skitch had said, but Newt had been too worried or too busy to notice it.

"Monsoon season should have started a couple of weeks ago," Skitch said.

While a desert country, the late-summer months usually brought scattered and fast-moving thunderstorms. Those storms occasionally dropped great amounts of rainfall to the point that they caused flooding along the rivers, washes, and canyons.

"I didn't think it ever rained here," said a new voice.

It was lawyer McPhee who spoke. He had come out from under the stagecoach and was crawling on his hands and knees toward them. The bandage wound around his head didn't allow his bowler hat to sit fully down on his head, and it leaned at a precarious angle.

Newt glanced at the storm clouds. "That thundercloud is as likely to miss us by ten miles as it is to leave a single drop on us."

"Such a dreadful country," McPhee said as he took a seat.

The lawyer was wearing his suit coat, despite the heat. He swung the leather satchel he carried off one shoulder and laid it in his lap.

"Does your head hurt much?" Newt asked.

"Terribly, but I intend to help where I can. Simon and Crusher would expect no less of me."

"You're in no shape to fight," Newt said. "I want you to go farther up the canyon. Wait in the rocks past the tanks. Ms. Blake will join you in time."

Skitch nodded at that, but then he must have seen something in Newt's expression that puzzled him. "What kind of idea is rattling around in your head?"

"We might have a chance if we could hold them off until nightfall," Newt said. "And it won't hurt us if that thundercloud keeps coming our way, either."

"If they don't rush us before then, they're sure to work close when the sun goes down," Skitch said.

"That's what I'm thinking, but they can't find us if we're not here."

"Go ahead."

Newt rubbed at the stubble of whiskers on his chin. "Might be we could load your gold on the horses and work our way out the back door."

Skitch glanced at the sheer bluff at the head of the canyon behind them and the mountain above it. "There's no way out of here."

"Not with the stage," Newt said. "But men on foot might make it."

"What about the horses and the gold?"

"It's been my experience that a horse can go anywhere a man can travel without having to use his hands. I've seen pack mules cross trails up in the Sierra Madres that you wouldn't believe a goat could cross."

"It won't work," Skitch said. "Even if there is a way up out of this canyon, Irish Jack would hear us."

"It's just something to think on."

"The mere fact that you are considering such leads me to believe you think our odds aren't good if we stay here," McPhee said.

"We've got cover and water, and it would be hard to dig us out," Newt said. "But those men out there know that, and it's why they're content to plunk away at us for the moment and not push the issue. But come dark, they'll get up on the bluffs, and come daylight tomorrow they can shoot down on us as easy as shooting fish in a barrel."

"I don't like the sound of that. Not at all," McPhee said.

"We stay," Skitch said. "Irish Jack is already wearing us down, and there's nothing but desert on the other side of these mountains. Maybe we make it over, but we're bound to lose horses. All those thieving bastards out there would have to do is follow along and pick up the pieces."

"I'm afraid I disagree," McPhee answered before Newt could.

"What's that?" Skitch asked.

The stubby-legged lawyer's voice was as squeaky as ever, but he seemed very assertive for once. "I have the authority . . ."

"You have what?" Skitch cut him off.

McPhee put a hand to his bandaged head as if talking was painful. "Simon and Crusher have granted me . . ."

"You're a pestering little bean counter, that's what you are. Tend to your books or puke in your hat, but stay out of business you don't understand." The anger was plain in Skitch's voice. He was on edge like the rest of them.

"I'm duly aware of your position as manager of the Vulture Mine," McPhee continued as if he hadn't been interrupted twice and as if he didn't notice how mad Skitch was getting, "but I'm afraid I haven't been fully honest with you. You, sir, are misinformed that you hold authority at this moment."

"That head wound has you talking silly."

"Easy, Skitch," Newt said. "I'm sure Mr. McPhee doesn't mean anything by it."

McPhee reached inside his leather satchel and pulled out a large envelope. "Mr. Skitch, this document grants me authority over the mine and its operations, should that become necessary."

"You? What do you know of mining? What do you know of anything, for that matter?" Skitch growled.

"I know nothing of mining, but I do take my job quite seriously. Mr. Simon and Mr. Crusher would take it quite unkindly if their gold shipment didn't make it to the railroad, and would frown on an employee who didn't do everything he could to prevent theft of their property," McPhee said as if he were talking over a formal dinner or presenting a case to a judge.

"What are you talking about?" Skitch asked.

"Mr. Skitch, you will do as this man says and we will attempt to escape this situation, or I'm afraid I will have to terminate your employment."

"I haven't made up my mind what we'll do, yet," Skitch said. "But I guarantee you one thing. You won't have any say in it. I had about enough of you before we left the mine, you snooping . . ."

Newt thought it was time to break in and maybe cool things off a little between the two men. "Mr. McPhee, I think what Mr. Skitch is trying to say is that you may be a little out of your element here. I assure you that we're all doing everything we can to get the company's gold to the railroad. And Mr. Skitch wants to see that done probably more than anyone."

"Three years I've put into getting that mine back on its feet, and what thanks have I ever gotten for it?" Skitch asked. "Now this lawyer sits here telling me what I'm going to do."

McPhee pulled a piece of paper from the envelope, unfolded it, and held it out to Skitch. "You will see that what I say is true, no matter how much you may dislike it."

From Newt's vantage point he could see only that the document contained one long, handwritten paragraph followed by some kind of stamped seal at the bottom of the page and several flourished signatures.

"What's this you're trying to pull?" Skitch snatched the letter from McPhee and made a show of reading it.

"As you can see, it's as I told you. Mr. Simon and Mr. Crusher have granted me authority over all mine operations should I deem there be need. And the other members of your board of directors have also signed."

"I never heard of any Simon and Crusher owning the mine," the Dutchman said.

The old German had come on them so quietly that Newt hadn't heard him. It was uncanny how quietly the man could move, despite his years.

"I've got no time for this." Skitch tossed the letter back at McPhee.

"What's that letter say?" Newt asked. "I'd be curious to know."

Skitch gave a sigh. "I never heard of this Simon and Crusher until two weeks ago. Not until I got a letter letting me know that they had purchased majority ownership in the Central Arizona Mining Company and that they would be sending out a man to check on their operations."

"I don't mean to antagonize you, Mr. Skitch," McPhee said. "But what Mr. Jones suggests sounds like our best chance. I'm perfectly fine with you remaining in charge of the mine and of this shipment, but I insist we not remain here and risk company assets in a fight we may not, or cannot, win."

"You insist?" Skitch was mad enough that his voice had a shake to it.

"Frankly, I think I'm being quite fair," McPhee said. "We'll have plenty of time when we get to the railroad to talk about the other matters I mentioned to you back in Vulture City."

"What's he talking about?" the Dutchman asked. "We don't know this lawyer from Adam. Anybody with a pen and a piece of paper could write up something making it look like he's somebody he ain't. And what's all his fool talk matter, even if he's the king of Egypt?"

Newt saw that the lawyer was going to keep talking, and where that might lead. "Mr. McPhee, in case you haven't noticed, you're making Skitch highly angry, and this is no time for us to be squabbling amongst ourselves. Right now we're chattering about what really doesn't matter at the moment, while we've left the Stutter brothers standing guard."

McPhee tucked the envelope and its letter back inside his satchel. "Very well, then."

"All right," Newt said. "How about you keep low and work your way back to the first of those water tanks and keep an eye on the horses?" Newt asked.

The lawyer nodded and started in the suggested direction. Instead of crouching, he crawled on his hands and knees as he had before.

"I can't abide by a fool," the Dutchman said. "Tom hired me, and Tom's who I work for."

"McPhee's out of his element, and he's scared and he's hurting," Newt said. "That's all."

The Dutchman scowled at that, but said nothing else and stalked back to his firing position, leaving Skitch and Newt alone. Newt twisted on his heels and made as if to leave.

"Where are you going?" Skitch asked.

"Thought I would go have a look at the head of this canyon," Newt replied.

"I told you we stay here."

"You call it, but it won't hurt to have a look at things. Could be you might change your mind before the day's over."

Skitch nodded and wiped at the sweat on his neck. "Damned, but it's a hot one."

Newt nodded. "And it's going to get hotter."

CHAPTER TWENTY-FIVE

Newt worked his way along the footpath to the two tanks at the head of the canyon, winding his way through the big boulders. He found McPhee sitting on a rock near the horses and polishing his eyeglasses with the corner of his coattail. He had no time for whatever business problems or company power struggles had caused the recent friction between McPhee and Skitch, and his intention was to go on past the lawyer without speaking. But McPhee wasn't finished talking.

"I was telling the truth back there," McPhee said.

"That's all between you and Skitch. None of my business."

"I fear that our situation is becoming more and more precarious," McPhee continued. "There may come a time when the success of this venture truly hangs in the balance, and I need to know I can count on you, Mr.

301

Jones. You seem a capable man, trustworthy man."

"Count on me for what?"

"I may ask you to take charge."

"Skitch has gotten you this far."

"Simon and Crusher intends the mine to become profitable, and of course, I have my own job at stake. The mine will not be profitable, nor will I long have a job should that Irish Jack and his cutthroats manage to steal that express box."

"What are you getting at?"

"I'll pay you a two-hundred-dollar bonus if you can put me and that strongbox on the train," McPhee said.

"First Skitch, and now you offering me a pay raise," Newt said. "I'd say neither one of you is very tight with the company's money." Newt didn't mention Jenny's offer of a bonus.

"Simon and Crusher will stand by my offer, but when . . . no, if the time should come that I need your help, then I will expect you to back me fully."

"I'm helping you now. That's what I hired on for."

McPhee shook his head. "Not this. What I mean is that I don't trust Mr. Skitch."

"You've already questioned his decision making."

"You don't understand," McPhee said. "You see, there were certain . . . let's say . . . irregularities in the mine's bookkeeping. Enough irregularities that gave me pause during my time in Vulture City."

Newt took a deep breath. "Be careful spreading that around, Mr. McPhee. Out here, a man's only as good as his word and his reputation, and an accusation like I think you're making is a serious one."

"Well and fine, but you see now why I don't trust him."

"I was hired to guard this express, that's all. And what's out there" — Newt pointed back toward where Irish Jack's gang was — "doesn't have a thing to do with whatever you think about Tom Skitch. Best thing you can do is save that trouble for another time and focus on the here and now."

Newt took up his rifle and went to check the horses. The picket line lay well hidden in the jumble of boulders and the stock was somewhat protected from the shots fired into camp, but he worried that a chance round might have struck one of them.

The horses were fine. He led all of them to water and let them drink again, and when he came back to the picket line he saddled the Circle Dot horse.

McPhee sat on his rock and watched him

the whole time. What an odd man he was, and as out of place with his baggy, pin-striped pants and his leather satchel and fancy coat folded across his lap as anything in the desert. At times, he looked lost, and at other times he was strangely bold for one such as he.

The head of the canyon wasn't like the almost sheer rock bluffs on either wall. Runoff water had gouged out a narrow slash that led from where he stood up to a higher point on the mountain — the very same water that had carved out the stone basins to create the pair of water holes. That erosion had left little but bare rock, and the cut was steep and just wide enough to perhaps allow a horse to pass as it neared the top. It would be rough going, but it might be done. He guessed it was maybe a two-hundred-feet climb — two hundred feet of slick, treacherous rock.

There was still no more gunfire, but he knew that it wouldn't be long before Irish Jack's gang made another try. He spent a moment scanning the canyon's walls to see if he could spot anyone trying to get to the high ground. The fight was over if Jack ever got a couple of his men up there.

Satisfied that, for the moment, nobody was moving around above him, he worked his way back to the stagecoach. Skitch saw him return, but didn't say anything.

Newt moved on to the Dutchman. The old German was still lying prone with his cheek to his Ballard rifle.

"Anything moving out there?"

The Dutchman shook his head.

Newt nodded at the Stutter brothers to encourage them and moved on until he found Jenny where he had left her.

"How's McPhee?" she asked.

"He's managing," he answered. "Sent him back to the tanks to watch the horses."

He settled down in a likely spot close to her where a big rock cast some shade and adjusted himself to where he was most comfortable. Occasionally, he leaned out a little to see between the rocks that sheltered him, watching for the outlaws' next move. The trouble with taking a look their way was that he risked making a target of himself, but Irish Jack's gang had the same problem. He glanced often up at the bluffs to either side of him, still worried about that weakness in their defensive position.

He checked his pocket watch twice while he waited and sipped occasionally at his canteen. The storm cloud to the southwest was larger than it was before, and even from a distance he could hear the dull boom of thunder and see the lightning crackling inside it and the dark curtain of rain beneath it. He was checking his watch for a third time when someone shouted from the thicket.

"You up there!" that voice called out.

Newt leaned out far enough to peer past the rock.

"I said, you up there!" it came a second time.

Neither Skitch nor any of the others answered the outlaw, and Newt eased his Winchester to his shoulder and waited.

"Aren't you going to answer him?" Jenny asked.

"Talking won't change this."

Jenny waited a time, and he could feel that she was staring her displeasure at him without looking to see that it was so.

"What do you want?" Jenny yelled back at the outlaws.

"Is that you, Jenny Silks?" the same voice from the thicket called back to her. "Heard a lot about you. Never had the pleasure of your acquaintance, but the boys here say you're a hell of a woman."

Whoever was out there was quieter that time, and there was definitely a healthy dose of the Irish brogue in that voice. Newt

306

wondered if it was Irish Jack doing the talking.

"You know damned well it's me," Jenny answered.

Newt heard her cock her pistol and glanced at her. "Old friends, huh?"

"Not hardly," she said.

"You men let a woman talk for you?" Irish Jack laughed.

Newt checked the canyon walls again. Jack might be trying to keep their attention while some of his men put the sneak on the stage party.

"What do you want?" Jenny asked.

"I want that gold, Jenny darling, and I aim to have it."

"Come and get it, then."

"We've got you hemmed in," Jack said. "Nowhere to go."

Newt thought he had located the general area at the edge of the thicket where Irish Jack's voice was coming from and shifted his aim that way. "Keep him talking."

Jenny nodded like she understood, and then called out again. "Save your Mick blarney for someone else."

"You only got two ways out of this canyon. You hear me?" Jack said. "Either you leave that stagecoach and I let you walk out of here, or I bury you right here and now. Your choice."

"No deal, Jack." Jenny moved to one end of the rock she was behind to where she could see a bit of the thicket.

"Don't let him draw you out," Newt said.

"You expect us to trust you? No thanks," she threw at Jack.

"What about you, Skitch?" Jack bellowed. "I don't expect a two-bit whore to have any sense, but are you willing to die for that gold?"

Newt saw movement in the brush first, and then he thought he saw what was the crown of Jack's hat through the fork in a clump of cholla. He took a sight picture slightly below that hat and put the pad of his finger on the trigger.

"Two-bit whore?" Jenny leaned out around the end of her rock and fired her pistol.

There was no way she should have been able to shoot like that, for she didn't even aim, and there was no way she should have been able to know exactly where Jack was speaking from without ever looking over that rock until then. Regardless, her shot knocked a head-sized clump of cholla off right above Jack's hat.

Jenny's pistol report had barely cleared the air when someone else off to the side of

Jack stood up out of the brush with a rifle aimed at them. Newt swung his own aim in that direction and found the outlaw with his front sight, but the Dutchman's Ballard boomed and a .38-55 round went through the outlaw front to back and knocked him over backward before Newt could fire.

And then there were so many guns firing and bullets scattering bits of rock and sand that it was hard to make sense of it all. A nasty ricochet smacked into the rock right behind Newt, but he wasn't aware of it because of the endless roar of the guns. He rose up and fanned the lever on his Winchester and put two fast shots into the same clump of cholla where Irish Jack had been standing, and then he ducked low and moved twenty feet closer to the stage with one hand on the ground to balance him. Jenny was hunkered behind her rock, and he grabbed her by the arm when he came to her and dragged her with him.

He and Jenny found a new spot of cover, but the rocks were barely big enough to shield both of them, and they had to huddle closely. Jenny's hat and veil had come off again, and her hair had come undone and fallen down to her shoulders. She gave him a wild, cornered look, her chest rising and falling out of fear and exertion.

"Now you did it!" Newt said to her.

Jenny popped up and fired her pistol again and was cocking it for another go when Newt pulled her back down. She swung her pistol at his face, but he caught her hand around the grips and yanked the weapon away from her and pushed her against the rock. He tucked the pistol behind his belt and looked toward the stagecoach in time to see Fred Stutter take a bullet in the forehead. The young Mississippian rolled over on one side and moved no more. Jenny saw that, too, and she stared at the body for a long moment while Newt took a quick look at the thicket.

"Get back to the tanks with McPhee and stay there," Newt said.

She shook her head and refused to go.

"Fighting's what you're paying me for, and I'll do better knowing I don't have to keep you from trying to get yourself killed." He gave her a shove toward the footpath leading to the tanks. "Go."

She made as if to resist, but decided otherwise and swung her hair out of her face and grabbed her hat. She took off toward the tanks, bent over at the waist and at a dead run. Newt rose up and fired two more fast shots. He had no targets in particular and only meant to draw attention and give her time to get clear.

Before he could duck low again, something struck him a wicked punch in the belly and he slapped at the wound and slumped to his knees. The force of the blow all but knocked the air from him, and he slumped forward and rested his head against the stone.

CHAPTER TWENTY-SIX

"I got the son of a bitch! I got the Widow-maker!" Ernie Sims cried.

Irish Jack winced at the cactus thorns digging into his neck when Ernie's shouting caused him to move his head too fast to look that way. A bullet scattered gravel over Ernie, and the marshal shut up and lunged backward to land flat on his back. His boot heels scrambled frantically at the ground as he crabbed backward until he found a shallow, eroded ditch that offered some safety from any more shots aimed his way.

The sight of Ernie scooting on his back like that would normally have given Jack some delight, but he was too mad and the cactus spines in his neck hurt too bad to laugh. Somebody had almost put a bullet in Ernie's skull, but it served him right for being foolish enough to call attention to himself by opening his big mouth.

But the cowardly marshal had managed

to gun down the Widowmaker. Jack had seen that with his own eyes. Jack wouldn't have guessed Ernie could hit anything with a pistol at sixty yards or better, but he had busted the big devil right through the boiler.

Jack looked back to the rocks where the stage party had taken its stand. Moving his neck again, no matter how slowly or gingerly, made it feel like his neck was on fire. He wanted to reach up and see if he could pluck the cactus needles away, but even so small a movement might get him killed. It didn't take much for whoever was shooting that big rifle out there in the rocks to see you, and Jack had already lost one of his men because he didn't have the good sense to keep well hidden and still.

Jack gritted his teeth against the pain in his neck, and the more it hurt the madder he got. That Jenny Silks had been the one who had done it. A bold whore, she was. Who would have thought that a woman could shoot like that? How she had even spotted him was a mystery. Yet, she had come so close to hitting him in the head that she had shot the top out of the cactus he was hiding behind and dropped a clump of it right on top of him. What was worse, that was the second time for the day that she had almost killed him. Being pierced by cactus thorns as a result of her shooting was even more exasperating than when she had sent him to the floor of the stage station back at Seymour.

Jack saw a shotgun barrel lifting up over the top of one of the rocks ahead and shouldered his rifle and took a shot at it. His wounded neck wouldn't allow him to get a good cheek rest on the rifle's stock and his shot was way off the mark. And the gun's recoil pushed a couple of those thorns deeper into his flesh. It hurt so bad he couldn't think properly.

He looked to his left and finally spotted another of his men, and when he had that one's attention he motioned him back deeper into the thicket. He retreated cautiously away from the fight without bothering to check if any of his gang were following him.

However, he soon heard the others working through the brush to either side of him, and the firing from his side withered away until it was nothing. The stage party aimed a few more searching shots at the sound of the gang's retreat, but none of them came close to Jack. When the gunshots finally ceased altogether, all Jack could hear were the ringing in his ears and the sound of panting men fighting their way through the thick brush.

It took the outlaws a long time to pick their way back to their horses. When the last of the gang showed up they found Jack had pulled his saddle off his big sorrel and had thrown it on the ground and was using it for a seat.

"One of you come pull these cactus thorns out of my neck," Jack said.

The other outlaws had already flopped on the ground and were guzzling from the canteens that they hadn't had the good sense to take with them to the fight. They seemed too hot and thirsty to honor Jack's request. Only Ten Mule was left standing. Being the biggest and weakened by his wound, it had taken him considerable time to work his way through the brush.

"I'll pull them out," Ten Mule said as he lumbered toward Jack.

"No, you're a clumsy bloke and you've only got one good arm, to boot," Jack said. "You would likely only push them in deeper."

Jack squinted at Ten Mule and wondered how such a big, dumb oaf could be related to him. And as bad as he felt, he was sure his nephew didn't feel much better. He was all stooped over as if he could barely stay on his feet, and Jack could see where his arm wound had bled through the bandage.

"Go sit down," Jack said. "You're likely to die, and I don't want you falling on me."

At that moment Ernie came into the little opening in the brush where they waited. Other than being sweatier and breathing harder than any of the others, he looked no worse for his wear.

"Get over here and pull these thorns out of my neck," Jack said.

Instead of heeding the order, Ernie simply stopped and stared at him. Killing the Widowmaker probably had him thinking too highly of himself. Jack shifted his rifle in Ernie's direction. He didn't exactly aim the weapon at the marshal, but the threat was there.

"Quit standing there like that and get over here," Jack said.

Ernie nodded and walked over. He was still puffing like he had just run two miles. He gave Jack's neck a dubious look.

"I don't know, Jack. Cholla stickers can be hard to pull out," he said.

"Hook them between your thumb and your knife blade, but you be damned easy about it," Jack replied.

Ernie produced a pocketknife and opened the blade. He bent over Jack and peered at his neck, clucking his tongue. "You got a good dose of them jumping needles."

"I don't want a count. Just pull them out, you fool."

Ernie reached out with the knife awkwardly. "This is going to hurt."

"Get it over with."

The fire feeling in Jack's neck came on hotter than ever, and he could tell by that feeling that Ernie had taken hold of one of the thorns. It felt like Ernie was wiggling the spine around in the wound rather than pulling it free.

"Got it." Ernie held the thorn in front of Jack's face so he could see it.

It was a nasty yellow thorn almost as long as a finger and with blood halfway up its length.

"Get back to it," Jack said. "And this time you better have the loving touch of Saint Mary herself."

Ernie had a harder time with the second thorn. Either he was as clumsy as Ten Mule, or he was still breathing so hard that it made him shaky. It felt like he was pushing a hot poker into Jack's flesh.

Jack whipped his own knife out of his boot top and pressed the point of it against Ernie's belly. "You hurt me like that again and I'll gut you."

Ernie nodded, but didn't make a move

toward Jack's neck. "I'm trying to help you."

"No, it feels like you're trying to kill me," Jack said. "Hurry up."

Jack kept the big knife against Ernie's belly while Ernie made another attempt. It took more time to free that thorn than it had the first one, but it also hurt Jack far less.

Ernie managed to pull out six more thorns, and Jack decided to lower his knife for the last five of them. Ernie straightened and folded his pocketknife.

"That's the last of them," he said.

"Are you sure? Feels like there's at least a dozen more still stuck in me," Jack replied.

Ernie shook his head and went to his horse to get his canteen. Jack reached up to his neck and probed tenderly at his raw flesh while Ernie guzzled water and managed to slop a good deal of it down the front of his shirt.

"Best you slap some kind of poultice on that neck," Ernie said when he emptied what was left in his canteen. "It'll fester if you don't."

Jack took up his own canteen from the ground beside him and poured a dab of water in his palm and pressed it to his neck. He repeated that several times.

The tin body of Ernie's empty canteen

318

banged against his saddle when he rehung it there, and every one of them except Jack turned and looked at that canteen. They all looked back at Jack.

"We've got to have more water before long." Ernie put words to what they were all thinking.

Jack took hold of his finger bone watch fob, lifted up the war medal pinned on his vest, and clutched both of them at the same time. He worked them absentmindedly in his hand for a while and said nothing.

"You rub those like they're charms," Ernie said.

Jack let go of the war medal and held up the finger bone. "Man in Albuquerque tried to sell me this. Claimed it belonged to Billy the Kid."

"That really the Kid's finger bone?" one of the outlaws asked.

"I doubt it's the Kid's finger bone," Jack replied. "That's why I didn't pay the five dollars the man was asking for it."

"How much did you pay for it?" Ernie sounded a bit impressed.

"Pay him? I cut his belly open for trying to play me the fool," Jack said.

Ernie found a good spot to sit under a tall yucca bush and leaned back against it and gestured at the finger bone. "It'd be something if that really was the Kid's finger."

"You're as bad as Ten Mule. That black-guard sold three more bones just like it that week, all with the same story, and a pair of glass baubles he was pawning off as diamonds," Jack said. "No, what this finger bone does is remind me, and everyone that sees it, that I'm not a man to be trifled with."

"How about that war medal?" Ernie asked. "Seen a few pin them on for dress-up on special occasions. You know, parades and holidays and such, but never anybody that wore one regular-like unless they were still a soldier."

Jack looked down at the bronzed medal. It was a flag ribbon holding up an eagle with a five-pointed star beneath.

"Are you saying I'm some kind of brag-gart?" Jack let go of the finger bone and dropped his hand to his rifle.

"I never said nothing of the kind."

Jack waited until Ernie looked down and broke eye contact before he spoke again. "The finger bone says I won't be trifled with. This" — he tapped the medal on his chest — "reminds me that I won't be killed."

The light breeze that had been blowing for the last hour or so instantly changed to a hard gust that rolled the dust through the thicket, and the brush swayed wildly. Jack looked up at the darkening sky like it was another thing to be fought, and then he nodded at the medal on his chest again.

"It was at Petersburg. Our boys tunneled under the rebel breastworks and lit four tons of black powder. Blew men and cannon and horses and guts a hundred feet in the air and left a hole in the line that was sixty or seventy feet wide and thirty feet deep," Jack said. "And then they sent us through the break and right into merciless hell itself.

"The rebels that weren't dead caught us down in that bloody, rotten pit. The bullets came like a hailstorm. Like that thundercloud about to blow up on us." Jack nodded at the sky to the south and squinted against the dust blowing in his face. "Men fell all around me, and there was nothing to do but keep on trying to climb out of that hole or die.

"When the rebels met us down in that pit, it wasn't the rifles that did the killing after a while, but man-to-man, rifle butt to rifle butt, and knife to knife. You could walk across the fallen and never touch the ground by the time our officers called for the retreat. Only seven men from my company climbed out of that hole alive, and they claimed I drug two of them back to our lines. I don't remember doing anything of the sort. All I remember was the dying, and biting the nose right off a rebel boy's face. They didn't mention that when they pinned this medal on me. All they talked about was what a fine fellow I was. Valor, they called it. Said I was full of valor."

Jack used his rifle butt braced against the ground to push himself to his feet, and he scowled some more at the oncoming storm. He clutched the finger bone and his war medal again like they were some kind of magic amulets.

"Valor doesn't have anything to do with why I keep this. It's not worth the price of a glass of whiskey, and there's been many a time I would have sold it for less. But it reminds me every day that there isn't one thing in this world that scares me, and if I lived through that pit I can live through anything."

Jack put away his rifle and took up his sawed-off shotgun from the pommel holster on his saddle instead. He gave a nod to the men watching him. "I won't be killed and I won't be trifled with. You hear me? Now, get on your feet. I want a couple of you to work your way up either side of the bluffs. Get up in the rocks if you can. Another hour, maybe less, it will be dark, and then the rest of us are going to go straight at them."

The other outlaws slowly got to their feet and checked their weapons. Ten Mule remained on the ground. While the rest of them had listened to Jack's story, the big redhead had lain down and appeared to be asleep.

"Get up," Jack said to him.

"I can't, Jack," Ten Mule said in a weak voice. "My head's swimmy, and I don't think my legs will work."

"Get up and fight or lay there and die," Jack said. "Because I'm going up there, right into that old, smoking pit, and we're going to kill everything in sight."

The outlaws started filtering through the thicket and back toward the stagecoach, but Ten Mule was still lying on the ground.

"What pit, Jack? I didn't see a pit up there," Ten Mule said.

"Get up and fight or die, nephew," Jack said to him from the brush. "Get up or die. That's all any of us get to do."

Sometime later, and after the other outlaws were gone and Ten Mule was left alone, he cried out. His eyes were closed and his breathing was shallow and ragged.

"I see the pit you're talking about, Jack,"

Ten Mule said. "I see it now."

And then he died.

CHAPTER TWENTY-SEVEN

Newt lay behind the rock and clutched at his belly. It hurt like the blue blazes and the blow had knocked the wind out of him. He looked down and expected to see blood while he wheezed and sucked for air, but there was nothing. When he could breathe better again, he moved his hands and untucked his shirt to get a better look at his wound. Instead of a bullet hole, there was only a hard red knot about the size of a fist. He glanced up at the rock above him where it was scored and nicked from more than one bullet impact and guessed that whoever had felled him had shot too low. Instead of punching a hole through him, the bullet that should have killed him had probably struck that rock and knocked a chunk of it free and drove it into his belly about three inches below his breastbone. The wound was going to be sore for a good long while, but he wasn't going to die, not yet.

The shooting had stopped while Newt lay behind the rock, and after a time he rose and moved toward the stagecoach. He passed the Stutter brothers. Ned was sitting beside his brother's body. He didn't even look up when Newt went by, and Newt didn't say anything, not wanting to interfere with the stage driver's grieving.

"Where you going?" the Dutchman asked.

"I'm going to get that strongbox," Newt said without stopping.

The black storm cloud coming from the south was almost on them and a clap of thunder rolled across the desert. Newt leaned his rifle against the rear wheel of the stagecoach and opened the door and took hold of the strongbox. He had dragged it to the edge of the floorboard by the time the Dutchman and Skitch walked up.

"Take the other end of this," Newt said.

Skitch took hold of one end of the box, and they held it between them. Newt took up his rifle and led Skitch toward the tanks. The Dutchman made as if to follow, but Newt shook his head.

"Go back and get Ned and bring him along," he told the German. "And get the water bags."

He and Skitch carried the strongbox up the boulder trail to where the horses were tied. Jenny and McPhee were waiting for them. McPhee held a palm-sized, nickel-plated, over-and-under derringer pointed at Newt and seemed surprised that it wasn't an outlaw come to kill him who had appeared out of the boulders.

"Do me a favor and go ahead and shoot me," Newt said as he and Skitch dropped the box.

McPhee lowered the gun. "I thought you were all dead."

"Not hardly," Newt said while he went to the Circle Dot horse.

Another gust of wind blew up the canyon, and this time it didn't settle down. It kept blowing. McPhee grabbed at his bowler hat to keep it in place, and the wind whipped Jenny's dress about her legs and her hair flew out from her back.

A bolt of lightning cracked the sky as Newt led the Circle Dot horse back to them, and the gelding spooked and tried to jerk away from him at the explosion of light and sound. Newt grabbed at his own hat as another hard gust of wind whipped up the dust. He faced the wind and took a look at the blackening sky and found the wall of rain marching toward them. That dark curtain was so dense that it blocked the view of all the countryside beyond it. The air was thick with the musty smell of rain and dust.

Newt steadied his horse and reached down for the strongbox. He didn't even wait for Skitch to help again, but heaved the heavy load up and tried to swing it one-handed onto the horse's back. Lightning cracked again and the gelding danced away from him and caused him to drop the box.

"Let me help you with that crazy horse," Skitch said as he reached for the bridle rein Newt clung to.

Newt brought the Circle Dot horse close and petted the animal's neck in an attempt to calm it. Then he and Skitch heaved the box up on the saddle. Ned and the Dutch-man, carrying Fred's body, came through the boulders.

It was then that the rain began to fall. It came not with a gentle buildup, but the sky simply opened up and poured on them. It rained so hard that Newt couldn't see past ten or twenty yards in any direction.

The Circle Dot horse flinched again at the sound of thunder, and Newt laid a hand against the gelding's shoulder and felt the quiver of fear rippling beneath his hide.

"Stand still. I thought you were supposed to be a spirit horse," Newt said to the geld-ing.

"He's a spirited devil, all right," Skitch said after he dodged a stamping hoof and he sputtered the water off his lips.

Newt started to tell Skitch that wasn't what he had meant about the horse and to mention how he had come by the animal on his way to Mexico one time, but didn't. It was raining too hard to talk properly, anyway.

They rigged a crude packer's hitch with Newt's rope to hold the box in place atop the saddle while big raindrops popped against their hat brims and the water ran off them in rivers. The wet rope was hard to bind tightly enough to make a good hitch, but it might hold for what Newt had planned.

The thunder and lightning hadn't let up, but the Circle Dot horse seemed to have calmed some. Newt was about to go get the other horses when the Dutchman motioned at him. Newt saw Ned sitting on the muddy ground over Fred's body like he had been earlier. The stage driver's hat brim was so wet that it had sagged down over his face so much that you couldn't see him. But to Newt, that sagging hat somehow made the young man look more forlorn.

"Ned, I know this isn't easy, but we've got to be going," Newt said.

Ned didn't look up. "I . . . I ain't lll . . . leaving him."

"Anytime now, or maybe after this storm breaks, they're going to come at us, and come at us hard," Newt said.

"Lll . . . let 'em come," Ned replied in a flat, emotionless voice.

"I know how you're feeling, but there's Ms. Jenny to think about," Newt said. "She's counting on you, and so is Skitch.'

Ned finally looked up at him. "I can't lll . . . leave him like this."

Newt started to say that there was no time to bury his brother, but knew he wouldn't be likely to leave if that had been his brother lying there. Time to spare was in short supply, but that was the way the chips fell. When things got hard, you simply did what you had to and hoped for the best.

"No time to dig a grave, but we could put some rocks over him," Newt said. "When this is all over you could come back and lay him to rest properly."

"Nnn . . . no, I think . . . I think I'll jjj . . . just stay here," Ned said. "Wuh . . . we always been together."

Newt knew there was no sense in arguing the matter. The young man's grief was too much. Newt headed to get the other horses.

When he came back with the horses the

Dutchman was returning from another trip to the stagecoach and carrying one of the coach's big canvas water bags over one shoulder.

"Where's the other one?" Newt asked.

"Shot full of holes," the Dutchman answered.

Newt turned the Circle Dot horse toward the head of the canyon.

"You aren't leaving him, are you?" Skitch nodded at Ned Stutter.

"We stay here, we probably all die." Newt had to talk louder than he liked to be heard over the wind and rain. "I don't like it, but he's a grown man. His choice."

"You're a hard man, Jones," Skitch said.

"You've said that before. Let's get moving."

"I don't know if McPhee can stay on one of them riding bareback," Jenny said as she looked at the horses. The Circle Dot horse had the only saddle, and it was in use to pack the strongbox.

"We won't be riding," Newt said. "At least not for a while."

Newt handed off the other horses to the Dutchman and Skitch and led the Circle Dot horse toward the head of the canyon.

"Where are we going?" Jenny called after him.

"Up," he said.

Although the sun had yet to fully set, the canyon was almost as dark as it would have been close to nightfall. With that and the rain, it was hard for him to see her when he paused among the boulders and looked back for her. In that kind of light and with the rain blowing sideways she looked like some kind of ghost standing there in her black veil.

"There's no way we can get horses up that," she said.

"We're going to try," he said. "I hired on to get you and this gold through to the railroad, and that's what I intend to do."

Newt took one last look at Ned Stutter. He couldn't see the Mississippian at first, but the lightning flashed again, and for an instant, the whole canyon lit up. Ned was still sitting where he had been with his head bowed and that sagging hat brim fallen even farther.

Newt grimaced and moved on. They would all likely die if they stayed where they were, but knowing that didn't make it any easier.

CHAPTER TWENTY-EIGHT

There was no trail that they could follow, only the narrow channel washed out of the mountainside that Newt had found earlier. Already, water was pouring down the cut ankle-deep, and when Newt looked up the slash in the mountainside appeared in places more like a waterfall.

"You seriously think we can get up that with the horses?" Skitch asked from behind him.

Newt started up the cut without answering. The climb was steep from the start, and there was nothing but bare, slick rock to walk on. The Circle Dot horse slipped and almost fell before they had gone ten yards, but managed somehow to keep its feet. The iron shoes on the horse's hooves made getting traction harder on the rocky ground. The angle was so steep that both Newt and the horse leaned far forward, scrambling ahead and fighting for a secure purchase for the next step.

"Don't follow too closely to each other," Newt called back at the rest of the party.

Twice, Newt had to stop briefly and catch his breath. And three times he had to stop and move rocks out of the way to get enough room for the Circle Dot horse to pass through the cut. After a time, neither he nor the horse could go any farther, and Newt stopped on a shelf of rock that provided a resting place. The horse's hind legs quivered from the strain while Newt looked back down the cut. Skitch was coming up after him, but was having a harder time with three horses in tow behind him. Jenny, despite Newt's suggestion to keep some spacing between each other, was right behind those horses, helping to urge them up the grade. McPhee waddled up the slope after her, his limping gait more pronounced than ever. The Dutchman was some ten yards below them with the last two horses.

Newt looked up the mountain and waited for the lightning to flash again. When it came, he almost decided to turn back. All his struggle, and he found that he was less than halfway up the cut. But he was committed by then, they all were, and there was no turning back. The narrow defile was barely wide enough for a single horse to pass at a time, and there was no way to turn them around.

He looked down at where the water tanks lay, but could see nothing of them. If Irish Jack and his men caught them in the cut it wasn't going to be pretty.

Newt started upward again with the Circle Dot horse scrambling behind him. They came to another ledge, almost waist-high and cut as squarely as a step on a set of stairs. Newt got up on the ledge and tugged and coaxed at the horse to try to make it come to him. The gelding balked at first, but finally squatted on its hindquarters and drew up its front legs and leapt for the top of the ledge. It landed on its belly on the brink of the precipice and its back hooves clattered and struck at the rock in an attempt to get its hind legs over the top. Newt jumped off the ledge, caught himself against one wall of the cut, and then leaned against the horse's rump and pushed with all his might. A thrashing leg almost knocked him down the mountain, but the horse finally made it up and over.

He bellied over the lip of the ledge and lay there for a moment. The Circle Dot horse stood above him with its legs shaking from the strain worse than before. Newt managed to get back to his feet and was almost afraid to look at what was above and ahead of them. But he saw that the worst of it seemed to be over — not easy, but nothing like what they had climbed so far. The mountain disappeared fifty yards above him, and he hoped that was the last of it.

He tied the bridle reins to the saddle to keep them from dragging, and then he gave the gelding a slap on the hip and sent it up the cut ahead of him. He looked below him and found Skitch almost to the lip of the ledge he stood on.

The Circle Dot horse's struggles knocked a head-sized rock loose and it bounded past Newt on its way down, went over the ledge, and barely missed Skitch's head. That rock clattered and bounced off the sides of the cut and then went out of sight. Newt could barely hear the Dutchman cursing and wondered if the old German had been hit by the falling stone.

Newt helped Skitch get the horses over the ledge, and then he took Jenny by the wrist and pulled her up with them. McPhee was almost harder to get up the ledge than the horses had been.

"Go ahead. I'll wait for the Dutchman," Newt said.

Thunder boomed so violently that it jarred Newt's heart, and he wasn't sure the others had heard him. However, the three of them and the horses they were leading moved up the cut.

A good while later, the Dutchman's hat appeared below the ledge, and then the rest of him. He was having a hard time with the two horses he led, and one of them was the one that had been wounded in one hind leg during the fight at Seymour.

"Let me catch my wind a bit," the Dutchman said as he leaned his shoulders back against one wall of the cut. He was breathing heavily and one side of his face was bleeding. Whether that falling rock had struck him a glancing blow, or he had hit his face some other way, Newt didn't know.

"How much farther?" the Dutchman asked when his breathing had slowed some.

Newt shrugged.

"That bad?"

"Can't be much worse."

The first of the two horses they put over the rock shelf was the hardest so far, but they managed it. The second horse couldn't make it because it refused to try. Either it was too exhausted or else that bullet wound in its hind leg was worse than Newt thought. Either way, they could do nothing to get it to move.

The Dutchman was up on the ledge, pulling on the lead rope for another try, and Newt slapped the horse with the flat of his palm above its tail head. The horse lunged upward but came nowhere near clearing the lip of the ledge. It thrashed wildly and almost flipped over backward. Newt threw up his arms in preparation to be crushed by the weight of the animal, for there was nowhere to dodge and nowhere to run in such tight confines.

The horse slid off and landed on its side at the foot of the ledge. It groaned pitifully. Under the lightning, Newt saw the white of bone revealed below one knee, and knew then that the horse had broken that leg.

"Go on," Newt said to the Dutchman.

And then he drew his pistol and shot the wounded horse between the eyes to end its suffering. He reholstered the pistol and climbed over the horse and started again up the cut. He hated to lose a horse — hated to cripple one — but there was no way that Irish Jack or any of the rest of that bunch was going to climb the cut with the dead stage horse blocking the gap, unless they left their own horses behind.

Skitch, Jenny, McPhee, and the Dutchman had gone out of sight. The last few yards of the cut felt like it was almost straight up, and Newt leaned so far forward that he had to reach out a hand to steady himself in several places.

He suddenly broke out on open, almost level ground. All four of them were sitting there in the rain watching him, but they were too tired to say anything, or else they had run out of words. Newt glanced down at the way they had come, and it looked worse and more impossible than it had seemed when looking up at it — a black slash in the mountain leading down into nothingness at an incredible angle.

Gunfire sounded from somewhere down in the canyon. Two gunshots fired by two different guns, and then a third shot later. They waited and listened, but the only sound after that was the falling of the rain.

"What do you think that was?" Skitch asked.

"You know what it was," the Dutchman answered. "Ned made his play."

"Are we going to wait for him?" Jenny asked.

The Dutchman looked at her and then shook his head. "Ned's dead, but maybe he took one or two of them with him."

They waited longer, each one of them either thinking about Ned Stutter or unable to summon the energy or the willpower to move again. The rain had slowed to a steady downpour and the lightning and the worst of the thundercloud had moved on.

"Where's your horse?" Skitch asked Newt. "Where's the gold?"

It was not yet nighttime and there was a hint of gray light left up on the mountain, but Newt could see no sign of the Circle Dot horse. He wanted to sit down and rest a spell with the rest of them, but instead, he trudged forward on heavy legs, starting along the spine of the mountain and headed west. He did not look back.

Behind him, the other four rose and followed.

Chapter Twenty-Nine

There was nobody at the stagecoach when Irish Jack came through the rocks. That surprised him some, but not as badly as finding that the express box was gone.

"They've gone farther up the canyon," Ernie said while he adjusted his hat brim to better block the rain and eyed the footpath through the jumble of boulders that led to the tanks. "No matter, we'll root them out."

Jack was determined, but he was cautious as well. Those boulders were as good a place to hole up as any the stage party could have chosen, and moving through that maze was going to be risky at best.

Jack was down to only four men, not counting himself, and he regretted sending three of them up on the bluffs. That had been a sound tactic if they were to wait until daylight to make their attack, but Jack wanted to get the matter over right then.

"Keep a close watch on those rocks," he

said to Ernie.

Keeping a close watch on anything was almost impossible with the rain coming down like it was. Jack knew he should wait until morning, but couldn't find the patience. And he felt that the advantage had shifted his way. Fights were like that, swaying back and forth from one side to the other. The trick was to feel when you had the advantage and to press the fight home when you did. Jack felt like he had Skitch's party on the run.

The Widowmaker's body was nowhere to be found, but the man was likely badly wounded, if not dead already, and one of the outlaws swore that he had gotten another of the stage party earlier in the afternoon. That left nothing but Skitch, the Dutchman, the whore, and maybe one of the Stutter brothers. And they had taken their box and crawled back farther into the rocks to lick their wounds. Yes, Jack sensed victory at hand, and that feeling had his blood up.

"Come on, let's get this done," Jack said.

Ernie gave him only a worried nod in return.

Jack hadn't taken three steps along the worn footpath leading to the tanks when someone appeared ahead of him between two boulders. Jack hoped the cover of the rain might let him approach the water holes without being seen, but he was fully expecting for that not to work and to be shot at. However, he hadn't expected anyone to step out and openly challenge him.

A gust of wind blew rain across the footpath in a blinding sheet, and the next moment there was someone standing there in front of him. A gun flamed and roared, then again. Jack thrust the sawed-off shotgun out before him. He fired one barrel and the man before him staggered forward and fell.

Jack glanced at Ernie. The marshal had his pistol held before him, but hadn't even fired a shot.

Jack stayed where he was, looking for other threats ahead. They would know he was coming now, but he didn't care.

He rose and went to the body between the boulders. "Isn't that one of the Stutter brothers?"

Ernie came up behind him. "That's Ned."

The body stirred and Jack leaned closer over it. A stream of water was running down the rutted footpath and it washed away Ned's hat. The charge of buckshot had hit him high on the chest, probably puncturing one or both lungs, and when he tried to speak it came out gargled and bubbly.

343

"What's he trying to say?" Ernie asked.

Jack leaned closer over Ned to hear better over the sound of the storm.

"That's for my brother," Ned managed to say when Jack could hear him.

"Was it now?" Jack straightened and fired his second barrel into Ned's face.

Ernie flinched and took a step backward. "Damn, Jack."

Jack broke open his shotgun and chambered two fresh cartridges. The sound of the breech snapping closed was sharp and brittle.

"Let's finish this," Jack said.

Jenny Silks led one of the horses and trudged behind the Widowmaker. It seemed like they had been walking for hours since the last time they had stopped to take a break, and yet, he hadn't looked back at them, not one time, and remained apart from them when they did stop. She wished they would get on the horses, for her boots were killing her feet, and McPhee was barely managing to keep up. The lawyer limped along far behind them. But the Widowmaker seemed to have no inclination to stop or to ride the horses and walked like he intended to foot it all night, if not all the way to the railroad.

She tried to remember all that she had heard of him, but not much came to mind other than what Skitch had said and the loose bits of talk that were spread around every mining camp in the Southwest. There was both good and bad in the man's reputation, depending on who you chose to listen to, but so far he was definitely a man who was hard to predict or sway to your wishes. She and Skitch had hired him to guard the gold, a hired hand and a hired gun. But it was his idea to climb out of the canyon, and he didn't ask their leave when he decided to act on that plan. And there he was now leading them along the mountain like he was in charge. A man like that was handy, but he was also worrisome. Who knew what he was thinking or planning next? He had left Ned in the canyon without hesitation. It might be that he intended to have the gold for himself. The more she thought about that, the more she came to believe it was true. Why wouldn't he?

She looked back at Skitch and the Dutchman, and McPhee waddling along in his oversized shoes in their wake. Which one of them could stop Jones? Her hand felt the empty pistol holster at her waist.

No one was going to take what was hers. Not this time. That's what the trip to the railroad was all about, really — not simply the gold, but winning.

The Widowmaker was wrong. You could set things right.

Widowmaker Jones — what a silly, awful name they called him. He was definitely a man you weren't likely to forget with those scars and the size of him, but it was still a preposterous name, like something out of the newspapers or one of those silly dime novels she had seen some reading in Vulture City.

But men were like that. Slapping a name on something like branding a calf or painting a sign, as if with the name or the mark they proved something, defined it, and took ownership. Whore, dove, sporting lady, she had heard them all herself, but she was going to rub that mark away like it never had been. There were men left back in Vulture City who might think they had bought a piece of her, and over the years she had felt herself being nibbled away until she worried that there would come a time when there wasn't enough woman left to matter anymore. In those times she felt empty as the desert. In her first years in Vulture City that feeling was the rank smell of man sweat and whiskey breath, crude laughter, and a silver coin clanking on a lamp table. It was that numb, unfeeling place between sadness and wrath, like dust in your mouth so dry that you couldn't swallow. It was wanting to quit and fade away like it was happening to someone else and not you. And then, after she had managed to build the Blind Drift, it was counting the coins in her money box every night and knowing that she might never save enough for it to really matter.

There was the faint hint of sunlight spilling over the eastern horizon. The rain had quit altogether, but the wind was still blowing, and it slowly dried her dress as they walked. She straightened her posture and smoothed the front of her dress to best show the curve of her breasts, and she folded back her veil over her hat and made her best attempt to gather her hair. The Widowmaker may have taken her gun, but she had other weapons. The years and the desert hadn't taken all of the woman out of her, and she knew that men still thought her beautiful. That was something. If her years in Vulture City had taught her one thing, it was how to use the weapons she was born with.

She quickened her stride and caught up to the Widowmaker, ignoring the blisters on her heels. He stopped when she came even with him, as if he was waiting to talk. She merely smiled at him, and then put a little

extra sway in her hips when she was ahead
of him.

CHAPTER THIRTY

They found the Circle Dot horse at daylight. The gelding was standing on the point of the mountain overlooking a wide swath of desert below. The express box was still tied to its back.

Newt went to the horse. He talked to it while he ran a hand over each leg and examined the gelding for any sign of injury or unsoundness.

Skitch had eyes only for the express box, but once he was satisfied that it was as it should be, he watched Newt fussing over the horse.

"You set a lot of store by that animal," Skitch said. "Forty thousand in gold in that box and you're worried about a thirty-dollar horse."

Newt let down the horse's hoof he had been examining and looked at Skitch. "He didn't cost me anything. Comanches gave him to me."

349

"Comanches?" Skitch asked like he hadn't heard Newt correctly.

The Dutchman and the others had heard the mention of the notoriously bloodthirsty tribe as well and came closer.

Newt saw the way they were waiting for more, and it embarrassed him. He turned his back to them and made a show of checking the horse once more. When he spoke again it was quietly.

"Apaches say he's a medicine horse," he said. "Brand on his hip is supposed to be some kind of spirit wheel."

"Apaches, you say?" Skitch asked. "First the Comanche and now Apache. Your horse gets around."

Newt turned to Skitch, and there was a hint of irritation in his voice. "We've seen some country, we have."

Skitch jiggled the lock on the express box, as if he was worried it had somehow come loose in the night. "I'm surprised we found your horse at all. That was a chancy thing letting him go."

"I knew he would be waiting," Newt said.

"Like I said, you set a lot of store by that horse," Skitch replied. "But that isn't your gold strapped to its back, either."

"And like I told you, me and this horse have covered a lot of country and he hasn't quit me yet."

"There's always a first time. A man that thinks too highly of a horse is bound to be let down, and he's lucky if it doesn't land him on the seat of his pants."

Newt said nothing else. Instead, he freed his saddlebags, slid his rifle out of the saddle scabbard, and went to a place at the point of the mountain and sat down. He took out a can of machine oil and a rag from the saddlebags and rubbed down his weapons while he watched the desert below. The Dutchman saw what he was doing and joined him and began cleaning his own guns. Tom Skitch held the horses off to one side of the group, holding them on loose leads so that they could graze on the sparse brown grass.

There wasn't a tree in sight on the whole mountain, nor on the mountains to either side of it. Nothing above shin height except for the occasional cactus or the brushy growth along the gullies scoring its slopes or down in the canyons between the mountains where an occasional dark splotch of green showed itself. The stage party could see for miles in all directions.

Jenny looked at McPhee beside her. The lawyer looked absolutely exhausted. He was standing so slumped that he was almost

351

shapeless. His coat was gone, his shirt had come untucked and the tail of it hung almost to his knees, and there was a big tear in the knee of one of his pant legs. He sat down and began to rub one foot through his shoe sole.

"What are you thinking about?" McPhee asked her while they watched the others oiling guns.

"I don't trust the Widowmaker," she said in a hushed voice.

"You think he wants the gold?" All of the stuffy, stumbling awkwardness was gone out of his speech. He sounded like a different man, although still with a comical formality about his speech.

"Of course he does."

McPhee nodded at that as if he was doing his own thinking and not liking the conclusions he came to. "He's gotten us this far, but you might be right that we should keep an eye on him. What is it we used to say in the business? Another bit player in this act of ours?"

She looked at the leather satchel he carried. "Have you still got that little pistol?"

"I do."

"You remember that if I need you to."

"I haven't forgotten the weapon, nor shall I. Do you remember old Sally? You were young then, but she was with us for a while and played a fine Ariel when she wasn't drunk."

"I remember her."

"Well, she gave me that pistol and claimed to have shot a drunken sailor with it once while playing her *Tempest* role in a Barbary Coast theatre."

"What about the Dutchman?" Jenny asked.

"Are you thinking how to thwart Skitch's own henchman? That grouchy old man makes an odd Banquo, don't you think?"

"Only you would compare this to *Macbeth*."

"Forgive my imagination. It tends to run wild on occasion, and I do so miss the crowd and a wordy bit of Shakespeare to wrap my tongue around."

She shook her head. "Tom wouldn't do as Macbeth. More of a King Duncan, if you ask me."

"King Duncan, hmm? Waiting for the knife he never sees coming? Who then are we in this tragedy? Witches over our cauldron weaving fate and casting prophecy?" he asked. "Do you ever miss performing for the crowds?"

"Sometimes."

"I guess your most recent profession calls

for a good bit of acting."

She snapped a cold look at him.

"No offense intended. We all do what we must to keep bread on the table," he added. "I only happened to notice that your skills aren't diminished in the least. You always were a talented girl, and you play the part of a lady in distress admirably."

"It isn't over, yet."

"No, but that's what makes this adventure so enticing," he said. "That and Solomon's own riches in that box, if what you say is true."

"There's forty thousand in the box. I heard Skitch say so."

McPhee looked off of the mountain as if he was searching for something in particular on the low country below. "Where are the hell twins? I would have thought they would be here by now. I'm not fond at all of those two demons, but it's high time they made an appearance, stage right."

"I wouldn't let them hear you call them that," she said. "They were always touchy, but they're worse since they're grown."

"No, I wouldn't think of insulting them. You've always been such a dear lass to me, but those two give me nothing but the chills. They've been that way since they were boys."

"They'll be along. All we need is a little more time."

Newt and the Dutchman had finished oiling their guns and were coming back toward Jenny and McPhee. Jenny pulled her dress front down tight across her chest, straightened her posture, and gave her hair a toss back over one shoulder. Those were only subtle, quick gestures, but McPhee noticed.

"Ah, you make an excellent witch," he said under his breath. "Bold Ulysses himself could not but heed your siren call before he crashed his ship to the rocks."

"Shut up and mind your part, lawyer," she hissed back at him.

"Simon and Crusher would have it no other way," he said in his former tone and with the shift to the subtle accent change he used with the others. "That's the way we do it in New York, you know."

"You've never played New York. Remember who you're talking to and mind your lies."

He gave her a mocking, offended look. "But that's the fun of a good character, girl. Making them believe you're somebody you're not."

Chapter Thirty-One

One of the horses was limping so badly that they decided to leave it behind. The injured horse's right hock was swollen badly after the arduous climb out of the canyon. That left four to ride and the Circle Dot horse to carry the box — five people with only four mounts to carry them and not a saddle for any of them.

Newt had kept them on foot throughout their night's travel, intending to save those horses as much as he could and have them ready for a fast run south when daylight came and when he could see the lay of the land and get his bearings. Now they were down another horse and he still wasn't sure of their next move. He busied himself with cutting down the reins on the harness bridles to a length manageable for riding those horses instead of driving them.

The Dutchman helped him trim the reins and he, like Newt, looked often at the countryside while he worked. "We could go west and strike the trail to Yuma. Leave it when we hit the Gila and cross over and follow the Southern Pacific to Maricopa Station."

"What about circling back and hitting the road we left farther down toward the crossing of the Salt?" Newt asked.

"I would expect that if I was Irish Jack," the Dutchman replied.

Newt looked at the single water bag lying on the ground not far from them and then did a mental count of the three canteens that he, the Dutchman, and Skitch carried. "How's the water between here and the Gila if we took the Yuma road?"

"Should be plenty of standing water down in these canyons after the rain if a man knew where to look, but not much once we hit the desert," the Dutchman said. "Deep Well is normally dependable and sometimes fit for a man to drink, but that's the last water going south until we hit the Gila if it's wet."

"How far if we go that way?"

"I don't know. Maybe ten, twelve miles to the river and another ten to Maricopa Station. Day's ride if luck goes our way."

Skitch was standing not far from them and overheard their conversation. "That's bad desert you're talking about, but I say we chance it. I think the Dutchman's right and Jack will likely expect us to double back to the freight road if he can't run us down."

Newt went to the Circle Dot horse and put his rifle in the saddle scabbard, and then he caught one of the stage horses and swung on it bareback. Skitch and the Dutchman had to help McPhee on a horse, and then they mounted the remaining two horses.

Jenny was left standing alone. McPhee guided his mount to her. He was unsteady and obviously unused to riding and clung to his horse's mane with his free hand as if he might fall off even sitting still. He looked down at Jenny as if expecting her to leap up behind him, regardless that it was a tall horse he rode and that she was wearing a dress.

Newt, too, expected her to ride with the lawyer. The two of them doubled up would free him and the Dutchman and Skitch if Irish Jack caught up to them and it came to a running fight. So, Newt was surprised and at a loss for words when she refused McPhee's offer and walked over to where he sat his own horse.

"Mind if I ride with you?" she asked. "I don't relish him falling off and taking me with him."

Newt could only nod.

"Well, are you going to get down and help me up?" she asked with that same hint of a smile she had given him earlier.

Again, he only nodded and swung down from the horse and stepped back out of her way. Rather than get on the horse, she faced him.

"Can I have my pistol back?" She held out an open hand.

He drew the nickel-plated Merwin Hulbert from behind his belt and handed it to her butt-first.

"I didn't appreciate you taking my gun," she said as she holstered the pistol.

"And I didn't appreciate you trying to whack me with it."

She tilted her head and looked up at him, but instead of arguing her point further, she turned to the horse and placed both hands on its back and waited there.

Newt was hesitant about how he should go about assisting her. When his sisters back in Tennessee were little he simply grabbed them and gave them a heave. He doubted such a technique would prove acceptable to a grown woman.

"Well, are you going to help?" she asked when he made no move.

He realized he must look like a fool standing there like that and stepped close to her, still unsure what to do and wishing she had asked to ride with one of the others. She wore her dress tighter than any woman he had ever known, and he could see lots of places where he shouldn't put his hands. He looked around for a rock or some hump of ground that he might lead the horse beside and use for a stepping block for her, but there was no such thing in sight.

Jenny hiked her dress high enough that he could see a bit of her bare knees above her boot tops, then bent one leg at the knee and held that foot up behind her. He was relieved to see an answer to his conundrum as to where to put his hands and took her around the ankle and gave her a boost to the horse's back. She landed astride the horse, and the dress crept farther up her legs. He looked away while she resituated her dress.

"Why, Mr. Jones, I never would have taken you for the modest type," she said when he looked back at her.

She was a good rider and put the horse back in place when it shied from the shake of her dress as she situated it. Newt was thinking how it was going to be difficult to swing on the horse in front of her, and waited for her to scoot farther back toward its tail to give him room to make the attempt. However, she didn't scoot back and kept hold of the bridle reins. All he could do was swing up behind her.

"Here, you take the reins," she said.

To do so, he was going to have to ride with one arm practically hugging her, and he was already pressed against her back. Despite the sweat and the heat, she smelled like some kind of flowers. The smell of that perfume was almost overpowering and made it even harder to forget the physical contact between them.

"No, you seem to be doing all right," he said, refusing her offer of the bridle reins.

Instead of easing the horse off at a walk, she tapped it in the belly with her spurs and caused it to make a quick jump forward and then go off at a hard trot. Newt had to grab hold of her with both hands to keep his seat, and he was pressed even closer against her back in the process. The smell of her perfume was even stronger with his cheek against her shoulder as he scrambled to regain his balance and to move his hands to her belt and away from places that would get him slapped. She was a lean woman, as hard as whipcord under that dress, but surprisingly soft in other places.

"Sorry," he said when he found a place for his hands on her belt leather.

"Sorry for what?" she asked. "I'm not made of glass."

Newt shook his head. No, she definitely wasn't made of glass.

She slowed the horse enough that he could reach out and catch one of the reins on the Circle Dot horse's bridle to lead it and the gold it carried along beside them. Skitch and then McPhee came behind them with the Dutchman bringing up the rear and keeping an eye on their back trail.

Newt tried to push himself back toward the horse's rump, but the downhill course of their travel kept sliding him against Jenny. And where the slope became steep, she leaned far back against him to keep her balance. Her fine blond hair and the lace of her veil tickled his cheek, and more than once he had to readjust his hold on her.

The White Tank Mountains ran northwest to southeast, and beyond them to the west lay a flat expanse of desert that went on and on as far as the eye could see. The stage party kept to the high places where they could, picking their way across the rough country and searching for a way through the maze of canyons. Only the Dutchman seemed to have any idea about the lay of the mountains, and he took the lead early in their march and chose their course. Even so, they were forced to backtrack more than once.

The sun was well up in the sky when a sharp spine of ridgeline led them down to the desert flats. Two miles farther on, they struck the Hassayampa River once more and the road to Yuma paralleling it. Another mile southward along its course and the Dutchman led them into a dry wash that came down off the mountains and emptied into the river channel.

There was no water in either the river channel or the wash they entered, but the sand bottom was damp and marked with signs of recent flooding caused by the thunderstorm of the previous night or other recent rains. Mounds of brush were piled in places on the wash's banks where those uprooted plants had tangled together and formed a drift. By the watermarks on the sides of the gully it appeared that the runoff from the mountains had reached the top of the banks before it subsided.

Newt had seen such floods before, short-lived often, but surprisingly violent in a desert with so few signs of anything wet. More than one traveler had made the mistake of camping in such a drainage or crossing one during the monsoon season, thinking that there was no danger without a single cloud in sight. But a rainstorm many, many miles away might send a wall of rushing water down a normally dry streambed, enough to wash away man or beast. He recalled once finding a freight wagon three-quarters buried in sand and silt and half hidden by a mound of logs and brush and rocks carried down a dry wash in such a flood. He had wondered then if the owners of that wagon had survived their ordeal, and what it must have been like to hear the roar of water coming down the wash like a freight train and then to look up and see a wall of water about to crash against you.

The mouth of the dry wash was fifty or sixty yards wide at its mouth, and not far up its course the army had dug a well in years gone by. It was a deep well, barely big enough for a man to crawl down to its bottom if he had a ladder to help him. There was no ladder and the sides were too steep to enter the hole and get out again. Newt couldn't clearly make out the bottom when he looked down into the hole, but he thought he caught the faint gleam of water.

They took the express box off the Circle Dot horse's saddle, set the box aside, and used Newt's lariat rope to tie onto their canvas water bag. They weighted the bag with a rock tied to its end and lowered it down the well. It was a slow process, but eventually the bag filled and they pulled it back up to them, hand over hand. The water was murky and floating with bits of debris that had washed into the well during the flood, and Newt wasn't fond of the thought of drinking it. However, he had drunk worse when he had to, and the horses wouldn't be bothered at all.

He took his knife and cut the seam loose on one end of the water bag and held it open for the horses to drink one by one. They were thirsty animals, and the men had to lower and pull the bag from the well ten times before the horses had drunk their fill. By that time the stage party had worked up a thirst themselves and partook of the brackish water with little hesitation. Even lawyer McPhee, often squeamish about such things, drank from the well.

"What say we take a short siesta here?" the Dutchman asked Newt. "Horses could use another rest, and that lawyer has been about to fall off for the last few miles coming off the mountain."

Truly, McPhee didn't look well. He had already lain down against one side of the wash where its high bank cast some shade. Jenny was taking the traveling especially well considering she was likely a woman not used to such overland horseback trips, but Newt knew that she had to be exhausted. He was. Miles of walking with no sleep, and then the morning's ride could sap the strength of anyone. The whole party by then was moving on nothing but guts and determination, and that would only get them so far.

"All right, but no more than an hour," Newt said. "And let's get out of this wash. That storm cloud to the east might bring more rain, and I don't fancy being caught down here if it comes."

"Come on, McPhee," Skitch said, "unless you intend to stay there and float down to the Gila instead of riding there."

McPhee reluctantly rose and followed them as they loaded the express box once again and led the horses out of the gully and back to the edge of the road. The lawyer's limping had worsened to the point that he could make nothing more than a few mincing steps without stopping to rest. Newt had first assumed that McPhee was dizzy due to his head wound and that was what made him so wobbly on his legs, but he realized that the lawyer must be suffering from some other wound to one or both of his feet. But then again, they were all nicked up and hurting, and there was nothing to be done about it until they reached Maricopa Station.

They could see for miles in any direction over the flat desert, and nobody was going to approach them without being seen far in advance. The sun was scorching hot by then, but all of them made do as best they could and either sat down or lay down to rest for a while. Newt took a seat against the Circle Dot horse's front legs, using the shade provided by its bulk. McPhee found a low clump of creosote to shelter him from the sun, and Skitch took the far side of the bush, obviously not wanting to have anything to do with the lawyer.

The Dutchman sat in the full sun watching the trail to the north with his Ballard rifle laid across his knees and holding the other horses close to him. He seemed not at all bothered by the sun beating down on him, and the leathery brown skin of his cheekbones above his beard wrinkled up to the bottom of his eyes against the glare.

Jenny Silks left the road and walked out into the brush away from them. Newt watched her go, but said nothing to her, assuming she needed the privacy to attend to personal matters that couldn't be handled in front of four men. She went out of sight in the low desert brush.

It was while she was gone that he saw the same flash of light that he thought he had seen back in the canyon at White Tank. The flash happened several times, and it was plain that it could be nothing but sunlight reflecting off glass. What's more, those flashes were coming from where Jenny had gone.

"Where's your looking glass?" Newt asked her when she came back.

"What?" she asked.

"Your mirror."

She stared at him for a moment and then pulled out the same hand mirror she had used back at White Tank. "I look a fright and thought I would touch up a little. I daresay the rest of you could use a bit of fixing up yourselves if you want to borrow my mirror. A razor and a comb wouldn't hurt you any, either."

Newt looked out over the desert but couldn't see much above the brush sitting on the ground like he was. "Keep that mirror in your pocket from here on out. I could see the sunlight reflecting off of it from here, and that means anybody else out there could, too."

"I only wanted to brush my hair and wipe my face," she said.

"None of us here care what you look like,"

Newt aid. "Better your hair gets unruly than you bring more trouble down on us."

Jenny gave him a cold look, but shifted it to some kind of sly smile. "Forgive me, but a girl in my business had better take care of her wares or she won't make a living for long. And I didn't hear you complaining any when you were riding with me. In fact, I think you don't mind these wares of mine at all."

"Keep that mirror put away," he said.

"I could use a good bath right now," McPhee spoke from the creosote bush. "A cold bath that I could soak in for a month. That's all I've thought about this morning, what the water would feel like if I was floating in it."

"Fool woman's gonna get us killed. Irish Jack could have seen that shine if he's anywhere this side of the mountains," the Dutchman said.

"Fool woman, you say?" Jenny scoffed. "Why, you old goat, I ought to scratch your eyes out."

The Circle Dot horse was already standing three-legged and hipshot with its eyes closed. Newt was too tired to listen to them if they were going to argue, and followed the gelding's lead. He lay down and put his hat over his eyes. His intention was only to rest for a spell and not to take a nap. But go to sleep he did, and he slept soundly. When he woke it was with a start and with that feeling you have when you know you fell asleep when you shouldn't have and have no clue how long you were out.

And then it dawned on him what had awakened him. It was the sound of the hammer cocking on some kind of firearm. He gently pushed his hat off his eyes and saw a man in a black hat and a long linen duster standing over him with a rifle aimed at him. Another man who looked so much like the first that they could have passed for twins was holding the Dutchman and Skitch at gunpoint.

"Make one move," the man standing over Newt said and shoved the barrel of his rifle closer to Newt's nose. "Give me an excuse."

Newt stared into the rifle bore and then at the man who wielded it. He was as fair skinned and blond as Jenny Silks, and his close-set eyes were so pale as to almost have no color at all. The other one over with the Dutchman and Skitch looked just like him, as if their bodies held neither pigmentation nor blood at all, and as if it weren't for the dusters they wore the sun would shine right through them.

Jenny Silks stepped into Newt's limited

field of vision and stood beside the one holding the gun on him. Her pistol dangled nonchalantly in her hand. "Watch this one, Sig."

"I'm watching him," the man with the rifle said. His voice was as striking as his appearance — high-pitched for a man and with a strange accent — an accent Newt had detected more faintly in Jenny's speech the first time he had met her.

"That mirror wasn't an accident, was it?" Newt asked her. "Not here and not back in that canyon."

"You're slow, Jones, but you're catching on," she said.

"You can't get away with this, Jenny," Skitch said.

Jenny kept watching Newt and never looked at Skitch when she answered him. "I already have, Tom, and there's not a thing you can do about it."

CHAPTER THIRTY-TWO

Jenny reached down and jerked Newt's Smith & Wesson from his holster. "How about this time I take your pistol, hmm?"

She handed Newt's .44 to the man in the duster standing beside her, the one she had called Sig, and he held his heavy Remington single-shot rifle with one hand while he tucked the pistol behind his belt.

"Pretty gun," Sig said. "Believe I'll keep it."

"Bjorn," Jenny called to the other man. "Get their weapons and the key to this box from Tom."

The one called Bjorn threw the Dutchman's Ballard rifle into the brush at the side of the road, and the old miner tensed and looked as if he was going to fight at the sight of his firearm being handled in such a fashion. Bjorn struck the Dutchman across the face with the barrel of the Webley revolver he held. The Dutchman fell to one knee in the road. When he looked up again he was bleeding from a deep cut over one eyebrow.

"You try me again, mate, and you'll get worse, and that's fair dinkum, I'm telling you," Bjorn said.

He pulled the Dutchman's pistol and slung it in the brush after the rifle and then did the same with Skitch's guns.

Sig, the one guarding Newt, backed away where he could cover the whole group with his rifle, and Bjorn, obviously his brother if not his twin, disappeared into the brush. He was gone only a short while before he came back leading two exceedingly fine and fast-looking black horses. The saddles on the two mounts were slung with quite the array of gear and weapons, including what looked like some kind of a sword hanging from one of the saddle horns, to various pistols in pommel holsters and a long, brass-tubed spyglass of the kind once used on sailing ships.

"Get the key," Jenny repeated.

Bjorn pointed his pistol at Skitch. "Hand it over."

Skitch reached slowly for his collar and pulled a leather string necklace over his head and withdrew the key on the end of the string from inside his shirt and handed it over. Bjorn pitched the key to Jenny, who caught it deftly and tucked it down the front of her dress between her breasts.

"Sorry, Tom," she said, "but the whole forty thousand sounds a lot better than only part of it."

"They'll hang you when they catch you," Tom said. "Won't matter that you're a woman."

Sig gave a shrill chuckle that sounded more like a child's giggle. "We're hard to catch. It's in our blood."

Bjorn nodded at that and gave a similar laugh of his own. "Constables and the redcoat army chased the pair of us over half of Queensland and never could stretch our necks."

Newt rose slowly to a sitting position.

"You stay down where you are, mate." Sig shifted the Hepburn rifle in Newt's direction.

Bjorn was stringing what remained of the stagecoach team together, and he pulled them alongside him when he mounted one of the black saddle horses. He looked across the desert, looked again, and then took up the brass-tubed spyglass. He scanned the horizon for a long moment and then looked to Sig.

"Riders coming our way," Bjorn said.

"Is it Irish Jack?" Jenny asked.

"Too far to make them out, but that's my guess."

"How far can you hit anything with that rifle?" Jenny asked Sig, and pointed at the heavy Remington Hepburn single-shot he held.

"Far enough, sister, but the best thing we can be doing now is to get on our horses and ride," Sig said.

"I told you I want Irish Jack," she threw back at him with a building fury already in her voice.

"Five riders, and they're coming fast," Bjorn called to them.

Sig gave Jenny a shrug. "There's the gold to think of and the fact that there are five of those blokes and only me and Bjorn to deal with it."

"You promised me," Jenny threw back at him.

"Did you think we came for anything but the gold?" Sig asked. "We haven't seen you since we were boys. Barely remembered you when we got your letter. And still you think we would sail across the seas just to help you kill a man?"

"Swallow your pride, sister, and settle for the prize," Bjorn said. "Your cut of what's in that box is enough for you to hire a dozen blokes to go after Irish Jack. Killing is cheap, and gold will buy you all you want."

Sig got on his own horse while Bjorn kept the stage party under his gun. Lawyer McPhee waddled out from under the creosote bush. He took one of the horses that Bjorn held and made a feeble and unsuccessful attempt to mount.

"Get on or get left," Sig said.

The short lawyer managed to get his belly across the horse's back and struggled mightily to get one leg swung to its other side. He grunted with the effort.

"Are you really a lawyer at all?" Skitch asked.

"I told you not to trust him," the Dutchman said. "Simon and Crusher, my ass."

McPhee managed to get upright on the horse's back and he looked down at Skitch and shrugged. "Begging your pardon, Mr. Skitch, but it appears this may be the best-paying role I've ever had the privilege of taking on, at your expense, of course."

"You dirty little dog," Skitch said.

"Ah, now, don't you think that hypocritical?" McPhee asked. "Remember, I've seen your mine books."

Bjorn looked through his spyglass again. "Best we hurry."

Jenny had been semi-modest before when

asking Newt's help to get on a bareback horse, but she had no such qualms now. She holstered her pistol, hiked her dress up her thighs, bundled the fabric in some kind of knot, and swung on one of the horses with the agility of a trick rider in a circus show.

Sig rode alongside the Circle Dot horse and pulled it to him. He gave the express box a good shake to make sure it was secure, and then he spurred southward along the road, leading the Circle Dot horse in his wake. Jenny and McPhee charged after him with Bjorn right behind them leading the rest of the horses.

Newt immediately jumped to his feet and stepped to the middle of the road to watch them recede in the distance. Behind him, Skitch and the Dutchman ran into the brush to try and find their weapons.

Newt turned to look to the east. Now standing, he could see the dust cloud coming their way and barely made out the growing figures of four horsemen coming at a run across the desert from the foot of the mountains.

The Dutchman had found his guns and came to stand beside Newt, and again his eyesight proved impressive. "That's Irish Jack's sorrel horse."

Newt was weaponless, but Skitch appeared out of the brush and pitched him his pistol. It was an old Starr single-action converted to take rimfire .44 cartridges, and Newt snapped the loading gate open and checked that it was loaded, more out of restlessness and habit than any fear that it wasn't.

The three of them ran for the wash and didn't stop until they were concealed behind and below its high bank. A better position, yes, but the bottom of the wash didn't allow them a view of the oncoming riders. They waited and they watched the sky for any hint of the dust cloud.

They didn't have long to wait. Horse hooves drummed on the road, and then that sound was almost on top of them. The Dutchman rested his Ballard rifle on the lip of the bank and squinted at the moving horses' legs he could see through the brush. The outlaws were passing within fifty yards of their location, but didn't stop. The three men listened to the sound of the hooves fade as the outlaws moved on.

The Dutchman pocketed the two extra .38-55 cartridges he had been holding between his fingers on the forearm of his rifle. "They saw Jenny leave and think that's all of us."

Newt moved cautiously out of the wash

and back to the road. As the Dutchman had said, Irish Jack and what remained of his gang were charging after Jenny and her brothers.

"Well, that's that," Skitch said.

Newt glanced at him. The mine foreman seemed less upset than he had expected, but maybe he was simply relieved to have avoided another fight or had given up in the face of such difficulties. Newt had long before come to learn that everyone had a breaking point.

"It's going to be a long walk to the Gila," the Dutchman said.

Newt was thinking the same thing. They were left in the middle of a desert without horses and ten miles or more between them and the nearest water, if the Gila was running wet after the rains.

"We can fill our canteens and the water bag," Skitch said. "That should see us through."

Newt turned to him. "My canteen and that water bag were hanging on my saddle."

"Yours?" Skitch asked the Dutchman.

The Dutchman walked to where his canteen lay on the ground at the edge of the road where he had been sitting earlier. He came back to them shaking and sloshing what little water remained in the canteen.

Skitch retrieved his own from the shade of the creosote, and it was less than half-full.

"Without a rope and that water bag we aren't going to be able to draw any more water out of that well," Skitch said.

"I say we go back to the mountains," the Dutchman said. "There's bound to be water in those canyons if a man has the sense to know where to look."

Newt started walking, not toward the White Tank Mountains, but toward the Gila River far to the south. The other two fell in behind him.

Skitch looked at the storm cloud drifting high over the White Tank Mountains, miles to the east. "Lord, I never wanted it to rain more than now."

The Dutchman took his own look at those dark clouds in the distance. "I wouldn't count on rain. Those clouds are moving away from us."

"Figures," Skitch muttered.

The two of them lengthened their strides. The Widowmaker was already far ahead of them.

CHAPTER THIRTY-THREE

Ernie Sims tried to prop his raw thighs up off the saddle. While his maneuvering did relieve the chafing somewhat, such a posture in the saddle was taxing and had the added disadvantage of often putting him off-balance on the back of his running horse. He had no doubt that Jack and the others would leave him behind in the desert if he fell off during their chase.

He soothed his mind by looking forward to the next time Jack slowed the horses to a walk. They couldn't keep going at such a pace much longer, no matter how close that dust cloud ahead of them seemed. Their horses were already winded and beginning to falter.

Ernie looked back at the mountains they had left behind. Neither he nor Jack had expected the stage party to be able to climb out of that canyon, but climb out they had. Ernie had seen the washed-out cut the stage party had climbed and the dead horse jammed between the rocks or he wouldn't have believed it could be done. However, he was learning that gold put the ambition in most men, leading to things you wouldn't expect otherwise.

Take Jack, for instance. He was so mad and crazy to have the gold that he was about to run his favorite horse to death. He normally set store by the sorrel, but now he was blind to anything but the chase. Ernie might have suspected that Ten Mule's death drove Jack to his current rash behavior, but Jack hadn't bothered to even take a look at his nephew's body, much less mourn over it. He had simply saddled his sorrel and took off to find a place to climb the mountain and go after the stage party. Ernie and the other two remaining members of Jack's gang had to ride hard to catch up, as if Jack thought himself fully capable of getting the gold by himself.

Ernie wished Jack hadn't rushed them off so quickly. He wanted his share of the gold, but he also would have liked to scavenge the bodies left in the canyon more thoroughly than he had. As it was, he barely had time to take a good pocket watch off Fred Stutter, a green silk neckerchief off Ned, and Ten Mule's brand-new Colt pistol. It was a better pistol than Ernie's current one and he would have enjoyed taking it out of his saddlebags and admiring it, but he was afraid Jack would notice the firearm and recognize who it had once belonged to.

They had camped that night in the mountains, and come daylight Jack and the rest of them had scattered out and searched for the stage party's tracks. Regardless of Jack's sizable reputation in the territory as a badman, he proved a surprisingly poor tracker. His skill at reading sign was as feeble as Ernie's own, and the other two outlaws were no better. Because of that it was well into the morning before they found where the stage party had ridden off the west side of the mountains. The horse tracks pointed to the Yuma road along the Hassayampa River.

But they had lost the trail again, and it was only by luck that they had come across the stage party again at a place Jack called Deep Well. Ernie had no idea where the scattered and often undependable water sources in the territory might be found, for he made it a practice to stick to towns where there was usually plenty of whiskey if the water ran short. Plump pretty whores, card games, and lonely widows and wives in need of some flattery and extra attention were also rarely to be found in deserts, and that was another reason to avoid such dry, difficult places. But like the desert, or not, there he was smack in the middle of it, saddle sore and thirsty and with his mouth full of the dust left behind by those they were chasing.

It had seemed like it was going to be a short chase when they had first flushed the stage party along the Yuma road, but the gang's horses were too tired to run with their normal speed. Instead of running down their prey, the stage party had increased the distance between themselves and the gang. Ernie wouldn't have thought that possible, and he began to think that perhaps Jack's luck had gone bad.

What Ernie had supposed would be a short stint of work that would earn him a share of the gold and some revenge on the Widowmaker had turned into a regular ordeal. Now, with the stage party outrunning Jack's gang, Ernie considered that he might not see a single ounce of the gold, nor was he going to get another chance at the Widowmaker.

It galled Ernie's pride almost as badly as his saddle galled his thighs that the Widowmaker had gotten away. People were probably already talking about how the Widowmaker beat up Skinny, Ernie's brother-in-law, and how Ernie hadn't done a thing about it. On his return from tending to the goat herder's wife, he had found out that Tom Skitch had gone to Wickenburg with his gold shipment and that the Widowmaker was one of the guards. Ernie was sure Skitch would go south to the Southern Pacific and that the pretense of taking the Wickenburg route was only a ruse. Accordingly, he had immediately raced across to Seymour with the intention first of perhaps getting a potshot at the Widowmaker from the brush, and second, to see if Jack might take him in on the robbery.

It was all Jack's fault that nothing had gone as planned. The Widowmaker might have gotten away, but Jack was right there ahead of him. The Irishman's presence made it easier to work up the proper wrath Ernie needed to imagine killing him. He shifted his thoughts to how to best him.

He first thought was to use his usual tactic and start shooting at Jack before Jack had any idea that a fight was at hand, for it had worked for him before. Nobody would remember that Ernie gave Jack no warning of his wish to fight, and the surprise factor might offset Jack's unsettling speed of hand and marksmanship. And shooting Jack in the front would lend far more credibility to

Ernie's reputation. However, the more he thought about it the more he became more certain that it was unnecessarily risky to shoot Jack facing him. Jack was as wary and suspicious as he was fast with his hands, and it would be just like him to be on edge and ready for anything, especially for Ernie coming out of nowhere with guns blazing.

No, the best thing to do would be to find the proper moment and shoot Jack in the back. With only three of the gang left other than Jack and himself, the odds of someone giving Jack warning before Ernie could kill him were lessened. Ernie could always tell that he had shot Jack in a stand-up fight, no matter how the event actually occurred. If he told enough people it was likely that his version of the matter would become the accepted truth. Regardless, Jack wouldn't be around to poke fun at his height, or his big belly, or any of the other countless, belittling things Jack liked to point out.

Jack eventually realized that the sprint had sapped the last strength from their horses and that he wasn't going to be able to outrun the stage party. He slowed his big sorrel gelding to a walk, and that gave more time for Ernie to think on ways to kill him.

"What are you looking so smug about?" Jack asked when Ernie accidentally rode alongside him. Jack always liked to ride in the lead and didn't tolerate anyone else trying to pass him.

"Why, nothing, Jack," Ernie said. "Bothers me as bad as it does you that Skitch got away with his express box."

Jack flashed him a hateful look, and Ernie immediately regretted pointing out Jack's failure. Jack liked his mistakes pointed out even less than he liked someone trying to take the lead when traveling.

"We quit when I say we quit," Jack said.

Jack kicked his sorrel ahead of Ernie, obviously finished talking about the matter. Ernie's recently improved mood began to fade until it dawned on him that if he killed Jack he could have the finger bone and war medal.

CHAPTER THIRTY-FOUR

Jenny Silks, sometimes Jenny Blake, went to the back door of the hotel and opened it to the dark alley behind her. Lightning flashed and revealed Sig and Bjorn holding the express box and waiting for her, while McPhee held the horses behind them. A few scattered raindrops began pelting the ground with dull thumps.

The room she had acquired for them was on the second floor, and she scouted the lobby to make sure no one was there before she led her brothers up the stairs to the room. The kerosene lamps on the walls cast tall thin shadows as they passed.

Bjorn and Sig went back downstairs and out the back door again to take the horses to the nearby livery, while McPhee trudged up the stairs on wooden legs and joined Jenny. He immediately flopped down on the single bed the room contained and sighed deeply as he sank into the feather mattress.

Jenny went to the window overlooking the street and waited for another lightning flash to reveal the train tracks and the Southern Pacific depot house a hundred yards away. The rain was coming down hard now, pelting the window glass.

"Quit your worrying," McPhee said with his eyes closed. "You've won."

"I haven't won," she said. "Not until I get on that train in the morning."

McPhee shifted to a more comfortable position, and his muddy shoes left mud streaks on the bedspread. "You're a bold wench to get on the very same train that was supposed to take the mine's shipment. You know that Wells Fargo was to take charge of the gold once it arrived, and I've no doubt one or more of their messengers is out there right now wondering why the Vulture City stage has yet to arrive."

"They'll be looking for a stagecoach and an express box."

"I assume you have some plan to fade into obscurity elsewhere, but someone recognizing you on the train won't help your cause. In case you haven't realized it, you don't exactly blend well in a crowd." McPhee gestured at her hat and veil lying on a table, and then at her boots and spurs.

"That's nothing that a trip to the dry

goods store won't solve," she said. "By tomorrow morning I intend to appear as nothing but your usual, demure woman traveling alone on her way to visit relatives back East."

"You, demure?"

"What do you think? Should I dye my hair brown or black?"

McPhee gave a weary smile. "Ah, now you're talking. I do so love costumes. Wish I were going east with you. Won't you rethink your plans and go with me to California?"

"No, there are too many there who might recognize me from the old days with the troupe."

"Those were the days, weren't they? All those lonely miners with pokes full of gold and starved for entertainment and hungry for anything that reminded them of home," McPhee said. "Remember the time that placer miner gave you that lovely nugget to stand up on a stool and sing 'Come Where My Love Lies Dreaming'? Big as the end of your thumb, it was, and you nothing but a snot-nosed girl with a squeaky voice and almost too shy to sing above a whisper."

"I remember that you took that nugget away from me," she said.

"That nugget fed the troupe for a week and fixed the wheel on one of the wagons so that we could get over the mountains to the next boom camp."

"I never saw any of the money I helped make." She turned from the window to face him. "And you left me in Tucson with Tulip without so much as a penny to my name."

"And you think I had a penny to leave you after what happened?" He rose to a sitting position and winced and touched a hand to his bandaged head when he bumped it against the bed's headboard.

"You shouldn't have left me with her, of all people."

"I had no clue how she was, and I was in no shape to take care of a girl," he said.

"Don't give me that. You knew how Tulip made her living."

"What's done is done."

Her stare was intense. "You know, there was a time when I swore I was going to get even with you. Tulip, too."

"Whatever happened to her?"

"She died."

"You?"

"No, it was pneumonia. By that time I had given up hating her so. Cruel as she was, she tried to show me how to survive the only way she knew how."

"There was a time when Tulip was better than she ended up."

"There was a time when we were all better."

"So you've been plotting your revenge all these years?" he said. "I wondered why you sent me that letter and put me in on this."

"Don't be so dramatic. I brought you here because I thought you could pull off your part, and I needed someone from outside the territory who wasn't likely to be recognized."

"Still . . ." McPhee looked at the express box.

"Oh, it's your share that has you worried I might double-cross you."

"That's enough to tempt anyone. I don't imagine those bushranger brothers of yours would have any compunction about doing me in if you asked them to," he said. "In case you haven't noticed it, I believe those two haven't spent their time in Australia learning to be choirboys. I wouldn't venture to guess what nasty habits they've picked up, but I can't help but imagine the worst."

"I think you overestimate their loyalty to me. It's been even longer since I've seen them than you. We were only children when I went off to the States with you."

"They came when you wrote them, didn't they? They are your siblings, and it's said there's no tie that binds like a blood tie."

"They came for their own reasons, and I've no doubt most of those reasons revolve around the gold I promised them."

McPhee leaned forward and smiled. "Speaking of gold, how about we take a look in that box?"

Sig and Bjorn came into the room at that very moment.

"Yeah, open the box," Sig said.

Jenny reached for the key hanging from her neck, but something outside the window distracted her — the shadows of four riders were coming down the street with their hats pulled low and their heads bowed against the blowing rain. She waited until they passed through the pool of lamplight cast out the windows of the saloon directly across the street from the hotel. In that same moment, the lead rider looked up toward her window and his face was revealed.

She ducked away from the window and turned to face her brothers. "Irish Jack is out there."

"Is he, now?" Bjorn passed a look to his brother.

Sig gave Jenny a wicked grin, and it spread even wider when he looked back at Bjorn. "You said you wanted him killed, and now here he is asking for it. What say we give him what he wants?"

Bjorn nodded and gave a quick chuckle that was as wicked as Sig's grin. "Sure, but let's have a little look in the box first and see what we're fighting for."

Jenny inserted the key and worked the lock open while McPhee got off the bed. They all hovered over her, anxious to have a look at the gold that Irish Jack's pursuit of them had thus far denied them.

The iron lid on the box creaked open, and she stepped back so they could all share the first look. The excited expressions on their faces disappeared immediately, and they stood there for a long moment trying to get their minds wrapped around what they were seeing.

McPhee gave a groan and went and flopped down on the bed, holding his bandaged head with both hands. "It was too good to be true."

"What are you trying to pull on us, sister?" Sig said.

"You bloody stupid sheila," Bjorn said. "Where's the damned gold?"

CHAPTER THIRTY-FIVE

Newt walked into the site of the abandoned Butterfield stage station at old Maricopa Wells an hour after sundown. Abandoned or not, he could see the glow of a fire burning through the almost blinding sheet of rain and the silhouette of the adobe brick walls of the stage station. Blind in the midst of the thunderstorm, he had no way of knowing whether it might be friend or foe at the fire, but he was too tired to care. He drew Skitch's pistol and staggered forward, not even waiting for Skitch and the Dutchman to catch up to him and discuss the matter.

He stopped five yards from the adobe with the rainwater running off his hat brim and the cocked revolver hanging at the end of his arm. The first thing he made out was the shape of a skinny horse standing with its head down and tied to a hitching rail. The front door was missing to the dilapidated adobe building, but he could see nothing of the inside beyond the flickering fire within its walls.

He raised the Starr pistol and went through the door. A young Mexican looked up from the fire he was staring at in the fireplace and then stood and moved back against the far wall with both hands raised. He was wearing a red serape over his shoulders and a straw sombrero that was unraveled at the edges of its wide brim.

"No me mates," the Mexican said, and then again in broken English, "Don't kill me."

Newt glanced at the Trapdoor Springfield carbine lying on the Mexican's saddle, and then he gestured at his waist. "Pull that blanket out of the way."

The Mexican acted as if he didn't understand.

Newt's Spanish had improved somewhat over the years, but he was far from fluent and too tired to think clearly. He stepped past the fireplace and jerked aside the young man's serape, revealing his waistline. There was no pistol there, only a sheath knife. Newt lowered the Starr revolver and went to stand in front of the fireplace. The Mexican stayed where he was with his hands still held at shoulder height.

"For Pete's sake, put your hands down," Newt said. "I'm not going to kill you."

The Mexican either didn't understand or simply didn't believe Newt's statement, and stayed where he was. Skitch and the Dutchman came through the open doorway and took in the scene.

"Little herd of goats out yonder under that shed," Skitch said.

The Dutchman found a spot against one wall where the roof wasn't leaking and sat down. Skitch flopped down beside him and closed his eyes and leaned his head back against the wall. The Dutchman looked haggard, but Skitch looked to be at his end.

After walking more than half a day across the desert they had come to the Gila River to find it running waist-deep and bank-to-bank. Neither Skitch nor the Dutchman had wanted to chance crossing it, but Newt had plunged in knowing that with the rain it was going to get nothing but worse and that it was liable to be days before they had a chance to cross once the river was in full flood.

It had been a tiring slog across the river channel, fighting the tug of the brown current and fearing that at any minute a wall of water was going to rush upon them and wash them away. Skitch had fallen and was almost carried downstream, but Newt barely managed to grab him and drag him to the far bank. The Dutchman had made it across the river without assistance, but he hadn't said two words since.

Newt gestured at the fire and then for the Mexican to take a seat. The goat herder squatted down over his heels, but came no closer. He looked from one of them to the other with his eyes large in the firelight.

"No tengo dinero," the Mexican said. *"No pesos, no dólares. Nada."*

"We're not here to rob you," Newt replied, and then struggled to find the words in Spanish. *"No te vamos a robar. ¿Comprende?"*

The Mexican nodded, but seemed no more at ease. Newt couldn't blame him. One minute the goat herder was enjoying the warmth of his fire out of the rain, and the next minute three gringos barge through the door and point a pistol at him.

Newt gestured at the coffeepot warming on some coals raked out in front of the firebox. The Mexican nodded vigorously and Newt poured a tin cup full of the boiled java. He watched the Mexican over the rim of the cup while he let the coffee's warmth flow through him.

"¿Cuánto comprar tu caballo?" Newt jerked

a thumb over his shoulder in the direction of the doorway and outside where the horse was tied.

"No está a la venta," the Mexican replied, and shook his head. *"El es el unico caballo que tengo."*

"Hey, Skitch," Newt said.

It took several seconds for the mine foreman to open one eye and look at Newt.

"How much money have you got on you?" Newt asked.

"I've a few dollars in my poke," Skitch answered.

"Buy this man's horse."

"What's he want for him?"

"He doesn't want to sell him, but maybe he'll change his mind if you show him the color of your coin."

Skitch took a leather drawstring bag from a pouch on his belt and held up two coins for the Mexican to see. "How's twenty dollars sound?"

The Mexican shook his head. *"No está a la venta."*

Skitch added another ten-dollar piece and held up the coins as before.

Again, the Mexican shook his head.

"Hard bargainer considering we could simply take that nag of his if we wanted," the Dutchman said.

399

The Mexican understood enough English that the Dutchman's words caused his eyes to expand again. He made a show of thinking the matter over, but finally held up four fingers. *"Cuarenta dólares."*

"Forty dollars? That pessel-tail nag of his ain't worth ten," Skitch muttered.

"Pay the man," Newt said.

"The gold is long gone," Skitch said. "You can buy all the Mexican ponies on the border and it will still be gone."

"There's a chance Jenny might have gone into Maricopa Station. That's the way her tracks were leading before the rain set in," Newt said. "One of us can ride into town and check things out. If she was there and gone, then whichever one of us goes can bring back fresh horses and we can start from there."

"I don't have another mile left in me." Skitch closed his eyes again. "I'm about done in."

"What about you?" Newt asked the Dutchman.

"You take the horse and do like you said. Me and Tom will stay here and rest a spell until you come back."

Skitch dug again in his purse and counted out a few greenbacks to add to the coins. He pitched the money across the room and it landed at the Mexican's feet. The Mexican picked up the money and smiled for the first time.

Skitch pointed at the grinning goat herder. "Acting like he's afraid we'll rob him, and here he is holding me up for forty dollars."

Newt barely heard Skitch. Like Skitch and the Dutchman, he found the urge to quit tempting. He wanted more than anything to curl up in a ball in front of the fire and give in to his exhaustion. It had been over thirty-six hours since he had last slept, most of that time either spent in the saddle or trudging across the desert. It felt as if there wasn't a bone or muscle in his body that didn't ache.

The young Mexican moved closer to the fireplace. He unbundled a package of corn tortillas wrapped in cloth, raked out more coals onto the hearth, and set a cast-iron skillet there to heat. When the first of the tortillas was warmed, he offered it to Newt and then gestured at a glass jar of *salsa verde* and a spoon. Newt spread a healthy dose of the salsa on the tortilla and wolfed it down in two bites.

There were only enough tortillas for each man to have one. It was a meager meal, but Newt nodded at the Mexican in thanks. Those tortillas had been meant as the goat herder's supper, and yet he had shared them.

"Gracias," Newt said.

"De nada." The Mexican fired off several rapid phrases in Spanish, but Newt couldn't follow him.

"He says his family has a little rancho on the Santa Cruz and he can bring more horses in the morning if we wish to buy them." Skitch's translation was half-slurred and drowsy.

Newt could barely keep his eyes open with the coffee and the tortilla hitting his belly. The fire crackled and a gust of wind blew spray of rainwater through the open doorway. It always amazed Newt how cold a desert could get once the sun went down. Only hours ago he had been wondering if he would die of thirst, and now he was soaking wet and concentrating to keep his teeth from chattering.

He pointed at the Mexican's serape. "You have a fire and I have a long ride."

The Mexican removed the serape and handed it to Newt. The garment was nothing more than a blanket with a slit cut in its middle, and what some called a poncho. But the wool of it was woven tightly and it would help to keep him warm and to repel some of the rain. Newt pulled the serape over his head and removed his gun belt and then buckled it over the top of the serape ends to hold it at his waist. The Starr pistol Skitch had loaned him wouldn't fit his holster, and he slid it back behind his belt buckle before he tugged his hat down tightly on his head. He took up the Mexican's saddle and saddle blanket from where they lay on the floor and hefted them over one shoulder.

"You won't make it to Maricopa Station in this storm," the Dutchman said. "Even if she's still there, Irish Jack is liable to be there, too."

"We lost," Skitch muttered. "We made a good try, but we lost. Might have made it if it hadn't been for that treacherous bitch."

"Pay the man for his saddle, or tell him I'll leave it for him at Maricopa Station," Newt said as he went back out into the storm.

CHAPTER THIRTY-SIX

The bodies of three dead men were propped on planks in front of the undertaker's shop when Newt crossed the Southern Pacific trains tracks and rode into Maricopa Station. He recognized none of the bodies, but had a good idea who they might be.

The storm had long passed by then and it was already promising to be another hot day. The skinny bay horse Newt rode was so short that his stirrups almost dragged on the ground. He pulled up when he came even with the mortuary and it was some time before the photographer setting up his camera tripod in front of the bodies noticed him.

"What happened?" Newt asked.

The photographer turned around and pointed at the bodies. "Irish Jack and his gang rode into town last night, and then two other fellows met them down at the livery and opened up on them. No warning,

404

no harsh words, no nothing, they just blew these boys out of their saddles. Damnedest thing to happen here since the railroad came."

"What did the two fellows look like?" Newt asked. "I mean, the two that started the fight?"

"How am I supposed to know? I heard shooting in the night and it was all but over by the time I looked out my window," the photographer said. "All I can tell you is that those men were wearing long coats that hung down around their legs. Looked like those driving dusters that the gents wear sometimes."

"What about Irish Jack?"

"Wasn't but Jack and one other left. They holed up in that saloon over there," the photographer said. "A few of the locals here got together, but they didn't want to tackle that kind of trouble in the dark and alone. By the time they had telegraphed the sheriff at Phoenix and worked up their courage to do something, Jack had licked his wounds and already pulled out for other parts."

Newt rubbed at his bloodshot eyes. "What about the two that killed these men?"

"They left as soon as Jack holed up. Went out of here popping their pistols like it was the Fourth of July," the photographer said with an incredulous shake of his head.

"Just two of them?"

"Two of them. There are some saying that there was a woman with them when they ran off, but I don't believe it. Maybe there was a third man and someone mistook him for a woman in the dark."

Newt rode closer to the bodies strapped with ropes to the planks leaning against the wall. The dead men rested with their arms across their chests in what was perhaps meant as a dignified pose, but nobody had bothered to close their eyes. Both men's firearms were on display, no doubt meant to show what desperate, violent outlaws they had been for the town gawkers already trickling by to have a look. Even a few passengers from the newly arrived train were coming that way to see the show.

"Yes, sir, it's been a one-of-a-kind morning," the photographer said. "And now there's a Wells Fargo express messenger down at the station saying how there was supposed to be a special stage run from Vulture City yesterday evening but it hasn't shown up yet. He's telegraphed the sheriff in Phoenix and wants to put a posse together to go up the road to Vulture City and have a look."

Newt looked at the train parked on the

tracks, debating on whether or not to go find the Wells Fargo messenger. And it crossed his mind that the best thing he could do was to ride away and get clear of the whole matter. He had been running on his last dregs of energy when he left Skitch and the Dutchman on the Gila, and the night's journey had left him in worse condition. What should have taken him a few hours to make the ride had ended up taking him four times that long. A few miles out from the train stop he had come across a wide, flooded wash leading down from the mountains, and he had lain down in the mud with his serape draped over his head and waited for the water to go down — a few miserable hours of fitful, soaking-wet sleep and nothing more.

The photographer glanced at the sky and seemed impatient to get back to fussing with his camera. "Light's going to be all wrong before long."

"Which way did the men in the long coats go?" Newt asked.

The photographer's head was already hidden beneath the hood of his camera and his answer was muffled. "Headed north on the Phoenix road when they jumped the tracks."

Newt rode on down the street. A group of men were gathered in front of an adobe saloon. Several horses with rifles hanging off their saddles were lined up behind the men, and it looked as if a posse was being formed, either to go after the culprits who had shot up the sleepy little train stop or to go in search of the Vulture City stagecoach.

Newt moved on past the gathering and found the livery farther down the street. The first thing he spotted when he dismounted and walked inside the hallway of the barn was the Circle Dot horse's head hanging out over the gate of one of the stalls. He also found his saddle atop the wall of the empty adjoining stall. His Winchester was still in the boot, and he shucked the weapon free and gave it a quick once-over. He was putting the gun back when the hostler came from his office at the front of the barn.

"What are you doing?" the hostler asked as he came down the aisle between the two rows of stalls.

Newt shoved the Winchester back in his scabbard. He didn't even turn to face the hostler, and instead moved to the gate at the Circle Dot horse's stall.

"I said, what are you doing?" the hostler repeated.

"I'm saddling my horse."

"You go on now," the hostler said. "That horse is confiscated property."

Newt took a deep breath as he often did when he felt his temper on the rise. What was it with every liveryman he ran across in the territory?

"You don't take that horse," the hostler said.

"The horse is mine." Newt kept his back to the hostler and worked the latch on the stall door.

"We'll see what Sheriff Orme has to say about that. He's on his way down from Phoenix this morning."

Newt turned and faced the hostler. The horse tender was a wide, thick man wearing a pair of short leather chaps to cover his thighs, and his hands were black with coal dust as if he might be the town's blacksmith as well. He had his sleeves rolled up, which revealed the kind of arm muscles a man gets swinging a hammer and pounding hot iron against an anvil.

Strong man or not, the hostler stopped halfway down the barn hallway when Newt turned around. He studied Newt's scarred face and then the pistol behind Newt's belt. From his expression, he liked the look of neither.

"Those men that shot up my livery left that horse behind," the hostler said. "Left it and four other worn-out, crippled nags back there in my corrals. Took a good chestnut gelding from me when they ran."

Newt swung the stall door open. "This horse was stolen from me yesterday."

The hostler took a hesitant step forward, but stopped again. "Letting you out of here with that horse could be the second animal stolen from me."

Newt didn't bother to bridle the horse in the stall, but simply stepped out of the way and went to his saddle without looking back. The Circle Dot horse followed him like a dog. Newt bridled the gelding and took his saddle and blanket down and swung them in place.

The hostler saw how the horse behaved. "I guess he's your horse, like you say."

"Depends on the day," Newt said as he cinched the saddle girth loosely and led the gelding by one rein toward the street. "Sometimes he thinks he owns me."

The hostler acted as if he was still contemplating putting up a fight over the horse, but stepped out of the way at the last second. Newt brushed by him and kept going.

"That horse ate twelve and a half cents' worth of corn and a manger full of hay," the hostler called after him.

Newt ignored him and led the horse out

on the street. He gathered the bay purchased from the Mexican back on the Gila and led both horses away.

"You going with the posse after those outlaws?" the hostler called again. "If you do, I'd appreciate if you looked out for that chestnut of mine. Bring him back and we'll call it even on your horse's keep."

He crossed the street to the Williams Hotel and left the Circle Dot horse and the bay at the hitching rail while he walked under the veranda and through the front door. The lobby was empty of people, including the hotel clerk. Perhaps the clerk was down the street with everyone else gawking at the dead outlaws. Newt pulled the open ledger book across the front desk and moved his pointer finger down the line of guest signatures until he found what he thought he was looking for. There, near the bottom of the page, was Cyrus McPhee's signature. Newt doubted that was the man's real name, and he was surprised that he hadn't adopted a different one to rent a room.

Newt glanced at the ledger page again and noted the room number, and then he went up the stairs to Room Seven, with his revolver in his fist. The doorknob wasn't

411

locked and he swung it open without knocking.

McPhee was sitting on the bed, looking out the window, and when he turned to see Newt standing in the open doorway the look on his face was not one of surprise or violence, but rather resignation. He sighed and slumped his shoulders.

"Well, you've found me," he said.

"Yes indeed," Newt replied.

McPhee looked at the open express box on the floor at the foot of the bed. "It was almost perfect."

Newt kept McPhee covered with the pistol while he stepped closer and looked down in the box. He didn't expect the gold to still be there, but what he found was perplexing. He reached down and picked up a heavy ingot of metal and hefted its weight in his hand. There were other similar bars left in the box.

"Nothing but cast lead," McPhee said. "No gold, just lead."

McPhee spoke the truth. It was nothing but a lead bar Newt held — heavy like gold and heavy enough to fool anyone who didn't look in the box.

"I see by the look on your face that you don't know what to make of that," McPhee

said. "I assure you, we were no less con-
fused."

Newt held up the lead bar. "This is all
there was?"

"That's all. It seems we underestimated
Mr. Skitch."

CHAPTER THIRTY-SEVEN

Newt leaned against the wall across the room. "So they left you behind?"

"Unfortunately, our most recent misfortune unraveled what few bonds Jenny and I have left," McPhee replied. "And I had no interest in partaking in her little vendetta. Gunfights aren't my thing, you know."

"I've been trying since we left Vulture City to place you," Newt said. "Had this feeling I had seen you before."

"I doubt it."

"No, it just came to me. I saw you acting in a play in Denver not long after I first came west," Newt said. "It's hard to recognize you without the costume and face paint."

"*Othello*," McPhee said.

"What?"

"Those lines I performed in Denver were from *Othello*. Playing the Moor was always a favorite of mine."

"How about you tell me how an actor comes to take part in a robbery?"

"Ah, it's a tangled web we weave."

"What's your real name?"

"Does it really matter? Take a seat there, Mr. Jones, and let me spin you a tale," McPhee said. "From the look on your face I fear it may be my last performance."

Newt remained standing and gave an impatient tip of his pistol barrel again.

"As you wish." McPhee gave a slight nod of his bandaged head. "Her real name is Jenny Larson. The Jenny Blake thing came about later because she thought it sounded more American and would make a better stage name. As for Jenny Silks, well, you know about that."

"Go ahead."

"I first met her in a little mining town in Queensland. She was ten years old."

"Australia?"

"Your knowledge of geography surprises me. I wouldn't have thought you much of a reader or so well traveled."

"Get on with your story."

McPhee cleared his throat. "Her parents were from the Faroe Islands in the North Sea between Scotland and Iceland, and they sailed to Australia in search of their fortune. But the mother got a bout of fever that was

415

sweeping the camp and the father got an aborigine's spear in his belly sometime not long afterward. That left young Jenny and her two brothers with no one to take care of them."

"The brothers would be the ones I met on the road?"

"Yes, Sig and Bjorn. A church orphanage took them in, and wild boys they were, even then."

"And Jenny?"

"Ah, what a pretty girl she was with a voice like an angel, and so unusual-looking. I knew the miners would flock to her like flies to sugar," McPhee said. "I was traveling with a regular troupe of actors at the time, and we adopted Jenny, if you will. Took her back to the States with us."

"And her brothers?"

"I heard they ran away from the orphanage before we sailed for San Francisco, but I don't know that for certain. I hadn't seen them again until yesterday. I assume Jenny somehow learned of their whereabouts and wrote to them same as she did with me."

"She wrote to you?"

"In time, Mr. Jones, in time. Hear me out," McPhee said. "Jenny traveled with the troupe for a number of years. We worked California, and then when the rush slowed

416

down we thought we would head elsewhere. The word was that there was a big strike on Lynx Creek in the Bradshaw Mountains near Prescott, and we loaded up the wagons and headed across the desert. That was in 1865. I remember it because the war ended that year, and because, well, that was the year it happened, what you might say put all this in motion."

"What happened?"

"We never made it to Lynx Creek. A band of outlaws caught us on the trail, vicious men. They were convinced we had more money than we did, and they tied poor El-rod to a cactus and lashed him with a coachwhip to get him to tell them where our money was hidden. He was our leader of a sort, and a gentler man you never knew. Played as fine a King Lear as I ever saw."

McPhee was staring at the window by then, not even glancing at Newt, as if his mind was rolling back the years and he was reliving that day all over again. His voice grew quieter. "They found some whiskey in one of the wagons. Maybe they would have let us go once they decided we didn't have any more money than they had already taken from us. Maybe they would have if it hadn't been for the whiskey."

"They whipped poor Elrod to death and

they did other things, horrible things. They kept us there all night, and the longer it went the worse it got. There was five women and four men in our troupe, and only Jenny and I were alive the next morning."

McPhee went silent for the space of several breaths before he continued. "Have you ever been scared? Really scared? I mean, scared to the point that there's no such thing as dignity and you'll beg and cry and do anything not to be afraid anymore?"

Newt didn't answer, waiting for the rest of the story and letting McPhee wrestle with the words.

McPhee looked down at his feet and those ridiculously large shoes for a man of his size. "They burned my feet with a hot knife. Burned me a little at a time and took all night doing it."

"Is that why you limp? Why you wear those big shoes?" Newt asked.

"It is. There hasn't been a day since that I can walk without pain."

"And Jenny?"

"At first I thought maybe they would let her be because she was only a kid, but that wasn't the reason. Maybe they were saving her for last, or maybe they were working up the evil in them and ran out of time," McPhee said. "I used to think that Jenny got through the ordeal better than any of us, but I've come to think she had it the worst. Can you a imagine a little girl having to see all that went on?"

Newt noticed that McPhee's hands had begun to shake ever so lightly.

"That scar on her face, did she get it then?" Newt asked.

"They put Jenny in one of the wagons and told her to stay put, but she heard me calling out and thought to help," McPhee said. "You might not guess it now, but she was once a sweet girl and as tenderhearted as can be. She tried to help me, and one of them, the outlaws' leader, knocked her into our campfire and then held her face down to the coals with a boot on her head. Burning a little girl, can you believe that? Burning a little girl and laughing while he did it?"

Newt's expression was grim, made even more so by the scars on his face and the clench of his jaws. "Hanging's too good for a man like that."

"But he didn't hang," McPhee said. "Do you know who that man was? It was none other than Irish Jack. I wonder now if the gold wasn't anything more than an excuse to get a chance to repay him for what he did to her."

"She tried to hire me to kill him."

"She made the same offer to your stage driver and his brother. And it's likely why Sig and Bjorn went down on the street last night and tried to kill Jack instead of simply running."

"What about you? I'd think you would have plenty of reason for revenge."

"Me? If I had known Irish Jack was around before I came to Vulture City I never would have answered her letter," McPhee said. "I've always been a coward, even before he caught us on the road, so I don't have a bit of shame telling you that I used to have dreams about him hovering over me and laughing while he burned me away bit by bloody bit.

"I begged Jack to kill me and put me out of my misery, but a party of freighters hauling goods to the mines came down the trail that morning and there was a fight. Those freighters ran Jack off before he could finish what he started, and then they buried our dead and hauled Jenny and me to Prescott."

"And after that?"

"I paid a man to go back into the Bradshaws to retrieve our wagons and whatever else I might recoup to sell to get Jenny and me back on our feet. He returned and said all the wagons had been burned along with everything in them. After that, there was no way I could take care of Jenny. I was a fool to think I could have even if it hadn't been for our financial loss. What did I know about raising a girl?

"For a time, we tried to make it as we always had, but the wounds in my feet were long in healing, and the people in Prescott soon tired of Jenny's acts. So, I loaded Jenny on a stagecoach and took her to Tucson. I had a sister there that I hadn't seen in years, and I was at my wits' end and didn't know what else to do."

"That sister wouldn't happen to be the Tulip that Jenny talks about?" Newt asked.

"The same."

"You left a kid with a prostitute?"

"I was out of options. She promised to take care of her until I could return."

"But you never came back, did you?"

"No, I didn't, and it's a bitter pill to swallow, even now."

Newt straightened from where he leaned against the wall. "Where's Jenny gone now?"

"Where do you think? I would assume she's gone after Tom Skitch or his gold."

Newt dropped the lead bar back in the box with a thump. "There is no gold. I would imagine that the real shipment is on its way to catch the train north of Prescott, if it isn't already there by now, and that the box we carried was nothing but a decoy to draw off Irish Jack."

"Is that what you think?" McPhee looked at him and gave an ironic smirk. "If there's one thing that this adventure of ours should have taught you it's that you can't trust anyone and nothing is as it seems. Have you forgotten what I told you about Mr. Skitch's business ledgers?"

Newt grimaced and stood over the bed, staring down at McPhee.

"I assume you are going to kill me now." McPhee looked once more toward the window.

"Why is it that everybody thinks I'm going to kill them?" Newt said more to himself than as a question for McPhee.

"You're going to let me go?" McPhee dared a glance at him.

"No, I'm going to tell that posse out there on the street where you're at, and I hope they lock you away for a long, long time." Newt's voice went cold and hard and cut flatly in the confines of the room. "Because for all your fancy talk and your excuses, you're rotten on the inside, where it matters."

"How easy it is for the strong to judge the

weak," McPhee said with a slight lift of his chin.

Newt gave a mocking grunt and then pointed at the bed pillow next to McPhee's right hand. "If you were going to make a try with that pistol you've got hidden under that pillow you would have already done it by now."

McPhee glanced at the pillow for a long moment, but finally pulled his hand back to his lap with a resigned sigh. Newt went out of the room and started down the stairs. He had barely reached the lobby floor when a gun went off — one shot, one dull pop.

"I didn't think you had that much guts," Newt said as he took a last look at the top of the stairs and then went through the lobby and out onto the street.

Above him, in Room Seven, McPhee lay slumped across the bed with a little bloody hole in one temple and a nickel-plated derringer still clutched in his lifeless hand.

CHAPTER THIRTY-EIGHT

He had been more than forty-eight hours without any sleep beyond a catnap when he rode back to the abandoned stage station at Maricopa Wells. The Mexican he had met the night before was doctoring a sick goat. Along with the herd of goats penned in the old stage company corrals, there were three horses that hadn't been there before. Newt dismounted and searched the inside of the adobe, but there was no sign of either Skitch or the Dutchman.

Newt walked over to the corral and hailed the Mexican.

"Buenas tardes," the Mexican said.

"Dos hombres . . ." Newt struggled for the Spanish he needed. *"¿Los gringos? ¿A dónde fueron?"*

The Mexican shrugged and pointed north across the river.

"¿Cuándo?" Newt asked.

"Esta mañana."

Newt looked toward the river, trying to determine what Skitch's early departure meant, and not liking the conclusions he came to. His eyes burned, and the desert was blurry before him.

"You want more horses?" the Mexican asked from behind him. "I sell you friends four horses. Good horses."

"Did they leave any word for me? *¿Me dejaron un mensaje?*"

The Mexican shook his head. *"Nada."*

Newt found the energy to unsaddle the horses and he turned them into the corral with the other stock. He nodded at the Mexican and then went to the adobe and lay down on the floor atop a straw pile in one corner and immediately went to sleep.

It was noon of the next day when he rode into the canyon at White Tank for a second time. He came by a different route, but the buzzards circling overhead would have led him to the water holes even if no other landmark had guided his navigation.

He found four bodies. First he found two of Irish Jack's outlaws in the brush, and he was mildly surprised to find that Ten Mule was one of them. Who would have thought when they fought in Vulture City that the big redhead would end up dead in a desert thicket not a few days later?

The Stutter brothers lay where they had fallen in the rocks. He wondered what the brothers' real last name was while he gathered stones to pile over them. He had no shovel, and the crude graves were all that he could manage. The two outlaws he left for the buzzards.

The stagecoach remained where they had left it, except that one of the doors was hanging open and the middle bench had been removed and tossed out on the ground. Newt went and looked inside.

Someone had ripped a section of floor out of the coach. No, not ripped. They had merely removed a lid off a small, hidden compartment beneath the bench. Newt immediately knew what had been hidden in that compartment.

He mounted again and headed down the trail through the thicket. The recent rains should have made it easy to track Skitch and the Dutchman, but another set of tracks were trampled over the top of their hoofprints. As near as Newt could tell, Skitch and the Dutchman were riding two horses and leading two more — likely packhorses. Before he left the Gila the Mexican goat herder had told him that he had sold the gringos two sets of *mochilas,* the long, pouchlike bags that Mexicans use for pack-saddle panniers.

Newt continued to study the tracks. His best guess was that three other horsemen had come along behind Skitch and the Dutchman. Like his earlier guesses, he was pretty sure who those three riders were. His theory was confirmed when he found a place where one of the riders had gotten down from the saddle to perhaps tighten a cinch. There were small boot prints in the sand there and the faint drag lines left by a set of spur rowels. Later on, he found a bit of red dress torn free and hanging from a limb where the brush encroached tightly on the trail.

He let the Circle Dot horse choose its own pace, and it was well into the afternoon before he waded the gelding across the Agua Fria and turned off the freight road onto another road leading up the Salt River to the northeast. It was two hours after night-fall when he rode into Phoenix.

CHAPTER THIRTY-NINE

Phoenix was a bigger town than he had imagined, more of a city than anything he had encountered in the territory, covering over a square mile and criss-crossed with numerous streets. He rode the Circle Dot horse past the Methodist church down the wide swath of Washington Street lined on either side with cottonwoods trees. He rode past Hancock's General Store and another tall adobe brick building with a sign on it proclaiming it the home of the *Phoenix Herald* newspaper. A big building rose up before him on one corner of a large intersection marked with street signs. The building was made of brick and mortar several stories high, and a covered porch ran down two sides of it, one along Washington Street and the other following Central Avenue. A sign hanging from the center of the porch roof proclaimed the monstrosity the NATIONAL BANK OF ARIZONA. Newt recalled the Stutter brothers mentioning the bank.

Newt pulled the horse up in front of the Tiger Saloon and left it tied to the hitching rail. He paused for a moment and studied the brick sidewalk fronting the establishment before he stepped onto it and went inside.

The place was crowded with men, some lining the long, polished hardwood bar, and others either standing in groups or sitting at tables. The clink of whiskey glasses and beer bottles sounded over the din of voices.

Newt found an opening at the bar and sidled up to it. The bartender who came to him had a handlebar mustache waxed to needle-fine points at the ends, and the white shirt he wore beneath his paisley print silk vest had sleeve garters above his elbows. The oil on the man's neatly parted hair shone under the lamplight.

Newt felt out of place in such a swanky saloon. It reminded him somewhat of Jenny Silks's Blind Drift back in Vulture City, and the nattily dressed men around him made him feel as dirty and ragged as he must look.

"What are you having?" The bartender gestured at the shelves of liquor on the wall behind him. There were almost too many choices, and Newt recognized none of the labels on the bottles.

The bartender must have noticed his consternation. "Are you a whiskey man?"

Newt nodded.

"How about a shot of Old Forester?" The bartender reached for one of the bottles.

"Make it a double."

"You want that on the rocks or straight?"

"On the rocks?"

The bartender chuckled. "I'm asking if you want a cube of ice."

"Ice? Where did you get ice?"

Again, the bartender laughed. "We've got an ice factory."

Newt absorbed that information while he tried to decide why anyone would want ice in their whiskey. He put his hand over the glass as soon as the bartender poured him two fingers of the bourbon.

"That'll be two bits," the bartender said.

Newt paid the man and took a sip of the whiskey.

"How's that suit you?" the bartender asked.

"It'll do." Newt took a second swallow that emptied the glass.

"You look like you've been out awhile."

"I have at that."

The bartender pointed at Newt's empty glass. "Have another?"

"No, but I'd take a beer if you have one."

The bartender opened a tin-lined chest and pulled forth a brown bottle of beer and uncapped it. When Newt took hold of the bottle he found it frosty to the touch.

"Help yourself if you're hungry." The bartender gestured at a table in the middle of the room with a platter of lunch meat, other sandwich fixings, and a loaf of bread laid out for the customers. "The food is on the house, and the bread is fresh. Got us a new bread factory and they make a delivery every day."

"Real high-toned place you've got here," Newt said.

"Depends on where you come from," the bartender replied.

"That's a fact," Newt said as he took up his beer and went to the table and began to make a ham sandwich.

He had barely taken his first bite of the sandwich when he heard someone mention the Dutchman. He listened closely to locate who had said it, and when he heard the name Waltz again he noticed the pair of soldiers standing at the far end of the bar.

"Did I hear you mention a man named Waltz?" Newt asked when he stepped close to the soldiers.

"Why, you a friend of his?" an old man with long sideburns who was standing

431

beside the soldiers asked.

"I'm looking for him."

"Everybody will be looking for that old codger if what they say is true," one of the soldiers said.

"You haven't heard, have you?" the other soldier asked.

"Heard what?" Newt asked.

"The rumor is that Waltz paid for a wagon down at the livery with a chunk of gold," the same soldier said. "They claim that gold looked like it had been hacked off an ingot with a knife. Pure, refined gold, it was."

"I knew the Dutchman when he was placer mining in the Bradshaws," the old man with them said. He sounded as if he had a few too many drinks. "He knows the business. Wouldn't take much to build a Spanish-style arrastra like we used to use. A little mercury and a good cast-iron pot and a mold, and a man could make his own ingots."

"Where can I find him?" Newt asked.

"That's the question that I bet a lot are asking right now," the old man answered. "There's already talk that the Dutchman has him a mine in the Superstitions that he's been keeping secret."

One of the soldiers finished his beer, belched, and then shook his head in disagreement. "The way I heard it, this Dutchman you're talking about has found the old lost Peralta Mines. Everybody knows that he's gone half the time prospecting the Superstitions. He knows those mountains like the back of his hand, if what they say is true. Could be that he found those mines. Could be."

The other soldier nodded. "Never met the fellow, but they're saying he always has money to spend when he comes to town. The assayer down the street was in here this afternoon telling how Waltz has brought gold ore to him more than once."

"Nothing makes people talk like the news of a find," Newt said.

The same soldier banged his beer bottle on the bar top for emphasis. "You got that right. Hell, there's a bunch down at the newspaper office right now talking about getting together and putting a watch on Waltz's farm so that they can follow him when he goes back to the mountains. If there's a gold strike, they want to be the first to put in their claims. I've got two more weeks left on my enlistment, and I might go prospecting in the Superstitions myself when my time is up."

"I wouldn't follow the Dutchman if I was them," the old man said. "He's the kind that likes to be left alone."

"Where's this farm of his?" Newt asked.

The old man leaned back from the bar and looked up at Newt like the whiskey was making it hard for his eyes to focus. "I don't know that I should tell you that."

One of the soldiers seemed not to have heard the old man. "I saw him not an hour ago, and he ain't at his farm."

"Where was he at?" Newt asked.

"Buy us a beer and I'll tell you."

Newt got the bartender's attention and paid for three more beers.

The soldier took up the beer and tipped his head at Newt in gratitude. "Now, that's what I like, a big spender. You must be getting the fever like everyone else."

"Where did you see Waltz?"

"He was driving that wagon he bought down past the end of Second Street along the river. Looked like he had bought himself a load of corn."

The old-timer and the soldiers gave Newt more precise directions to the area the soldier had mentioned, and then Newt left the saloon. He mounted the Circle Dot horse and followed the main thoroughfare two blocks east and then turned south toward the river. The outskirts of the city became nothing more than a scattering of houses and occasional farm fields. He rode slowly and stopped often, looking for anything that might hint of the Dutchman's whereabouts. A dog barked at him from the dark as he passed.

The city street faded to a faint set of wagon ruts visible under the moonlight. When those ruts ended at an irrigation canal, Newt turned off on a narrow trace that led through a mesquite thicket. It was at the end of that lane that he found the freight wagon parked in front of a small adobe shack. A team of four mules was hitched to the wagon, and two horses with big-horned Mexican saddles on their backs stood tied to the tailgate.

Newt tied the Circle Dot horse to a tree and moved through the dark until he stood against the side of the wagon. The bed of the wagon was mounded with freshly picked ears of corn.

The adobe on the other side of the wagon had only a single window, and no light shone from within. Newt went back to the Circle Dot horse not twenty yards from the wagon and sat down with his back against the tree, where he could keep a watch on the house. He slept sitting up and woke often to check the house.

CHAPTER FORTY

Newt woke an hour before daylight to see a light burning in the adobe's window. He rose and stretched the kinks from his muscles before slipping off through the morning darkness. He stopped to one side of the window and took a quick glance inside. Tom Skitch and the Dutchman sat at a table across from each other with a kerosene lamp between them. The lamp wick was trimmed low and gave off only the dimmest of lights.

Newt drew the Starr from behind his belt and laid a hand to the door latch. He took one deep breath before he swung the door inward and lunged into the room. Startled, Tom Skitch scooted backward in his chair, but made no attempt to lay hand to a weapon. The Dutchman, on the other hand, reached for the Ballard rifle propped against a chair beside him. Newt eared back the Starr's spur hammer and pressed the pistol barrel against the Dutchman's temple. The blued steel puckered the flesh behind the Dutchman's left eye and he froze in place.

"Don't you so much as twitch," Newt said.

He yanked the Dutchman's pistol from its holster and pointed it in Skitch's direction while he kept the Starr in his right hand pressed against the Dutchman's head. Skitch glanced at the coach gun leaning against the wall, but instead of making a move for it he put both palms on the tabletop in plain sight.

"Have you lost your mind?" Skitch asked loudly.

Newt motioned for Skitch to join the Dutchman, and then moved to where Skitch had been when the mine foreman complied. Newt piled the shotgun and the Dutchman's pistol on the table before him and then sat down. At the other end of the table, the Dutchman rubbed his temple and eyed the cocked revolver Newt held resting on the tabletop and pointing at him.

"You two about pulled it off," Newt said.

"Pulled off what?" Skitch asked. "If this is about the wages I owe you . . ."

"You've already played me the fool once," Newt said. "Don't try it again."

"There has been some misunderstanding here," Skitch sputtered.

Newt drummed the fingers of his free

hand on the tabletop. "Would you believe it? I found an express box in Maricopa Station full of lead bars and then I went back to White Tanks after I found you two gone. Want to guess what I found there?"

"I'm telling you, you don't understand."

"I found your little hidden compartment in the bottom of the coach."

"All right, all right." Skitch leaned back in his chair. "I guess I should have told you before now, but I didn't know if I could trust you then. We built that compartment under the bench as insurance in case the stage was robbed."

"You let me ride into Maricopa Station without telling me."

"We were going to wait for you to come back, but I was worried about the stage-coach sitting alone and someone stumbling across it and finding the shipment."

"Then how come you didn't bring that gold on into Maricopa Station after you got it back?"

"Because the gold was gone. When we got back to the stagecoach somebody had already beaten us there."

Newt frowned, and again he drummed his fingers on the tabletop. "I spent my whole way here trying to figure how you thought you could get away with it. The only thing that came to mind was that you planned to slip off somewhere along the way or to run when we got to Maricopa Station and before Wells Fargo took a look in the express box, but Irish Jack and Jenny spoiled all your scheming. Or maybe you and the Dutchman planned to kill us all. I even wondered if Irish Jack might be working for you. Whatever you intended, you're a bald-faced liar and a thief."

"Those are harsh words. Now, why don't you calm down and listen to reason?"

"Where's the gold?"

"I don't know."

"I think you do. I think that's why you bought that wagon out there," Newt said.

"I'm telling you, the gold was gone when we got back to the stage."

"That's not how I read the sign at White Tank. Jenny and those brothers of hers came along, but not until after the two of you had already been there."

The Dutchman had been looking down at the table, but his head came up when Newt mentioned Jenny. "That whore's here?"

Newt shrugged. "It wouldn't surprise me if she was out there on the streets looking for you right now. Maybe she started getting the same suspicions as me when she found what was in that express box."

Skitch and the Dutchman passed a quick glance between them.

"You're a fool, same as she is," Skitch said. "And I'm beginning to believe you intend to have the gold for yourself. That's the real reason you're here, isn't it?"

The three of them sat at the table in silence for a long time. Skitch was nervous and fidgety, but the Dutchman only glared at Newt from under his bushy white eyebrows.

Newt returned the Dutchman's hard gaze. "You know, I wondered why Skitch there would hire a man to guard his gold shipment that everyone said was a high-grader."

"You say that easy with a gun in your hand," the Dutchman said.

Newt went on as if he hadn't heard the threat. "Was that how it was at first? A man that had the mine foreman looking out for him might lay hand to a good bit of ore. Mighty profitable. How big of a cut did he take for looking the other way?"

"Don't let him bait you, Jacob," Skitch said.

"But high-grading what you could carry out in your pockets or your lunch pail wasn't enough, was it?" Newt added. "You wanted more."

For a second time, there was a long silence

440

in the room. Newt let Skitch get up and feed another chunk of mesquite wood in the stove. Skitch started to sit down, but Newt took up the shotgun with his left hand and cocked one of its hammers. He pointed the double-barreled weapon at the two of them while he shoved the revolver back behind his belt. The gray light of morning was beginning to shine through the window.

He stood and skidded the chair out of his way and motioned for the Dutchman to get up. "Time we took us a little ride."

He followed them out the door. Tom Skitch started to gather one of the saddle horses tied to the tailgate of the wagon.

"No, get up on the seat, both of you," Newt said.

The Dutchman climbed up on the wagon, followed by Skitch, while Newt freed the horses tied to the tailgate. Newt retrieved the Circle Dot horse and swung into the saddle. There was a moment as he mounted when the horse was between him and the men on the wagon seat, and when he put the shotgun back on them he saw the Dutchman leaning out with his hand on the belt knife at his waist.

Newt cocked the other hammer on the shotgun. "A quick man with a knife might beat a man with a gun if the distance between them wasn't too far. Man with the gun might flinch, you know, hesitate instead of pulling the trigger. But then again, he might not. I guess it depends on if you're feeling reckless."

The Dutchman's eyes shone with hatred in the hollows of his skull.

"Are you feeling reckless, Dutchman? Because I guarantee you I won't flinch. This old scattergun will put a hole through you big as your hat," Newt said.

The Dutchman let go of his knife.

"Go ahead and throw it down," Newt said.

The Dutchman drew the knife and pitched it to the ground.

"You drive."

The Dutchman scowled at him one last time before he took up the lines and started the team moving. The wagon jostled and rattled over the rutted lane leading out to the street. Newt kept the Circle Dot horse even with the wagon seat and the shotgun's buttstock resting on his thigh.

"You've got nothing but a wild story," Skitch said to Newt. "I did everything I could to see the gold to the railroad. Took every precaution to protect the company's property."

"Save your talking for the city marshal. I suspect he shouldn't be too hard to find,"

442

Newt said.

"I'm too old to let them lock me away," the Dutchman muttered.

"I hear the prison at Yuma is hotter than hell in the summertime," Newt said. "But they might go easier on a man if he told where the gold he stole was at."

"How much will it cost me for you to let us turn this wagon around?" Skitch asked.

Newt gave a bitter chuckle. "I let you buy me once, but I'd as soon eat glass as do it again."

"Give him a cut, Tom," the Dutchman said.

"It's your word against ours," Skitch said to Newt. "You think they'll believe a hard case like you? Well, I promise you they won't, not after I tell them that you were riding with Irish Jack."

"Save your lies for the law," Newt replied.

"Give him a cut before you get us both hanged," the Dutchman said. "There's too many that saw him leaving Vulture City with us, and word is bound to have already spread about the attempted holdup at Seymour."

Skitch hung his head for a moment, and it was obvious that he was feeling all his plans fading away. When he lifted his head again he looked at Newt and his words had a

443

resigned but bitter bite to them. "Forty thousand split three ways still makes a healthy stake for all of us. What say you, Jones? That's what you're after anyway."

Newt gave nothing in reply.

"You're a born loser if I ever saw one, but here's your chance to change that," Skitch continued.

"That's the difference between you and me, Skitch," Newt said. "Your word isn't worth a damn to you or anybody else."

The Dutchman turned the wagon onto Madison Street. It was early enough in the morning that the city's residents were only beginning to stir. A woman came out of her house and started across her yard to her chicken pen to gather the morning's eggs, but turned and ran back inside when she caught sight of Newt holding the shotgun. Two young boys on the other side of the street saw the same thing, gawked at Newt for a moment, and then ran ahead and disappeared inside one of the businesses a block away.

Ahead, a group of workers were taking advantage of the cooler morning hours and unloading a wagonload of hay at the Grand Central Livery. The last of the hay was pulled up by the haymow to the loft and the wagon pulled out, revealing what was beyond it. Two men were just then dismounting in front of the livery, but they stayed on their horses when they saw Newt and his prisoners coming down the street. It was a good hundred yards to the livery, but Newt instantly recognized the two men by the long linen dusters they wore and the two black horses they sat on.

"Looks like things are about to get interesting," Newt said.

CHAPTER FORTY-ONE

Skitch and the Dutchman noticed Jenny's brothers at the same time Newt did.

"Give me a gun," the Dutchman said.

"Keep moving," Newt replied while he watched the brothers ahead of them.

Sig and Bjorn took a last look their way and then turned their black horses around and disappeared around the corner where Madison Street bisected Central Avenue. The Dutchman kept the team of mules to a slow walk.

"They wouldn't try anything in the middle of town," Skitch said.

The Dutchman was too busy trying to watch both sides of the street to talk, as if he expected a bullet to strike him at any moment. He swung the wagon onto the wide swath of Central Avenue where Jenny's brothers had gone. The street had been recently graded, and the freshly scraped dirt was dark and smooth. Still, the wagon creaked and rattled, and for some reason the sound of it was suddenly too loud in the quietness of the morning.

Ahead at the next street intersection, Newt spotted the big brick bank he had seen the night before. If he remembered correctly, the city jail wasn't far west of that. By then, he, too, was searching both sides of the street for any sign of Jenny or her brothers.

They turned the corner onto Washington at the same time that a man came down the sidewalk in front of the Tiger Saloon. It was Ernie Sims walking down the sidewalk, and when he looked up and saw Newt and the wagon he stopped in his tracks. Newt barely had time to wonder what the marshal from Vulture City was doing there when Irish Jack, leading his big sorrel horse, came out of an alley beside the saloon. It was the first time that Newt had laid eyes on the outlaw, but he instantly recognized the horse.

Newt twisted in the saddle to keep watch on the saloon while the Dutchman kept the horses moving westward. Skitch, like Newt, had seen Irish Jack and Ernie Sims, and faced backward on the wagon seat and studied them with worried eyes.

Boot steps sounded on the wooden decking of the balcony over the bank's front porch, and Newt looked up and saw Sig Hanson there, aiming his big-bore rifle at them. The rifle boomed and Skitch fell off the wagon seat with a groan. Newt spun the Circle Dot horse around to face the bank, at the same time bringing the shotgun to bear. He fired the first barrel one-handed, and the charge of buckshot knocked splinters out of the balcony railing near Sig. The Aussie bushranger was struggling to reload his single-shot rifle, and that bought Newt a little time.

He sank his spurs into the Circle Dot horse's belly and charged toward the bank. He shouldered the shotgun and took aim at Sig for a second time. But Bjorn Larson stepped out from an alley to Newt's right at that very moment and fired a shot at him. The bullet aimed for Newt missed, and without slowing his horse, Newt swiveled at the waist and put a charge of buckshot into Bjorn's chest. The range was short, only half the width of the street, and Bjorn took a staggering step backward and then slowly crumpled to one knee.

Newt looked back to the balcony in time to see Sig bring the loaded rifle back to bear on him. He spurred the Circle Dot horse again and reined it directly at the bank's front doors. The horse didn't slow as it leapt onto the sidewalk. Man and horse went under the porch roof just before a heavy bullet passed over them and thumped a hole in the street beyond them. Newt ducked low and braced for impact as the Circle Dot horse hit the double doors with its shoulder. The gelding's weight and momentum carried it inside the bank lobby in a shower of glass and the groan of busted wood.

The horse scrambled to keep its footing on the hardwood floor and scattered furniture and knocked out a front window before it came to a stop beneath the large chandelier hanging from the molded tin ceiling in the center of the lobby. Newt swung from the saddle, slipped on the broken glass, and almost fell.

One of the bank doors was lying on the lobby floor and the other sagged on its hinges and swung slowly back and forth in the wind. Newt drew the Starr single-action and charged into that opening. The first thing he saw was the Dutchman whipping the mules, and the wagon bouncing and skidding wildly as it raced away from the fight. Sig's rifle boomed from the balcony again, and Newt thought he saw the Dutchman flinch. The wagon fishtailed wildly, skidded broadside, and then tipped over on its side. The Dutchman was flung from the wagon seat and sailed through the air with arms flailing and still holding on to the leather bridle lines. He hit the dirt at the same time the kingpin broke free. The mules, loose from the wagon, kept on down the street at a dead run. The Dutchman clung to the lines and skidded on his belly behind the runaway team. A bullet kicked up dirt behind him just before he went out of sight.

Bjorn was still down on his knee across the intersection and Newt was about to take a shot at him when another gun boomed twice from somewhere near the saloon. Bjorn clutched at his face and fell over on his side, and at the same time a woman screamed.

Newt could hear Sig moving around on the balcony above him. He took his best guess where the bushranger stood and thumbed three quick shots into the roof decking above him. The .44 caliber bullets punched cleanly through the one-inch lumber and Sig gave a cry of pain or surprise. Newt shifted his aim to one side, tracking the sound of Sig's movement, and emptied the revolver. The boots went quiet on the balcony, and then after a few seconds Sig's body fell to the street in front of Newt. He was dead before he hit the ground.

Newt had no spare ammunition for the Starr rim-fire, and he dropped the pistol and lunged for the edge of the sidewalk where Sig's body lay. The grips of Newt's Smith & Wesson with their blue turquoise crosses were visible at Sig's belt where his duster lay open. Newt pulled the pistol free just as a bullet whipped past him and smacked into the brick wall behind him. He ducked and dropped to one knee.

Ernie Sims was running across the street away from the bank and the saloon and firing his pistol wildly over one shoulder. Newt brought the Smith & Wesson to arm's length and squinted down the barrel. He had time to fire one shot before Ernie leapt over a yard fence and disappeared from sight. Newt knew that he had missed, and he waited for Ernie to reappear. The street had suddenly gone quiet again.

Newt glanced toward the jail again at the wrecked wagon, and then where Skitch lay in the street. The mine foreman wasn't moving.

Newt rose and moved along the sidewalk to the corner of the bank wall. He cocked the Smith & Wesson and waited a count of three before he stepped around the corner.

Irish Jack stepped out of the alley on the far side of the Tiger Saloon at the same time

451

Newt came around the corner of the bank. Jack was looking at something across the street and didn't notice Newt for an instant. The redheaded outlaw had a pistol-sized, cut-down shotgun broken open and was reaching for fresh cartridges. Newt's revolver hung at the end of his arm beside his right leg. Less than thirty yards separated the two men.

"You've played hell, Widowmaker," Jack said as he dropped the empty shotgun.

Newt said nothing and wished that he dared a glance to where Ernie had gone over the fence. He was caught in a cross fire if Ernie decided to get back in the fight. And he was sure that Jack intended to fight. The man was a killer, and his eyes were as crazy then as any Newt had ever encountered.

"You got anything to say before you die?" There was an odd quaver to Jack's voice.

"Come and have you some," Newt said as he swung his .44 up.

Irish Jack reached for both his shoulder holsters at once. His hands were faster than any man's had a right to be. Newt turned sideways to the outlaw and extended the Smith & Wesson at arm's length. The revolver bucked in his hand, and he put his first bullet right above Jack's belt buckle. Jack grunted with the impact and staggered against the saloon's front wall.

But he righted himself somehow, bellowed his rage, and charged forward with both pistols blazing. Newt gritted his teeth, ignoring the bullets flying past him, and put a second shot into Jack's chest at point-blank range. Jack fell to his knees and both of his arms sagged to his sides. He gave an animal-like growl and tried to raise his right-hand gun. Newt strode forward and stepped on the gun, pinning it to the sidewalk.

Jack wobbled and fell over on his side, staring upward at Newt with one eye twitching. His mouth worked like he was trying to say something, but no words came out. Newt kicked the Remington pistols off the sidewalk and took a step back from the downed outlaw and waited for him to die.

Instead of dying, Jack slowly squirmed across the sidewalk and then got his knees back under him and pushed himself up the wall. Newt kept the Smith & Wesson pointed at him but did not shoot.

"Damn you." Jack staggered off the sidewalk and started across the street, wobbling left and right and at times looking like he would fall again.

Newt broke his pistol open, shucked the spent brass, and loaded the empty chambers with fresh cartridges from his belt. He was about to turn away when Jenny Silks came running onto the street. She screamed, and Newt knew then that it had been her cry he heard earlier when Bjorn was killed. Again, she let out that banshee wail somewhere between anguish and wrath. Tears rolled down her pale cheeks. Her nickel-plated pistol was held before her in a shaking hand.

"Turn around!" she screamed. "I said, turn around and face me."

Jack glanced over his shoulder at her, but staggered on. She stopped in the middle of the street, raised the pistol, and fired once, and then a second time into Jack's back. Newt could tell by the way Jack's body jerked that both rounds had struck him, but he kept going. He disappeared into the hotel on the far side of the street. Jenny's pistol arm fell to her side, and she went quiet and still except for the uneven heave of her chest.

She dropped the pistol in the street, glanced at Newt once as she started back the way she had come, but looked away quickly and went on. Newt watched her until she was gone, holstered his pistol, and then turned and started down the street in the opposite direction.

He came first to Skitch's body. The mine foreman lay facedown in the street. The heavy bullet from Sig's rifle had taken him between the shoulder blades.

Newt moved on to the wagon. A good portion of the load of corn had spilled from the wagon bed, more than enough of it to reveal a patch of leather among the ears. He dug in the corn until he pulled out a large canvas and leather bag. More digging brought forth two more identical bags. He hefted one of them, judging its weight.

He gathered all three of the bags and turned and started walking back to the bank. He was almost there when he heard someone coming behind him. And then came the sound of a cocking pistol.

He turned slowly and found a short Mexican holding a pistol pointed at him. There was a marshal's badge pinned to the breast of the man's shirt.

"Stop right there," the marshal said.

"You're a little late, Marshal," Newt replied.

The lawman looked at the wrecked wagon, the bodies strewn about his city street, and the busted bank doors behind Newt. "You've got a lot to answer for."

"Most of us do."

The marshal's eyes narrowed. "What's in the bags?"

"How's forty thousand in stolen gold

sound?"

The marshal looked at Newt like he didn't believe him. "Is that so? Mind telling me where you were going with it?"

Newt jerked his head at the bank behind him. "I was about to put this in your bank."

The marshal looked again at the bank's destroyed front doors.

Newt saw where he was looking and gave as much of a shrug of his shoulders as the heavy bags would allow him. "Your bank opens too late to suit me. Never could tolerate a banker's hours."

"You're a calm one considering the bind you're in," the marshal said. "You keep hold of those bags, now. I imagine I'd be doing the territory a favor if I shot you, so don't give me an excuse."

The marshal stepped forward and pulled Newt's pistol from its holster and then stepped back to put more distance between them. He flinched when Newt dropped the bags. The sound of metal clanking together was plain in the silence around them. Somebody gave a gasp of surprise, and only then did Newt realize that people had come out of their houses or businesses all up and down the street now that the shooting was over. He and the marshal looked down at the bags at the same time. The fasteners on

456

one of the bags had broken, and two gold ingots the length of a man's palm had spilled forth.

"How much gold did you say?" the marshal asked.

"Enough to cause all of this."

"From the way you're acting, I'd say I ought to hear the rest of your story."

"That could take some time. It's complicated," Newt said. "You might want to go up the street first and have a look in that hotel yonder. Irish Jack went in there. He's shot to doll rags, but I'd go careful if I was you."

"Irish Jack, you say? I suppose you shot him, too."

"I did."

"Anything else you want to confess to?"

"There a woman up somewhere in town, a dove from over at Vulture City. Jenny Silks is what some call her."

"I know Jenny, or at least I know of her. What's she got to do with this?"

Newt pointed at the gold at his feet. "She and Irish Jack got the notion that they might rob a stagecoach. Those two in the dusters were her brothers."

"And that one over by the wagon? I believe that's Tom Skitch."

"That'd be him."

457

The marshal laid a hand to one end of his mustache, smoothing it, and then he shoved his hat back on his head a little and gave Newt a wry look. "Anything else I ought to know about?"

"Not that I can think of."

At that same instant the Circle Dot horse clomped out of the bank doors and stopped on the sidewalk. It gaped open its mouth and gave a great yawn.

"We frown on riding horses indoors," the marshal said with that same wry look.

"He was helping me make a deposit."

The marshal tugged at the ends of his mustache again. "Call it a hunch, but I think it might be all right if I left you here while I go have a look in that hotel."

"I'm not going anywhere," Newt said. "But would you mind if I had a seat over there by my horse? This morning has taken the starch out of me."

The marshal kept Newt's pistol, but holstered his own. Shaking his head, he went past Newt, then stopped when he was only a short ways off and looked back. "You're either the nerviest liar or the damnedest innocent man I think I ever came across."

"Marshal, I don't know if there's such a thing as an innocent man," Newt said. "Not a one of us."

Chapter Forty-Two

Ernie Sims slipped into the hotel by the back door after he saw Jack retreat inside. He would have gone to Jack sooner, but it took some time for his hands to stop shaking. The whole morning had been one shocking occurrence after the other. Even Jack had given up on the gold, and it had been by mere chance that they happened to ride into Phoenix. Even more against the odds, in Ernie's opinion, was the fact that upon their arrival they had gone looking for a saloon that might open up early only to run into the Widowmaker, Skitch, and the Dutchman instead, not to mention those men in the long coats showing up at the same time and doing their best to kill everyone in sight. Gunfights were unsettling enough when you had time to plan for them, but surprise gunfights so early in the morning bothered him greatly.

Ernie had been sure that he was going to

die through the whole ordeal, but somehow he had gotten through it without a scratch. Considering the amount of shooting that had gone on, that was a great stroke of luck, indeed, if not a miracle on a level to impress a priest.

And then, the greatest surprise of all had happened. That crazy whore had walked out on the street and shot Jack full of holes. The Widowmaker had already all but finished Jack off, but then she went and did what she did. It was nothing short of an execution. She had always seemed an average whore other than looking so odd, and he had never guessed that she was crazy. He preferred his doves far more sane and less likely to shoot you in the back. He reminded himself to make sure he searched for calm, predictable women in the future, even if that meant they might be ugly and less interesting.

He found his way to the lobby and heard Jack's ragged breathing before he saw him. The outlaw was lying on the floor in the shadows against the front wall. When Ernie came closer he saw the bloody bubbles inflating over Jack's lips every time he exhaled. Jack lay on his back, and the whole front of him was bloody, both entry wounds and exit wounds. He looked like he was shot in more places than he wasn't.

Ernie glanced out the front window and saw the marshal coming toward the hotel, and he saw the Widowmaker sit down on the sidewalk in front of the bank. It would have been a relatively easy thing to step out the front door and take a shot at the Widowmaker, but Ernie had suddenly decided that he didn't care to try and kill him anymore. All he wanted was to get out of Phoenix and go back to Vulture City, where things were much more predictable.

Jack's eyes were open. At first Ernie thought Jack was staring at him, but he realized when he leaned closer that Jack's stare was blank. The only movement of his eyes was the strange but usual tic in one of his eyelids.

"You're about done for," Ernie said.

Jack didn't reply. If it hadn't been for the ragged and uneven heave of his chest and that ticking eyelid Ernie wouldn't have believed him alive at all. Truly, Jack's tolerance for lead was impressive.

But no matter how Jack swore he couldn't be killed, it wasn't helping him now. Jack was as good as dead already, and no amount of stubborn nature was going to do anything but drag things out. But the fact that Jack was still in the realm of the living was a fine opportunity to say a few things that Ernie had dearly wanted to say to him for years.

"Can you hear me, Jack?" Ernie said.

Jack gave no indication that he heard Ernie, and that was disappointing to Ernie, while it also emboldened him. "What's the matter, Jack? You don't look so tough now."

Jack's chest heaved, his lungs expelled a raspy hiss, and he blew an exceptionally large bubble.

"I hope it hurts, you arrogant bastard," Ernie said. "The only thing I wish is that I could have been the one to put a bullet in you."

Jack's eyelid spasmed more wildly, the way it often did when he was mad. Ernie hoped that meant Jack heard him.

"Why don't you have the good graces to go ahead and die, you stupid Irish bastard?" Ernie said.

The words had no effect on Jack's condition, but the eyelid's twitching did slow some. Ernie was trying to think of something else to say to Jack that was especially mean and clever when his attention was drawn to the finger bone hanging on the watch chain draped across Jack's vest. And then his gaze shifted to the war medal pinned on the vest lapel above the watch chain.

Ernie's hand reached for the finger bone first. "You won't be needing this, will you now, Jackie boy?"

Jack's big knife flashed upward and drove into Ernie's belly right beneath his breastbone. Ernie's eyes expanded in shock and pain before he fell across Jack's body, driving the knife blade in deeper. He grabbed frantically at the pistol on his hip, but suddenly he couldn't make his arm work. And then his whole body began to shake and he felt something warm soaking through his shirtfront. One of those convulsions flopped his head around and he found himself staring into Jack's eyes. Jack's eyelid had quit twitching and his mouth slowly changed its shape into something that definitely resembled a satisfied smirk.

"Oh, you . . ." Ernie never finished what he started to say, for he died then and there.

Irish Jack died a few seconds later.

CHAPTER FORTY-THREE

City Marshal Henry Garfias propped his boots up on his office desk and scribbled something down in the little notebook he held. Across the desk from him, Newt finished the last of his story and took a sip from his coffee mug. It was the third time since the previous morning that the marshal had asked him to explain the events that had taken place with the Vulture City stagecoach.

"I've known Tom Skitch since he came to the territory two years ago," the marshal finally said. "Hard to believe he did what you say he did, but people never cease to surprise me."

"In my experience, some people don't deal with temptation as well as they ought to," Newt answered.

"The only hole I can pick in your story is that every witness that might corroborate it is dead," the marshal said as he reached for his own coffee mug on the desk.

"There's the Dutchman if you can find him."

"No need to find him. Sheriff Orme telegraphed me that he's on his way up from Maricopa Station, and that Waltz met him there and turned himself in."

Newt didn't attempt to hide his surprise. "He's a cunning, bitter man. I wouldn't have thought you would take him without a fight."

The marshal put his feet back on the floor and closed his notebook and set it on the desk. "I'll have to talk to the sheriff to get the details, but from what I gathered from his rather long message, Waltz claims he ran because he was in fear of his life from those that were trying to steal the mine shipment he was hired to guard."

"He's as guilty as sin."

"Yes, I suspect you're right."

"You suspect? They had the gold hidden under that load of corn," Newt said. "Something's bothering you that you aren't saying."

"No way to prove where he and Skitch were going with it. You said yourself that Skitch claimed he was going to put the money in the bank."

"They offered me a cut to let them slip

out of town."

"It's your word against Waltz's."

"No, I'm telling you how it was." Up until then, Newt sounded only tired, but now his temper rose in his voice.

The marshal held up a hand. "You misunderstand me. Apparently you have little experience with our court system. We've got a local horse thief that I've caught two times since I took this job. Caught him red-handed, but each time he managed to find a lawyer better than the prosecutor. His last lawyer somehow convinced the jury that he rode off on someone else's horse in a state of drunkenness because he mistook it for his own, despite the fact that I caught him dead sober on that horse a day after he stole it and sixty miles from here."

"All anyone was talking about when I hit town was how the Dutchman had paid for that wagon with gold."

"It wouldn't be the first time Waltz has spent a little gold in Phoenix. He keeps to himself most of the time, but not enough that most around here don't know of his obsession with prospecting. Half the town is convinced that he's mined a major find."

"He paid for that wagon with refined gold," Newt said. "And his so-called finds before that were likely what he high-graded

466

from the Vulture Mine."

"Can you prove that?"

"I don't have to prove anything. I was hired to guard that shipment, and that's what I did. You deal with his lies. Stretch his neck or let him go, as bad as the thought of that galls me," Newt said. "As soon's we're done here I'm going to go find me a saloon and get good and drunk, and then I'm going to sleep for about a week."

"You may not get the chance," the marshal said. "At least not without more trouble than you want."

Newt didn't like what the change in the marshal's tone hinted at. "Tell me the rest of it."

"How much gold did you say was put on the stage at Vulture City?" the marshal asked.

"Forty thousand dollars' worth."

"Well, what's bothering me, and what's bothering the sheriff, is that there was only about thirty thousand worth in those bags under that wagonload of corn."

Newt absorbed that information and its implications. "Skitch told me there was forty thousand worth of gold in the shipment, and that's all I know. I'd guess he lied to me for one reason or the other, or maybe he and the Dutchman took a part of

467

the gold and stashed it as a little insurance in case they got caught trying to get away with the main haul. Who knows?"

The marshal nodded as if he might have already considered the same possibilities. "When I wired the sheriff back and told him that I had thirty thousand in gold from the Vulture City stage he wired me back and said that Waltz swore that he had personally helped load the gold on the stage and that there was forty thousand dollars' worth to the ounce. Fifty-two ingots, to be exact."

"I never laid eyes on the gold until you did out there on the street yesterday morning," Newt said. "I told you there was nothing but lead bars in the express box when I looked in it at Maricopa Station, and that hidden compartment in the bottom of the stage was empty when I got back to White Tank."

"According to the sheriff, Waltz claims you must have taken some of the gold. And he also claims that you were never hired as a shotgun guard and that you were with Irish Jack's gang when they tried to rob the stage. Says you hunted down him and Skitch here and forced them to drive that wagon. Says you were going to kill them as soon as you got free from town."

"That's a damned lie. You don't believe that."

"Won't matter what I believe. You're a man with a reputation, and a lot of those stories about you don't show you in the best light," the marshal said. "You haven't been here much more than a day and already there are some that are telling how you used to work for the mining companies over in the New Mexico Territory doing their dirty work. They're saying how it's common knowledge that for the right price you'll bust a man's head or put a bullet in him and never bat an eye, and how you came here and turned that street out there into a slaughterhouse."

"You're saying they'll believe that thieving Dutchman and not me?"

"I'm saying that the sheriff wants me to lock you up until he can get here and we get to the bottom of this."

Newt glanced at his Smith & Wesson lying on the marshal's desk. The marshal saw him looking at the pistol and gave a slight frown.

"She can tell you that I wasn't with Irish Jack." Newt pointed behind the marshal's desk.

The marshal turned in his chair to look at Jenny Silks sitting on her cot behind the iron bars enclosing the front of the tiny

469

brick cell. She had undoubtedly overheard their whole conversation, but gave no indication that she had. She had been staring at the wall across from her the whole morning. The breakfast the marshal had brought her earlier lay cold and untouched on the floor at her feet.

"Be my guest," the marshal said to Newt. "But I don't think she'll talk. Only words she said when I locked her up were to ask if Irish Jack was dead. Hasn't said a word since."

Newt got up out of his chair and went across the room to stand in front of the bars. She didn't look up at him and simply kept staring at the wall. Her face was drawn and haggard, and her pale hair, usually combed until every fine strand of it shone like it had a light of its own, was tangled and hung across her face.

"Tell him," Newt said. "Tell him how you and Skitch hired me, and that I didn't ride with Irish Jack. Tell him the truth."

She didn't move, nor did she answer him, but he saw her eyes cut quickly to him for an instant. She held one hand in the other on her lap, slowly kneading it.

"McPhee is dead," Newt said. "Thought you might want to know that."

She rose and went to the single window at

the back of the cell. It was a small window and too high on the wall to let her see out of it, but she stood in the sunlight that spilled through it.

"What makes you think I care?" she asked after a time.

"Just thought you might want to know."

She turned to him, and instead of sadness there was nothing but bitter hate in her expression. "If I had a gun I would kill you right now."

"I don't doubt you would."

She began to pace back and forth across the narrow width of the cell, two steps one way, two steps the other. Her dress hissed where it dragged against the floor.

"I was so close I could taste it," she said without stopping her pacing. "Almost beat the lot of you."

"Your brothers are dead, and so are a lot of others, and you're looking at a long stretch in the territorial prison. I think in time you'll ask yourself how much gold is worth that."

"You don't know me," she spat at him. "You want me to apologize? Want me to say what a bad girl I've been? Well, I won't, damn you. I'd do it all over again if I had the chance."

She sat back down on the cot again with

her jaw tense and stubborn and trembling with anger, and her gaze focused on nothing but the wall in front of her. It was plain to him that she would speak no more to him.

He glanced at the marshal, but the peace officer only shrugged and shook his head. "I told you."

Newt went back to the other side of the marshal's desk, but didn't sit this time. He stood looking out the front window at the Circle Dot horse standing tied to the hitching rail.

"So what next?" he asked.

The marshal cleared his throat. "What might interest you as much as the sheriff's request to detain you is that I believe there's usually a lot of distance between a man's reputation and the truth of him. And it so happens I know some things about you that people aren't saying. For instance, I happen to have a certain friend who holds an interest in the Southern Pacific Railroad, and he hasn't forgotten how you went down to Mexico and got his boy back from the Apaches when the army wouldn't or couldn't. You've got a lot of dead men behind you, Jones, if the border talk is true, but as harsh as it sounds, I don't see any good men in your graveyard, and that says something in itself.

"Myself, I'm a married man, hope to have children one day, pay my taxes, and tip my hat to the ladies on the street. I try not to lie and say a prayer or two on occasion. Like to think I'm a good man, but I've killed three men in the line of duty since I started wearing this badge. Think about that a lot when I lay down at night, and the conclusion that I've come to is that this territory needs good men strong enough and hard enough to stand against the other kind, at least until this country grows up. I think you might be one of the good kind, no matter what they call you."

Newt glanced again at his pistol lying on the desk.

"Take it," the marshal said. "A man with your habits is likely to need it again."

Newt took up the gun and shoved it down in his holster. "You're letting me go?"

"I advise you to forget getting drunk and that nap you were planning to take," the marshal said. "Because no matter what my gut tells me, the next time I go down that street and I find you still in town I'm going to play it by the book. I'm going to lock you up in that other cell beside Jenny there and I'm going to forget this little talk of ours."

Newt looked out the front window at the

473

street. "Think I'll go to California. Always did want to see that country."

"I think that's a good idea."

"What about the Dutchman?"

"Maybe he'll pay for what he's done, maybe he won't. Either way, the sun will rise and set tomorrow just like any other day and we'll move on."

Newt started for the door.

"Ha! You think you're a good man?" It was Jenny who called to him.

Newt turned to see that she had gotten up from her cot again and was standing at the front of her cell with both hands clenching the bars and her eyes boring into him like red, wet gun barrels. "You stand there acting high-and-mighty, but what did you get for all your troubles? Huh? A few dollars in wages that you'll throw away on whiskey and women, and then you'll wake up tomorrow morning the same miserable, ugly, murderous son of a bitch that I see standing before me right now. Nothing changed, nothing different, every day the same as the day before."

"You know, there are things uglier than scars. So long, Jenny." He put a hand to the doorknob and stepped out onto the street.

"You didn't break me. None of you did," she called after him.

He shut the door behind him and went to the Circle Dot horse at the hitching rail. He swung into the saddle and reined the horse out onto the street.

"Come on now, we've got a bit of traveling to do," he said.

The Circle Dot horse pricked its ears forward and sped up to a trot without being asked to, as if it understood what Newt had said, and as if it was equally anxious to see some new country. Several people on the street had come to recognize Newt and his horse, and they stopped to watch him as he passed. None of them waved or offered a greeting. He sat tall in the saddle, ignoring their stares with his thoughts and cares hidden behind his scars and beneath the shadows of his hat brim. At the first opportunity he reined onto a side street that led west. He never looked back as he urged the gelding to a ground-eating, rocking-chair lope.

"I don't suppose you know the way to California, do you?" he asked the horse when they were well out on the desert.

As usual the horse had no answer.

HISTORICAL NOTES

The Vulture Mine

Nobody knows exactly how the mine, the settlement that grew up around it, and the nearby Vulture Peak came to be named after vultures. Some claim that Henry Wickenburg saw one or more of the scavenging birds flying overhead at the time of his discovery of the ore vein, but what is for certain is that the Vulture Mine, at times, was one of the richest gold mines in the Arizona Territory. In the earliest days, Henry Wickenburg simply allowed miners to work the vein and charged them a percentage of their findings. An old mule-drawn, Spanish-style arrastra with a stone grinder originally processed the ore at Wickenburg, but later there were several stamp mills that serviced the mine, first at Smith's Mill, and then Seymour before the Arizona Mining Company took ownership and built the water pipeline from Seymour and moved the stamp mill to the mine. The mine itself changed ownership several times. While rich with ore, the mine always proved challenging when it came to producing a profit, due to no nearby water source (the Hassayampa River at Seymour was ten miles away), among other things. Wickenburg himself sold the mine to a New York company for $75,000. He received $25,000 of the sale price, but never received full payment, despite a years-long court battle. From that point on, the mine's history is one of off-and-on operation, and from approximately 1863 to 1942, subsequent owners all went bankrupt or shut down operations for various reasons. However, profitable or not, certain historians estimate that the Vulture Mine produced 340,000 ounces of gold and 260,000 ounces of silver in its lifetime. By 1884, the time setting of this novel, Vulture City had sixty to eighty stamps crushing its ore, an assay office, blacksmith shop, five or six boardinghouses, carpenter shop, cookhouse and mess hall, laundries, stores, warehouses, and at least three saloons. And, of course, it had a stagecoach road to transport the gold the mine produced.

The Gunpowder Express

The Southwest deserts are rife with tall stories and legends, but my naming of the trail from Maricopa Station (modern-day Maricopa) northward through Phoenix and Wickenburg to Prescott and points nearby as the Gunpowder Express was purely of my own creation. However, had such a name been given in its day, it would have fit quite nicely. During the course of my research and perusal of old newspaper articles and historical pieces I was able to identify numerous stagecoach robberies or attempted robberies along this route, all of which occurred during the general time period of this novel's setting. The worst spell of robberies began in the mid to late 1870s and continued for several years. In 1883 alone, the *Salt River Herald* and the *Arizona Gazette* reported how robbers successfully took the Wells Fargo express boxes off stagecoaches at Ash Fork, and twice between Phoenix and Prescott. And out of the scattershot of my research came one such holdup story that was, in large part, the genesis of my concept for this third Widowmaker Jones novel. According to this particular folktale from the area, in 1876 or thereabouts, two holdup men, names unknown, supposedly robbed a stagecoach from the Vulture Mine of $40,000 in gold bars. Lawmen were soon hot on their trail, and the outlaws were apparently not as good at evasion as they were at robbing stagecoaches. They were shot and killed in Thompson Valley. Part of the loot was recovered several days later, but as is common with many such treasure tales, the remainder was hidden in the mountains somewhere between the Vulture Mine and where the town of Hillside is located today. If it exists at all, it has yet to be found. As the Widowmaker says, gold seems easier to find than it is keep.

White Tank and White Tank Mountains

The White Tank, a watering hole that gave the mountains their name, was located somewhere in the northeast end of the mountain range bearing its name and was the only easily accessible year-round source of water for miles. Early travelers along this desert route needed to know where it was. The wagon road going past it stretched from Maricopa south of the Gila River to Wickenburg, and then continued north to the new territorial capital in Prescott. Remnants of the road are few, and the watering hole itself is now gone. The white granite cliffs surrounding the large natural basin caved in and obliterated the White Tank as a water source, and there is nobody left alive who knows the location of the tank, although mention of it appears in several journals and writings from those days, as well as being marked on most maps of the time period. That blank space in geographical history allowed me to create my own fictionalized location for the tank, and I placed it in a canyon similar to other runoff basins found in the White Tank Mountains.

The Dutchman

Jacob Waltz, or Walz, depending on which historian you believe, is a name that is associated with perhaps the most famous and most written-about gold story in the West, the Lost Dutchman Mine. Called the Dutchman, slang in that era for those of German descent, he is known to have mined and prospected over portions of California and the Bradshaw Mountains of the Arizona Territory before coming to the Phoenix area. Beyond that, the few known facts get murky.

According to the legend, the old prospector showed up numerous times in Phoenix and paid for his purchases with some of the richest gold ore anyone in those parts had ever seen. When questioned about his riches, the cagey old German only hinted about a mine he had in the Superstition Mountains and gave contradictory directions as to its general location. Again, according to legend, several men attempted to follow him into the Superstitions to find the source of his gold, but he always managed to elude them in the rugged terrain of those desert mountains. Some of those would-be trackers were even said to have been murdered or simply disappeared under mysterious circumstances. Waltz died in 1891, but on his deathbed he supposedly spoke of his mine to a Mexican baker woman and two brothers who had befriended him. All three tried to find the source of the gold, but were unsuccessful in their many attempts over the years. Following their failure, the legend continued to grow. Maps and supposed leads that identified the location of the mine were sold or swapped hands by the dozens. To this day, people are still traipsing out into the Superstitions in search of treasure, and historians and amateur sleuths still squabble and bicker over what is actually the truth within the legend.

However, my interest in the Lost Dutchman Mine for the sake of this novel formed when learning that Waltz likely worked for the Vulture Mine at one time, and that there are some who suppose that his gold may have come from high-grading ore from his employers there, if he truly had any gold at all.

Bushrangers

While the California gold rush of 1849 has become synonymous with the quest for riches and adventure in the American lore of manifest destiny, Australia had gold rushes of its own during its wild colonial days. Like California, people flocked to Australia from all over the world to get in on the action once rumors of any kind of gold find hit the newspapers. And in any such rush, there soon came those who were more interested in stealing gold than they were in digging or panning for it. The American Old West had its outlaws and road agents, but Australia's inhabitants, in their usual, sometimes colorful, way with the English language, gave that kind of predator a new name. Bushrangers, those robbers and cutthroats were called. For the sake of the story, I needed Jenny to have been long separated from her brothers, the twins Sig and Bjorn Larson, and I needed those twin brothers to have developed some skill with weapons and outlawry during their time away from her in order to make them suitable adversaries in the narrative's struggle to see who wound up with the gold shipment from the Vulture Mine. Historical pieces and movies about the most famous of the bushrangers, Ned Kelly, and his demise in a gunfight against peace officers where he wore a homemade suit of armor long ago caught my fancy and left me wanting to find a place in a story for similar such villains or characters from the Land Down Under.

Enrique "Henry" Garfias

The Californio son of a Mexican army general, Garfias, the first city marshal of Phoenix, is one of the lesser-known gunfighters and lawmen of his era. It is hard to believe that Old West historians and writers of western fiction such as myself have written so little about Henry, and that he doesn't get the attention of other frontier lawmen such as Wyatt Earp, Wild Bill Hickok, Bat Masterson, or others whose claim to fame was their daring deeds with a pistol while wearing a badge. Henry was known to be a quiet-spoken, modest, fair-minded man. He stood only five feet nine inches tall, yet he was deadly quick with a pistol and brazenly brave. From the start of his career as a peace officer working as a Maricopa County deputy, through his days as the marshal of Phoenix, Henry is sometimes credited with killing as many as seven men in the line of duty. He engaged in numerous gunfights and always came out on top, even though often outnumbered or fighting against men who had the drop on him. The *Phoenix Herald* once wrote about Henry, stating, "Henry Garfias had the reputation of never going after a man that did not return with him, dead or alive."

ABOUT THE AUTHOR

Some folks are just born to tell tall tales. **Brett Cogburn** was reared in Texas and the mountains of Southeastern Oklahoma. He was fortunate enough for many years to make his living from the back of a horse, where on cold mornings cowboys still straddled frisky broncs and dragged calves to the branding fire on the end of a rope from their saddlehorns. Growing up around ranches, livestock auctions, and backwoods hunting camps filled Brett's head with stories, and he never forgot a one. In his own words: "My grandfather taught me to ride a bucking horse, my mother gave me a love of reading, and my father taught me how to hunt my own meat and shoot straight. Cowboys are just as wild as they ever were, and I've been damn lucky to have known more than a few." The West is still teaching him how to write. Brett Cogburn lives in Oklahoma with his family.

The employees of Thorndike Press hope you have enjoyed this Large Print book. All our Thorndike, Wheeler, and Kennebec Large Print titles are designed for easy reading, and all our books are made to last. Other Thorndike Press Large Print books are available at your library, through selected bookstores, or directly from us.

For information about titles, please call:
(800) 223-1244

or visit our website at:
gale.com/thorndike

To share your comments, please write:

Publisher
Thorndike Press
10 Water St., Suite 310
Waterville, ME 04901